There Was a Time

GEORGE H. WITTMAN

CASEMATE

Philadelphia & Oxford

Published in the United States of America and Great Britain in 2021 by
CASEMATE PUBLISHERS
1950 Lawrence Road, Havertown, PA 19083, US
and
The Old Music Hall, 106–108 Cowley Road, Oxford OX4 1JE, UK

Copyright 2021 © George H. Wittman

Paperback Edition: ISBN 978-1-63624-044-2
Digital Edition: ISBN 978-1-63624-045-9

A CIP record for this book is available from the British Library

Printed and bound in the United States by Integrated Books International

Typeset in India by Lapiz Digital Services.

For a complete list of Casemate titles, please contact:
CASEMATE PUBLISHERS (US)
Telephone (610) 853-9131
Fax (610) 853-9146
Email: casemate@casematepublishers.com
www.casematepublishers.com

CASEMATE PUBLISHERS (UK)
Telephone (01865) 241249
Email: casemate-uk@casematepublishers.co.uk
www.casematepublishers.co.uk

To Joyce and Geraldine

Author's Note

I was assigned to the Indochina Branch after returning from Europe on my first assignment as an intelligence officer. I was supposed to go directly to the Far East in the summer of 1954 but was assigned to the Vietnam desk and subsequently the newly created Cambodia/Laos desk. About a year later, I went out to the field in covert operations for the Indochina Branch. Not once did I hear from official sources of the extensive contact that Office of Strategic Services (OSS) had had with Ho Chi Minh and other leaders of the Viet Minh. I learned about that years later. It was a matter never discussed during the 1950s and never taken advantage of in the 1960s. This book is about that period in spring/summer 1945 when the principal American intelligence organization of that time, the OSS, was in close and cooperative contact with Ho Chi Minh, personally, and fighting cadre of the Viet Minh, organizationally. These were the last and very dangerous days of World War II and the battle against the Japanese.

While this story is told in the form of a novel, it nonetheless is based on actual events and exploits of various OSS officers and enlisted men. I have chosen to fictionalize these individuals because so many of them sought in later years to avoid public awareness of their roles in northern Vietnam and their working relationship with Ho Chi Minh and his staff in the field. Similarly, for literary purposes, I have combined the activities of several of the teams and their operational leaders. I have tried to remain true to the action and the situation of the history of the operation. These missions and the events which drove them occurred some 20 years before the Gulf of Tonkin Resolution that marked the justification for the escalation of American involvement in Vietnam.

There was a time.

George H. Wittman

Preface

After the last remnants of the Battle of the Bulge had been cleared away in the winter of early 1945, and the expectation grew that Berlin would fall by springtime, the attention of the American military command turned toward the Pacific. The priority that the European theater had held was now shifted to destroying the Japanese in Asia. MacArthur had already landed in the Philippines in October 1944 and the Marines were to secure Iwo Jima by March 1945. The United States could then bomb the home islands of Japan with increasing frequency from land bases.

With the alteration of operational priority, military and intelligence assets from Europe were diverted to Asia. DeGaulle's Free French government, back in power since the fall of Paris in August 1944, was eager to put their stamp on the recovery of their former colony of Indochina, made up of Vietnam, Cambodia, and Laos. The status of the Vichy French administration and military forces that had collaborated with the Japanese was now in doubt. If there was to be an American invasion of Vietnam as part of the piecemeal successful advance across the Pacific, DeGaulle's people wanted to be able to claim they had done something, anything, to encourage anti-Japanese resistance. The future of France as a colonial power in Indochina depended on it.

From the American standpoint the future of Indochina lay in some form of trusteeship, as President Roosevelt had intimated as early as the Cairo and Teheran summit conferences. Politically, the Americans had also recognized a special interest in Vietnam held by the Chinese Nationalist government of Chiang Kai-shek. The British tended to side with French ambitions to regain their old colony on the principle that they intended to return to take over theirs. Needless to say, the result of this was a great deal of behind-the-scenes tension.

Into all this was thrust the newly reinforced American covert intelligence unit of the OSS assigned to Kunming, China. With the arrival of a cadre of experienced behind-the-lines operatives from Europe and a few eager young men trained in Vietnamese, the Americans launched themselves directly into the complicated politics and dangerous operations that marked Vietnam's northern region during the last six months of World War II.

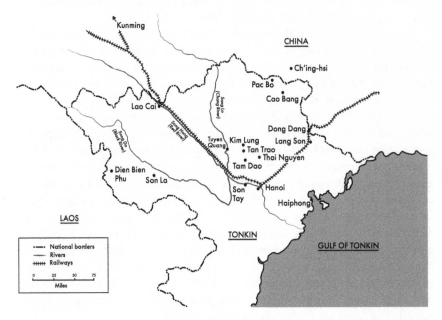

Northern Vietnam, 1945

* * *

The number of people who died from famine and flood in the Red River area of Tonkin in the disasters of 1944–1945 ranged from 500,000 to one and a half million. It depends on who tells the story. It really doesn't matter. It was horrific. This monumental tragedy which affected the entire region of northern Vietnam nonetheless became a backdrop to the political and military events during the last months of World War II.

The delta flood plain had been created over the millennium by the yearly monsoons which fed the red-brown wildness that poured down from China to Vietnam. This life blood of the northern part of Vietnam is drawn from the mountains of China's Yunnan Province. The *Song Hong*, as the Red River is called in Vietnamese, flows in great rushes south and east aided in its march to the Gulf of Tonkin by its equally ungentle cousins *Song Da*, the Black River, and *Song Lo*, the Clear River. Three typhoons welcomed by the furnace of air off the Gobi Desert accompanied the annual south-westerly monsoon season of May to October 1944. The Tonkin harvest of that year was destroyed. The farmers who should have been working to replant for the second harvest the following spring of 1945 had been decimated by the floods that inundated the delta. Even if they had been able to do so, there was little seed to plant. All this devastation and at this point the war's military action had barely touched this part of Indochina.

Hanoi, sitting on the right bank of the Red River, was protected by a series of dikes. The capital city of French Indochina was reasonably safe from the floods. Not so the thousands of villages southeast in the lowland of the delta plain. Most of the dikes protecting this rice-growing area had been swamped by the rain-swollen rivers. The sidewalk cafe attached to the magnificent old Metropole Hotel still held its usual collection of French *colons* and their wives and mistresses. Japanese and French officers sitting in self-imposed segregation from each other talked in hushed tones of the progress of the war these first couple of months of 1945. They tried to ignore the seemingly endless lines of peasants pushed along by police to clear the street for the occasional vehicle. The garbage from the hotel and the many spacious villas in the "European" sector of the city became the principal feeding centers. Sickly farm families roamed the city carrying their small children in baskets and their meager possessions in cloth bags hung at each end of a *don ganh*, the split bamboo pole which, when balanced on the shoulder, becomes the primary mode of goods carrier for the Vietnamese peasant. These were the *ban co*, the class of people who had been poor for many generations and who nonetheless made up the backbone of the population.

In the delta itself, those villages that had not been swept away had used this "dry season" to try to rebuild, but they had very little with which to work. The simplest task was a burden for bodies wracked by disease and starvation. The old colonial administration either ignored the plight of the impoverished Tonkinese or were incapable of relieving such a massive catastrophe. The Japanese Army personnel were under strict orders to leave these civil matters to the colonial French authorities. In any case, they and the Vichy French army units found it hard enough to protect their own stores of food supplies from marauding bands. At night, shots could be heard as sentries picked off thieves. In the morning, carts roamed about the city picking up the bodies of dead from the night before.

For the French *colons*, the poorest of whom were wealthy by comparison to the delta farmers, this was a period of considerable disadvantage, but nothing more. Prices of necessities were sky high but could be obtained. Hanoi's Vietnamese merchants found ways to acquire supplies, as merchants seem to be able to do in many crises. They paid top prices and passed it on to the customer. It was an economic equation for a political sea change. And the amazing thing was that the supposedly politically sophisticated French colonial administration, then and in the future, never recognized the full impact of what had occurred before their eyes.

* * *

The Japanese had been quick to take advantage of the French capitulation to the Germans in 1940. Tokyo found the new Vichy government most accommodating when it came to Indochina. Their agreement with the collaborationist French allowed the colonial government to remain in administrative control of Vietnam, Cambodia, and Laos. The French, in turn, gave the Japanese all they wanted militarily: full transit rights, stationing of Imperial Japanese troops, and access to all required support facilities. Economically, Japan had first call on strategic minerals and agricultural products. Ironically, Japan won the admiration of the *indigènes*, especially the nationalist Vietnamese, for the humbling of their colonial master. The communists, always politically more acute, were conflicted in their reaction after Germany, Japan's ally, attacked Soviet Russia. Nonetheless, the Japanese played their Asia solidarity card with finesse and major incidents were avoided. However, the scene changed drastically on March 9, 1945. At 7pm on that day, Ambassador Matsumoto delivered the demand that all French troops be placed under Japanese control. The French were given two hours in which to reply. The Japanese Army moved with speed and precision. Most French units surrendered immediately. Some "for the honor of France" fought briefly; then they surrendered, honor satisfied. These units were treated with "appropriate military courtesy," disarmed and interned. However, in the north at Lang Son a combined force of Legionnaires, French regular soldiers, and Vietnamese colonial troops held out for two days until they had run out of ammunition and water. The Japanese slaughtered them after their attempt to finally surrender. The same thing happened to the garrison at Dong Dan that had held out for three days. The message had been sent!

Some similar combined forces in the south and central highlands made it to Laos. These small units were harbored by Laotian tribesmen and purposefully ignored by Lao officials. Effectively, these groups of regular military now became partisans. They raided across the border for the next six months, providing the only such military operations against the Japanese in Vietnam originated and commanded by the French during the entire war.

A larger force, again made up of Foreign Legionnaires, regular French, and colonial Vietnamese troopers staged what their commanding officers, Generals Sabattier and Alessandri, called a "fighting retreat." In fact, this sizeable force of over 6,000-plus horse-drawn artillery gathered together in the region around Son Tay 20 miles northwest of Hanoi. From there they headed toward Dien Bien Phu about 200 miles away by air, but at least 300 or more on foot. They were harassed all along the way, but the Japanese never wanted to commit the size of force necessary to seriously block and defeat Sabattier and his troops. Instead they encouraged tribal hill people by offering bounties for captured or killed soldiers of the Sabattier force. The Japanese forces locally along the route were positioned to ambush and otherwise impede, but there was no sustained Japanese offensive. It really wasn't needed. The French did not want to fight unless it was to defend themselves. The march through the mountainous terrain often covered by near-impenetrable bamboo forests and dense jungle-like foliage took its toll. Disease, fatigue, and lack of food plagued the fleeing force. They arrived on the plain of Dien Bien Phu with one objective: to contact the Allied headquarters in Kunming, China, and plead with them for help.

The American headquarters in Kunming for the OSS learned of the emergency message from liaison with 14th Air Force who received the signal. They also found out that word had come from the top, "the real top, in Washington," that no assistance should be given to this, or any other Vichy French force in Indochina!

Chapter One

The sound of heavy fire reverberated through the stone walls of the church. A small group of men dressed in traditional, working-class, civilian clothes huddled against the protective sides of the ancient walls. Each man was wrapped with bandoliers of ammunition and carried a rifle. Some had German "potato masher" grenades attached to their belts. They had made their way down from the Vosges Mountains to a small town southeast of Nancy as soon as they had heard the Americans were close. The Germans still put up a serious defense as they withdrew in order. This group of *maquis* eagerly looked forward to greeting their liberators. It had been a long and bloody fight between the elusive *maquisards* and the relentless Germans. No quarter given—none asked.

The American tanks had to be just a few blocks away. The tallest of the men, speaking French with an unmistakable American accent, shouted above the din of the exploding tank shells that everyone should stay where they were. The old church shook from the impact of the firing on nearby buildings. The tall, gaunt American looked around the doorway to see exactly where the tanks were. They could all hear the rumble and metallic grinding of gears in between the noise of the detonations. One of the *maquisards*, an older man with a large grey mustache typical of the region, disregarding the advice of the American, dashed around him with a white flag made of a dingy grey scarf. The old man was oblivious to the voices screaming at him as he joyously jumped up and down with the rag attached to his rifle. A Sherman tank turned the corner. The machine gun mounted on the turret sprayed down the street as the gunner swept all moving objects in range. The old man died instantly as the tank rolled on, unmindful of what had just happened. The gunner thought he was taking fire from one of the roofs and directed his weapon upwards. Another tank followed and blew away the entire tile roof. The little town was completely "liberated" within the next 15 minutes.

Slowly townspeople appeared from the rubble of their destroyed homes and the cellars of those left standing. They cheered the infantry that followed the tanks. No one blamed the Americans for what had happened to their town. They were liberated now and that was all that mattered. The American dragged the body of the old man to the side of the road and, with the help of one of the *maquisards*, carried the corpse back into the church. No one said anything. The rifle with the scarf still attached was laid by the old man's side. The American untied the scarf and slipped it around the dead man's neck. They all crossed themselves—even the American, who wasn't even Catholic. Their war had ended.

* * *

Major John Guthrie was tired, annoyed, and generally in a bad mood. It was nothing new. He had been this way all the way from England, a week of very uncomfortable and unreliable wartime air transport. Of course, it all had begun before that. Trying to convince a moronic American infantry officer he was part of the same army and not a German had been the beginning of the downhill slide. It was his choice swearing and waving of his dog tags in the captain's face that finally convinced the company commander that John was a bona fide Yank. Eventually the OSS liaison apparatus swung into motion and John finally completed the round trip which had begun six months before with the flight from England and the jump into the Vosges to link up with the French resistance.

It hadn't been easy to leave his *maquisards*. It had been only six months, but it was literally a lifetime for some of them. The absurd death of old Emile on the day the Americans finally reached their sector was the worst of all their casualties. He was just so happy he couldn't keep from rushing out. The *maquisards* took it in their stride. They held nothing against the American in the tank. It was Emile's own fault they said, but for John it was a terrible ending for his mission.

Back in England there had been the period of decompression, of debriefings, of after-action reports, of just about everything that no longer seemed to have any meaning. Slowly the fatigue of months with little sleep and constant danger gave way to an overriding sense of irritation—at little things, big things, the war, the OSS, just about everything. It was time for a rest. Some cushy assignment where you didn't have to think. Paris would have been nice. He deserved it. They'd even agreed with him on that.

Then there was that talk with the pompous bird colonel who actually said, "You know, son, there's a war on…." He was lucky John hadn't busted him in the mouth. His experience, the non-combat colonel had said, was needed out in the Pacific Theater, in Indochina ops. There his French knowledge and guerrilla warfare skills would be invaluable. "Bullshit!" was John's instant reply. It hadn't mattered. The orders already had been cut. So much for the accolades, the Silver Star, the promotion.

The flight over the Hump had been horrendous. Mercifully, it was comparatively short, though freezing cold. At the airfield's reception hut a sergeant called out his name, and he was soon bouncing around the front seat of a jeep on his way to the OSS Detachment HQ in Kunming, China. The sergeant's determined cheerfulness made John's bad mood even worse. And the drive through a cold rain slanting with a strong wind on slippery and dangerous mud and rock roads hardly improved John's disposition. The supposedly reassuring statement by the driver that February in Kunming was usually dry and moderate only convinced John Guthrie that this was an assignment from hell.

The dusty ground of the OSS compound had been turned into mire. The jeep couldn't pull up closer than 50 feet to the headquarters building because of a useless wall of sandbags that had been constructed as someone's idea of protection for the HQ. John slid out of the jeep and made his way up the mud pathway to the building. He stopped for a moment on its wooden porch in order to stomp out some of the muck collected from the short walk from the jeep. He shook the rain off his trench coat and adjusted his tie before going in.

A blank-faced staff sergeant led the new arrival into the C.O.'s surprisingly comfortable office. There were framed photos on the wall of some apparently important officers, most of whom John did not know. He did notice that a serious-faced Chiang Kai-shek stared out beside a photo of an easily recognizable General Claire Chennault leaning casually against one of his Flying Tiger P-40s. A florid and pudgy lieutenant colonel stood up from behind his desk, returned John's salute, and offered his hand. John shook the hand. It was as pudgy as the rest of the man.

"I'm Edgar Hallstrom," he said.

"John Guthrie reporting for duty, sir."

"So, how's everything in London, Major? They called me from the reception office at the airfield to let me know you were coming in. I sent a jeep. I take it he found you."

John stood at a relaxed form of attention, which is as close to strict military bearing as could be expected of an OSS officer. Hallstrom gestured for him to sit down. John took off his trench coat and seeing no place to hang it, laid it carefully on the floor.

"London is fine, sir. Thank you for the jeep."

"Well, I'm glad you're here now. We can use you. I've already received your 201 file. It says you're a big hero, Major. They gave you a Silver Star, I see. What did you do?"

"I'm sure the basic stuff is in the file. They dropped me into the Vosges Mountains. I made contact with the French Resistance. We blew some things up, and then I got out when Georgie Patton and some of his Third Army tankers rolled into the area. I think London was surprised to see me again, so they gave me a medal. As simple as that, Colonel."

"Well, I'm sure you'll have plenty of chances for more medals here, if that's what you want. We need some hard chargers like you, Guthrie. A lot of good things are going to happen here."

Who the hell wants medals? What a jerk this guy is, John thought, though he said nothing. It didn't matter, Lt. Col. Edgar Hallstrom just steamrolled along.

"Chungking told me you were sent here because of your experience with the reds in France. And you speak French, of course. You do, don't you?"

"Yes, sir. I speak French. OSS French—a year in college and our immersion course in England. I used it in France with the *maquis*, who were all communists. That's my big experience."

"Well, there you are. That's what I said. You may not be an expert, but you know them, right?" said the acting commander of the OSS detachment in Kunming.

Again John decided not to reply. It was the only way to avoid getting in trouble on his first day in China. Hallstrom was obviously one of those people who brought out John's least diplomatic instincts. With a great effort, John's better judgement told him that it was best to grit his teeth and keep the trap shut.

"What did you do in civilian life, John?" Shifting to the OSS custom of informality was Hallstrom's next idea of a clever conversational gambit.

"I was a lawyer… in Chicago, Edgar." What's good for the goose….

"Really, so was I… not in Chicago, of course. Cleveland is my home base. What firm were you with?"

"The United Steelworkers," John answered savoring the expectation of the reaction he got.

"Jesus, that's why they sent you. Of course. A labor lawyer!"

John Guthrie did the only thing he could. He smiled—a great big grin. It was the first time in days that he'd been amused. A perverse amusement, but still. The red-nosed, puffy-faced, overweight Hallstrom had divined the answer. Guthrie was a bomb-throwing, rabble-rousing, Bolshevik labor lawyer. The worst of the worst. There was nothing else left to do but laugh, which he did. To Hallstrom's credit he saw the humor and also laughed.

"Well, whatever, John. We're going to want you to get into Indochina—the northern part of Vietnam to be exact—make contact with some commie guerrillas there and turn them into an effective partisan force. They're already picking up our downed fliers and getting them out. The AGAS (Air Ground Aid Section) people who run those exfiltration ops may want some help in

4

that regard also. But the main thing is to get these reds out kicking some Jap ass …." Hallstrom paused for effect. It was as if he enjoyed his own tough talk. "Of course, that's after you read in, get acquainted with everyone, so on and so forth. I figure a month or so should do it. Sound colorful enough? Maybe not like the Detroit auto riots, but it's the best we can offer you. Ha ha."

John took a deep breath, congratulated himself on his self-control and answered, "Well, Edgar, it'll just have to do, I guess." Unspoken but even clearer in feeling than before was the realization he had just flown over 6,000 miles to end up with this jackass. What a war!

John completed his reporting-in formalities and left Hallstrom happily stuffed in his swivel chair reaching for something that clinked in his bottom desk drawer. It had stopped raining and a weak sun began to reflect through the clouds. The jeep seemed to have disappeared. Where the hell was that driver? John looked around for Hallstrom's staff sergeant, but he, too, was missing. At the other end of the compound he could see a small truck being loaded. It seemed that one of the two men was in uniform. It was too far away to be sure, but that figure appeared to be Hallstrom's sergeant. The other was Chinese.

John tried to get the attention of the two men but they were intent on stuffing cartons in the back of the truck. He was about to venture onto the muddy parade ground when the jeep slid around the corner of the compound to a splashing stop in front of the headquarters building.

"Where the hell did you disappear to, Sergeant?" John said after crawling back into the jeep's front seat.

"Sorry, Major. I thought you'd be in with the old man for a while, so I took off to deliver a package to the CQ which came in on the same flight you did. It was for Capt. Parnell and I knew he'd been lookin' out for it. I guess I shoulda waited, but what with the rain pourin' down, an' all…."

The sergeant guided the jeep carefully around the corner he had just slid through, not wanting to further incur the wrath of an already obviously pissed-off major. They passed by the two men and the truck. John could see that one of them was the staff sergeant. He didn't look up when the jeep drove by, but the other man, a gap-toothed Chinese, gave a big smile and waved.

"Friend of yours?" John asked his driver.

"Naw, not really. He and his old man handle all local stuff. They sorta have the concession around here."

"So what's the sergeant doing with him?"

"I don't really know. He's the colonel's eyes 'n ears as well as the detachment's admin sergeant."

The sergeant driving the jeep was clearly not at ease talking about the loading of the truck. John backed off. If what appeared to be obvious was true, he didn't want to know anything about it. One thing was sure though:

this assignment was getting to look like one of those things that had snafu written all over it.

Ten minutes of careful driving to avoid potholes and the jeep drew up in front of a sturdy low building with an American flag in the center of a spacious courtyard. Two other smaller buildings were on each side.

"This used to be some sort of Christian mission, but they moved and we got it. That's the Officers' Quarters. The EMs are billeted in the two other buildings. There's an NCO club and an Officers' club just down about a block or so. All the comforts of home, Major."

A corporal sat behind a desk sorting forms. John signed a register and received a key to a small but adequate room with a view of the courtyard.

"We're pretty crowded now, sir. This is the best we got," the corporal said.

"It's fine. Thank you, Corporal. Where's the mess?"

"It's right in the back of this building. The whole rear end. It's both the Officers' and the EMs' mess. Separate rooms but the same food. A lot of people eat locally."

John set about pulling things out of his duffel bag. He hadn't brought much along. Outside of the new blouse and set of pinks he'd had made for himself in London, there wasn't much else than what was on his back and some fatigue gear and extra jump boots.

"They've got some great tailors here, if you ever need anything," a voice said from the doorway. "I see you've got old Bergen's room. The poor bastard was transferred off to liaison duty in Chungking. There's a definite disadvantage in knowing the local language. Do you?"

"Do I what? And who are you?" John had been surprised by the newcomer and reacted immediately. He never liked being surprised. It was an old reflex.

"Oh, I'm sorry," said a well-built, blond man in a sweatshirt with "Princeton Crew" printed on it. "Parnell, Edouard Parnell. Captain to be exact. Welcome to China, Major. You must be Guthrie. They said you'd be coming in today. I meant do you speak Chinese? Cantonese, Mandarin, whatever?"

"No, I don't speak any Chinese, Captain."

"That sounds great. Captain, that is. I just got my promotion and it's still a treat," said the smiling Parnell. To John he looked like the typical eastern Ivy Leaguer that his sweatshirt announced. The perennial schoolboy. Another bad mark for the day.

"You might be wondering what I'm doing lounging about in the morn like this. The answer, Major Guthrie, is that there is nothing else to do. In fact, your arrival may be the most exciting thing that will happen this week. I'm speaking, of course, of work-related matters. There are many things to do here in lovely, exotic Kunming. You will find the fly boys over at 14th Air Force are quite generous with their excellent stock of Scotch whiskey flown in over the Hump. And there are the wonderful but woefully outnumbered belles of the nursing corps attached to the 14th's general hospital. Of course, the Chinese food is quite good, if you like that sort of thing."

John knew this Parnell character was just trying to be friendly, but that was of absolutely no interest to him at this juncture. He wasn't there to make friends. Get in, do a job, get out. That's all he wanted to do. This was not where he wanted to be, and he had no intention of pretending it was. It was best that all concerned knew that from the beginning. He didn't give a shit about the booze, the nurses, or the goddamn Chinese food. He had the urge to say just that but held back.

"Thanks, I'll remember that," he said and turned back to his duffel.

"Well, I've the room right next door, so if you need anything…. I'm off for a run now that it's stopped raining. I'll see you when I get back. Lunch maybe?"

John grunted noncommittally. He could hear Parnell go out the front door and saw him lope out the courtyard. He closed his own door and stretched out on the metal cot. He was so tired his eyes hurt, yet he was a long way from sleeping. The pain in his stomach had returned, but he no longer had any of the compound that he had been given by the medical officer in London. It would go away he told himself. It was just a dull pain, nothing of importance. He would concentrate on other things, good things. He thought about his father who swore by his own ulcer remedy of whiskey and milk. The Guthrie men were too perverse to admit frailty. Evelyn had said that.

It seemed like such a long time ago. He thought about receiving the divorce papers in England. It wasn't that there had been any surprise involved; he had expected the final paperwork for quite a while. Even before he jumped into France, he knew the marriage was finished. But he still couldn't stop thinking about it. Even lying on a cot in damn Kunming, he still thought about it—and her. In truth the marriage was all over before he had even received his commission. He could hear her saying it wasn't his fault. What the hell was that supposed to mean? He tried to push it all out of his mind. Concentrate on willing the pain to go away, he ordered himself. He could do that and Evelyn would disappear—for a while.

The cot was comfortable enough, but like most cots it was too short for him. He propped his heels over the end of the bed, aided by a folded blanket acting as a footrest against the metal end of the cot. At least he could stretch out completely that way. Fatigue took over. When he awoke from a dead sleep of what seemed to be hardly more than an hour or so, he had no idea where he was. Very slowly he reoriented. John could hear voices coming from somewhere in the building, but he couldn't make out what was being said. Soon there was a polite knock on the door and someone announced something about dinner. Still groggy, John rose and headed for his door just as there was more knocking. He opened the door and found Parnell on the other side.

"Chow time, Major. I hear it's chicken and you shouldn't miss that. It's just about the only thing the mess sergeant can't ruin. I'll introduce you around. You missed lunch but I told the CQ not to bother you." Parnell was neatly turned out in his khakis and a sweater.

"We're quite informal in the mess, Major. Lord Edgar rarely dines with us. That's what we call our acting C.O. You've met, I imagine. He's quite a study in military demeanor, if I may venture an opinion. I'm afraid dear Edgar could never make it in a real Army outfit. However, in the Office of Silly Services, as I've dubbed our organization, he fits right in."

"From what I've seen so far this certainly isn't much of a military unit, and that includes you, Captain Parnell," said John as he splashed water on his face.

"*Touché*, Major Guthrie. I was being quite rude. You are right to chastise me. I apologize. However, I've been here for three months sitting on my arse and so has everyone else. Hallstrom is quite content with all this as he plans to make full colonel by never doing anything and therefore never making any errors. They haven't made his command position permanent yet, so we're all hoping he'll fall over his bottle of Johnny Walker and get himself booted upstairs somewhere. Isn't that always what happens to his kind? They never get the paddling they deserve."

"I wouldn't know about that," John said as the two of them ambled down the corridor to the mess.

The dining area was divided into two sections. The larger part contained the long tables and benches of the enlisted men's area. They went through a cafeteria-style line at one end of an enormous room. Walled off on the opposite end in a smaller area was the officers' mess. One long table with a tablecloth and chairs was served by Chinese waiters.

"All quite civilized, eh Major?" remarked Parnell. "Allow me to introduce the man in charge."

An elderly Chinese man came forward from the corner of the room where he had been keeping an eye on the assembling crowd. He wore a traditional short jacket with a high collar. It was black silk and clearly marked his status. Edouard Parnell introduced the man to John.

"It is a great honor to have you join us, Major. We hope you will enjoy your stay."

The old man's English was accented but perfect. John responded with a perfunctory, "Thank you." As John was led over to the officers' mess section by Parnell, the captain, in a confidential tone said, "That guy runs the show around here. I'll tell you more about him and his operation later."

What followed was the expected round of introductions to the assembled officers of the OSS detachment. There were about a dozen present and John could not remember a single name after the formalities had been completed. He knew he should care more about who they were, but for the moment it didn't matter a damn. There was another major present—a big guy, bigger than John. He had a brown sweater on just like Parnell, but John could see the gold leaf on his collar peeking through. His nose had the mashed-in look of a boxer or football player, though the eyes were soft. All in all, John decided it was an interesting mix of faces. He had plenty of time to learn more about them if he wanted to.

The meal was surprisingly excellent. The fact that John had barely eaten during the last two-day leg of his trip certainly was a factor—he was famished. Parnell kept up a polite chatter attempting to draw John into the dinner conversation with little success. After dinner, John allowed himself to be dragged along to their so-called officers' club down the street from the quarters. By that time, John had begun to feel slightly more friendly toward the world in general and Edouard Parnell in particular. Parnell had refused to be deterred by John's steadfastly irritable manner. A couple of straight shots of something that came from a bottle appearing to be Haig & Haig convinced John that half of his father's ulcer recipe definitely had a value of its own. Any discussion of the war was scrupulously avoided, as was any inquiry into John's experiences in Europe. This suited him perfectly and by the end of the evening he felt no pain in any sense of the term. Parnell guided his charge safely back to the quarters and deposited the unstable John Guthrie onto his cot. The new arrival instantly fell asleep, a turning, twisting, disturbed sleep.

The long crawl across the muddy ploughed field. Wet, soggy dirt clawing at his body, holding him back. The objective far away lit only by the night's pale glow. The lone figure of the German sentry set against the criss-cross pattern of chain-link fencing, innocent and unsuspecting. The pylon of the radio tower stood like a magnet drawing him and his three comrades wriggling toward it. Halfway there the sentry moved away from the gate and began his regular tour of the fenced perimeter. His back turned, it's the moment for a scramble forward and then a quick flop again to the ground. All timed to be able to greet the guard as he completes the circumvention of his post. The combat knife drawn from its scabbard was now simply an extension of the arm; his body flattened against ground smelling of the sweetness of newly turned earth. Sensing even more than seeing the sentry as he draws within a few strides of turning the corner of the fence, the body springs up and into the German. The upward thrust of the knife catches the sentry just above his belt and is driven on up through the solar plexus. A maquisard *swiftly steps behind the German and snaps his head back in a strangle hold. The arm with the knife is covered with blood as the sentry is lowered quietly to the ground. And then John sees himself, once again arm and knife dripping with the young man's blood. A sharp, driving pain in his own stomach.*

John woke up at that point in the scene, as he always did. The dream was always the same because it was less a dream than it was a reliving of a nightmare, a memory not to be forgotten. The pain in his gut would be there as would the sweat soaking his skin. Sleep after that carried only fear and was fitful and unnourishing. The first light of dawn came eventually to save him from further terror.

The next few days passed by with great swiftness as John learned from Parnell details of the detachment's current status and expected role in OSS/China's operations. John had a chance to meet and talk with the major with the boxer's face, Bob Simpson. The soft-spoken and soft-eyed Simpson showed none of the competitiveness that John had expected from an officer of equal rank toward a newcomer. Bob Simpson was one of those really large men whose physical strength never needed to be displayed and whose quiet manner and common sense marked him as a natural leader. John judged the 250 lb. Simpson to be very useful in a bar fight, not unlike John's father's buddies back at the mill in Gary. Big Jack Guthrie had been one of those hard men until he hurt his back on the job. That's when he went full time with the steel union and pushed his son out of the mills and on to college and law school. Father and son both owed a lot to the union and the men who built it. It turned out that Simpson came from Youngstown, so there was an instant understanding between the two majors.

"Bob was a tackle for Notre Dame back in the twenties, I think. He's pushing forty now, but he doesn't look it does he?" Edouard Parnell had the story on almost everyone in the detachment and was determined to brief John on all of it. As interesting as the social biographies may have been, John knew Parnell was really only looking for an opening to learn more about him. Good technique, John thought, but wrong target. John didn't like to talk about himself and avoided Parnell's sly inducements to do so.

According to Parnell, the most important guy in the detachment was Tony Castelli. Captain Antonio Castelli was Hallstrom's adjutant and the key to getting anything done or obstacle removed. To the extent that Hallstrom was involved in any complicated decision making, Castelli was the source of the thinking. A five-foot, seven-inch perpetual motion machine, according to Parnell, Tony Castelli reveled in paperwork—reports, analysis, memos.

"And what's more," Parnell said, "Tony remembers everything he reads or writes. He's the perfect staff intelligence officer. If we ever get to do anything around here, he'll be invaluable. As it is, he knows every black marketeer in town and can get anything you want. He's the one who rounded up that old crook and his son. Tony's got the touch alright."

It was Edouard Parnell that John found the most interesting. Not at first, of course, but in later days when bits and pieces of the young man's own background filtered through. First, and most importantly, Parnell was the only other one in the detachment who had previous combat experience. As much as Parnell would use information about people to draw others out on themselves, he used the same device to deflect inquiry into his own life. Eventually, though, it came out that Parnell spoke fluent French and that he had spent 1943 to 1944 in Belgium working with Resistance members to develop sabotage ops prior to the Normandy invasion. That he was a New York socialite was quite true, but the guise of artificiality with which he protected himself was just that—a camouflage.

"Tell me, Edouard, why do you play the 'hale-fellow-well-met' routine? You've obviously got more on the ball than that." John had a Scotsman's proclivity for going straight to the point. That, too, he'd inherited from his dad—that and a taste for whiskey. He was sipping a drink at the Officers' club with Parnell. It was one of the rare times that no one was around other than the Chinese barman.

"Ah, you noticed. What makes you think differently?"

"Come on. I worked for the United Steelworkers. We don't trust anyone."

"A pleasant facade opens many doors. My mother taught me that. She's French, you know. She understands these things. Now you know my secret."

"How was it in Belgium?"

"Shitty. How was it in France?"

"Equally."

"So there it is. We all have our camouflage. You have yours and I mine. Let's drink to dissemblement."

"*A la votre.*"

"*Salut.*"

* * *

A group of tribesmen stood around the inert form on the straw mat. The men were short, slight but tautly muscled. Some had filed their front teeth to points which flashed brightly against deep brown skin while they talked animatedly but softly. They all carried knives or machetes except for one who was the obvious leader. He authoritatively cradled an old French army rifle. The weapon was a distinguished totem. It was well oiled to protect its venerable bolt action from rusting in the heavy humidity. Other than homemade shorts which were nothing more than stitched-up loin cloths, the only other accoutrements were strings of cowrie shells and shiny bits of metal draped around the men's necks. They were Tho tribesmen of North-Central Vietnam along the Chinese border—rugged, forested, hill country. These and other tribespeople had lived for scores of generations in this tangled and ofttimes dangerously wild land stretching westward to Laos.

The hut sheltering the prostrate form on the mat was made of a combination of bamboo and wood slats. The structure was the largest in the compound. A strong ginger odor emanating from smoking pots in the corners of the room hung heavily in the air. On the dirt floor were strewn bits of animal skin which the men carefully avoided. By the side of the still-living body was a collection of his personal possessions. These were neatly arranged, as were pieces of the bloody flight suit they had cut off of him. His head was wrapped carefully in a poultice of ground herbs held on by an applique of fine leaves. His broken arm and leg were similarly covered but also rendered immobile by strips of split bamboo tied together by an intricate web of vines. It was all the excellent work of the clan shaman. He had come from his own village nearby to treat the man the tribe's hunters had found unconscious, hanging from his large white cloth in the trees. That beautiful thing with its useful thin ropes attached was also folded by the pilot's side. They all thought the parachute, something of which they had heard but did not know the name, and until then had not seen, was a wonderful object that could be made into any number of valuable things. This they had learned from the shaman. He knew a great deal beside his medicinal arts. He knew all the stories of the several clans he served in the tribe. He was truly a learned man.

They were careful not to go further than look at the collected items. It was forbidden to take this man's property while he was still alive, but of course they could talk about them. That was acceptable to the shaman, who was also their ethical arbiter. It was the village chief's job to keep everyone in line. His ancient rifle acted both as a symbol of his office as well as an excellent club for the enforcement of discipline.

There were three items of particular interest to the group. First, of course, was the beautiful white cloth with its many uses. After that there was an item they all knew—a large pistol. They had never seen a .45 cal. automatic before, but they knew it was a pistol. What a find! Then there were the three coins. These had been wrapped in a piece of silk with writing on it. They couldn't read, so it didn't matter that it was written in Chinese characters. They knew one thing, though. The coins were gold. They knew gold when they saw it. That was the shiny metal some of them had strung with the cowrie shells. The three fine gold pieces were certainly going to be a matter for considerable bargaining if this man died. Only the shaman's stern warning had kept them from picking up the coins to determine their weight. Yes, gold was something they knew about.

The white man moaned but remained asleep. The shaman had left strict instructions that he should be called immediately if the man woke up. The village chief told everyone to leave the hut. It was not a popular instruction. The younger hunters were eager to just sit and wait in the hut. After all, this was exciting. The headman quickly silenced the grumbling with a wave of his rifle. The group trooped outside, again avoiding the small animal skins that the shaman had left to act as guardians of his patient. The hunters had left their bows and deadly fire-hardened arrows outside as a sign of respect for the medical magic of the process going on within the hut. These were their hunting tools and thereby instruments of death. The shaman's work was to give life. It was important to keep the two separate in times such as this. Their knives were personal symbols of manhood not dissimilar to the chief's rifle. As such these weapons carried a powerful positive character which could only help in the stranger's recovery.

The injured man was receiving the best treatment available. Two young women acting as nurses remained squatting outside the hut's entrance to be relieved by two others every few hours. Thus it had gone ever since the broken but breathing body had been brought in by the hunters. The vigil had been maintained day and night; it was a highly honored duty in which one garnered much respect. The shaman's local assistant was in charge of the nurses and responsible for calling back the shaman if there was a change in the patient's state. Although this white man was a special case, like all doctors, the shaman had many duties. He counted on his staff to monitor his patient's condition and keep him informed.

The news of the arrival of the downed pilot spread quickly by word of mouth across the hidden paths that traversed the region. The information swiftly reached the rag-tag guerrilla force of the communist-dominated Viet Minh nationalist league. Tho tribesmen were at the core of this force so it was natural that they had a special interest in this new prospect. Instructions were quickly sent to the village to take particularly good care of the flier. The contacts made by the Allied air/ground recovery unit, AGAS, had already considerably benefited Tho villages elsewhere.

The attentive care of the shaman and the clan that found the American was crucial to the reward. It wasn't so much a humane act as it was a practical one. It was always more advantageous to return a healthy individual than a dead one. The reward was much higher. This information was passed back to the village. It never had to be explained to them. For the ever-pragmatic people of the village, the pilot was a gift from the spirits. They knew it was their responsibility to be worthy of the gift. It was only logical.

The white man made excellent progress under their careful nursing. In a few weeks he could even stand with the aid of a conveniently shaped tree limb as a crutch under his good arm. He seemed like a happy person for he appeared always to be smiling. Importantly, he had also been very generous with his goods, though he had kept his very powerful-looking pistol. The pilot had given the beautiful soft cloth with the excellent ropes to the assistant shaman, who, in turn, shared it with the nurses. He wanted to give his gold coins to the headman with the rifle whom he presumed was in charge of such things. The shaman was there at the time and made it clear that he would handle the distribution. This didn't sit well with the village head, but he deferred to his spiritual advisor. That was an intelligent move in light of the special powers which the shaman had with the spirit world. The headman had to be satisfied with the colored piece of silk with the Chinese characters on it. Tied around his rifle or his neck it made a very clear statement of his status.

While the pilot could move about well enough with his crutch, he certainly couldn't walk the 60 miles to China. It was decided to transport the flier by a form of a chair slung between two poles. There was quite an argument as to which of the men of the village would accompany and protect their honored guest on his way "home." A Tho tribesman who was a Viet Minh guerrilla arrived to act as a guide and contact with the Chinese. A system had begun to develop for the returning of downed Allied personnel. Occasional Japanese patrols would have to be avoided and great care exercised so as not to injure the treasured passenger. Two four man shifts changed every 30 minutes carrying the Tho version of a combination litter and sedan chair. The pilot estimated that they were able to carry him steadily in this manner at a solid walking pace, perhaps three miles an hour. Even with having to hunker down at one point as a patrol went by, it took only three days before they arrived at a designated transfer point at a medical missionary's station under Chinese military protection.

The village headman had decided to accompany the group in order to ensure the safe arrival of his charge and also represent his clan when the expected rewards were doled out. He wasn't disappointed. The Viet Minh representative, however, claimed the two long boxes of rifles the Chinese soldiers offered. He also took the lion's share of the Chinese dollars that went with the successful return of the live flier. This was the village's tribute to the Viet Minh as acknowledged protectors. It was merely tradition. Paying tribute was as old as the Tho themselves. There were others who paid it to them. For the village that had actually rescued and cared for the pilot went a small fraction of the money. That could be used for something good in the future. They knew not what. Best were the several bolts of cotton cloth of different colors and boxes of salt.

The following morning the happy group swung off down the trail from which they had just come. The porters carried the heavy rifle boxes slung beneath *don ganh*, the poles that earlier had supported the pilot's sling chair. The bolts of cloth were similarly hung. The village headman this time led the way back with the Viet Minh guerrilla taking the rear covering position. The headman as usual carried his ancient rifle, but now he also had the .45 automatic pistol which the thankful airman had given him as the ultimate sign of his gratitude. The shoulder holster was hung twice over the slight man's chest and back. It was awkward, but never did any soldier carry more proudly this badge of honor—and power. He also had learned to say the pilot's name, which he would repeat often in the future: Ah-mer-i-can!

* * *

14

Bui Dac Thanh was the head of a *to dang*, the basic cell of the Indochinese Communist Party. They met once a month at one of the cheap cafes in Hanoi. Thanh was always careful about security. His cell was small, with only five including himself in the group. He was the only soldier. The others were civilians, although all had a military connection even if it was only through a relative. Two were army food packers who worked in the Vichy government warehouse in Hanoi. The other two were workers in the communications center. They were all fiercely loyal to the Party and their country. The Party someday would bring freedom and independence to Vietnam. Of this they were certain. And they would be in the vanguard.

Thanh had been in the Party since he was 18. It was they who had urged him to join the French Colonial Army six years before. It had been hard at first because Thanh was better educated than most recruits. He could read and write and was quite good at arithmetic. He had risen to the rank of *soldat de première classe*. Unusually tall and athletic, Thanh was marked for even higher rank by his superiors. That evening's discussion had been quite lively.

"Why doesn't the Army do something?" one of the warehousemen asked Thanh. The subject was the catastrophic flooding that had decimated the villages of the Red River Delta. "Many thousand have no homes or food. It's terrible. I see people roaming streets in the city looking for garbage to eat. The Army could do something." The packer was quite agitated.

"They have to await orders," Thanh replied, conflicted in loyalty to his military command and his revolutionary political instinct. "I mean the ordinary soldiers. All the men in my unit would want to help, I'm sure. What can they do? The French don't care any more than the Japanese. It's a terrible situation."

"The Japanese say they're our friends," said one of the communications workers.

"I asked about that at our regular *chi bo* chapter meeting. The leader told us that the Japanese just want to push the French out and take over. He says they are imperialists just like the French. So there's your answer," replied Thanh, happy to be able to supply a Party viewpoint on the subject.

"I know that two people were killed by Japanese sentries over at their warehouse. Those Japanese guards just shot them dead. They were only trying to get a little food. There's very little food in our stores but the Japanese have plenty in their supply sections. They're bastards, just like the French. It is our socialist responsibility to help the unfortunates of the delta," said the other communications worker. Always eager to show initiative, his manner bordered on insolence.

"What do you suggest comrade?" Thanh asked.

"I, well, I suggest that we, the Party, do something."

"And what would that be, comrade?"

"We should demonstrate. We should go out into the streets and protest."

"And get mowed down, I suspect."

"Well, we shouldn't sit around and do nothing. This is why we joined the Party—to be able to fight against the imperialists. This is the time to do something." The man's voice had become very high pitched and some of the other patrons began to look at him over their shoulders. Thanh held his own voice even and spoke very slowly and carefully in order to exercise control.

"There is a time to act and there is a time to wait. This is the time to wait. We will be told when to take action and where. Would the comrade have us jump into the fire just because there is a fire? If the people rise up on their own, I am sure the Party will want us to lead them. However, until the time is right, we must reserve our energies."

"I say we should lead the people in the uprising, not wait like a bunch of clucking old ladies."

"I'm sure that our female comrades would dislike how you speak of their sex, comrade, or more to the point, I believe our leaders know far better than we when the moment is right for such action. I, for one, wait for their signal. It may come today, tomorrow, or sometime in the future. But when it does come, we must be ready, ready for the sacrifice, whatever it may be."

Thanh liked to give these talks emphasizing discipline and Party order. He believed every word and sought through that belief to infuse the others with his commitment. He was the cell leader and that was his job. The problem was that his better education and way of speaking could be resented by some. The communications worker was one of these.

"Perhaps if Comrade Thanh had to work to put bread into his mouth and those of his family, he would better understand what I am talking about. Marching around playing soldier with the French doesn't impress me."

"I'm not trying to impress anyone," said Thanh, barely holding his temper. "I'm just telling the truth."

It was not the first time the two men had disagreed. The other man was ten years older than Thanh and resented the fact that the soldier had been chosen as *to dang* leader. For his part, Thanh knew he couldn't afford to allow the baiting to get to him.

"The comrade's frustration at not being able to do anything about this great tragedy is most understandable. We are all frustrated. I will make a point of bringing the matter up at the next *chi bo* meeting."

Grumpily, the man settled back in silence. The other communications worker tried to change the subject.

"I've heard that some comrades have left the city to join our brothers preparing for resistance in the countryside. What does Comrade Thanh think of that?"

"I think that we must all stay where we are supposed to be until we are called upon to do something else. What good is an organization if everyone just goes off to do what they want?"

"There's more food up north in the countryside. Why stay here in the city starving?" asked one of the packers.

"Are you starving?" shot back Thanh, now thoroughly annoyed.

The whole group went silent. Thanh knew it was his responsibility to wipe away the conflict. He smiled his best smile.

"If you are starving, you should eat your shoes, comrade."

"The soles are rubber, comrade," said the packer going along with the joke.

"Then just eat the straps and think of them as chewy noodles," countered the still-smiling Thanh.

This produced the desired laughter all around, though some without quite as much enthusiasm as the others. Thanh was happy he had brought them back together as a group. As their leader this too was part of his job. He knew, though, that he could not leave the situation as it was. To have even one man in this discontented state was not good for group solidarity, one of the first principles of revolutionary organization. The basic unit, the cell, must be solid and on that relies the expanded development. He had been taught that early on and Thanh was proud of his ability to learn and put into practice the lessons in which the Party instructed him. As the leader of a *to dang* he must always think of the group first.

"I believe that in these very dangerous times we should recognize that anything could happen, and above all that we remain a functioning unit under all circumstances. Who knows what can happen? I suggest, therefore, that we elect an assistant head of our *to dang*—just in case, who knows. I would like to recommend our comrade, here." Thanh pointed to his recent adversary, who smiled in acceptance.

Several shots a distance away interrupted the celebration of Thanh's welcome political stroke. They all agreed it must be Japanese sentries shooting at hungry looters again. Yes, they said, these were dangerous times.

* * *

In the days following John's arrival in Kunming, he and Edouard worked together on their future area of operations. Edouard had been over the files before, so he was able to take John through the basic material rather quickly. Reports from French and Chinese sources made up the bulk of the files. The trouble was that the French material was old, and the Chinese reports carried only very rough translations, and those were quite suspect.

"My impression has been that the Chinese military in general view our presence here with mixed reactions. I don't think they want us fooling around

17

with Vietnamese matters too much. They've got plans themselves for the post-war—or at least that's what I've heard," said Edouard.

Where did you pick that up?" asked John.

"I admit they're most likely biased, but it came from some of DeGaulle's guys over in M.5 (French Intelligence in Kunming). I don't think it's a big secret that Chiang Kai-shek's people are always looking out for future economic advantage. As it is, most of their military around here are involved in one type of scam or another. That's the old Chinaman's big connection."

"I wanted to ask you about that. The day I first arrived I saw his son and Hallstrom's sergeant loading up a truck with what looked like GI packing crates of some sort."

"It wouldn't surprise me at all. The only question is whether or not Hallstrom is in on the deal. The fact is that maybe half of what comes up here from the Ledo Road ends up in the black market. I mean everything that comes into Kunming. That's a helluva lot of stuff. And guess who controls those shipments? The Chinese Army, of course. Castelli told me that. He knows this stuff."

"Is he in with this Hallstrom thing?"

"Well, I don't know that Edgar himself is actually making anything, but his sergeant obviously has something going on. As far as Tony Castelli is concerned, I figure him for a pretty straight shooter. I can't see him tied into anything. Tony's the one who told me about the sergeant, the old Chink and the Chinese Army connection. I don't figure that Tony would tell me about all this business if he was involved himself."

"Sounds right. Is the sergeant also Hallstrom's orderly? Isn't he supposed to be detachment admin noncom?" John asked.

"He's a bit of everything. He's got his fingers in everything and Edgar is wound around one of them. The old man can't make a move without him. That's why I call him the Colonel's dog robber. He's valet, orderly, paper pusher and organizer."

Both men were squeezed into a small room, one of several attached to the side of the main office of the detachment. There was very little office space, and this had been created by shifting out accumulated broken furniture and other useless junk that had been stored there. It had been Edouard's initiative that had created this new useable space; he laid claim as a result. He and John were now among the handful of operations officers who had a place to sit down and quietly pore over collected files. Castelli dropped in with a small pile of papers.

"This is background stuff on the communist Ho Chi Minh and his Viet Minh. There's a lot of interest in these people, so don't lose anything."

"Tony, we may lose our minds in here, but never your files," Edouard said as John signed the classified distribution sheet. Anything new was welcome.

These first weeks in Kunming turned into a pleasant surprise for John. The weather at 6,200 ft. in the first days of March could be quite brisk. More importantly, Edouard Parnell's unflagging upbeat view of life was an effective antidote to John's black moods. John found himself thinking of his Vietnam assignment with unexpected interest. Edouard had already put a great deal of work into the region's history and presented his findings to John as if each new fact was unearthed from long secret sources. There was nothing that Edouard Parnell could not turn into theater, and John soon became a captured but approving audience.

However, the easy-going life changed dramatically as news of new Japanese moves in Vietnam began to filter in.

"The word is that most of the Vichy forces in the south just allowed themselves to be interned without a fight," Edouard said to John. "I find that surprising, don't you?"

"Hell, they rolled over for the Germans, why should they act differently with the Japs? The Japs have been playing with them all along."

John's time with the *maquis* had left him bereft of understanding of anything Vichy. That forces loyal to the collaborationist French government should find themselves discarded by Imperial Japan simply served them right. These were not the same Frenchmen he had fought alongside in the Vosges. This now became the subject of discussion between the two in their cubbyhole office.

"Would you have hung around in that damn army after they caved in 1940, or would you have made the choice to fight on elsewhere?" John challenged Edouard.

"Fight, of course," Edouard replied. "But out here in Indochina, away from Europe… well, maybe it might not have been that clear cut."

"Hell, it wasn't. Just maybe a little harder to make the jump."

"That's just it. The ordinary *poilu* never really had a choice, did he? And it had to be hard for the junior officers. In the higher ranks… perhaps they had a choice—certainly more opportunity. They say the Vichy forces in Tonkin are trying to get out."

"Now they're making a move. They could have done that a long time ago. They would've had Chinese help. They might have been able to control at least the northwest corner of Tonkin. But they didn't do it. They just wanted to live fat and happy just like they'd been doing before the war. They certainly didn't want to fight the Japs. My *maquisards* wouldn't even call them Frenchmen."

"A lot of them are Legionnaires. They just do what they're told."

"Ha, all the more reason to pull out and set up a corner of Vietnam for De Gaulle's Free French. It would have driven the Nips crazy to have a force stuck up there, always some form of threat. And the Foreign Legion is supposed to fight. It would have been a *beau geste*."

"I loved the movie."

"So did I. Brian Donlevy was great."

"He would've been Vichy," Edouard exclaimed triumphantly.

"Hmm, I guess you're right. The hell with him. I change my mind. I'm changing the subject now also," said John.

"Okay."

"Tell me, what's the purpose of this war?"

"To beat Hitler and Tojo and so on. Avenge Pearl Harbor?"

"No, I don't mean that. I mean the purpose for us, the individual, you and I us?"

"The purpose of the war is… nothing. It's just a matter of staying alive. There's no personal gain—only the attempt not to become one of the losses."

"And at the same time do it with enough balls so as to make yourself feel you're a man."

"Sounds right to me."

"Not much of an ambition…."

"Hell, John, it's a damn hard job. Unless, of course, you're in the Special Services. I could use a weekend with one of those USO girls."

"If we were in one of those wars in the 1700s, we might pick up some treasure."

"Not the Revolution."

"OK. Wrong century, wrong army. The point I'm making, Edouard, is that we get shit out of the war except the possibility of living through it."

"Actually, that looks pretty good to me at this point."

"Come to think about it, you're absolutely right."

"Let's head over to the 'O' club and have a drink on that."

"To our health and continued existence."

"And to the USO girls, John. Don't forget them."

In these few short weeks, the two men, so different in background and temperament, had become friends. Wartime makes such things possible. In the case of John Guthrie, the loner, it was a new experience. To have a friend requires trust, and for someone brought up in the rough and tumble of the strikes of the 1930s, trust did not come easily. His was the mentality natural to an intelligence officer. Wartime finds a place for such people.

Chapter Two

For the sake of the briefing the mess hall had been cleared of tables. The Special Operations (SO) officers and Secret Intelligence (SI) officers concerned with Indochina activities sat toward the front of the room supposedly divided into their two sections. All enlisted men regardless of their assignment were in the rear. This had been at the specific instruction of Lt.Col. Hallstrom, who, as it was explained by the adjutant, Tony Castelli, was unable to attend because of pressing business related to the current Tonkin crisis. Groans of derision arose from both sides of the room. The section signs, so carefully prepared by Hallstrom's sergeant, were quickly converted into paper airplanes winging their way across the room. Everyone sat where they wanted to after the horsing around ended. It took about 20 minutes for that to be accomplished. Patiently, Tony Castelli waited out the ruckus. It's doubtful that things would have been much different if Hallstrom had been there, but his absence was a good signal for the schoolboy shenanigans to begin.

Castelli finally mounted an improvised step made of a large wooden crate in order to be seen from the back of the room. With a stick he pointed to a large map that had been pinned to the wall.

"Gentlemen, today we—meaning me—are going to brief you on the current situation in this area known to us all as the Vietnam portion of Indochina. Now a lot of this stuff you guys most likely already have heard about in one form or another, but this is the straight scoop and therefore as official as anything gets around here. Now is that part clear?"

This was a mistake because it merely brought another round of catcalls. Castelli waited them out and began again.

"On the evening of March 9th, the Japanese Ambassador in Saigon delivered the demand that all French troops be placed under Jap control. A two-hour period was given for the Vichy general in charge to officially react. The Japs moved in after that time. Most of the French units surrendered immediately though some put up some light resistance—primarily for show. These were quickly disarmed and interned. However, here in the north—Tonkin—at Lang Son, a combined force of Foreign Legionnaires, French regulars, and Vietnamese colonial troops held out for two days until they were out of water and ammo. The Japs slaughtered them after their attempt to surrender. The same thing happened at Dong Dan where they had held out for three days."

The room was silent. There wasn't even a shuffling of feet. Castelli allowed the effect of his remarks to sink in.

"Now we gather that some mix of Legionnaires, regulars and Vietnamese colonials from the garrisons in the south and central highlands have filtered into Laos. Efforts are underway to make contact with the aim of maybe regrouping these guys into some sort of partisan unit. That's a hope rather than an actual plan. I don't even know how many there are—I don't think many. Any questions so far?"

The room remained silent.

"Okay, here's the part that will concern us most. A large force in Tonkin made up of the same three types of Vichy forces under the command of two generals, with their full staffs, have begun an organized withdrawal. The best figure we have is around 6,000. They started from Son Tay—over here near Hanoi—and have headed toward Dien Bien Phu—a crossroads point over here. They may already be there, but it's a hell of a long way—over 200 miles on foot. Air Recon says they're strung out to hell and gone. We have another report that says one of the Vichy generals somehow is no longer with the main force but has struck out for northern Laos. If this is confusing, you're right on the mark."

John and Edouard exchanged glances. John spoke up.

"How fresh is this information, Tony?"

"Okay, Major Guthrie has put his finger on the vulnerability here. He asks about the time element—how fresh this info is. The answer is that the air recon is a result of photos taken at some height and then analyzed. That's got to be maybe a week old before we get it. If we had an immediate ops need I'm informed it could be speeded up. For some reason, everything goes to Chungking first and then back here."

"So, these troops could be at least a week beyond where the photos are showing them," John added.

"Correct, Major. In fact, M.5, the French Intel boys, tell me their reports show two columns have been formed. One heading northwest toward Laos—that's where the missing general most likely is. The main body led by a General Alessandri is headed more straight north. I've learned Chungking has a couple of high-level people who either are or are planning to fly into Dien Bien Phu to get the picture on the ground. In other words, yes, we're sort of out of the loop for the moment."

"Aren't we supposed to be the Indochina people, Tony?" Edouard asked the question that was on everybody's mind.

"Ah, Capt. Parnell has won the Kewpie doll. Yes, we are, as you so quaintly put it, supposed to be the Indochina people. I suspect that is what the old man is at this very moment attempting to ascertain. I shall continue, if I may. A little background on General Alessandri. He's a Foreign Legion officer and he has a loyal contingent as a sort of personal guard. The good guys of the 14th Air Force have done what they can by dropping food and medical supplies to the various elements they could find, but the suspicion is that they're generally in bad shape. Overflights report that the heavy artillery has been abandoned along the way."

A voice called out from the back of the room. "The Japs, what are the Japs doing?"

"There've been no major Jap Army movements, so it seems both sides are avoiding a serious battle. Again, the Free French M.5 guys report that their info shows the Japs laying ambushes but no large-scale confrontation. There are other reports that the Japs have offered the tribal hill people bounties for killed or captured soldiers of the Vichy force: All this stuff has little or no confirmation but seems logical."

The murmuring around the room had become louder as the audience debated the impact these developments might have on them. John and Edouard said nothing but waited for Castelli to continue. There seemed to be a punchline missing. They weren't disappointed.

"Okay, so much for the SITREP. Here's the kicker: The War Department in Washington has signaled Chungking, who passed it to us and the 14th, that we are to do nothing—repeat nothing—to aid these Vichy people. This includes their Vietnamese colonial troops also, of course. General Chennault hit the ceiling on that one, I hear, and finally got permission to bomb any Jap forces harassing the Frenchies. There is big time international politics going on here. The Free French Intel people at M.5 here in Kunming say they are in contact with DeGaulle himself, in Paris. They may be stretching things a bit, but maybe not. They've got a serious problem because they say loads of civilians are also trying to get out now that the Vichy gravy train has come to a screeching halt. Meanwhile we are to sit and wait. Oh, yes. We're on alert."

A groan came from the audience. Questions came from all sides. Castelli held up his hand like a schoolteacher quieting down his class. Finally, he responded to the tumult.

"I have no more information than what I've given you. I'm sorry, that's it."

The grumbling continued, but the diminutive adjutant simply collected his maps and pointer and headed for the door. One shouted question did, however, get his attention.

"What the shit does 'on alert' mean?"

Castelli turned at the door and shouted to no one in particular, "On alert means we sit on our collective asses and await orders. Whaddya think it means?"

* * *

Lord Edgar Hallstrom's dream had come true. Now attention would be paid to his area of operations. Taking advantage of this, he was able to get approval for the formation of a team to reconnoiter a few of the key trails northeast from Dien Bien Phu in an attempt to make contact with some of the Vichy units. This was deemed acceptable under the War Department restrictions as the mission was characterized as strictly for intelligence purposes. From Hallstrom's viewpoint, the important thing was that he would have a team in the area and that fact in itself would bring official attention to him. As the irreverent Edouard Parnell put it, he could smell the eagles of a full colonelcy already.

Not unexpectedly, John and Edouard were tipped to go on what was to be called Gorilla Mission. What was surprising, and annoying to Edouard, was that John was not named as team leader. That position had been given to Bob Simpson.

"He doesn't even speak French. He's got no actual combat experience. This isn't a damn football game."

John didn't really care one way or the other. "If the truth be told, Edouard, I am pleased to not have the responsibility."

Edouard wasn't mollified and only kept his mouth shut at the demand of his friend. Tony Castelli explained what led to the decision to put Simpson in command.

"It's very simple, really. Simpson has date of rank on you by a couple of years. That's how Edgar made up his mind. There's nothing personal at all. It was the safe way to go. That's Edgar. I pointed out that Bob never has heard a shot fired in anger, but that didn't matter. 'Date of rank, m'boy,' he said. So that's it. You'll have no trouble with Horse. Did you know that was Simpson's nickname at Notre Dame? The old man told me that. Edgar was very impressed when Bob first came here. I gather he was a big football fan. But when Horse didn't seem to want to play Edgar's game, the old man lost interest. Bob Simpson hasn't a political bone in his body. You guys'll do just great."

The whole matter ended there. There was no time to dwell on something that John didn't care about, especially when there were so many other things to worry over in an assignment in which no one had any real preparation. They drew weapons from the armorer and the rest of their gear from Supply. For John's part, the brief time before they jumped off kept him from thinking about the past. There was just too much to do. Edouard was his usual high-morale self, and treated the mission as he might a hunting weekend in Westchester. The only really disturbing note as far as John was concerned was the fact that everyone in the outfit seemed to know what the Gorilla team was going to do and where and when they'd do it. Who was in command might not have bothered John, but the total lack of proper security was inexcusable. He mentioned it to Simpson, but they both knew nothing could be done about it.

The "stick" of four SO officers and one enlisted man was night-dropped about 125 miles west of Cao Bang near the Hanoi–Kunming rail line. The plan was for the Gorilla team to head southwest, seeking to make contact with the Vichy units heading northeast from the crossroads town of Dien Bien Phu, the route that M.5 reports showed might be used. From the outset the team ran into trouble. Night drops are difficult in any case, but drops into an area not previously scouted, and with no friendly reception forces, compounds the problem. On top of this was the rugged terrain of a heavily forested mountain area into which they parachuted.

Three of the team were hung up in the trees. Luckily, none were seriously hurt, and they were cut down by the other more fortunate ones. John scrambled out on a limb to free Edouard entangled in the branches. Later he put a bandage over Edouard's gashed eyebrow.

"So, how bad is it, boss? Don't hold back. I can take it," said the irrepressible Edouard.

"Well, it's not quite Purple Heart depth, but definitely an acceptable scar. It'll add character," John replied as he adjusted the brown field dressing after pouring on sulfa powder.

There had been discussion with staff planners before they left Kunming about the best way to widen the search area by dividing into two units. It was useless to argue with the well-meaning planners, but the first thing they did upon landing was to agree to stay together and wait until first light so they at least could see where they were going in the heavy forest. Fortunately, they had good maps from the old colonial department of mines which M.5 shared with OSS. It had been agreed that John would be the map reader and navigator. Simpson didn't know how to read the French cartographic symbols and abbreviations. Even if he had known French, he never could have seen the fine print without his glasses. He may have been a horse, but he was a bit of a blind horse when it came to reading anything. That he'd been able to get into OSS at all was possible only with waivers on his weight and eyesight.

At nearly 40, Bob Simpson was several years older than John. He had played team sports since childhood and found the transition to OSS special operations just another athletic event. Simpson had cornered John one night before they left Kunming with the suggestion that they needed a "skull session."

"John, let's face it. You've got combat experience and can speak French. You should be the quarterback of this show. You know it and I know it. But they stuck me with the command, so that's it."

"I've got no problem with that, Bob," John said honestly.

"I'm countin' on you to kick my ass if I'm off base on anything. It's like I'm captain of the team, but you're the quarterback."

Without fully understanding what Simpson meant by that sports analogy, John replied, "I'm sure everything's going to be just fine."

"You'll let me know, right?"

"Absolutely."

"John, we're goin' t' have some fun, right?"

"I guess you could call it that, Bob."

Thin streaks of yellow light slanted in from the east after a restless few hours. They checked Edouard's wound and found it had stopped bleeding. A smaller plaster bandage was put on primarily to keep the cut closed and covered. The team formed up to move out. Simpson carried extra ammunition for his favorite weapon, the Thompson sub-machine gun. In fact, Horse Simpson's pack must have weighed nearly twice that of the other team members as he insisted on carrying the extra items like rope and additional tarps. As it was, they all carried more than usual for a five-day to one-week patrol mission. They didn't know what might arise that could delay getting to the small bush landing strip where they were to be picked up.

John checked the area just to be sure the buried parachutes were adequately hidden from sight. He pulled some branches over the newly turned earth and, when satisfied, gave a signal to Simpson he was ready to take the point. Everyone had been warned to keep the chatter down.

They moved slowly, single file through the dense undergrowth. A heavy fog settled in and the canopy of trees prevented the early pale sun from making any but the barest inroads. The light was adequate to see by and it was good to get going. The group slashed its way with machetes through heavy foliage and interwoven hanging vines. To the best of John's judgement, the map indicated—if they had been dropped in the place—they would soon come upon a well-defined logging trail. The team made more noise than it should have, but there was no alternative when you're forced to cut your way through. They did not expect to meet anyone at this stage other than perhaps some tribesmen. At least that was what they had been told to expect. The French were judged still to be some distance off. With this in mind, they were more than a little surprised when they heard the sounds of a vigorous fire fight in the distance, hardly 45 minutes after they had started out. John, ten yards ahead, held up his hand, signifying halt. He needn't have because the little column had automatically stopped at the first sound of fire. The easily distinguished clump of small mortars was bracketed by bursts of a machine gun. Individual rifle shots beat staccato in the early morning air. The entire Gorilla group hit the ground even though the sounds were a distance off. The firing continued for about 15 minutes and then petered out.

The team gathered around John, the "veteran," as if they expected him to tell them what the shooting was about. He, of course, knew no more than they did. Edouard decided, as he always did, the time was ripe for a little light humor.

"I think this satisfies the requirements for a battle star on our theater ribbon. I already have my Purple Heart from the jump, so I think it's time to go home now."

No one laughed. Bob Simpson shot him a dirty look.

"Shut up, Eddy. What the hell do ya think that is, John?"

"Haven't the faintest, Bob. But it's certainly military weapons with some firepower. I wouldn't think it's tribesmen, unless they're damned well-armed. I can't tell if two sides are firing at each other or that one side is simply giving it to someone else. There's no way in hell to know."

Simpson spoke in a hoarse whisper.

"Whoever it is, they're pretty damn trigger happy. That was a hell of a ruckus. We might get shot the same way, even if they're friendly, before we could identify ourselves. And in this jungle how do we do that—identify ourselves I mean?"

The larger meaning of what he had said sunk in. That the five of them were there at all now seemed rather absurd. The thought was recognized by an exchange of sheepish grins and a few shakings of heads. No one else spoke. They didn't have to. They all knew what their job was at that point. It was obvious. Get the hell out of there!

John, with the briefest hesitation, suggested that they simply head directly for the designated landing strip.

"If we meet any Vichy units on the way, swell. Otherwise we're just wasting time. Sorry, Bob, but that's the way I see it. We're just stomping around in the woods without a clue."

"No, I agree, John. This is definitely one of those 'it seemed like a good idea at the time.' It's embarrassing, but that's it. I should have seen it. Maybe just too eager for some action. It looks a lot different on the ground. A typical OSS balls up."

"Hell, we all could have said something. It's not your fault, Bob. We'll do our job. We'll be looking for the French column. They might be the ones shooting that we just heard," John said encouragingly.

"It could also be the Japs," someone mumbled.

It was the always sophisticated French American Edouard Parnell who got them moving. In his very best prep school accent he said, "Well, enough of this fucking around. Let's move our collective asses!" The key words were as clearly and properly enunciated as if he was reciting Shakespeare. It certainly cut through to the essential element. John checked his compass and the map, and the little troop formed up with him in the lead and Edouard covering the rear. John smiled to himself at his friend's juxtaposition of aristocratic air and soldierly vulgarity. This time the team proceeded with as little noise as possible.

There were no regrets at the new plan of action. It wasn't as if they had been sent to rescue anyone. All they were supposed to do was locate the French column, if there was one, and report back. No one had suggested that they should expect to fight their way into anything. They all had the same thought. They were bugging out to avoid having to fight their way out. From what, they weren't going to hang around and find out. It could have been Vichyites or Japanese giving or taking a pasting. The firepower was pretty heavy, certainly out of the league of the Gorilla team. What they were doing was the prudent thing. Hell, they weren't even sure they had been dropped in the right place!

Each was submersed in his own thoughts as they picked their way through the vine-entangled forest, slowly working down the side of the small plateau on which they had been dropped. They moved obliquely from the sound of the firing. It was difficult going because the slopes of the flattened mountain were sharp-angled and hard to traverse. John was very aware that they had not run across the trail they expected. This was just as well, as far as he was concerned. It was best to steer clear of beaten pathways. The welcoming gunfire had forced that. After an hour of sliding and stumbling down the hillside, they came upon some discarded old French military equipment. There were also signs that a small band, presumably French, had trudged through this same area. They halted to discuss the find.

"As the crow flies, we haven't gone very far, but we've been moving at a steady clip, so I figure we've covered about three miles on the ground. What we want to do is stay in this valley for another ten miles—then we'll have to hump it up and over some hills west by northwest."

John showed the kneeling group the positions he was talking about on the map. They all perspired heavily even though the mountain temperature was comparatively mild. Bob Simpson already looked as if he had lost a few of his excess pounds, but otherwise he seemed in good shape. Aside from some heavy breathing, everyone else was quite fit. John continued:

"I'd like to make it here by nightfall." He pointed to the map again. "That would mean we'd be in striking distance of the strip in maybe another day and a half."

"Sounds good to me," said Simpson in response to his "quarterback." The others assented.

During this brief break, John had a chance to talk with Edouard who had been holding down the job of rear trailer, a task which required constant turning backward to check movement behind.

"How ya doin' pardner?"

"Well enough, masked man. I guess old Horse doesn't care for my sense of humor."

"He's just not used to your unique comic ability," John replied soothingly. "I take it you agree with my assessment. You can read the map as well as I can. Don't worry about my feelings."

"No, John, you're right in all respects. That is, if we were dropped where we were supposed to. I think we were, so you're okay. I was just a little annoyed at Simpson telling me to shut up when I was trying to lighten the scene."

"He's a bit tense. It's his first time out. Forget about it."

"Anything you say, Dad."

Edouard dropped the matter, but it obviously had bothered him. John wanted Edouard to get his mind back to the situation at hand.

"Keep a wary eye open in your tail gun position. If we're goin' to be hit, the chances are it'll come from the rear—at least that's what I'd do."

"I'm your obedient servant, m'lord. Roger, Wilco, and all that good stuff."

Edouard dashed to the rear of the group as they pulled out, his mood swiftly back to its usual good humor. In front of him was another captain, Paul Schreymann, a fluent French and German speaker who had been born in Alsace and came to the US as a teenager. The lone enlisted man of the five-man team was Sgt. Ted Applegate of Anniston, Alabama, a former Ft. Benning instructor who had been transferred to the OSS training cadre. He had fought to be assigned to the field. Definitely "Old Army," Applegate had 15 years' service and long experience serving pre-war in the Philippines. He was the ordnance expert among the team members—all of whom he considered amateurs. Applegate had trained scores of OSS candidates of all ranks. Rank, as such, meant little in the field for OSS or Applegate. There, respect was earned and maintained by performance. He wasn't much impressed with anything other than combat experience.

The Gorilla crew set out on their next ten-mile jaunt in determined fashion. They were in as much control of the situation as they could be and were committed to marching out of this part of Vietnam in one piece. If any Vichy units crossed their path, all well and good. For the first while a small stream trickled along the route they traveled. Birds they disturbed flittered through the trees, but they saw no other signs along the way. The ground was soft enough to show if anyone had passed by. From time to time they would stop and rest for five minutes, splash some water on their faces, have a drink from their canteens, and move on. Drinking from the crystal-clear stream was taboo unless mixed with the water purification tablets popped into the canteen. That was the one thing they all remembered from their training. What types of berries to eat and roots to chew on were long forgotten from their survival courses.

Because the direction was right, they stayed along the natural path the stream created. That relatively unimpeded route allowed them to make very good time. They hiked for about three hours on ground that was damp but firm underfoot. John calculated how much longer he should push them to make the ten miles he had reckoned they should travel from his kilometer conversion. There were no landmarks to check against. Once again, he was reminded how stupid it was to be dropped in without a good local guide. He went over the map with Edouard and they agreed that another hour's march would bring them to where they should begin the west by northwest climb. Bob Simpson suggested that it would be best to take a chow break before they went on. From their packs each team member pulled out one of the rectangular cartons of so-called K rations and tore open the brown wax paper covering. Edouard couldn't resist remarking on how much he enjoyed a picnic *al fresco* as he happily munched away on a dry biscuit of supposedly high nutritional value.

They were gathered together in a group exchanging stories of great meals they had eaten in the past when the first shots splintered the trees around them. Why none of them were hit was a testament to the poor marksmanship of the ambushers, as well as deflections of rifle rounds fired through heavy tree cover. They all grabbed their weapons and returned fire. Simpson fired a long burst of his tommy gun in the direction of the incoming rounds as the others let loose with their carbines. No one had the faintest idea what they were firing at. Without saying a word Horse Simpson lumbered forward toward the incoming fire, blasting away. Crouching and running he was soon followed by the rest of the "Gorillas" screaming at the top of their lungs. Later they would admit that they had been so shocked and scared that the screaming came without any thought. They heard a few shouted commands and the firing stopped. They could hear the attackers retreat back up the high ground. The OSS team ceased their firing and checked on each other. All five were untouched. Bob Simpson had a broad grin on his leathery face. They spread out in intervals of about ten feet and slowly began to move up the hill sweeping the area and ready for another round. They stopped after going about 30 yards at a shout from Sgt. Applegate.

"Y'all bettah have a look at this," he drawled.

The lanky Applegate prodded a form on the ground with his boot, then with a broken tree limb. The body didn't move. "He's daid," the sergeant announced with finality. "He's damned daid." It was a Japanese soldier. They had been ambushed by a squad of Japs. There couldn't have been any more or they wouldn't have run away. John also realized that he had been stupid to simply follow the stream. Their direction was easily given away, and this allowed the Japs to track them with ease and hit them when and where they wanted. Applegate sidled over to him and said very quietly so no one else could hear:

"Ah, missed it too, Major. Next time we don't make the same mistake." He then turned to Simpson who was still focused on the surrounding high ground searching for any movement, and in a louder voice said, "Well, Major, you sure got lucky with that Thompson. If you'd have anythin' t'aim at, you'd missed by a mile. But it sure does spray good, don't it?"

Applegate picked up the dead man's rifle, inspected it and said, "Arisaka, 99. Seven point seven millimeter. Ah guess they had nuthin' automatic 'n they didn't have no grenades neither or we'd most be daid by now." He then spat to emphasize his instruction.

"Well, we aren't dead, and that's good enough for me, Sarge," Edouard said with conviction.

They went back down the hill to retrieve their packs which had been left behind in the charge. At John's suggestion they started off at an angle up the height and then moved on a parallel line with the valley stream below. It was harder going, but it made them less of a target. Applegate volunteered to range higher and forward as both point and flanker while Edouard continued his rear cover assignment. The three others were careful to keep an adequate interval between themselves. John would lead them west by northwest after a calculated period, while the old "Bama coon hunter," as Ted Applegate called himself, scouted forward, never losing sound contact with the group. He couldn't see their movement from his distance, but his hearing always kept him appraised of their pace and direction. In the same way, by frequent stops to listen, he was able to pick up unrelated sounds that might be hostile. He was an experienced woodsman and was at ease in the forest—any forest.

Applegate rejoined the team as the evening light dimmed. The night dark descended as if a curtain closed. They fell exhausted to the ground by a rock outcropping that provided some cover. Bob Simpson designated the shift time for each to act as pickets as the others slept. There were no fires to boil water or heat the canned rations of glutinous sausage patties and spaghetti, but they were washed down hungrily with canteens of water. Crackers and candies rounded out the meal which Applegate pronounced satisfactory and Edouard characterized as cold garbage. Cigarette smoking was out of the question; the smoke could be smelled at a long distance. They knew a larger Jap unit was out there somewhere.

No one had any trouble falling asleep, though after two or so hours any sleep was fitful. At first light they broke camp with a breakfast of water and leftover nutrition crackers. As the team dragged their stiffened bodies into action for another day's hard march, John inquired about Edouard's gashed brow.

"You should let me look at it," he said.

"It's fine, really. Anyhow if we take the bandage off it's liable to start bleeding. It may be swollen but it's not hot, so I don't think there's any infection. I can see out of the eye well enough. Anything changes I'll let you know."

"Be sure you do that, kid." For the first time John asserted recognition of the six-year difference in their ages. Edouard was too sore and tired even to pretend to object. They went over the map together, agreeing on the route of the day's march, confident that the direction was correct.

The morning was spent climbing. It was particularly tough moving cross country on an angle up the side of a hill, but there was no alternative if the direction was to be maintained. Applegate again took the point but recommended that the trailer position be shared instead of leaving it to Captain Eddy, as he called him. Edouard was grateful for the break in the particularly tiring task of always turning and sometimes walking backward. The sergeant advised that it was best to change the rear guard trailer every half hour to keep him sharp. Applegate never relinquished his self-appointed status as team instructor.

During the mid-day break, the Alabaman regaled them with lessons he learned while serving with the Filipino Scouts. Always hit the last man first, a Moro tracker had taught him. The best way was to silently take out the last guy with your bolo knife, then quietly work your way down the line. That was the Moro way, said Applegate, as he worked on the barely chewable fruit bar he stowed in the side of his mouth like chewing tobacco. He was well aware of his image and intended to keep it that way, even if it scared these amateurs every now and then.

Other than Applegate's remark about the Thompson sub-machine gun, nobody had said anything to Bob Simpson after his charge up the hill. He would have made light of it if they had. It was very much on John's mind as he pushed branches from his face after resuming the march through the brush and low-hanging tree limbs. Simpson's reaction to being fired on was one of pure fury. Obviously the Japs never expected it, John decided. Nor did they expect the wild Indian attack from the rest of them. John couldn't recall who was the first one to turn screaming up the hill. It all happened so fast; there was no thought to it. It wasn't like his calculated and very personal killing of that sentry. This time there was only exhilaration. There was nothing to agonize over. There was the unexpected crash of gunfire, and then he and the others became just a crazed bunch of guys bent on obliterating whatever was shooting at them. A primal urge. Not calculated, not the premeditated murder that had been expected of him before. And yet this time he hadn't really had a sense of defending himself, although he knew that would be a later explanation. No, he and the others were out just to annihilate the source of those shots. They hadn't even known the shooters were Japs. It hadn't mattered who or what they were. How is that explained?

Why was he even thinking about such things? Concentrate on the slogging forward, listen for other sounds, of Applegate up front or other foreign noises. Be alert! But the images of their rush kept coming back, demanding explanation. It must have all happened before, somewhere. The Danish berserkers, that's who they were. The wild Norsemen who gave their name to the word. Screaming and yelling in full voice of their madness and thus to throw themselves on their enemy. For them it was a planned tactic and, at the same time, the warrior's psychic armor. It was the explanation he wanted, needed. For that moment he had joined with his Viking Scots forbearers. They all had.

Ted Applegate had thoroughly enjoyed the entire experience. This was what he had volunteered for. He had more than paid his dues on the dusty red clay of Ft. Benning and the heat and wet of endlessly boring duty in the Philippines. He had been told he'd have his war, and goddammit here it was. His had been the rebel yell that drove them wildly up that hill—just like his ancestors at a dozen battles in the Civil War. Raw-boned farm boys like him, and nothing could stop them once they got going. He had been the first one to rise up to follow his major, and the others quickly joined. But it was "Johnny Reb" who knew exactly what he was doing, and he would do it again if need be. Well, that Yankee major and the rest of them had passed their first test. He'd make them soldiers yet!

The rain had started about halfway through the afternoon, bringing with it a damp chill which soaked their overheated, sweating bodies. At first it was refreshing, and then it just added to the discomfort of tramping heavily burdened through the primeval forest of upland trees, bushes and vines. By the end of the day they were all yearning for hot, dry sunlight, but at least nobody had shot at them. Again, a picket guard was set, with each man trying to avoid the wetness as best he could. The trek that day had actually been easier, in that they seemed to have been developing some conditioning. That night, though, they were colder and hungrier than the previous day. A couple of days' growth of beard added to gauntness. Shaving hadn't even entered their minds, except for Ted Applegate, who contemplated using his bowie knife as a straight razor the following morning. He discarded the idea with the military logic that if the two majors and two captains didn't shave, who was he to give them direction on personal hygiene. Damn, if they'd been Regular Army... But hell, OSS was practically not in the Army anyhow! He found solace in a healthy bite of the candy bar in his pocket.

Along with all the usual equipment they carried on their person and in their packs, as well as their weapons and ammo, each of the Gorilla team members had added a personal touch to their supplies. In Applegate's case it was several Baby Ruth bars he had somehow obtained from the incredibly stocked black market in Kunming. Every now and then on the trail he would give himself a treat of a bite of one of the bars. For John's part, satisfaction came in the form of a dozen packets of chalky tablets for his ulcer pain. He was going through his store rather quickly. Edouard, never lacking in *joie de vivre*, had an extra canteen filled with a quite serviceable *vin ordinaire rouge* which he had procured from a French liaison officer. He husbanded this supply by rationing himself only a few sips at a time. The others had brought along their own favored tasty treats as a reminder of the world left behind. Unlike food rations or ammo which were unhesitatingly shared, these were personal sensory memories privately held and as individually important as photos from home. John had neither—nor sought them; it was part of his armament.

The next day did not start well. Theoretically, they should have been able to see several landmarks that the map indicated in the form of twin sugar loaf peaks directly in their march path. Even waiting for the fog to lift did not reveal the required peaks. The map could be wrong, or they could be reading it wrong. John, with Edouard's help, decided that they must have miscalculated the distance marched, but they didn't want to make a big thing out of it and get everyone's spirit down. They decided it was best to carry on as if they knew exactly where they were and where they were going. For most of the day John led them as before, showing nothing but confidence. In a whispered conference with Edouard during a break, John admitted he was completely lost.

"I haven't the faintest idea where we are other than I think we've gone in the right general direction. Here, look at the map. See if you can figure it out."

Edouard squinted with his good eye as John traced the route he thought they had been following.

"If here's where we're supposed to be right now, I certainly can't see any recognizable topography," said Edouard after studying the map. "Hell, the map couldn't be that wrong. It's a French Indochina Government map. If they don't know this place, who would? With all due respect, Admiral Columbus, the moment might be near to tell the rest of the crew."

"Okay, I agree. But I think we should put in another couple of hours of hiking. I still feel we're on the right path. If nothing changes after that, I'll call a general palaver."

The team was about to form up to continue their trek when it happened. They never saw or heard them coming. They just seemed to materialize from the forest. If the tribesmen had wanted to, they could have killed every last one of the Gorilla team and the Americans never would have known what had hit them. There were about 15 fighters, all dressed in different collections of pieces of uniforms, some French, some Japanese, some in dirty civilian bush jackets. None wore shoes. The tallest among them, a man wearing the closest thing to a complete battle dress uniform, held his hand up palm forward. It was the universal sign of peaceful intentions. It didn't matter what his intentions were; his people had the drop on the Gorilla team even though they were armed only with ancient single shot bolt action French rifles. They also carried a lethal assortment of knives and machetes. Later the team would learn that they had four grenades spread around the group. Several of the men had bows and arrows slung across their backs. There was no question about it, this crowd was a serious bunch of cutthroats. The tall man, presumably their leader, spoke, in okay French.

"*Bonjour messieurs. Cherchez-vous quelque chose?*" He meant it as a sort of a joke. That he emphasized with a broad grin. John immediately grasped the situation, but wasn't sure the others would, especially the ones who spoke no French. He was particularly worried about Simpson and Applegate. Quickly he responded, first in English directed to their spokesman, but really meant for his own people.

"I think they're friendlies. Stand easy." In French he returned the greeting saying also that they were Americans and had been sent to help. He made no attempt to explain who it was they were supposed to help. He aimed at a nice, generally helpful manner. It seemed the smartest approach when confronted at three to one by a group of guys who might not have been armed with the most advanced weapons, but certainly looked like they could well use the ones they had. The leader seemed to accept the explanation. He asked only one question. "Americans?" He had no idea what that was. He knew about the French—far too well. He had heard about *les Anglais*, though he had never seen one. And in recent times he had come to know the Japanese, not kindly. But Americans… "Are you friends of the French?" he asked John in his oddly accented French. John sputtered. He didn't know how to answer that question. There was no simple answer, and that was what this man wanted. Edouard came to his rescue.

"*Il y a deux types des Français.* There are the good French and the bad French. The bad French are the ones who want to rule the people, and the good French want the people to rule themselves. We are friends of the good French. Are you friends of the good French, too?"

The man didn't answer. He turned to his tribesmen and spoke in their tongue. Their smiles became even broader. The leader turned back to speak to Edouard and John who had moved together. Applegate had tried to edge off to the side, and Simpson was hefting his Thompson ominously. John quickly explained in English what was going on and told them to relax. It was important that the whole team remain calm.

"You don't like the Japanese?" the tall one asked John.

"No, we don't. We are fighting a big war against them. They came to our country and attacked us, so now we are fighting them." That was the best he could think of.

"Are you winning?"

"Oh, yes, we are winning."

"We saw them attack you."

"Attack us?"

"Yes, the other day. We were following them. They followed you. They ran away."

At that he turned around and spoke again to his fighters. This time they all roared with laughter. He turned back to John and Edouard.

"We thought it was very funny how they ran. He made them afraid," pointing toward Bob Simpson. "You all made them afraid." He turned and translated again to his men. This time they shook their weapons in the air in approval.

John explained what had just gone on. Simpson smiled and Applegate let out one of his patented rebel yells, but in a softer tone than before. The tribesmen loved it and waved their rifles again in response.

These were Meo tribesmen a long distance east of their Laotian highlands. The leader had served in the French Colonial Army. As far as John could make out, they were essentially mercenaries. What he would have no way of knowing was that these tribesmen were part of a protective force of the Meo. This was the small but effective private army that "King" Touby Lyfong, of this sizeable tribe, maintained to secure the overland northern routes for his opium poppy products. From time to time they would take on odd jobs for the French colonial forces. A new wrinkle had been added to their employment of which John would hear soon from the tall Meo leader, who liked to be called "Lieutenant." He explained that a segment of the Meo tribe of which he and his men were part had established an alliance with the Tho tribe of the Cao Bang region far to the east. They were all going to be part of a "liberation army" for Indochina. Lieutenant didn't know too much about this "army," but he had a pamphlet that explained it all. The Meo leader was eager to show John the tract which he kept safely tucked away in a small leather pouch with other valuables. It was as if he was displaying his official orders. His pride in having such documentation was evident. The trouble was that he couldn't translate what the pamphlet said because it was in Vietnamese, which he didn't read—and, of course, neither did any of the Gorilla team. John looked at the paper to be polite. He did notice the depiction of a flag in the corner of one of the pages. The flag was red and it had a yellow star in it.

John thought he recognized the symbol but checked it with Edouard.

"Isn't this the same as some of that stuff Castelli showed us? What did he call it? Viet Minh, right?"

"That's it. The same thing. They're led by this communist guy, Ho something."

John turned back to Lieutenant. "Viet Minh," he said authoritatively.

"*Oui, Viet Minh*," replied Lieutenant eagerly, pleased that John had recognized the symbol. "*Nous sommes tous Viet Minh maintenant. C'est bien ça?*"

"*Ah, oui, tres bien. Pour la liberation, bien sûr*," was John's reply.

Each man then turned to his own group and translated the exchange. John addressed himself to Bob Simpson who had been waiting patiently—contrary to his normal instincts.

"Somehow these guys are connected to the Vietnamese guy, Ho, who we were briefed about back in Kunming. Remember? He is some sort of communist nationalist who has this outfit called the Viet Minh which has been helping us and AGAS in the pilot rescue operation. The Ho guy is trying to get the French to give up their claims on Indochina altogether. You know, independence."

"Does this mean these guys are on our side?" Simpson said motioning to the Meo.

"For the moment, I think. They're trying to be friendly." Both Edouard and Paul Schreymann, who understood the French exchange that had been going on, nodded their heads in accord with John's assessment.

Lieutenant seemed to sense the confusion of the big man who was obviously a chief. He was used to "Europeans" not understanding the obvious. He had run across that sort of thing a great deal during his tour in the French colonial military. He spoke to John slowly, as if he were instructing a child.

"First the Japanese came to us to pay us to attack the French Army. There are many French soldiers now trying to get away from them. The French are not in charge anymore. The Japanese told us that." He waited a moment to see if what he had said had been understood. Then he continued:

"Then we were told by our chiefs that we were now allied with other tribes, and we should not attack the French who were trying to get away, but we should try and help them leave. Then we would have the independence, all the tribes." It all made clear sense to Lieutenant.

"So, you will now attack the Japanese?" It was less clear to John.

The Meo leader appeared to cogitate over that question. His forehead wrinkled in exaggerated thought. Finally, he said, "You want us to be your allies?"

It was John's turn to ponder his answer. Both Edouard and Paul exchanged glances but offered no help to him. Ted Applegate spat in a supreme gesture of indifference to whatever was happening. He had already picked out the two guys he was going to take down first if any of these little characters turned bad. Bob Simpson was more sanguine; the quarterback seemed to have this matter in hand. Edouard was fascinated with the assorted uniforms and weapons of the tribesmen. Some had the faces of teenagers but were most likely adults. None showed any sign of tension that he could discern. Just a happy bunch. He wondered if they smiled that same way when they were cutting your throat.

John began slowly, speaking as clearly as he could in his basic French.

"We know of the leader of the Viet Minh. He is a Dr. Ho. That is his name. He is an old and wise man, I am sure. We know that there are many groups like yours that are part of the Viet Minh, and that you are all fighting for independence, freedom. The Japanese are against freedom. They want to rule everywhere. We would hope that you would fight them with us. I am sure Dr. Ho would agree."

It was a grandstand play tossing in this Ho guy like that. Lieutenant may not have ever heard of him, but at least it was a way to tie in the Viet Minh angle. Lieutenant seemed rather proud of that connection, not that he seemed to have the slightest comprehension of the broader political ramifications.

"I think we need more weapons if we are to be your allies," Lieutenant responded. He was a hell of a lot cleverer than he appeared, with or without the political sophistication. He delivered another broad grin. "We need better guns. Guns like his." He pointed to Simpson's tommy gun. "But like yours would be good," motioning toward John's carbine.

The Meo leader still smiled, but John sensed a hardness. There was a pause and Edouard spoke in English.

"Tell him we have many weapons of both these types for him that will come by airplane. Tell him he must lead us to the airstrip so we can send for the weapons."

John did exactly as Edouard suggested. Lieutenant turned and spoke to his band of cutthroats. One, the oldest and most grizzled, spoke back sharply. Lieutenant answered calmly but firmly. He turned back to John, no longer smiling. He was strictly business now.

"There is a big Japanese company. They are looking for you. They have many weapons including mortars. They have attacked some French the other day. The soldiers you chased away were from that company. But they do not know this place as well as we do. We can help you as you ask, but you must promise that we will get the weapons when we take you to that landing place. And you must give us something now to prove your trust. It is our way," he added solemnly. There was no room for negotiation.

"I shall talk with my friends," John said diplomatically. The Meo nodded in agreement. He went back to his group as John drew the Gorillas around him.

"Look, we have to give them something to show us the way to the strip. We then have to give them some weapons when we get there. It's ticklish to trust them, but we don't have much choice."

"We can kill the bastards," drawled Applegate.

"Then we don't have them as guides, and we'd certainly take casualties," Edouard responded quickly.

"But we don't really need them—or do we, John?" asked Simpson.

John then briefly explained the problems he had been having with the map. He looked directly at Simpson who responded with the authority of team leader, something he hadn't done that often.

"So we damn well need them or at the very least have a better chance with them than without." The discussion was over.

"Let's see what we can give them now. We'll work on the weapons when we get to the strip. How's that, John?" Edouard offered to his friend.

"Sounds good to me." John looked toward Bob Simpson who shook his head affirmatively. It was settled.

They pooled their resources. They set aside two machetes and two entrenching tools. Applegate put in his remaining candy bar. That was a real sacrifice. Edouard offered up his extra canteen with the wine in it. He had been planning to pass it around to celebrate with when they reached the landing strip anyhow. Lieutenant came over while they were putting together their pile. He looked over the collected stuff with a critical eye. Edouard opened the canteen and gave him a drink to show what it was. The wine was clearly a hit, but the Meo leader still hesitated.

"I need more, for them." He moved his head in the direction of his own group. He seemed to be saying he was happy with the offering, but he needed more to sell his companions. He took another swig of wine. It was obvious who was getting that little gift.

"Who's got a GI watch or something that wasn't their grandmother's present?" John asked. "Let's see if we can give him a couple of watches. Mine was my Dad's, but I guess...."

"Hell," said Applegate. "This is GI. They'll issue me another. Right, Major?"

"Here take this one," Schreymann said, pulling off an expensive Patek Philippe. "The lady who gave me this took a two-carat diamond engagement ring with her when she left me for a damn tennis instructor. They'll love it. It's gold."

He was right. Lieutenant took it. He gave the stainless steel one of Applegate to the grizzled old fighter who had complained earlier. The two shovels and two machetes went to four tribesmen chosen by Lieutenant. Nobody wanted the Sergeant's candy bar. He took it back and stuffed it in his pocket. Edouard, always amused by the manner and accent of the Alabaman, thought that Applegate's gesture in grabbing back the Baby Ruth bar qualified as haughty. Pissed off was more the way Ted Applegate would have explained it. Turning down his treasured candy bar was downright insulting. Edouard, who had stood nonchalantly with his arms behind his back as if at ease, relaxed and reholstered his .45 which he had somehow withdrawn without anyone noticing. His carbine had been left on the ground when the tribesmen made their original entrance, and he was not going to be caught with nothing, as he put it, but a smile on his face.

Lieutenant gave orders to his band who spread out before and behind the Gorilla team. Bob Simpson took the lead now. He wanted to have the tall Meo in his sights, he said. Applegate, now in a bad mood, took up the rear. He didn't trust these "damned little bastards," and said so. John, relieved of his duties as pathfinder, nonetheless tried to keep track of the direction and timing of the march so as to be able to check where he might be on the map. Lieutenant couldn't read the map, so he was no help in that regard. He mentioned a few landmarks that John should look for, however. As far as John could tell, the men moved by sheer dead reckoning. The topography of the area must have been solidly implanted in their brain, providing their own mental map. He mentioned this to Edouard who suggested that was most likely why both the French and the Japanese wanted them to work with them. "Very capable chaps," was his estimation.

For his part, Lieutenant knew these white men could not find their way through the mountains. They had no sense of the memory of sound and sight. They knew nothing of the movement of game in certain patterns nor of prevailing cloud flow at certain times of year. They really were amazingly stupid for people who possessed so many things and were so rich.

The Meo scouts returned from an extensive patrol late in the afternoon to report no sign of the Japanese. Lieutenant reported to John and Bob Simpson that they would make camp early in order to do some hunting. The news was greeted with considerable joy by most of the Gorillas who had become drained by lack of sleep and nothing but cold rations. Edouard and Ted Applegate seemed to have survived so far best of all. In fact, they appeared to thrive on the privations. All happily greeted the news that it was safe enough to start cooking fires. It was the first hot meal the OSS men had had in days. The two groups ate separately, though the tribesmen offered to share part of the day's hunt. The OSS consensus was to avoid eating the game for fear of the potential of developing a dose of dysentery, the dreaded GI runs. The team shared their cigarettes with the Meo, and that was a major social success. Slowly the mutual wariness began to dissolve. After eating, Lieutenant came over to talk. It was as uncomplicated as that. After eating there is conversation, a universal tradition.

The Americans sat around with Edouard translating. The Meo leader told them of his experiences in the French colonial military. He told of the beatings he had endured by the French sergeant for minor disciplinary infractions, and, in the same breath, of the respect he had gained in his own community for his military service. The conflict within him was obvious. The love/hate relationship with the colonial master was apparent. Edouard tried to make that clear to his audience.

"He's very proud, you see, of having been a member of the French Army. But at the same time, he doesn't want to be treated as a lesser person. They may not look very sophisticated, these tribal people, but they have a very old culture, and they want it respected."

"He don't seem to me to have no great culture. No disrespect, Cap'n Eddy, but he 'n his compadres here look like they're a long way from bein' cultured. This ain't sayin' I don't have a lotta regard for their huntin' n' trackin' ability, 'cause I hold those skills very highly."

For Ted Applegate that had been a lengthy speech. There was no point in going into detail in reply at this time, but Edouard didn't want to leave the matter entirely.

"I'll ask him what he and his people would do if they could rule themselves with no interference."

Lieutenant listened carefully as Edouard phrased his question into French. After some moments' thought, the Meo leader replied very carefully:

"I have thought about that, myself. Of course, everyone wants to have a ruler from their own people. I think I would be a good ruler, but then so do other people in my tribe. Of course, we already have a king. Touby Lyfong, we call "King," but that is the old way, and there are others in our tribe who are head men like him. We are a big tribe. No one person is over us all. But it could all be worked out. We would need time to work it out, but we could do it. We don't need the French. We would need help, though. We need many things. Do you think your rulers would want to help us?"

Edouard made the translation as meaningful as possible, and then assured Lieutenant that his country, America, would certainly be willing to help—if they could. He didn't want to get involved in further specifics. He'd already seen Lieutenant's highly developed negotiating skills. Also, John gave him a warning glance that clearly indicated he thought they had begun to tread in difficult territory.

Lieutenant returned to his own group with no regret from Ted Applegate. "Ah jes' don't like that bastard, no way."

None of the other Gorillas tried to change his opinion. Edouard was clearly the most sympathetic and actually interested in the tribespeople, but he too made no effort to disagree. Paul Schreymann, who had well understood the French exchange, said he shared the Alabaman's dislike of the Meo leader.

"I can't explain it, but the man's manner, as well as that of his people over there. Well, I just don't trust them. One minute they're all smiling, the next they're hard as nails. I'm not sure they won't cut our throats tonight the first chance they get."

While Bob Simpson joined Edouard and John in downplaying that danger, they all did agree that it was smart to take carefully divided shifts on individual guard duty. The sergeant immediately reminded everyone he had given up his watch, a situation which increasingly annoyed him. The others offered to supply him and Schreymann with theirs as needed. Simpson offered his sub-machine gun as the guard weapon.

"If we're going to do this, then it's best we do it right," he counseled.

"Ah say use it right now an' take our chances on findin' the strip," Applegate directed his remark toward John.

"Ted, these guys are our best chance to get the hell out of here without us getting mowed down by the Japs. I trust them to do that. We'll keep our eyes open and a good watch on our stuff. But it's important we don't show them—in any way—that we aren't going to trust them. You know that, dammit." John Guthrie was annoyed. Perhaps it was also because he felt responsible for being unable to handle his allotted map-reading task, though none of the others, including Edouard, could have done better. Sgt. Applegate shrugged acceptance of his superior officer's direction, though it was quite clear that his mind hadn't changed. He offered to take the first shift of guard duty, as any smart old soldier would do. He also wanted to check on just how the Meo were setting up their own guards.

The last two shifts were John's and Bob Simpson's. John knew he wouldn't be able to go back to sleep, so he stayed up with Bob talking about their situation. From the beginning theirs had been an easy relationship. Although Simpson was in command, the fact that he had respected John's field experience smoothed over what might have been a sore point. For John's part he was always careful not to overstep his role as subordinate to the other major. So far, it had been an effective division of authority, though they both well knew it would be the ex-ball player who would be blamed if anything went seriously wrong.

"Y'know, John, if we get out of here okay, we're gonna be heroes. Of course, if it all turns to crap, this horse is gonna be hung out to dry. I mean even if we get back."

"Hell, Bob, this was a stupid assignment in the first place."

"You know it and I know it, but sure as hell they'll never admit it. But who cares? There will be another game tomorrow. It ain't like it's the end of the season. But we got a good team here, and with a little luck... well, you know."

"If we handle these little guys right, these tribesmen..." John started to say.

"The sergeant doesn't trust these guys too much, and I can't say I blame him," Bob confided.

"We don't have any choice, as we said before. Frankly, even with those antique rifles they could take us down if they really wanted to. This is their part of the world and they know how to operate in it. The big thing we've got going for us is their expectation of a big payoff if they get us out of here. I think the Lieutenant guy is smart enough to realize that even if the others don't. And he seems very much in charge, don't you think?"

"Well, one thing's for damn sure, we ain't in charge. By the way, who do you think they'd line up with in a fight? The French or the Japs or is it just a question of who paid them last? And we're now the most recent... payers that is."

"He more or less told us. They were all set to nail the Vichy French in their retreat. They may have already done that until they got the word to lay off. Obviously, the Japs would have tried to pay them to help against the French. The interesting thing is that they have enough discipline to make the turn. He seemed pretty proud of the Viet Minh connection. Hallstrom has already told me he's supposed to be building up contacts with these Viet Minh even though they're communists or whatever. I can see now why that's a good idea if these tribespeople are so *gung ho* for them. So, the long short answer is that if these little guys are part of the Viet Minh, and they seem so, they're prepared to follow this Ho's line, at least as long as it promises them the independence they seem to want. That means if we make friends with the Viet Minh, we also get a whole bunch of these tribal guys. If Lieutenant and his people here are any example, they can be trained into an effective guerrilla force. They're forest people and they clearly have a natural talent."

"So, for the moment we're the good guys. And also, we have some stuff they want, right?"

"You got it, Robert. And maybe it could make a nice connection with the Viet Minh. I hope it's as simple as that."

The camp began stirring by 0530 hours. Only Edouard had to be awakened. Nothing much bothered him. He could nap at the drop of a hat and falling to sleep in the bush was no trouble at all. He had won Applegate's approval for his ability to relax on cue. "A perfect field soldier," had been the veteran sergeant's comment on Edouard. Compliments such as that did not come easily from Applegate. Schreymann kidded Edouard for winning the award of "best sleeper" among the team members. He responded that it had taken him years to perfect his talent. A hot meal and a little better sack time had brought back the banter that had marked their earlier morale. The little Meo had brought with them a return of an expectation of success, even if it was simply the perception that they might find the air strip before getting killed in the attempt.

The morning's march covered a great deal of ground. The tribesmen moved with a steady pace through terrain that would have taken the OSS team twice as long to cover. It helps to know where you're going, John thought. It also helped that the Americans by now had all become accustomed to the rough conditions, even though they remained uniformly hungry. The rations they carried were adequate in terms of basic nutrition, but that was about as far as it went. The relief from the pain in John's gut was only temporarily attained by the tablets he had been given by the detachment's medical officer. Being

43

constantly hungry added to the distress. He tried to hide it, but Edouard noticed his periodic grimace. Nothing was said other than through eye contact. There was nothing Edouard could do even if John had shared his secret.

Lieutenant announced they were now about only one more day's march from the strip. They had stopped for a midday break when he amended his statement in conversation with John. "Maybe one and a half," the Meo said. John passed the new information on to the other Gorillas. Applegate groaned upon hearing about the light change.

"That sonofabitch don' know shit from Shinola. You sure he's not walkin' us in circles, Major?"

"It's okay, Sarge. I keep track of the direction with the compass," John replied soothingly, but without effect. Nothing was going to change the Alabaman's opinion of Lieutenant and his fellow tribesmen.

John had pored over his map with Edouard and they thought they could discern where their progress was leading them. They were able to pick up some landmarks now and relate them to the map, but that wasn't a positive confirmation. They no longer had the confidence in their own ability with which they had started. Nonetheless they agreed that, as best they could tell, things seemed to be on track. They had spied a major height off about ten miles to the west. They were able to line that up with a small waterway clearly marked on the map and had forded the stream that morning. At least it all seemed right.

They had been moving along at a regular pace when, an hour after the noon break, one of the Meo scouts slipped out of the heavy foliage and the column came to a halt. Simpson and John moved forward to find out what was going on. The scout was in animated conversation with Lieutenant. After the exchange, the Meo leader explained the situation to John who translated.

"The scout says he saw a patrol—that he thinks is French—ahead of us. He says there are about eight of them, one European, the others colonial troops most likely Vietnamese. The scout says they're well-armed with a light machine gun and they carried grenades in addition to their rifles. Lieutenant says he thinks it may be a forward scouting party for a larger body of troops. I figure it could also be a small unit that's broken away from the main force."

"We have to make contact with these guys, John," Simpson said excitedly. "We have to find out what unit they're with and what they might know about the rest of them."

"Right. I'll tell Lieutenant that I'll go on ahead with his scout and try not to get shot before we have a chance to palaver with this 'European' who is most likely an officer or noncom in charge."

"Better take another one of our guys with you. Take Schreymann."

John would have preferred Edouard to go along with him, but there was no point in making an issue of it. After all, Simpson was the team "captain."

They explained the new situation to the rest of their group. Paul Schreymann joined John and they went together to the head of the column to explain to Lieutenant what they wanted to do. The Meo was not happy.

"I do not trust these people," Lieutenant said firmly.

"But the French are running away. They don't want to make any more trouble." John sought to dissuade the Meo leader from his antagonism to his former colonial masters.

"I don't mean the French. I mean the Annamite flunkeys."

He used the word *l'aquais* which John didn't understand until Paul Schreymann explained.

"It means he sees these Vietnamese colonial soldiers as simply toadies of the French, and that is pretty low in his estimation. It actually means 'lackeys.'"

Lieutenant, wanting to make sure John truly understood his reaction, explained further in his most simple, though strongly accented, French that he didn't trust the Vietnamese in general.

"These are lowland people. We are from the mountains. We don't like the lowland people. Anyhow they treat us badly. We never trust them. I do not trust these soldiers. They steal everything."

Eventually, the Meo capitulated but insisted the Americans be accompanied by two of his men—the scout and the grizzled old man with the bad attitude. They learned later the reason for his choice. The four men set forth at a dog trot through the heavy brush. The two Americans followed the lead of the Meo scout. He ran bent over; they ran bent over. He fell to the ground; they did the same. The scout would run and fall, and then get up and go another hundred yards or so and then hit the dirt again. They finally realized what he was doing. He was listening. He could hear better close to the ground. Sometimes he actually would put his ear down on the floor of the jungle-like entanglement of growth. They did the same but couldn't hear a thing. The two Meo murmured directly into each other's ear; they could not be heard even lying close to them. They then motioned the Americans forward and repeated the same procedure for about a mile. John sensed they were not going in a straight line but circling the target. Finally, the scout pointed ahead. Neither John nor Paul Schreymann could see a thing. Eventually, some movement in the distance could be observed. Then, carefully edging through the brush and foliage, the French patrol slipped within their sight. John was about to hail in French when the old Meo stood up and called out. John surmised the old man was speaking in Vietnamese because the sounds seemed quite different from the Meo tribal language he had heard spoken by the Lieutenant and his men. The scout motioned for the Americans to stay down.

At the first sound of the old Meo's voice the patrol stopped dead and then fell to the ground taking up firing positions. After a moment, a Vietnamese soldier shouted back. The old man standing exposed never moved, but he did shout in reply. At that point, the white "officer" stood up and called out something in what seemed the same language which presumably was Vietnamese. The white man raised his hands showing he had no weapon. He was, however, well covered by his unit lying prone around him with their rifles at the ready. John could see the man carrying the barrel of the light machine gun ease it into place as the soldier with the tripod carefully, without quick movement, pushed the mount closer to his partner with the barrel. Another soldier with two boxes of ammo wriggled nearby, getting set to complete the firing team. This was a well-trained group, thought John. The old Meo now motioned for John and Paul to get up so the European could see them. The Meo dropped to the ground when they stood up. He and the scout had their sights dead set on the white man.

John called out in French, "We are friends. We are Americans. We have been sent to find you." The white officer replied in heavily accented French something that John couldn't understand. "*Comment?*" he asked politely. The man shouted louder in French. This time his German accent was obvious. "We are French soldiers. *Nous sommes soldats français.* We have been looking for you. We wish to come to fight with you. We want to fight the Japanese." At least that was what John thought the man said. His accent was nearly impenetrable. "He's German," Paul whispered hoarsely. "I can talk with him. He's most likely a Legionnaire. *Ich spreche Deutsch.*"

"Go to it, Paul," John agreed.

What followed was bizarre by any measure. Upon hearing Paul greet him in his Alsatian German, the white man seemed as if he had been shot. He actually took a step backward. The two men began shouting at each other in German. They walked quickly toward each other and met halfway, at which time they hugged and laughed. Or rather, the Legionnaire still yammering in German was doing the hugging and Paul was allowing himself to be hugged. More loud German followed, then some serious talk. Paul motioned for John to come forward. No one else moved. The Vietnamese continued to remain in prone firing position and so did the Meo. The white men obviously had all gone crazy. John would have agreed with them. Paul introduced John to the German as his superior officer. At that the Legionnaire snapped to attention and sharply saluted. John spoke in English and Paul translated into German. They could have spoken in French in spite of the German's incredibly heavy accent, but the language of the moment was German. The Alsatian American and the German were *landsmänner* and only the German language would suffice at this important moment as far as Sgt. Manfred Vogel, 10th Regt. Légion Étrangère, was concerned.

John explained through Paul the purpose of the Gorilla Mission in finding the location and disposition of the fleeing Vichy French forces. Sgt. Vogel said that his patrol was about a day's march ahead of a regiment of mixed units of the colonial and regular French forces. They had been hoping to receive more aid from the Allies, he said, ever since they had been parachuted some supplies weeks earlier. John didn't go into the change of orders which had forced the limitation of further drops. Vogel knew about the landing strip, and, in fact, had been ordered to reconnoiter the area to determine if it could be used.

"What we found out, Herr Major, is not very good news. The Japanese have about 100 men holding that strip." The German Legionnaire had shifted to French in order to speak directly to John. He spoke very slowly so that he would be understood. It was an important aid to John who had extreme difficulty with Vogel's heavy German accent. Paul interrupted from time to time to make sure things were clear.

"I don't see how you'll be able to use the airstrip, Herr Major. I can assure you, sir, that my regiment will not want to take on the Japanese. We've been avoiding them ever since we left Son Tay—even when we outnumber them. As a Legionnaire, I am embarrassed to say this, but you must know."

Back with the Vichy patrol, Acting Corporal Bui Dac Thanh kept his attention on his sergeant as Vogel talked with the two foreigners. They weren't French. From the language, one seemed to be a German like the sergeant. Maybe they were Legionnaires, though they had strange uniforms and foreign weapons. There was some whispering among the patrol and Thanh hissed at them to be quiet. He wondered if these were the Americans he had heard about.

Thanh tried to hear what the foreigners said. It was important to remember these things just in case something might be important later to the Party. Thoughts of his obligation in that respect were never far from his mind. He had had to leave Hanoi with virtually no notice to his *to dang*. The deputy was finally going to get to be in charge. Thanh's army unit moved out without notice, but he had been able to smuggle a note to the communications center. That's all he could do. The party leader of the *chi bo* would figure out what happened even without word from him. The Party would contact him again when he arrived at wherever he was going—or he would find a way to send them a message. Of that he was confident. All this trouble might turn out to be to the Party's advantage. The Party would be ready, in any case. Thanh would do his best to keep his eyes and ears open. He didn't need specific instructions in that regard. It was a very secure feeling amidst all this chaos. He also would be ready.

The news about the Japs at the airstrip effectively denied the Gorilla team the ability to make contact with AGAS which was supposed to arrange the exfiltration. The plan had been for a reconnaissance plane to circle the area twice a day on a regular schedule a few days after the original jump. When the team had arrived at the strip and sighted the plane, the Gorillas were supposed to signal with a V-ray pistol that fired a small colored rocket. The plane would communicate with the AGAS listening station just across the border in southern Yunnan about 100 miles away. A small transport plane then would be sent in to pick them up. With radio communications so difficult in mountainous terrain it had seemed a logical plan. With the Japanese sitting on the airfield, the entire extraction process had broken down.

John's thoughts sped ahead to the alternative of the long trek to the sanctuary of the first Chinese lines. A week, at least, was his calculation—and that would be with very low food supplies and no trouble from the Japs.

Sgt. Vogel's voice broke into John's thinking.

"If I may offer some advice, *mon Commandant*, I think it would be best if you and your party remained here, giving me time to return to the regiment and see what we can do to help. With all due respect, sir, your companions, the *indigènes* here, are not a trustworthy lot. These are opium traders, bandits."

John didn't want to get into a discussion of either his Meo "companions" or where the team would encamp for the next few days.

"Thank you for your advice, Sergeant. Unfortunately, we are soon going to run out of supplies, and I would prefer to get closer to the strip before we make any decisions. In any case, I want to discuss this with the rest of our unit."

The German, in proper Legion manner, drew himself to attention and replied, "*Oui, mon Commandant!*"

The old Meo's ability to speak Vietnamese made it possible for John to communicate with him through translation by Sgt. Vogel. John explained in French and the German translated into Vietnamese that the Meo should return to the OSS group and bring them forward. The grim-faced old man nodded and raced off with the scout. He was not at all unhappy at the chance to get out from under the guns of Thanh and the rest of the colonial troops. The departure of the two Meo tribesmen was the signal for the entire patrol to relax for the moment. In quiet voices the Vietnamese soldiers who made up Vogel's command talked among themselves of what they might expect next. Thanh silenced the murmuring with a brief explanation.

"The two foreign 'Europeans' are Americans, I believe. They are the ones who dropped us some supplies. Remember? These must be officers. Be quiet. Show some discipline. Are we not soldiers?"

Sgt. Vogel called to Thanh to have the troops take a short break. He sat with John and Paul, killing time in conversation until the rest of the Gorillas came along. It was easier to understand his French now in relaxed exchange.

"So, tell me, Sergeant, as a German with the war on and everything, how do you get along in a French unit?" It might have been a ticklish question, but it was an obvious one.

"Sir, I've been in the Légion Étrangère for nearly 20 years. I left Germany during the bad times in the late twenties. The German government then could do nothing for us. I was young and did not want to hang around a crumbling country. *La Légion* took me in, no questions asked. I served first in North Africa then down to Brazzaville in the Congo. Then they sent me to Indochina. I was here when the war in Europe started, and now I'm here in the woods with you. I am a *Légionnaire*. That is my citizenship.

"Do you have any views on the war at all?" John asked.

"Sir, for me life is very simple. I go where *La Légion* sends me. I fight who they want me to fight. It is a respected profession. Someday I shall retire, but for now I go on. I think I might like to fight the Japs, though. I have met them, and I don't like them."

John and Paul exchanged glances, both thinking the last comment was for their benefit. John restrained himself from asking Vogel what he would have done if *La Légion* asked him to kill Americans. He knew what the real answer was without asking.

The rest of the Gorillas arrived, accompanied by Lieutenant and about half the Meo force. Schreymann briefed Simpson and the others while John gave the same details in French to the Meo leader. Bob Simpson spoke up quickly and forcefully.

"Send this guy back to his unit. He can tell them what's gone on here. I agree that we go on closer to the strip. One way or another we have to make a move. If we can't get picked up we'll have to join with the Frenchies and march up to China with them."

"Should I tell him that, that we might join up with them?" John asked.

"Hell, I don't know. What do you think? Are you sure what side these Vichy guys are on?"

It was a fair question and John didn't know the answer. Back in France they would have been considered on the Germans' side. Edouard broke in:

"I think they would love to have us with them. It would be their free ticket home."

Schreymann, after a moment's thought, agreed with him. Applegate looked away and said nothing. This was officer talk. He just wanted to get going and stop all this bullshit. Finally, it was agreed that Sgt. Vogel should be given the straight story; that they would move on to get a look-see of the strip. When John suggested to the German that he might mention to his superiors the possibility of a meeting with the American team at some rendezvous near the strip, the sergeant shook his head.

"They wouldn't want to do that, sir, with respect," he said in his proper military French. "They do not wish to risk any contact with the Japs, *mon Commandant*. They've been avoiding a fight all along the way. For many of us it has been an unhappy decision—among the Legionnaires, that is."

"But you must outnumber this small group, only a hundred. How many are you?" said John incredulously.

"Oh, yes sir, we are many more—a combined 500 maybe. But we also have many civilians. Too many. Anyhow, with respect, sir, the officers do not want to fight. Not here, not now. Maybe later after we get to China and you Americans supply us with more weapons."

Politely, the German sergeant asked John if he had a map. John pulled out his not-so-trustworthy colonial government map. Vogel looked at it and immediately pointed out where they were. John was annoyed at the realization a German noncom could read the map better than he. Vogel pointed to where the strip was located and marked the route he expected the Vichy column would take to avoid the Japanese encampment. He suggested a rendezvous site on that path for the American team. Never looking up from the map he spoke to Schreymann in German, "And tell *Herr Major* not to bring these bandits with you. My officers won't like them." Paul said to John that he would tell him what Vogel had said later on.

Goodbyes were said with Vogel and Schreymann hugging again. The Legionnaire snapped off a sharp salute to the American party, ordered his men to follow him, and trudged off into the bush. John quickly borrowed a pencil from Edouard and noted the places Vogel had pointed to on the map. This time he would not make any mistakes!

"It was lucky you had me take Paul along. I'm sure we got more out of that Kraut as a result," John complimented Simpson.

"Hell, I wasn't about to send my back-up quarterback, Eddy, with you. What if they dusted off you guys? Had to hold my French-speakin' combat guy for later in the game if we needed to substitute. The German thing was pure luck—like interceptin' a pass or somethin'. All part of the game, m'boy." Bob Simpson's disclaimer was honest, but he was nonetheless pleased at the praise.

The map showed, and the Legion sergeant had confirmed, there was an escarpment overlooking the small valley containing the landing strip. The height would provide an excellent vantage point to observe the Japanese position. By working their way up the cliff they would have a clear view of the entire valley. John explained the intended route to Lieutenant. He indicated he was in agreement with the strategy. He called in the rest of his Meo fighters who had remained outside the perimeter. All the while the legionnaire and his Vietnamese troops were engaged in the talks with the Americans, the Meo had the entire scene covered. It was a reminder of the natural military talent of the Meo. No wonder the colonial army feared them.

It took the Americans and their Meo escort all the rest of that day and half of the next to reach within striking distance of the landing strip. By noon time they could smell the distinctive odor of napalm even as they heard heavy explosions interspersed with sounds of aircraft strafing ground targets. Though tired from five hours of hard trekking that morning, the OSS team along with the Meo tribesmen scrambled up the escarpment to get a view of what was happening. By the time they got into position, most of the action had subsided, though one end of the landing area was still ablaze. It was the northeast edge of the strip—exactly where Vogel had said the Japanese unit was bivouacked.

At that point they only could guess at what had occurred, but it was a pretty good guess. The L-5 which the OSS used as a spotter plane undoubtedly had been making its planned passes over the strip. The Japanese troops naturally decided to have some target practice with the slow-moving US aircraft and the observation plane would have come under heavy ground fire. The Gorillas all agreed that the L-5 must have reported back to AGAS and the air controller at 14th Air Force. It wouldn't have taken much urging from OSS HQ to call in the full strike to remove the Jap unit endangering the use of the air strip. The small Japanese force most likely never knew what hit them, the Americans conjectured.

"What a bunch of idjits t'give up their position like that," commented the former and forever Ft. Benning instructor, Ted Applegate.

"If they're any Japs left after that hoorah, they're runnin' as far as they can into that jungle. And I bet they're not in too good shape even if they got away." Bob Simpson made that pronouncement as he studied the area with his binoculars.

Lieutenant volunteered his Meo to scout the area. He recommended the Americans remain out of sight on the escarpment. The Gorillas watched as the tribesmen stealthily made their way down the slope. In about five minutes nothing could be seen or heard of them and the Americans once again were completely alone. To be on the safe side, John recommended that they post two men at a time as pickets about 50 yards upland. They would be replaced every half hour; it kept them sharp. Those left behind talked softly with each other or rested, wrapped in their thoughts.

It wasn't a good time for John Guthrie. Having too much time to think about matters always increased the pain in his gut. Too much exertion also bothered him, but at least then he had something else on which to concentrate. He slowly chewed some of his tablets. He knew Edouard had noticed his grimacing but was being the good friend by saying nothing. What the hell could he do anyhow? Go out and get a bottle of milk? That always helped. One of the advantages of the Vosges was the availability of plentiful milk supplies from the farms. What a different war. It seemed so much more familiar. Familiar farmland, familiar seasons, and familiar smells. In a way, even the enemy was familiar. Nothing was familiar now. Nothing fit. Everything seemed to carry a mystery. Japs you couldn't see, but you knew were there. Hard little tribesmen who were your temporary allies, until when you never knew. A French Army patrol made up of Vietnamese and led by a German who owed allegiance to no nation but would fight to the death for his Legion. And somewhere out there were a people organizing to create their own country—or so you were told. Where were these people? Who were they? Communists? How the hell could simple Asian farmers be communists? Communists were guys like his *maquisards*—mechanics, welders, factory workers—not illiterate peasants. Nothing fit.

John looked around and saw the old soldier Applegate concentrating on cleaning his carbine. He went over to bum some oily patches to work on his own. It didn't take much to field strip the carbine, but if you cleaned it carefully it could be relaxing. It was an old soldier's trick. The same result could be attained by sharpening your combat knife, the veteran sergeant had assured him, not knowing it was the last thing John ever wanted to do. He understood the logic, though.

The half-hour shifts made the time pass quickly and they were preparing for the beginning of the third hour of picketing when they heard the Meo rollicking up the cliffside pathway like a bunch of noisy teenagers coming back from a beer party. Their raucous laughter could be heard working its way up the climb. Several came into view waving bottles of what turned out to be sake. All of them carried extra rifles and ammo boxes. One lugged a small mortar, and another had a light machine gun with its ammo belt slung like a bandolier around his neck. Lieutenant had acquired an officer's Nambu pistol and holster. He beamed.

The Meo leader reported what by that juncture was obvious. The entire Jap force had been wiped out or fled. Proudly he announced his men had "taken care of" the remaining wounded. Bob Simpson wanted to leave immediately to inspect the site. John disagreed.

"The rain is beginning," he pointed out, "and that means we'll be in the dark in another hour or so. I don't think it's a good idea to go roaring off at this time. I also don't think our Meo friends are in any mood for anything but a celebration."

"We don't need 'em. Let them celebrate," Simpson said, eager to get on with the game.

"I beg yuh pardon, Major Bob, but Major John has a good point." That was all Applegate said, then he spat. Simpson shrugged.

"What the hell. It'll all be there tomorrow," he said.

Camp was set up on the bluff. All the Americans were excited over the prospect of getting out of their situation. As Simpson said, it was a good time to call a time out and start the war again some other place. The Meo threw caution to the winds and had cooking fires crackling in a matter of moments. They protected the low fires with hastily built lean-tos to keep out the rain. Larger constructions of similar style were built with amazing speed. The Americans followed suit, recognizing their value in providing protection against the elements. The Gorilla team's effort lacked the speed and competence of the tribesmen who were much amused at the "Europeans'" ineptitude. Generously, several Meo came over at Lieutenant's instruction and helped the OSS men put together their shelter. It was a happy time.

For Lieutenant and his men, the venture with their new friends had turned out very successfully. They would have plenty of booty with which to return to their villages. And, perhaps more importantly, these new friends might not know very much about fighting in these mountains, but they apparently were very rich and willing to work with the Meo. For Lieutenant himself, this was going to be a great coup among the leadership of his mountain people, the *montagnards* as the French called all the hill tribes.

The Meo leader regaled his American friends with the history and lore of the Meo in a festive evening of victory toasts drunk to each other in captured sake. The Americans were invited to come someday to visit the Meo in their home villages. Lieutenant was impressed at the way these Americans treated him and his men as equals, not like the treacherous Annamites or the lordly French. His final toast to them was telling. Edouard translated:

"He says, we are friends forever of his people, the Meo. He says this is so because we are men of our word; that we are trustworthy."

"Tell him we think the same of him, of all of them," said Simpson.

The sake ran out and the toasts ended as the rain drove everyone into their lean-tos.

Dawn came sticky and wet. There hadn't been that much sake to drink, but it was powerful on unaccustomed stomachs of the OSS team. It hadn't seemed to bother the tribesmen at all. One way or another, the Americans all complained about headaches and queasy feelings in the pit of the stomach—all except Applegate.

"It's nuthin' compared to the white lightnin' we make back home," he boasted as they made their way down the escarpment to the valley below, slipping and sliding on the wet earth and leaves underfoot. The Meo led the team to a path, eventually arriving at the far end of the strip still smoldering from the devastation of the napalm. The heavy perfume of the mountain verdancy gave way to the stink of burnt petroleum products. Further on charred corpses, unrecognizable, littered the ground. The Japanese had been caught flat-footed. They must have been bivouacked in a group instead of dispersing. In a small area there were scores of corpses. They were completely unprepared for the fury of the sudden air attack. There really had been no need for the strafing and explosives; the napalm had incinerated the target and most of the Japanese were standing in the bullseye.

None of the Americans spoke. The Meo kept up a determined chatter. They were soon off looking for more loot. This was war and they understood it. Simpson broke the silence.

"We better get cracking and keep an eye out for our spotter plane. Here, Sergeant, take this V-ray pistol. We only have two rocket shells, so don't waste them." The major pulled the signal weapon from his pack and handed it to Applegate.

"I think we should check around to see if there's any stuff useful for intelligence," John said. "Obviously there's nothing here—we've got to look beyond the burned area. There might just be some papers, orders, or something, if it didn't all go up in smoke. We better count the bodies and make a record of the arms and equipment. They're sure to ask us about that when we get back."

John was as business-like as he could be. It was necessary in order to get through the carnage.

"They should have known that they would give away their position by shooting at the observation plane, if that's what happened," Edouard suggested.

"Who knows, maybe the plane just saw them and took off," Simpson replied. "It doesn't seem to really matter."

They moved beyond the burnt perimeter following the Meo who had already located a storage area the night before. It was here that the tribesmen had picked up their souvenirs. It was also obvious this was where they had come across a clutch of petrified Japanese soldiers, shell-shocked by the air attack.

The Meo had dispatched them with their knives in their usual competent manner. There may have been some resistance, but it didn't seem so. The tribesmen proudly showed off their handiwork and began to collect items they had missed the day before. They gathered what they wanted and placed it in a pile to be later allocated for carrying. They found a food storage bin and began arguing over whether or not they should take some of the rice. They already had more stuff than they could carry. Lieutenant gave some orders and the men began separating the piles into military equipment and just plain useful junk.

Schreymann, who up to that point had barely uttered a word, shouted out that he had found something. The rest of the Gorillas found him standing beside a shack with an open door. Inside was a radio. This meant the Japs maintained regular contact with this airstrip. It also meant that if this unit didn't reply, this alone certainly would bring up questions. There was discussion over using the radio, but Paul Schreymann wisely suggested that it was best they leave it as it was.

"If we just leave it, there's always the possibility the Japs on the other side will think something is broken or atmospherics are bad. That's always a possibility in these mountains," he said.

"Well, I don't know one way or the other," said Bob Simpson turning expectantly to John.

"Sure, I guess that can happen. There were plenty of times we didn't pick up signals in France, but we used to think most of the time the Germans were trying to jam London. But then the distances were much greater. I don't really know anything about here, though the idea that commo is always difficult in mountainous areas is something you would expect," John said.

"The real question in my mind," said Edouard, "is whether their radioman sent a message and then bugged out. This shack wasn't hit, so he could have been in it… or, on the other hand, he could be one of those guys over there." He pointed in the general direction of the killing ground.

Bob Simpson knew it was his responsibility at this time to take charge, but there wasn't much he could do.

"Okay, well, hell, we've got to go on the basis that something got through to some sort of main headquarters, and there could be a relief column on the way. Right, John?"

"You got it, Bob. We have to go on that basis. We've no other choice."

They looked around for any code books but found none.

"I don't think the fact that there's no paper here means much," said Edouard. "Their CO might have had them as well as the radio man, and they could all be burnt up. I say one thing's for sure."

"And that is?" said John knowing exactly what Edouard was about to say.

"It's time to get the hell out of here."

A simple statement of the obvious that was typical battleground conversation. It bore no relationship to the Hollywood version of men in battle. The stink of napalm and putrefying corpses effectively blocks all but essential thoughts. Fear overrides everything else. Standing in the grey dark of the unburnt portion of the Japanese encampment was fearful indeed. They headed back to the open space of the landing strip. The smell was the same, but at least there was cleansing light.

All this while, Applegate was out on the strip keeping his eyes peeled for an approaching L-5. He sat on the ground chewing the end of a twig, his mind whirring: The strip looks in pretty good shape… it's about two-and-a-half football fields long… they must've wanted to use it, but what for…? I should mention that to the majors… that Major John might think about that, but I'm not sure of the others…. They're decent guys, though… but not real Army…. What sort of plane will they bring in to take us out? It better happen soon 'cause I don't trust those tribal guys further than I could throw 'em.

The Alabaman smiled at the image of him tossing the Meo into the air. In his many years in the Regular Army, he had imagined many funny things. It was a way to get through the boredom. It was his secret trick. He learned to do it sitting silently still-hunting deer. Ten-year-old country boys are very inventive.

It was around 0900 hours when Applegate first spotted the circling L-5. He shouted for the rest of the team and ran into the open, fumbling to shove the rocket shell into the pistol. He fired the weapon when the plane was some distance away. "Ah, shit," he said realizing his mistake. He took the second, and last, shell from his pocket preparing to load and fire when the reconnaissance plane came closer. Slowly the plane lost altitude while making ever-decreasing circles around the field. The rest of the Gorilla team came running from the other end of the field waving their arms. The L-5 made a full-length pass at the strip before pulling up and around. They could see a figure in the passenger side but could not make out the face.

"They're going to have to get some altitude if they want to come back around," said a concerned Edouard. But the plane never gained any height. It simply came straight in and landed. They all ran shouting toward the L-5 as it taxied back in their direction. The side door opened even before the plane came to a stop. Broadly smiling, Capt. Antonio Castelli, Hallstrom's deputy, jumped out when the aircraft came to a stop. He was talking before he hit the ground.

"Oh Jesus, I am glad to see you guys. After the strike we all of a sudden thought we might have gotten you guys, too, if the Japs had caught you. I can't tell you what we've been going through since yesterday. It was all so stupid, we...."

"What the hell are you doing here? Where's our transport plane?" demanded Simpson.

"I had to talk to you to explain...."

"What, that you hadn't killed us?"

"No, no. That this strip is too short to pull you all out!"

Tony Castelli's face had the concerned look of an Italian barber who had just cut his client's chin. The laughter and smiles stopped. Applegate swore loudly. He could be heard over the throttled back but still roaring engine of the plane. They moved back from the noise and the prop wash. Patiently and apologetically, Castelli explained the situation. He said he had to talk fast because he didn't want to waste time.

"After you guys took off, we heard—it was too late to contact you—from air recon at 14th HQ that some analyst had gone over their photos of the strip. And, well, he analyzed the length and also that he had picked up signs of a Jap concentration at one end, at least that's what he thought. You can imagine how everyone went apeshit on that news."

"C'mon, Tony, get to the point of all this," Bob Simpson interrupted.

"Okay, so they sent out two other sorties of observation planes with better photographic capability to confirm. As soon as the confirmation came in, we hit the bastards."

"And after that you worried about if they had caught us, right? What a bunch of idiots," Simpson said shaking his head.

The rest of the Gorillas listened tight-lipped. They were all thinking the same thing. Why wasn't this seen before they left on the mission? Tony Castelli was only the messenger, but they all could have killed him.

"How the hell do we get out then?" Bob Simpson was in no mood for what he saw was staff officer waffling. The little Italian captain handled it as best he could. He got right to the point, finally.

"You've got to cut down at least 200 feet of trees at the far end of the strip. Just cut them down, not dig them up. We need to have an extended flight path. Landing they tell me is not that big a problem. It's the take-off. They think they can get airborne in 800 feet, which is what you've got. But they need the extra 200 to 300 for clearance. We have to use a C-45. It can get all you guys in, but nothing else—no equipment, guns, anything. The plane's going to be stripped and carrying the absolute minimum fuel load. One pilot, no co-pilot. I mean, stripped down to an absolute minimum weight."

"Y'all said 200, then ya said three. Which is it, Captain? And why can't ya send in five L-5s each carryin' out one man?" Applegate in his most prolonged drawl was barely civil. The others all nodded in agreement with the lowest-ranking but most veteran GI.

"Well, we don't but have two L-5s, this one and one that's having its engine repaired. Even if I took out one of you stuffed in the back of this one—and we're not too sure you'd fit in or if we could handle the extra weight—that would mean too many more trips to get the rest of you out. The big thing is that our reports say that there's a Jap column already on the way. We've got a radio intercept. Can you cut down that stuff at the end of the runway?"

"When do you figure it's got to be done?" asked John.

"I hate to say this, but the safest would be today," Castelli replied taking a deep breath. He had a lousy job and was doing the best he could.

"John, you get out Lieutenant and tell him what we need. If he can get that damn stuff down in five or six hours, tell him he can have everything we've got—including my Thompson. We'll still have adequate light at 1600 hours, right?"

Bob Simpson "captain of the team" was in charge now, and he intended to get out of there come hell or high water. He said just that.

"What do you think? We don't need but a little more than the width of the plane's wing span, right? How wide is that? Would 60 feet do?"

"Sounds good to me," replied Castelli, not having the faintest idea of the C-45 wingspan or who the ferocious-looking tribesmen were on the side of the strip staring in fascination at the airplane. He climbed back into the L-5 to check with the pilot. "Buzz says 60 feet will be plenty," he shouted above the engine noise.

"We better have a look at how thick that stuff is at the end of the strip," Simpson said. Without waiting, Paul Schreymann raced off in the direction of the end of the runway. He disappeared into the heavy growth. Edouard joined John in talking with Lieutenant and his entranced band of cutthroats.

The negotiation did not take long. John and Edouard dashed back. John reported the result.

"He says he can do it. But I think he'd say anything to get that tommy gun. He did say that it wasn't that heavy, the growth. They passed through it circling the Japanese position. He says no big trees. Anyway, that's what he said. They can do it, he says."

Paul sprinted back from the end of the strip to breathlessly declare the strip had once been longer and was now overgrown.

"That's good, you see," said Paul. "Cutting saplings and second growth stuff is definitely doable."

"It also explains why maps show it longer than it is," added John instinctively coming to the defense of map reading.

Bob Simpson turned toward Tony Castelli and fixed him with a look that must have sent shivers down the back of opposing linemen in a Notre Dame football game years before.

"Listen to me, squirt," he growled at the diminutive captain. "If you don't get that plane here and us out by 1600 hours, I will personally walk back to Kunming and break you in two. Is that clear?"

The others smiled but Tony did not. "Yes, sir," he responded like the West Point cadet he had dreamed of being as a child. "It'll be here, and we'll get you all out." With that, he hauled himself back into the little Piper L-5, and the flight officer with the stereotypical name of Buzz gunned the motor. Speeding down the short runway, they were soon airborne.

Altogether the entire group, the OSS team and the Meo, had eight machetes. Lieutenant explained what had to be done to his men. There was some grumbling until they heard the eventual reward. Clearing forest was second nature to these iron-hard men. That's what they had done since childhood in creating new fields for poppy cultivation. They worked in two teams; one cut while the other rested. They were in perpetual motion. Simpson, protecting his nickname of Horse, insisted on taking his turn with one of the machetes, and that created a contest among the Gorillas as to who among them was the best chopper. None of them could keep up with the Meo. Lieutenant was amused at the American antics, but his fellow tribesmen disdainfully ignored their feeble efforts. Lieutenant stayed on the sideline fondly rubbing down the Thompson that soon would be his. John took the time to give the Meo leader rudimentary instruction on loading and firing the weapon which tended to rise up against a target. Lieutenant showed his appreciation by yelling at his men to go faster.

For once on this escapade the Gorilla team had some luck. It did not rain. In fact, it was an exceptionally sunny, dry day for that time of year. By midafternoon, the landing strip was as dry as could be expected in that part of the world. It was a break, and they all knew it. By 1530 hours the Meo had created a swath for the Twin Beech, the C-45, to fly through on take-off. There wasn't much time for a lengthy goodbye because by 1545 the plane was circling and shortly after landed. Every bit of their equipment was left in neat piles by the OSS team, including the carbines. The Thompson was already cradled in Lieutenant's arms. The ammo clips for the carbines were stacked next to each weapon, as were the packs and webbing. The Gorillas were stripped down to their now filthy uniforms—except for Applegate who refused to give up his bowie knife.

The Meo were quickly drawn up by Lieutenant, who wanted them to look as militarily sharp as they could. He and they were real soldiers now. They were proud men. They had done a good job, and these new "Europeans," these Americans, respected them. Lieutenant stood holding a salute until the plane raced down the strip at full power. Inside the stripped-down C-45 the OSS team held on the best they could with their backs against the side of the fuselage; all the chairs had been removed. About halfway down the dirt and gravel airstrip the pilot partially lowered his flaps and the plane struggled against the drag to get airborne. They were a foot off the ground and then two feet and more as the aircraft threaded its way through the pathway cut by the Meo. There was about ten feet to spare on each side, as Edouard shouted out from his vantage point next to a window. None of them saw what the pilot did as he cleared the end cut by only about one yard.

There was no fuel for a fly-by. The Meo were already picking up the packs and weapons shortly after the plane began gaining altitude, and Lieutenant had them off into the bush quickly.

"Well, Gorilla Mission is over," declared Edouard above the engine roar.

"I say we won the game. It was close, but we won," Simpson announced with triumph.

"In spite of some sloppy ball handling, eh Horse?" said John, uncharacteristically willing to join in the sports analogy.

"They always say, 'a win is a win,' and this qualifies," Simpson shouted back.

He didn't voice it aloud, but John was thinking, "A typical OSS screw-up. But then we also had that dumb OSS luck." Big Jack Guthrie would have warned him, "You get out what you put in, my son." Next time he would prepare better, he told himself. He looked over at Edouard, who, unlike the others, looked amazingly fit after the sojourn in the Vietnamese forests. Edouard caught John's glance and responded with a smile and a thumbs-up gesture. When the C-45 had gained altitude, Edouard crawled closer to where John was propped up against the side of the plane. By the expression on his face John knew that his friend had something important to say.

"I didn't have a chance to say before, but I wonder if you noticed what I did about that Legionnaire sergeant."

"What? He was German. So...?"

"He didn't look anything like Brian Donlevy. In fact, he didn't even have one of those nice white caps with the thing on the back to keep the sun off."

The line was delivered with a perfectly straight face. John started laughing, and then controlled himself enough to pretend to be serious.

"So that means…?" he asked.

"Well, at the very least he's miscast and…."

"And at worst he's an imposter."

"Worse than that. He might be a non-union actor. What do you say to that?"

"I say this is a matter I shall have to refer to higher union authority. This could be big, Edouard. Thanks for bringing it to my attention, Junior."

With that John broke into uncontrolled laughter. Edouard joined in and added a not-so-gentle nudge in John's ribs. The strain of the past several days melted. The others did not know what had been said but enjoyed the unheard joke anyhow. Soon they were all laughing to the point of tears.

Edouard leaned over and shouted in John's ear:

"It ain't much of a war; John, but it's the only one we've got."

Chapter Three

Thanh had a military respect for Sgt. Vogel. He had decided that the Légionnaire knew what he was doing when it came to things important to soldiers, such as eating, sleeping and fighting. Other than that, Thanh's view of the German was distinctly negative. He knew that for Vogel, a Vietnamese soldier was simply a witless automaton who needed to be told what to do at every juncture. Vogel was not alone among the sergeants in the Colonial Army with this view, but it was the obvious disdain he had for all things Vietnamese which truly galled Thanh. What was worse was that Vogel seemed to revel in his disrespect.

Thanh worked himself up with these thoughts whenever he was faced with a long, hard march such as the one they had been on since leaving those Americans. It had been the first time he had seen an American, and even then he was not absolutely sure until Sgt. Vogel had announced their nationality. They seemed bigger than the usual French officers. One was positively enormous. Why were they tied in with the *montagnards*? What a terrible bunch those primitive tribal people were, he thought. Opium bandits! Maybe the Americans were working with them in the opium business. It would all make a very interesting report when he next made contact with his comrades. Certainly, they would seek him out once he arrived in China, he encouraged himself once again.

Thanh's appointment as Acting Corporal during the long march escaping the Japanese had been well received by the other members of his squad. He was a buffer between them and Platoon Sgt. Vogel. Thanh was pleased with their reaction but fearful of the implications if the German began to suspect that his own authority was undercut by Thanh's popularity. Thanh had to be particularly careful in his reactions to Vogel's discipline measures. Punishment for even minor infractions in the Colonial Army often was physical. Thanh urged his men to maintain their control and avoid any conflict. He had seen soldiers flogged till their backs were blood striped and didn't want it to happen to those he considered his men. As a result of Thanh's commitment to his unit, Vogel benefited as Platoon Sergeant. Naturally, the German was convinced that the excellence of his command was due to his own leadership and that the patrol had been an example of the superb control he had over the men. They were all handpicked from the platoon and even though he had driven them till they nearly dropped, they all stayed the course. He would be commended by his captain.

Both Thanh and Vogel had been thinking the same thing. The meeting with the Americans was a very important matter to report. However, Thanh would have to wait until he made contact with the Party in China, while for the German it was simply a matter of getting back to the regiment. Vogel pushed his men mercilessly in order to speed up their return. When they finally rendezvoused with the main unit, Vogel had driven them to exhaustion even though he also barely could stand. It all made a great impression on his superiors as Vogel and his men stumbled into camp with news of contact with the Americans. It was sadomasochism at its most productive. With a bit of embellishment as to Vogel tracking down the Americans and outwitting the Meo, the escapade became worthy of a regimental commendation.

Within a couple of days Thanh and his squad were back out on their usual assignment, ranging ahead of the main force as both scouts and foragers. Thanh was particularly good in presenting a pleasant face to any of the tribespeople with whom they might come into contact. The truth was that he had a very low opinion of these *montagnards*, but never allowed it to show. His political perceptions of equality did not extend to this underclass of mountain people. His city background and lowland Tonkinese heritage ensured his preconceived negative opinions.

The village that Thanh's squad cautiously entered initially appeared empty. There was the usual stray mongrel and hastily extinguished cooking fire, but nothing else to set this encampment aside from others he had seen. Some of the huts were set above ground on stilts. Swiftly the squad members moved about the huts searching for food or other useable items. They were in luck; the villagers had fled so quickly they left behind newly killed game as well as most of their personal possessions. Although Thanh and his men sensed something out of the ordinary, they were too happy at finding the large quantity of meat hanging from wooden drying poles to pay adequate attention. Under Thanh's direction the soldiers began to cut pieces of bamboo to act as *don ganh* for carrying back the meat. The first fusillade coming from the edge of the village was deadly. Three of the six squad members went down.

Thanh threw himself behind one of the huts for cover, but it provided little protection from the rifle and automatic fire coming from several directions. One of the men who had been shot tried to drag himself out of the open ground to some shelter, but he never made it. He was hit again and lay still. The others who had been hit never moved. Thanh decided they already were dead. He shouted to his remaining three men to fall back to the trail they had come from. One by one they rose from their prone firing positions and dashed back in the woods. Two made it to safety in the trees. The third was hit but kept firing to give cover to Thanh as he rolled out from behind the hut and ran bent over to make a smaller target. The wounded man kept firing from behind a felled log that had served as a communal bench near a cooking fire.

From the protective tree cover, Thanh called to the wounded man to try and crawl away, but the soldier just stayed behind the log. Gathered together in the heavy brush and trees, Thanh and the two other survivors fired at any movement they could discern on the perimeter of the village. The incoming fire petered out and Thanh with his two soldiers inched forward one at a time toward their wounded buddy. Finally, they stood up and leapfrogged over to the downed soldier. The man's pant leg was soaked in blood. Thanh quickly cut a vine as a tourniquet and twisted the vine tight with a small piece of wood until the bleeding stopped. The man never uttered a word, but he gave Thanh a smile. The two other troopers knelt, weapon at the ready, back-to-back providing a screen. But there was no further need. Whoever had attacked them had disappeared.

Thanh's first thought had been that they were under attack by the vanished villagers. He realized quickly that the firing was too accurate and well controlled for a group of untrained tribesmen. It had to be a Japanese raiding party, but they could have had help from the village. Certainly, the *montagnards* had done nothing before to help Thanh and his squad unless they were cajoled with gifts. Even then they had taken every opportunity to steal whatever they could. Compassion for frightened mountain people was not high on Thanh's list of reactions at this juncture. He was steaming mad—at the Japanese, at the village, and at himself for letting his guard down allowing his squad to be ambushed like amateurs. His job now was to get his wounded comrade back to the regiment for medical treatment.

After some searching in the huts, they found a suitably strong piece of cloth. It was dirty, but that didn't matter. They laid the cloth on the ground and moved their friend onto it. He groaned slightly, but otherwise gave no indication of the excruciating pain that drove through his groin. Thanh collected all the rifles including those of the two unscathed soldiers. He bound the weapons, three together, and slung one bundle over each shoulder. His own weapon he carried at the ready. To the extent he could, he added the leftover ammo to his own belt. The cloth was knotted at both ends and a strong pole slipped through the length of the stretcher. The two soldiers raised their wounded companion so that each balanced the end of the pole on his shoulder. The soldier still had not said a word.

At a slow dogtrot, the two stretcher bearers struggled down the path that had brought them to the village. Thanh, heavily burdened with the rifles and ammunition, followed behind protecting their rear. The three dead soldiers remained where they had fallen. Nothing would be said about them until much later when they would be remembered as brothers, as soldiers do their dead.

The villagers would also remember the dead soldiers. They would speak of them often in the stories they would tell of the Japanese invaders, whom they would call "harsh mixed men," meaning that they were oriental and European at the same time. They would tell of the day the Japanese soldiers came into their village and chased them out. They would speak of the Annamite soldiers who were ambushed, and their dead left behind. They would remember that their shaman had counselled them to bury the dead soldiers in the forest so as to cleanse the village of their murder and release their souls to go home. They would remember these and other events of their village in song and story which would be told and retold in future times. Thus, the dead live in many ways for the people of the mountains.

* * *

The ubiquitous AGAS, formally a unit of the Army Air Corps, had been operating for some time in northern Vietnam with the assistance of existing contacts of the Chinese. Prominent among these had been Ho Chi Minh and through him the apparat known as the Viet Minh. The activities of the Viet Minh in AGAS' exfiltration system for downed air crews had grown considerably and thus had come to the attention of the OSS headquarters in Chungking, which aimed to utilize the communist-led league in further intelligence activity. It was an ambition that had also occurred to Ho Chi Minh.

"I have some good news to report, Uncle," said a rather officious but good-looking young man in a white suit. His suit and tie were quite out of place in the rustic tropical surroundings of Ho's hidden encampment, 55 miles north of Hanoi near the village of Kim Lung.

Sitting cross legged on a straw mat set on the floor of a typical peasant's stilted hut was the gaunt leader of the Viet Minh, the founder of the Indochinese Communist Party, Ho Chi Minh.

"Excellent, Comrade Van. I enjoy good news. What is it?"

It was tradition as well as good security procedure to never use true names in discussion. Vo Nguyen Giap had been known for so long by his pseudonym that compatriots in the Party leadership never thought of him as anything other than "Comrade Van."

"I have a confirmed report that the American flyer whom our Tho brothers were caring for has been successfully transported to safe hands in Kwangsi. I was worried that he would not have recovered well enough to make the trip, but apparently all went well."

"That is good news, indeed. It is very auspicious timing for us. I believe we should make a strong effort to become more involved with the Americans at this point. You understand, comrade?"

"Yes, of course, Uncle. We have shown our utility to them and so this is a good time to attempt to involve them in our struggle. The theory is excellent, of course. But are you convinced we can trust them?"

The older man sipped some tea while considering his reply. It wasn't for effect that he delayed his response. Giap was a loyal and thoughtful lieutenant whose question was perhaps even more apt than he realized.

"I admit, Comrade Van, to a certain liking for America. You know I've been there. I am impressed with their plan to give the Philippines their independence after the war is over. That is a good sign. I'm counting on them having the same anti-colonial sentiment in our regard. But you are right... there is an element of trust here. *Il faut qu'avoir une peu de la patience, et après du courage, comme toujours.*"

It was not unusual for Ho to speak French with Giap when he wanted to make a point of delicacy. For a man whose appearance showed a personal disregard for the niceties of dress, Ho often chose to be quite formal in language—no matter which it was of the several he spoke.

"And if I may ask, Uncle, how are we to become more—as you say—involved?"

At 33 years old, Giap was hardly a child, but the 22 years that separated him and Ho were far greater in reality of experience. That Ho was addressed as "uncle" was both an indication of a sense of traditional respect, as well as a recognition of the elder man's role as head of a political family.

"I shall travel to China to visit with them. Kunming I would think. We can get word to them that I'm coming through our Chinese friends or perhaps through the more direct channel we now have with their rescue people."

"Uncle, this is very dangerous to tell people you will be on the way. It becomes much easier to intercept you—something our enemies would dearly love to do. I am perhaps less trusting than you are of our Chinese 'friends,' and who knows what the security of the Americans is like."

"So, what do you suggest? We must give them some notice of my intentions."

"Perhaps you could travel secretly to China. We have assets in Kwangsi that could harbor you while getting word on to the Americans. It seems a safer way."

"It would give the Americans less notice, but perhaps that is not such a disadvantage. It is important though that we do not appear impolite."

Preparations for the trip were minimal. Food would be obtained along the way and overnight stays in friendly villages provided lodging. Practicality of travel along narrow trails demanded nothing more mobile than an oxcart. Most of the time the bone-thin Ho walked accompanied by a few staff and an experienced team of Tho guerrillas. The march of about 115 miles took nearly eight days to the border at Pac Bo. There they were met by several trusted agents who transported their leader by truck eventually to Kunming. Ho pronounced it a pleasant excursion.

* * *

The letter arrived unexpectedly. John hadn't received any mail since leaving London and hadn't written even to his family. The Guthries weren't much for letter writing. This letter from his mother—which unopened seemed to carry such import—turned out to be simply an inquiry as to his health and welfare, as well as a brief report on local happenings in and around Gary, Indiana. A perfectly ordinary, chatty letter—six weeks old. He'd neglected to send his new APO address. Nonetheless the letter was a shock. He had been able to thrust all thoughts of home from his mind. Evelyn had disappeared. In fact, he had blanked out any memory since he had returned from the Gorilla Mission that touched on the past, including his trauma in the Vosges. He had made a complete transition to the new life in Kunming and what it might bring. He'd come to accept his new world and thus benefit by it. The letter, as innocuous as it was, had the effect of reintroducing another reality, an old reality—something best forgotten.

John sat at a corner table of the Restaurant Deux Chapeaux, Edouard's favorite eating establishment in Kunming as well as a general hangout for Allied Intel types. John had sought refuge in the restaurant well after lunch was over when he knew the place would be nearly empty. He hadn't wanted to sit alone in his room, not wanting to be without human contact. Having a coffee and perhaps a Chinese brandy at the Deux Chapeaux allowed him to read his letter again and maybe shake off his weariness and the sense of despair that had so unexpectedly returned.

"Monsieur would perhaps like another coffee?" The question came from the café's owner, Liu Chi Roget, a Vietnamese of Chinese and French ancestry—or a Chinese of French and Vietnamese ancestry. It was all a matter of outlook and the prominence which Chi-chi, which is what he was always called, wished to emphasize at the moment. He held passports with all three surnames and citizenship. It was well known that Chi-chi had originally come from Cholon, the Chinese city within a city in Saigon. How he had arrived in Kunming was a matter of considerable speculation. The more generally accepted version was that Chi-chi had fled north after an unfortunate affair involving the shooting of a member of the *Binh Xuyen*, a criminal gang that held Cholon and the wealthy suburbs of Saigon in terror. The police and drug traffic were in their control, so when one of their enforcers was killed in Chi-chi's family's restaurant, his execution was ordered. None of the regular customers of Deux Chapeaux knew the real story, but this one sufficed. It was also accepted that Chi-chi had to be well-connected in order to operate such a restaurant that catered to foreign military officers.

"Yes, please, another cup of coffee. By the way, where do you get it?" John asked.

"The same place you do, Major," said Chi-chi mischievously. "Except that I pay quite a bit more." They were speaking in French, though Chi-chi was known also to have a smattering of English to go along with his three other languages.

"May I ask you another stupid question, Chi-chi?" asked John eager to get his mind freed of the blackness which enshrouded it.

"Of course, sir. But your question is hardly stupid."

"What is this brandy made of?"

"See, not a stupid question at all. It is made of apples, or apricots, or perhaps even some sort of grape. It's mystery brandy. *Specialité de la maison.*"

"All right, now I have a tougher question. What are you going to do when this war is over?"

The seriousness of John's question took the restaurant owner by surprise. The look on the American officer's face was without humor. Chi-chi hesitated.

"I don't know," answered Chi-chi. "And you, Major?"

"That's why I asked. I don't know either. Should we know?" John sipped his coffee. "Suppose I told you I was in no hurry to go home? Would that mean anything?"

"It might tell me you like Kunming. But then it might also tell me that you don't like going back to your old life. It is an interesting question."

"You didn't answer about your own post-war plans."

"No, I didn't. Perhaps it's because we in Asia do not plan as you do. Too much happens over which one has so little control. Perhaps you wish to become more Asian, Major." Chi-chi sat down at the empty table nearby. He leaned over and poured John another brandy. "An Asian custom, Major. An interesting question deserves a toast. In English I believe you say, 'In the house.' Is that correct?"

"On the house, actually. Thank you. An old Asian custom, eh?"

"Well, not so old… but appropriate. Allow me to ask you a question?"

"Another Asian custom?"

"I think so. What will your country do after the war? I mean what interest does America have here?"

John found it hard to concentrate. No lunch and several brandies and coffee tended to befuddle.

"I don't think America has any interest here. Where's here? China? Asia? What?"

"I mean this part of Asia. Maybe China, maybe Indochina. The English and the French always had a big interest."

As foggy as John had become, he was aware that the question he had been asked was quite serious. He was being asked a serious question. What to answer?

"I think America wants democracy, that's what I think it wants."

"And what is democracy?"

"I don't know. I mean I know, but I can't explain it right now. Too many brandies. It means the people get to choose their own leaders. That's basically it. I'll be more eloquent some other time. Your apple, apricot, whatever brandy does work wonders with the mind. Everything's gone soft. My brain's too soft."

"Perhaps you should have something to eat. Nothing too heavy. Would you care for an omelet? I should not have bothered you with such a question. Excuse me, please."

"Not at all. It was a good question. We have an old American custom. A good question deserves another good question. What do you think?"

"I think perhaps we should have this conversation again at a later date. I do not think it is good for you to drive. I will get a rickshaw for you."

"I have my jeep. I can't leave my jeep."

"Your jeep is safe with me. I will protect your jeep. No one will touch your jeep around here."

Chi-chi helped John to his feet and put him into a pedicab. He gave instructions to the driver in Chinese and John was whisked off toward the OSS compound a mile away. Chi-chi had known exactly where to direct the pedicab operator. John was not so inebriated that he missed that point. Now he'd see how good the instructions were.

The jostling of the pedicab through the streets kept John awake. The little Chinese Frenchman was right. The old life was out. Had to get a new life. Can't plan these things. Had to think more like an Asian. Gotta think Chinese. An interesting man this Chi guy. Too smart to be just a restaurant guy. That's obvious. A philosopher, too. Have to tell Edouard about this.

A brief but bumpy ride of about ten minutes through crowded Kunming brought John and the pedicab to the gate of the OSS compound. John offered to pay the driver, but he declined saying something in Chinese that seemed to mean it all had been taken care of. Yes, there was something very civilized about Mr. Chi—and something very uncivilized about his exotic brandy that had the kick of a mule, a Chinese/French/Vietnamese mule. As he teetered toward the Officers' Quarters, John decided that Asian ways most definitely fit him.

68

Chapter Four

"Thank you very much," said the slight figure in grey-brown shorts and white shirt as he accepted another American cigarette.

"Here, sir, keep the pack. If you enjoy them, we'll get some more for you." Tony Castelli was at his unctuous best.

A storeroom that had been converted into an administrative office was reconverted for this conference. Hallstrom wanted his deputy to "make it impressive, something that you might find in a corporate headquarters or maybe at the War Department." They had brought in several tables from the officers' mess and covered them with some dark green cloth purchased at one of Kunming's textile stalls.

The flag that Hallstrom had in his office was moved to the new conference room. Tony had tried unsuccessfully to create a circle with the mess tables, but in the end had to settle for four of them pushed together in a rectangle. Much discussion had gone into the seating arrangements. In the end it was decided that Lt. Col. Edgar Hallstrom would be at the head of the table, signified by the flag behind him, and the Vietnamese leader, Dr. Ho Chi Minh, would directly face him. Castelli was the one who recommended that the title "Doctor" be used. Little cards had been lettered with each of the attendees' names on them. John Guthrie was appalled.

"Tony, this is crazy. This man is a Communist partisan leader. Ours is a covert relationship—or at least as covert as anything is here in China. You don't use true names with people like this. He could be on the other side tomorrow. We don't know these Viet Minh people."

"John, I said virtually the same damn thing to Hallstrom, but he'd have none of it. Too complicated he said."

"I'll speak to him."

"Go ahead if you want to, but I tell you his mind is set. To tell you the truth, I think he's afraid he'll have trouble remembering all of our phony names."

"But you've got these cute little party cards in case he's stuck."

"He insists we use our own names."

"Look, Tony, Hallstrom is the guy who is so worried about our dealing with communists he's afraid of becoming associated with a project to arm them. I would think he'd want to cover his role."

"Ah yes, but you're missing the main point, sir. He's been ordered by Chungking to proceed with this operation, and he wants to look good doing it. Also, in spite of not trusting these communists, he wants to get full credit if they are successful and really take on the Japs. John, you know the guy well enough by now. He's scared of being tainted as a pro-communist, but at the same time he wants to make sure they know who he is when kudos time comes around. Hell, there's a Russian mission in Chungking—maybe he thinks they'll give him a medal. The point is—and I'm trying to warn you—he gets stuck on these small things and that's it. You'll only hurt yourself by pursuing it, I assure you."

"It's against all security procedures."

"You know it. I know it. But so what?"

"You know he got a commendation for the Gorilla Mission."

"I wrote it up for him. He put himself up for a meritorious service award. They have a medal for that now. It's green, looks nice."

"He didn't do anything. He wasn't there."

"He commanded the unit that did the job. Or if not commanded, 'had effective supervision of....' Good for one of the new greenies."

"Incredible."

The meeting itself was attended by Bob Simpson, John, Edouard, Paul Schreymann, and Tony Castelli. Hallstrom had not announced his guest list until the last moment.

"Lord Edgar considers you Gorillas his Vietnamese experts now," Castelli announced.

Head Gorilla, Bob Simpson, now awaiting a sure promotion, had been named acting chief of the SO section in Kunming. With his new glasses that the MO said he now had to wear all the time, "Horse" had taken on the look of a hulking professor. Because of his clearly worsened sight he was restricted to admin duty. Paul was now his deputy and principal buffer with Hallstrom.

With four people in the room capable in French—Castelli also spoke the language—it had been expected that the discussion with the Vietnamese would be in French. They had heard from their Chinese sources that Dr. Ho had some English, but they were not prepared for his fluency.

"First, gentlemen, I would like to thank you sincerely for this opportunity to meet with you. I have long admired America. I have travelled to New York several times and visited Boston and other places. I was working on a ship then and got to see many things. When I was a young man, of course."

The look on Hallstrom's face was a picture. He literally sat with his mouth open. This communist gook spoke English. By Edgar Hallstrom's rules, if a person spoke English—and this Ho spoke good English—he had to be taken seriously, at least, and perhaps was therefore truly pro-American. This time bigoted, self-righteous Edgar Hallstrom was correct on both counts.

"The briefing that Major Guthrie and Captain Parnell have just given regarding the situation with the Vichy forces was quite interesting and is consistent with what our own—Viet Minh—sources tell us." Ho smiled, reinforcing his statement.

The meeting had opened with John and Edouard reluctantly giving an update in French of the current status of the Vichy and colonial troops. Hallstrom had insisted that the session open in that manner. John's protests on security grounds were overruled. Hallstrom believed it would indicate American goodwill. John had argued that one didn't give up something to a new contact without something guaranteed in return. He tried to explain the element of control—unsuccessfully.

The little man with the wispy beard and the jaundiced, thin body had listened politely but asked no questions. John gave him full marks for not showing any of his hand. Unlike the Lt. Colonel from Cleveland, this Vietnamese was a pro. John watched as Ho sat apparently at ease in a straight wooden chair. He would turn every so often to flick the ash from his cigarette into the tin can on the table in front of him. John found the deliberation of the man fascinating as he carefully snuffed out the shortened cigarette. In about five minutes from the last one he would light another with one of the wooden matches in a box that had been placed by Castelli next to the package of Lucky Strikes. He seemed to be thoroughly enjoying himself. He listened carefully as Hallstrom droned on about the progress of the war against Japan. To give Lord Edgar credit, John thought, he's doing a good job of building the scene for the eventual suggestion of Viet Minh guerrilla operations against the Japs.

"So that brings us to the big question. Would you agree, Dr. Ho, that the time is right for an active campaign to begin against the Japs in Tonkin? But allow me again to thank you and your organization for what you have already done in helping our downed fliers to escape. Just the other day another one was brought over. We were told by the people at 14th Air Force that he had received wonderful treatment."

"Colonel, ours is a humanitarian as well as political mission. The Japanese are not our friends, even though they would like us to believe so. They made a very big—what is that called—performance of their coup d'état against the Vichy French administration just a few weeks ago, but have taken no real steps to bring independence to Indochina. But to answer your question directly, if you Americans have landed so close to Japan…. What is the name, Iwo Jima?

Then, yes, it would seem that this would now be a good time to put pressure on the Japanese in Vietnam."

Edgar Hallstrom beamed happily. As far as he was concerned his mission was accomplished. He would report to Chungking that he had convinced this important Vietnamese leader with his own guerrilla army to fight the Japanese. That's how he would characterize it. Play down the communist thing would be the approach. Anyhow, this little guy looked more like some middle-aged scholar with his chin hair and pleasant smile—maybe a professor of something. And he spoke damn good English even if it did sound a bit like one of those Hollywood Chinese actors speaking American. He hadn't said one sort of communist thing during the whole meeting. You would have thought he'd have mentioned something about how well the Russians were doing, or something. No mention of "the masses" and the usual "revolution" crap. Just seemed like a real nice guy, not full of himself like so many of the Chinese generals he had to deal with to get the barest bit of cooperation.

"Our people in the Viet Minh are from various nationalist and ethnic groups. It is a loose league, very democratic, working hard for our independence. That I'm sure you know. Our people are all very motivated, but we do not have the arms and equipment necessary to make the attacks on the Japanese that you suggest. We are happy to continue to help with rescuing your pilots, but we need many supplies and training for what you suggest. I also have to convince the other members of our council. I am simply the coordinator. As I said, we are very democratic."

Edouard and John looked at each other. This guy Ho was a master and he was playing Hallstrom with ease, but there wasn't a thing they could do. They needed to know more about this obviously smart old man. It was clear that Hallstrom was already in love with him. Edouard scribbled a note on a piece of paper from the pad Castelli had placed in front of each seat, along with pencils and a glass of water. "Lord Edgar loves agents who speak English!" he had written.

"Well, Dr. Ho, I can't go into details with you at this moment regarding such matters as arms and equipment, but Major Simpson and Guthrie are responsible for such things and I'm sure they'll be happy to discuss this with you later. Right, Gentlemen? My interest, and responsibility, is just to collect information."

John was livid and he could see Bob Simpson wasn't too happy either. That SOB Hallstrom had slipped out of the position of responsibility for supplying these Viet Minh people with weapons, shifting any future blame for arming communist partisans over to SO.

Bob Simpson gave a look to John that cried out, "Help!" Before John could come up with a clever way to turn the tables on the SI chief, Hallstrom sprung forth with what they later referred to as his *pièce de la résistance*.

"Dr. Ho, I think it is about time that you met our great American flier, General Claire Chennault of our Air Corps here in China. I know he will be pleased to meet the leader of the Viet Minh who have done so much to help our downed air crews. As you may know, sir, the General started the American Volunteer Group—they called them the Flying Tigers. He is highly respected by Washington and, of course, the Generalissimo—Chiang Kai-shek. But I expect you knew that."

"I certainly know of your General Chennault. He is quite famous. I would be delighted to meet him," Ho replied with sincerity. This was after all what he had been hoping would occur. A step up the American ladder, an excellent political step. At the same time, he sensed that the voluble lieutenant colonel was over his head. Ho knew he must keep him secure. It was time for a compliment. Compliments like names were of passing value, but sometimes they were useful. "Colonel, you are indeed an excellent host and clearly a fine military officer. It will be my privilege to work with you."

The room went quite silent. Hallstrom's chest literally expanded with a large intake of breath.

"I am honored, sir," Hallstrom said.

Tony Castelli's face was studiously blank. Edouard looked down at his boots inspecting them for pieces of dust. John, Bob, and Paul sat motionless. Their reaction was noted by the ever-alert Ho even while Edgar Hallstrom was totally oblivious. Ho lit another of the delicious American cigarettes and inhaled, deeply savoring the flavor.

"I really like your cigarettes, very much," he said. "I thank you again for this wonderful... *rejouissance.*"

"Delight, treat," Edouard quickly said.

"Yes, that's it. A treat," responded Ho, now in total command.

* * *

The promised meeting with Chennault was arranged quickly. The general liked to have a broad range of contacts outside of his immediate responsibilities. His private relationship with Generalissimo Chiang Kai-shek and Madame Chiang had already become a source of annoyance to Washington. A meeting with a Vietnamese nationalist leader might perturb his immediate superiors, but that did not bother the hero of the Flying Tigers.

Hallstrom and Castelli accompanied Ho to the general's office, a large, well-appointed suite in the headquarters building of the 14th Air Force. A quiet bustle reverberated through the halls. An immense anteroom lined with photographs of warplanes contained a large conference table and chairs. Ho was fascinated with the impressive display of fighting aircraft. He carefully studied each one before he moved on to the next.

"I have to admit that this is very exciting," Ho said in his typically ingenuous way. They waited only briefly before being ushered into the general's private office. Ho was offered a chair while Hallstrom and Castelli remained standing.

"How very nice of you to come to visit me, Your Excellency. I have so wanted to thank you personally for all the help that you have given to our pilots and crew," Chennault said as he smiled welcomingly.

Not only had Chennault already been well briefed by his own S-2 who was the liaison with Hallstrom, but he was practiced in dealing with Chinese officials. He treated Ho the same as he would a visiting Chinese general. It didn't matter that the scrawny little figure in a clean but tired jacket with a tieless shirt and khaki shorts carried none of the ostentation of the usual Kuomintang visitor.

"General, it is my honor to be so graciously received by you. We, the Viet Minh, are committed to assisting your poor unfortunate flyers. It is the humanitarian thing to do. We appreciate all that you and your men are doing to fight against foreign domination of Vietnam and all of Indochina."

Chennault had been told of Ho's English-language ability but was not prepared for his eloquence. Combined with the little man's unpretentious garb, the effect was quite disarming. For Ho's part, the tall, craggy, handsome American flyer seemed the prototypical American straight from the Hollywood films he remembered seeing. He was just as impressed with the American general's diplomatic courtesy.

"I would like very much to hear your view on how things are going in Tonkin since the Japanese coup. Has life changed much?" Chennault asked.

An intelligently phrased question, thought Ho. He judged the man *un homme très serieuse*. Ho answered with appropriate gravity.

"The Japanese had a chance to make many friends among the Vietnamese people. They have shown no signs of doing so. They could have shown that they were very different from the French. They have not done so. They wish only to rule us as the French have. The people will fight that. The Viet Minh will lead that fight."

"That's excellent. Colonel, are we doing anything to help the friends of Mr. Ho here?" Chennault fixed Hallstrom as one would pin a fly to the wall.

"Yes, sir. We have been discussing just that. Yes, sir." If there had been any way the hefty Cleveland lawyer could have fallen to his knees and groveled, he would have. Tony Castelli satisfied himself with a small smile. He knew the scene would be great in the telling. Chennault waved both OSS officers into side chairs.

The conversation between Chennault and Ho Chi Minh continued on for about five minutes more with the general explaining how well the war was going in the Pacific. Ho listened attentively and asked a few intelligent questions.

"Well, it truly has been wonderful meeting you, Your Excellency. Is there anything we can do for you while you're here in Kunming...?"

"Yes, General. I very much would like a picture of you. I would like to show my friends a photo of a great American general who understands the problems of us Vietnamese."

"I would be delighted," said Claire Chennault, charmed by the openness of his visitor.

An aide was summoned, and he quickly produced several 8 × 11 glossy photographs that were kept for the many journalists passing through. Ho chose one. The general reached for the photo and wrote on the bottom, "Yours sincerely, Claire L. Chennault." Years later, the Vietnamese leader would still have that photo.

The entire scene was rerun in the officers' club by Tony Castelli doing his best imitation of his boss. He had to be careful because Hallstrom could drop in at any moment.

"Okay, so we're there and Edgar is standing so stiff at attention I thought his back would break. Old Chennault is gabbing away with the old man telling him about all the good stuff.... MacArthur coming back to the Philippines and all that.... I can see Edgar is dying to say something, you know, important. He can't stand to not speak. You know that. He's got this screwed-up look on his face. I figure any minute he's going to burst out with something like how terrific he was during some big bridge tournament. You know how he talks about that all the time. Then I realize when we sit down that he's got his legs crossed real tightly... he's got to go to the latrine and he's dyin'. We were in there maybe fifteen, twenty minutes total. The second we're out of his office, the general's office, Edgar mumbles something and dashes off for the latrine. The old guy didn't know what was going on and asked me. What could I do but tell him? And he, funny little guy, was concerned. He said it was... get this... 'a problem of age' and that one should always be understanding with the problems of the elderly. I nearly split a gut. Here is this little old man, who looks like death warmed over, talking about Edgar like he's some ancient relic. Well, maybe he's right. Compared to Edgar this old guy is as spry as they come. I bet he doesn't even know what a swivel chair is. I tell you he's hard as nails... but a nice guy. I liked him. He walked off with a nice photo of Chennault. I wonder what he'll do with it?"

John had been listening and smiling with the others, but now he spoke up.

"He'll use it to show his people that he's got the support of an American general behind him. It's a big political weapon for him. He's in with the big guys. That old fellow doesn't keep a scrap book. That I guarantee you."

"We should try and meet with him separately, if we're going to work with him," Edouard said.

"Good idea," said Castelli. "There's a Vietnamese who contacted us through AGAS. I'll get hold of him, and he can set it up. I have to let Edgar know, of course."

"That's fine," said John. "It's got to be a legit meeting, but not in our offices anymore. I'll talk to Bob and we'll use our new safe house. Sometimes I wonder if Hallstrom knows what business we're in. Maybe you're right. To him it's just one big bridge tournament."

"I say let's have old Tony here get on to AGAS and arrange our meeting," said Edouard. "But we better do it fast before the little guy goes running off with his photo of Chennault and back to where he came from."

It took several days to iron out all the details, but finally arrangements were made for Edouard to pick up the Vietnamese leader nearby a crowded vegetable stall in a busy part of town. An old man getting into a jeep would either be ignored or simply be taken for a servant being picked up in the afternoon to go to work for the long noses.

The safe house was located across town near the university far away from the OSS compound with its wonderfully complex cover name on a large sign at the gate—"Air Ground Force Resources Technical Staff (Provisional), 5329th." Of course, any decent rickshaw puller in Kunming would know it as AGFRTS—or "those American intelligence people." John had gone to great pains to make sure the newly obtained safe house was as secure as could be arranged, but that wasn't saying much. The important thing was that its one large room was reasonably clean. It was furnished with a bed, some small chairs around a table, and an overstuffed chair covered in a sort of blue fabric. It was functional, if dingy.

"If we'd had some more time, we could have given this place a coat of paint," commented Edouard.

"If we'd had the paint," responded John trying to peer out of the dirt-grimed window.

"I've got the feeling that this guy, Ho, doesn't deal much in externals," said Edouard.

"He seemed to enjoy his visit with Chennault—at least according to Tony," John said, while arranging a pile of magazines he had borrowed from the officers' club.

"True, but he gives me the impression of a man who has seen and done it all. Of course, what the hell do I know? It's just my impression. I have to admit I've never met anyone like him—not that I've really met many Asians to talk with before we came here. He's certainly not like any of the Chinese officials we've met." Edouard lowered himself into the large club chair. "This is comfortable, if a little seedy."

"It goes with the rest of the place, but we were lucky to get our hands on it. Otherwise this dump would look like a large prison cell," replied John.

"You'd think our outfit could afford something a bit more… luxurious. Oh well, beggars can't be—and so forth. I think it's time for me to take off for the pick up. I want to leave a little time to case the area. It's useless, I know, but just for form's sake if nothing else," said Edouard heaving himself out of the chair and heading for the door.

"Take care," John said as Edouard left.

The street in front of the safe house was relatively quiet in comparison to the usual bustle of Kunming. John opened the door to let in some air. The few passers-by studiously ignored the "foreign devil" smoking a cigarette and lounging in the doorway. Their calculated disinterest was the essence of Chinese courtesy. It was not polite to appear to be aware of the presence of a white man in an environment quite inappropriate to that presence. Hear and see no evil guided the ordinary person's life, especially in a city teeming with war refugees and an ever-increasing number of military from many nations.

John thought about this as he watched a flight of B-25s of the 14th Air Force overhead. Every now and then he allowed the incongruity of his life to penetrate his wartime armor. The odd smells of a Chinese city, rickshaws pulling silk-clad doll women, coolies struggling along with immense burdens—these and a hundred other sights he allowed to invest his senses for a short while, just a short while. To see and smell and hear without anyone knowing. A child's illusion and, sometimes, an adult's protection.

Unexpectedly, Edouard appeared around the corner and screeched to a halt just in front of John. His passenger, Dr. Ho, held on for dear life in the jeep's front seat, but he was laughing quite happily.

"That was quick, Edouard. I hope he didn't scare you, Dr. Ho?"

"No, no, the Captain was just showing me how he avoids being followed. Most amusing."

"Don't worry. There wasn't anybody following us. I thought I'd show Dr. Ho a bit of fun. He's a good sport."

"Please come in, both of you. You came back so swiftly, Edouard. I wasn't expecting you for at least a half an hour," said John looking at his watch. "I don't know what I was thinking. It is half an hour. I completely lost track of time."

"That is the sign of a mind hard at work, Major."

"My mother used to say that I was daydreaming. Did you ever do that, doctor?"

"I still do. It is very pleasant to have *la rêverie*. Is it the same word in English?" asked Ho, accepting the seat of honor in the overstuffed chair.

"Oh, this is a very comfortable chair. I think though it is for someone much bigger than I. I feel I am in the arms of a large soft bear." Ho's small frame sunk into the folds of the chair.

"Would you care for a drink, sir? We have some nice wine. At least I've been told so by our mess sergeant who traded for it with the chef at the French mission," Edouard showed the bottle to Ho so he could see the vintage.

"I'm sure it is an excellent wine, Captain, though I'm no expert. I rarely drink alcohol in any form these days. But I did enjoy wine when I was much younger. Thank you. This chair is enough comfort for me. I assure you it is far more than I'm used to."

"This place is not much, Dr. Ho, but it is out of the way and more pleasant to chat in than our offices," John explained.

"Yes, it is quite pleasant, but what is this word 'chat'?"

"*Bavarder, en français,*" said Edouard quickly.

"Oh, another very good word. 'Chat.' Yes, we can chat very well here." The old man showed every sign of enjoying himself.

John was impatient to move the conversation on to operational subjects. He perceived that the Vietnamese could continue on with this small talk as long as they did. He was very polite. He was most likely lying about the chair that was enfolding him just to be courteous.

"Perhaps it would be best if I explained something about our getting together today," John began in his most diplomatic tone. "Our interests are a bit different than... uh... the Colonel's interests who you met the other day...."

"You mean Lt. Col. Hallstrom who took me to visit Gen. Chennault?"

"Yes, him. You may have gathered that from what he said. At any rate, we are more interested in your, well, unit, in regard to its fighting capability. Not that the colonel's requirements of intelligence gathering aren't important.... It's just that our section focuses more on *l'action directe, comme on dit en français.*"

Ho smiled at John's use of French. "*Oui, je comprend,*" he said for the first time using any French in his talks with the Americans. Edouard mistook the older man's quick minimal response in French perhaps to be a preference. He launched into rapid French defining SO branch needs as opposed to SI. Ho held up a finger indicating he would like to ask a question. In English he asked Edouard, "Are you French, perhaps Parisian?"

Embarrassed, Edouard replied, "My mother was French. My father is American and so am I."

Ho smiled at his patriotic emphasis. "It is that you speak so perfectly. You would make most Frenchmen feel quite, what is the term, low class. I mean this as a compliment. I assure you that in Indochina we indigenes do not get to hear many Frenchmen who speak the language as well as you do. That is what I like about American English. You can speak good English in many accents. American democracy, right?"

"And where did you learn your English, sir? It's excellent," asked John.

"Oh, not excellent at all, major. As I mentioned at our earlier meeting, I used to work on ships as a young man. Then I worked in some restaurants. I worked in New York, as I mentioned. I've worked in many places. I have read quite a bit, too." And that was all he said about himself. He was content to be silent.

All the while John had been studying this man called Ho Chi Minh. He watched him as he would a witness, trying to discern some telltale sign. It passed through John's mind that the man of indeterminate age who sat before him was doing the same as he. What was most disturbing to John was the sense that this wizened Vietnamese with the scraggly goatee was better at it than he. Ho had the look of a man who had known many interrogations—soft ones and hard. Anyone who worked with him, and certainly those who worked for him, would have to be able to respond to that deep knowledge and experience. Instinctively, John looked over at Edouard. The younger man was totally enthralled by the Vietnamese leader. It was easy to see. Ho most likely saw it, too. John quickly tried to regain control both of his own thoughts and the physical scene in front of him.

"Specifically, then Mr. Ho [an artful and purposeful reduction in rank] it's important for us to know exactly what your people can and are willing to do." A no-nonsense question demanding a clear answer.

"We have the capability of *l'action directe*, but it is just as I have been saying. We need supplies, equipment, weapons—military weapons. You heard about our successful attack on the French garrison in December?" Ho didn't wait for a reply, nor did he explain that the attack by his scholarly military lieutenant, Vo Nguyen Giap, and 34 selected Viet Minh cadre decimated two small Vichy French garrisons on Christmas Eve, 1944. He put it in more palatable terms.

"The aim of our small group was to capture military hardware and ammunition, as well as make the statement that we could do so. We were successful in all respects. We have the complete support of the populace. They understand that we represent the people."

John shook his head in disapproval.

"We are not interested in actions for political effect. We are also not interested in attacks for the purpose of revenge against the former colonial governing body. We are interested in one thing only—killing Japs and disrupting their fighting capabilities. This could mean such things as blowing bridges, rail lines, communications, etc. It's quite straight forward, Mr. Ho. Do you want to help the United States in its war with Japan?"

"The simple answer is yes, Major, but the situation is not that simple."

Ho stopped there, letting his statement sink in. This Major Guthrie was an experienced man, older than he looked. This was a very important meeting, perhaps more important than the previous ones. He understood, this Guthrie.

He understood what he was attempting to do. But at the same time the larger point was to gain American support for the political aims of the Viet Minh. That was his agenda, and the question was whether that was reconcilable with the limited military aims so directly put by the forceful Major.

"I understand well the point of your focus, and I respect it, Major. However, the reason why there is a Viet Minh to assist America in its war against the Japanese is political—our desire for independence. That must be understood as part of the... I don't know the word... the structure perhaps... of any future relationship. We do not ask you to help us gain that independence, but I know about what your President Roosevelt said about the independence for the Philippines. I would think he would think the same way about Vietnam and the rest of Indochina."

John decided that it was best to say nothing. This old man was a practiced debater, and this was his argumentative turf. It was best to accept what he had just given and ignore the rest—also a good debating technique.

"Dr. Ho [promoted again] that is all we ask; that the Viet Minh work with us to fight the Japanese. We do not wish to become involved in your politics. We certainly do not want to be seen as supporters of French colonialism. That's their business... and your business," John said as forcefully as he could.

The two men smiled at each other, both experienced negotiators enjoying once again the bloodless battle of verbal and mental contest. Ever so briefly, John Guthrie was transported back to his meetings with the hard-nosed steel plant managers. Ho sensed the competence of his adversary, and in his own way was pleased to have the exchange with this bright young American who apparently blew up bridges and other things as his country ordered.

"I think we understand each other quite well, Major. You must excuse me if I seem so fixed on our—Vietnam's—interests. I do see the larger issues. At the same time it is my hope to be able to pass on to you," Ho gestured to both John and Edouard, "some idea of the struggle of our people. Did you know, for example that the floods of the past year destroyed all the dikes in the Red River Delta and destroyed thousands of peasant farms? Our people in the Colonial Administration offices reported to us that perhaps over a million people lost their lives—maybe more—in Tonkin alone. Now this year there is no seed to replant nor farmers to work the rice fields, if they could plant. The flood didn't kill all of them. Most died from the famine that followed. And what did the French do—nothing. Neither did the Japanese who made such a big show of being our friends and fellow Asians. This is our world. This is the world we have to live in. This is what I want you, need you, to understand about us."

The sincerity of the little man perched in the soft cushions of the large club chair was eloquent. But Ho had not finished with his lesson. He pulled himself from the confines of the chair. Edouard thought for a moment he was going to leave. He glanced at John, who shot back a worried look. Struggling out of the chair with its deeply sunken seat, Ho finally gained his feet. The two American officers rose simultaneously.

"No, no, please sit. I'm just trying to get something I carry with me," Ho said reaching into his pants pocket. "I have made many copies of this. I give it to my people, but it is good for everyone, maybe, I think. It is in Vietnamese. You do not speak Vietnamese?" He asked the last as courtesy. Ho was always conscious of the niceties and would not insult his hosts by taking their ignorance for granted. Both Americans shook their heads acknowledging their lack of the language. They sat down again like attentive school children.

"First, I must tell you that the struggle to get back our independence has been going on over 80 years, so this is not a new thing. This poem, which I shall translate for you, is by a man who was executed by the French in about 1864, or so. His name was Nguyen Huu Huan, and he was a dedicated member of what you would call today a resistance group. I would tell you more about them if you want, but what I want you to hear is what he wrote. I believe in it. I think maybe you do also. I think you should. I tell all my young friends that. Huan wrote:

> The more I see my duty, the more I feel
> On my shoulders its infinite weight.
> A man worthy of the name must blush
> If he cannot pay the debt with his life.

"I believe that. You are soldiers—you understand that. You are Americans, and isn't that why you had your revolution? I have read about it, you know. I also have read your Declaration of Independence. Someday, maybe soon, Vietnam will have its own declaration of independence. But first, we Vietnamese must remember what Huan wrote before the French executed him." Ho sat back down, this time on the edge of the seat so his feet could touch the floor.

There really was nothing John or Edouard could say after such a heartfelt lesson, for it was that—a lesson from a master. John knew instinctively that he was about to lose control of the meeting and moved quickly to overcome the disadvantage.

"I have something for you to take back with you as a symbol of our, American, willingness to work with you, the Viet Minh."

"Should I get them, John?" Edouard asked.

"Yes, please do," he replied.

The young captain reached under the bed and brought out a leather suitcase. The ever-resourceful Tony Castelli had obtained the valise through one of his numerous contacts among Kunming's merchants. With a grand gesture, as if he were a conjurer about to uncover a secret treasure, Edouard flung open the cover revealing six US Army issue Colt .45 cal. semi-automatic pistols, with extra clips. Ho's face, as John would later tell the story, was a picture of delight. "Like a kid in front of the Christmas tree," he would say.

"These are for you and your staff as a gift from the United States Army as a symbol of the cooperation which we hope will develop between us and the Viet Minh fighting forces. We have additional ammunition so that they may have some target practice as well." John was satisfied he had regained the initiative.

* * *

Ho Chi Minh would return to Vietnam armed with valuable indications of his success in dealing with the Americans—a signed photo of Major General Claire Chennault and the six brand-new .45 automatics. Soon, it had been agreed, John would arrange to send an advance team with which to maintain direct radio contact. That would be followed by himself and a training cadre to teach Viet Minh fighters both tactics and weapon use. The objectives of both sides had been accomplished. Everyone was happy.

Hallstrom signaled Chungking he had succeeded in getting Ho to agree to incorporate the Viet Minh into an OSS-directed Intel net. Bob Simpson envisaged the possible beginning of serious SO operations against Japanese infrastructure targets. Ho Chi Minh himself believed he had not only reinforced the role of the Viet Minh politically, but he had opened up a new potential source of material aid and assistance from the OSS. Edouard was imbued with the spirit of his Parnell family revolutionary heritage. Even the usually reticent John Guthrie had to admit he had been impressed with the leader of the Viet Minh. Only the normally ebullient Tony Castelli sounded a warning:

"We're going to start up with this guy, okay. But can we see it through? You know he's in this for the duration."

Chapter Five

"Okay, here's what I've got on him so far." Tony Castelli, sporting a nascent mustache, rifled through a file on his desk. John and Edouard sat opposite, tilting backward on their wooden chairs. Castelli's room was filled with grey metal filing cabinets and a large map stand. He called it his ammunition bunker. That was how he saw his enormous collection of paper—the weaponry of an SI deputy chief.

The subject of the meeting was Commandant Jean Sainteny, head of Mission 5 (M.5) of the Free French Forces in Kunming. Major Sainteny, his equivalent rank in US Army terms, directed his group with the implied—if not actual—direct backing of DeGaulle's own staff in Paris. He was their man for all matters Vietnamese.

"Sainteny has already made it clear to me that he knows about the little meeting with Ho Chi Minh, and he's pissed off he wasn't invited. I of course lied and told him it was all on such short notice, etc." Castelli finally found what he was looking for and began reading from the file.

"Sainteny... age mid-thirties, blah, blah, blah. Son-in-law of former Governor General of Indochina. Banker before the war in Indochina. Returned to France—he says—to fight Germans 1939. It seems logical, so we don't really question it. But he says he was captured and escaped to join the Resistance. I've checked all the way back to London, and nobody has any record of him as a member of a resistance group. London is willing to give him the benefit of the doubt, though. I guess the reason for that is he was accepted as a part of the inner circle around DeGaulle's intelligence chief. That's basically it. The rest is just correspondence."

"That's not too much, Tony," John commented.

"It's all between the lines. You have to read between the lines, John."

"Fine. He's well connected on both the political and economic front."

"Exactly. I would look at everything this guy does from the standpoint of how it benefits him and his connections. He's not just a French intelligence group commander. He's a guy with a substantial personal interest in how things turn out. Vietnam represents a lot of post-war moolah for all concerned."

"So what have we got then… we meaning OSS in Kunming?"

"John, Sainteny has to do everything he can to make sure we—you, Edouard, me, Horse, and even Lord Edgar—are kept in check. That's a main part of his job."

"How is he going to do that?" asked Edouard.

"You haven't met him, have you? This guy is smooth—and plenty devious. He'll figure something out."

"Is he vulnerable to the old buttering-up technique?" Edouard asked.

"Oh, I'm sure he's as vulnerable as the next guy, but that's not going to mean much," Tony answered. "It's not going to make him less suspicious about American intentions. Remember, the French always think we're after their colonies."

"So what do you suggest?" asked John. "Should we include them in on the deal—you know, offer them some role in any Viet Minh operation?"

"The problem then wouldn't be with the French—it's the Viet Minh. Ho wouldn't be happy with a combined American/French team. Remember, they're in the business of getting rid of the French."

"So we're stuck one way or the other," said Edouard.

"Looks like it, buddy."

"What's the situation with the Vichy French forces working their way north?" asked John.

"According to M.5, whom I would expect have the best info on this, there are units approaching Lao Cai on the border."

"And this is a main force?"

"They say they think they're led by a contingent of Foreign Legion troopers. No one seems to know what these Vichy losses have been, but they've got to be considerable. Sorry, but that's all I have. Like I said, they don't share too much."

"You've got to find out what M.5 wants, Tony," suggested Edouard. "Time for a little cumshaw in the right places."

"You think I haven't tried?" replied Castelli.

* * *

The M.5 headquarters was not more than a mile away from the OSS compound. Unlike the Spartan facilities of the Americans, however, French intelligence was housed in what once had been a district tax building, a comparatively sumptuous facility. Jean Sainteny sat in the large office of the former head tax collector ranting to his adjutant.

"I can't believe it," he said. "Why not send me to find out what's going on? The chief knows nothing about Indochina. He comes all the way out to Dien Bien Phu from Paris. What's the point in that? Just to have a meeting with those Vichy generals?"

"The signal from Calcutta indicated he was already on the way back to Paris. Perhaps, sir, something important came up and he had no chance to contact you," said the aide trying to soothe his boss.

"I'll tell you what came up. One minute they're informing me that the column is ready to launch some big attack on the Japs, and the next we are told that the same useless Vichy people are in no shape to fight and we should get the Americans to drop supplies to them or else they won't even be able to make it to China. Absurd! Which is it? Are they going to stay and fight or aren't they? Do they need ammunition and guns or food and medicine? And what about their generals? Where are they? Alessandri has to be with his Legion unit, but is the other fool in Laos yet? If the columns are in no condition to fight, I need details. How can I ever get the Americans to help if we don't know where the columns are nor what shape they're in. *Absolument absurde!*"

"Well, sir, we do know some are heading to Lao Cai."

"Yes, of course I know that. That's what we told that American, Castelli. But how many and which units? These columns are spread out for miles maybe a hundred miles, perhaps even more. I'll have to take a chance and get down to Lao Cai and see for myself. We can't afford to wait to hear from someone else where our own forces are. The latest information we have now is weeks old. It would not take much for us to look very stupid."

"How will you get to Lao Cai, sir?"

"I'd like the Americans to fly me down. The roads are terrible this time of year. Castelli could arrange it… if he wanted to. But then I'd have to come up with something in exchange. I don't really like that little Italian, but he's useful. Maybe if I just offer to take him along…?"

The simple flight to Lao Cai, only 200 air miles away, became far more complicated from the outset. Castelli agreed immediately to arrange transport from the 14th Air Force liaison but suggested he would also like to bring along two of his colleagues, a Major Guthrie and Capt. Parnell. Jean Sainteny had not met these two yet, but he had heard about them as part of the American operation to make contact with the Vichy column. Rumor had it that the younger one, Parnell, was half French and that could prove interesting. Sainteny decided he was pleased to have them along—not that he had much choice if he wanted Castelli's help.

The real problem which arose was the news that Major General Marcel Alessandri, who commanded all Foreign Legion forces in Tonkin, was reported to be with the advance column heading toward Lao Cai, if not already there. Sainteny knew Alessandri from before the war, though they had not been on the same social plane. Legion officers, especially ranking officers, had little time for civilian bankers, even if they were son-in-law of the Governor General. Sainteny suspected that now as a mere commandant he would be considered even more lowly. This prospect made him doubly annoyed long before anything had actually occurred. He was, however, still the ranking Gaulliste officer in the area and had no intention of having this Vichy general attempt to pull rank. The fact that Alessandri had never given the slightest thought to the young banker, Jean Sainteny, either pro or con, might have annoyed him even more if he had known about it.

For John and Edouard, the trip to Lao Cai was just what they had been looking for—a chance to make contact with Sainteny and M.5 outside of the usual Kunming liaison circuit. The combination of his usual charm and excellent French established an instant rapport for Edouard with Sainteny. By the time the C-45, the same aircraft type but differently appointed than the one that rescued the Gorillas, landed in the airstrip near the border not far from Lao Cai, Edouard and Jean Sainteny had worked up a very satisfactory acquaintance. Both men were quite pleased with themselves. Tony Castelli and John exchanged knowing glances in recognition of the Gallic dance they had just witnessed.

They hadn't expected much at the airstrip and certainly weren't disappointed. Steel tracking had been laid down to firm up the landing area. Each track was perforated in order to lighten their weight and also add to the friction which assisted a plane's wheels to grasp the surface. The result was an extra roar in landing and considerable loss of rubber on the tires. The jury was still out on the efficacy of the invention, although during rainy season it was a great deal better than landing in wallows of mud. The group of four officers from Kunming off-loaded and immediately began a search for some sort of vehicle. Supposedly, there was a Chinese construction brigade stationed nearby that might be able to provide some transportation. That's what Castelli had said before they took off. Aside from some coolies shifting sand from one pile to another, there was no one in sight. The pilot of their plane joined them on the ground and expressed his surprise at the lack of a reception party. He had flown in several times before and there had always been a crowd at the field. There were scores of barrels of aviation fuel lined up in neat squat rows, but no one to roll them out to siphon their contents into arriving aircraft. That part didn't bother him. He had plenty of fuel for the return trip to Kunming. It was the total absence of people that was surprising.

The airstrip was never supposed to be anything but an emergency landing place or a refueling stopover. There was no regular radio contact. Just another bush airstrip with some qualitative improvements for the military aircraft. Jean Sainteny felt a bit of a fool in arranging for this expedition and began to apologize.

"Not at all," said John dismissing the Frenchman's apology. "We all wanted to come down and see what was going on. We're here now, so why don't Edouard and I do some scouting around down that road to see what, if anything, is going on."

The suggestion that the two SO officers take on the responsibility of reconnoitering the area was not really a matter of courtesy. Neither Sainteny nor Castelli were field men. They were strictly staff intelligence, and as such were far more at home with their charts, reports and dispatches than they were with the physical aspects of stomping about the countryside. They also weren't dressed for anything but the office with their starched "sun tans," ties, and comfortable shined dress shoes.

"I wonder what was in their minds when they dressed this morning," said John, as he and Edouard took off across the strip headed for the road on the other side.

"My guess is that it was either suiting up in their normal way or going whole hog in a full combat kit. Obviously, Tony and Sainteny share a certain similar fashion sense."

"Or lack of common sense would be more like it," said John, always annoyed at situations showing lack of forethought. "It was fairly obvious that we were not going to be traipsing about downtown Kunming and having drinks at the Os' club."

Both John and Edouard had on their jump boots and webbing with holster, first aid packet, and canteen. John even had his small compass attached to his belt. It was his new rule: Never go anywhere in the boondocks without your compass. He even had a small map of the region in his back pocket. Even for this simple day's outing, the lessons of the Gorilla Mission had been well learned. Edouard had smiled at his friend's precautions, but he understood well what had prompted him. He had his own little field compulsions. In his field jacket he had stuffed the contents of a couple of K-rations. John needed his compass and he needed his snacks. It was all a matter of personal choice and survival needs. Presumably, Tony Castelli and Jean Sainteny had come with expectations of a full-service safari. "Oh well," he said aloud.

"What?" asked John. "What did you say?"

"Nothing. I was just thinking about our two comrades back at the strip. They're both very smart, but certainly like fish out of water out here without their usual accommodations."

"I don't know what Tony was thinking. Do you think those two guys coordinated their outfits? My God, they couldn't have done that, could they?" John asked with a smile on his face.

"Yes, they do sort of look twinsy today, don't they? Ties and shined shoes. What the well-dressed warrior will wear in Yunnan today. By the way, what the hell are we looking for?"

"Frenchmen, Vietnamese, at this stage somebody, anybody."

A little further down the dirt road strewn with potholes they came upon a Chinese couple pulling a cart. The attempts at communication were a total failure, but the man kept pointing back along the road as if that was where the two officers should go. John and Edouard thanked the couple, who giggled in return. Soon the two Americans saw more people heading toward them, some pulling empty carts just as the first did.

"Maybe it's market day," said Edouard.

"It's something," John responded. "I think we're close to finding out what."

After a turn in the road a large crowd of Chinese peasants milled around what appeared to be a tent. There was a great deal of chattering and some laughter. All the Chinese seemed to be trying to sell something, mostly foodstuffs. John and Edouard pushed through the press of people. In the middle was a tall white man in a military uniform of some sort. He haggled with several of the peasants good naturedly in Chinese and then apparently settled on a figure for some of the vegetables. He wore khaki shorts and a floppy hat, but he was definitely an officer in uniform—clearly a French officer. Both John and Edouard spied his insignia and rank on his rather ragged but clean shirt. They both called loudly in French to get his attention.

"Commandant, Commandant," they shouted together.

The French major turned quickly to the sound of their voices, smiled broadly and waved them over while pushing himself away from some eager new food sellers. He greeted both Americans with his best salute and immediately launched into a barrage of French which only Edouard understood completely because of the man's effusive language and speed of speaking. When he had slowed down, John also began to understand what was going on. The two Americans introduced themselves.

"It is a great pleasure to meet you both," the Frenchman said, barely stopping for a breath. "The general will be so pleased to know you are here. Yes, he will be very pleased. You will want to meet him, of course. Please excuse my miserable appearance, but you understand from where we have just come. At least we have a few days in which to get a bit cleaned up and some of our clothes washed by these very nice people." He gestured to the still milling crowd. "I am buying their produce for our men. It's been so long since there has been such abundance."

Two French soldiers arrived with an empty cart and began piling in some of the vegetables and fruits that the officer had purchased. They looked haggard, but both were clean shaven and bright eyed. They had been through a great deal. That could be easily seen. The officer saw John and Edouard eyeing his men.

"They may not look like much now, but they are still soldiers, I assure you. They are Legionnaires."

John explained that they had flown down from Kunming in hopes of just this meeting. He explained that Commandant Jean Sainteny of M.5 was with them and would want to welcome *la Légion* himself. It was a neat way of avoiding reference to Vichy and the questionable loyalty of the column. He could tell by Edouard's nodding head that he had achieved the proper diplomatic balance in his serviceable but admittedly unpolished French. The Legion major insisted that General Alessandri would want to meet them immediately, but John, with Edouard's polite assistance, explained that he thought it more appropriate if Sainteny be the first to welcome le Générale de Division Alessandri. The use of the correct military rank for a major general was quite intentional and had been Edouard's subtle addition. It established a certain official character to a most unofficial meeting.

The French major stopped the two Legionnaires who were about to depart with their cart of produce and ordered them to immediately double-time to the airstrip and return with Commandant Sainteny of the French Army and Captain Castelli of the American Army. He said that they should remember to apologize for their lack of proper transportation and scruffy appearance.

The Americans went into the tent to wait while the French officer finished his bargaining. He came in well-satisfied with his efforts.

"I knew my bad Cantonese would come in handy one day," he explained. "I am sorry that my English is not up to even that level of Chinese." For a man who had just marched about 300 miles through tortuous terrain with bare subsistence rations—and being repeatedly harassed by the Japanese and sometimes local tribesmen—this Legion officer had lost not one bit of his military bearing. As the three of them waited for the arrival of "the two other guests from Kunming," the officer told of the recent days of unit's *l'Expédition*, as he called it.

"This has been the best part of the trip," he said. "We were able to buy some of this Chinese money with the gold coins the general had been carrying all the way from Son Tay. Otherwise I don't think our greeting here would have been so cordial, eh? We've had a couple of days here to regain a bit of our strength, but I assure you most of the force is pretty ragged. We have people straggling by squads, by twos and threes. To have a whole company come in is rare. The general spread us Legionnaires throughout the column—you know we have both French Army and Colonial Army troops. He wanted to tighten up the column that way, but it didn't work too well. We lost—the whole column that is—a lot of people. I think more to sickness and bad food than to the Japs."

As the major continued on, happy to have a chance to tell his story, his voice became more tired. It was clear that it was only the excitement of meeting the Americans that had buoyed his strength. He shouldn't have been telling them everything that he was. He was just so relieved finally to be out of the hell that they had marched through. Even officers of *la Légion* could be excused for talking of their ordeal. He admitted all their heavy weapons and ammunition had been abandoned along the way. They had eaten most of the horses and pack animals they had started with. He didn't want to, but the picture he created for John and Edouard was of a dispirited rabble that was lucky the Japanese had decided it wasn't worth the major effort required to mount a serious offensive against them.

"My general preceded us across the border here. He is located only about a kilometer away. I know he has been hoping to make contact with the Allied authorities. I am responsible for these food purchases. That's all I've been doing for the past three days—that and getting myself and my men cleaned up a bit. The general relaxed our normal standards while we were on the trail, but now he wants us back in shape. We're stretched from here to over on the other side of the border. I mean the whole column is stretched. We have a company of about 100 Legionnaires on the other side of Lao Cai as a rear guard, but they're due to come over shortly. It might even be today."

It was clear the Legion major was exhausted. Edouard broke out some of the K-ration high energy fruit bars he had brought along and offered it to the officer. He did not ask what the dark, mysterious-looking rectangles were. He quickly accepted the gift and tried to bite off a chunk. Edouard counseled him to be careful about biting into the bar which could easily dislodge a tooth. He also explained what it was that the man was so eagerly chewing.

"*Délicieux... absolument délicieux,*" said the major, savoring the sweet, gummy glob in his mouth.

The sounds of the Chinese vendors gathering again outside the tent reminded the major that he had not completed his purchasing. He excused himself and returned to his task while John and Edouard remained sitting comfortably on the two crates that served as chairs. The sounds of the haggling outside resumed in the same manner as when they had first come upon the scene.

"You know, we've got more or less what we came for already. A pretty good order of battle report he gave us. I'd still like a look at the troops, themselves, though," said John in a somewhat conspiratorial tone. "We should pass this on to Tony as soon as we can, or at least tell him that we've got it."

"I think our major would be crucified if his general knew what he had given us. I suspect these Legion people don't talk much to outsiders... about anything," said Edouard in agreement.

"He's on his last legs," John said in explanation.

"But I bet he's a hell of a lot better than he was a few days ago...."

Their conversation was interrupted by some loud greetings in French and a quick downturn in the bustle of Chinese trading voices. A quick look outside the tent showed that the messengers had returned with their quarry. Castelli and Sainteny had arrived flushed with their hurrying, perspiring profusely, and with their carefully shined shoes caked with dust.

Unsurprisingly, Sainteny quickly led off the Legion major for a private exchange. John and Edouard took advantage of this less than polite but operationally understandable demeanor to give Tony a quick briefing on what they had learned about the status of the Vichy column.

"Did he say anything about any Japanese deployment?" asked Tony.

"Not a word," Edouard answered.

"Nothing," added John. "But he did mention about Alessandri most likely wanting to meet us. If that's the case, I suggest that you take the diplomatic honors, Tony, and we'll shift off to have a gander at some of these troops to see with our own eyes just what state they're in."

"Good idea, John. If they'll let us divide up like that...."

"We'll be discreet. I'll figure out a line. If I can't, Prince Edouard of the Blarney Stone certainly will."

They didn't have any more time to discuss their plans. Sainteny returned with the major and the announcement that they would leave immediately to meet with Alessandri. It wasn't an invitation. Edouard looked at John who looked at Tony. A command performance. With a shrug, John said they would be delighted to meet the famous Legion general. So much for their clever division of labor.

With the major of the Foreign Legion as their guide, the little group made its way over to a small encampment of three tents. A rather soiled flag, presumably signifying the headquarters of a major general stood on one side of the largest tent. On the other was the tricolor of France, a bit faded and slightly tattered but in overall better shape. John immediately noticed the difference and wondered the reason for the disparity. His curiosity was satisfied unexpectedly by the major who pointed to the general's standard.

"That is the ensign of the 10th Regt. of the Foreign Legion. They say it is nearly 50 years old. It has been in 27 battles and never been taken. It is our proudest possession."

No comment was made on the French flag which apparently did not have the same meaning for those in the Legion's 10th Regiment. John thought about that discrepancy as he also wondered about the protocol of saluting a general of the Vichy Army. He had decided he wouldn't initiate such a salute, but then began to worry how to communicate his decision to the other two Americans. They had all stopped in front of the main tent, the flags hanging limply by the door flap. John took a careful step forward, establishing himself as ranking officer. Sainteny could do what he wanted. In boots and breeches, a sharp-faced officer strode out of the tent. In a strong voice as if introducing someone at a royal gathering their major announced:

"I have the honor, *mon Générale*, to present Major John of the American Army and Commandant Sainteny of the Army of France."

The general reached his hand forward with a smile and John grasped it for a warm handshake. Sainteny snapped to attention and saluted. Alessandri responded as any major general would when saluted by a major. His return salute was somewhere between casual and pro forma. He spoke in heavily accented English to John.

"I have been waiting for quite some weeks for this moment, Major. I... am very... pleased that you have come to meet us. You and your staff. Would you please... introduce me?"

Edouard and Tony Castelli, John's "staff," stepped forward to be presented.

"Captains Parnell and Castelli, sir."

The general offered his hand to each American. He let Sainteny cool his heels. John stole a sideways glance at Jean Sainteny. The chief of M.5 still stood at attention, unblinking. He was in the presence of the man who had commanded all Foreign Legion forces in Tonkin. One waited until such a man spoke to you—as long as it took.

John had made no attempt to get his last name correct. He had never given it to the major. He was fascinated by the interplay between Alessandri and Sainteny. He knew Edouard and Tony were watching the same thing. They both seemed to be enjoying themselves and had nice smiles plastered on their faces.

"I have a thousand questions for you, Major John, but I'm sure you have just as many for me. Is there something I can do for you? I apologize that our hospitality is somewhat limited."

John observed Alessandri's eyes dart over to Sainteny and back again. They were a pale green, maybe onetime blue. The sharpness of the face was due to a thin scar that pulled one cheek inward past the mouth. It had been a good stitching job, John thought. How many of those 27 battles had he been in?

"Perhaps you would like to visit some of our rather unfortunate column? I'm sure you would like to know what sort of... what is the word... how we are? Situation, what is our situation, correct?"

"General, that would be an excellent idea. And I will leave Captain Castelli here to discuss whatever you wish. He is most knowledgeable on all matters *logistique* which will be important to you at this time."

Alessandri indicated he was quite happy with the arrangement and urged John and Edouard on their way, assuring John he would "take very good care of your Captain Castelli."

The decrepit state of the column of French and Colonial Army Vietnamese soldiers that made up the surviving echelon of Vichy's military force in Vietnam was obvious. As the trio of John, Edouard, and the Legion major as escort officer moved down the road to Lao Cai, the filthy remnants of what had been a sizeable and well-armed force huddled in clutches by the side of the road. There was little attempt at order, to say nothing of military discipline. Even John, who had little regard for anything Vichy, was horrified at the state of these poor troops. He didn't ask where the officers were. He didn't have to. They were there among the rest of the ravaged army that had not even fought a major battle. Every now and then an attempt could be observed of some unit commander who tried to set up, in a fashion, a form of HQ. At least there were some cooking fires going and signs that food had begun to reach the ranks. John didn't want to say anything in front of their escort, but the looks exchanged with Edouard communicated how appalled they both were. There was something fundamentally wrong with the scene as it stood.

Seemingly in anticipation of the Americans' reactions, the Legion officer sought to disassociate himself and his fellow Legionnaires from the debacle that was so evident.

"They lost all motivation. The colonials have no idea of what country they are serving, and the strictly French units and their men are not much better. They were told that Vichy represented the lawful government of France and now that's all changed."

John thought about what had just been said. It was a valuable assessment. This Legion major had provided information and analysis that it would have taken considerable effort to gain otherwise. Dumb luck, he thought.

"And the Legionnaires? What's held them together, if they are?" asked Edouard provocatively.

The major simply smiled wryly. It was a question he savored in answering.

"They are, as you say, together, most definitely. For one thing our general stayed with us all the way, not like that other one who has flown off like a sparrow to Laos. He wasn't *Légion*."

This was the first reference to the Legion versus Regular Army, and it certainly wasn't favorable. Another glance between the two OSS officers catalogued the intelligence—more good information for Castelli and SI.

"The fact is that we, the men and officers of la Légion Étrangere, have been cut off from our brethren in Africa since early in the war. We here in Indochina automatically became part of the Vichy army, but what has held us together, our *raison dêtre*, is our pride—our military pride. You know our motto is "March or Die," and I assure you we die well. But we die as Legionnaires. Does that answer your question, Captain? In any case, you will soon see for yourself the difference."

The major seemed to have regained his strength. John realized he must have done the same thing day in and day out during the long march. Exhaustion was used as a fuel in such men. The drawn face and hollowed eyes were a testament to the pride of which he spoke. John remembered the look in the faces of the steel workers with whom he had grown up. He remembered it in his father who would work every extra shift he could. And the unity among these men—he had seen that, too, before.

The Americans had been alerted to what they might expect. The major had told them that much. The 100-man rear guard would make the crossing. The other Legionnaires were too scattered among the other units to participate, but the "centurions" would represent them all. As fatigued and hungry as they were, this last cohesive Legion unit had no intention of arriving in China as a foul and defeated army, no matter what the others looked like. They had rested for an entire day within a gunshot's range of the roiling *Song Hong*, the Red River that rushed down from the northwest past Lao Cai. The Legionnaires washed and shaved. With the food the major had procured they ate whatever their shrunken bellies could stuff in that day. They cleaned their uniforms and weapons as best they could, paying careful attention to their *képis blancs*, the white dress hats each had stuffed in his pack—the distinctive headgear of the Legion.

When John and Edouard came upon the Legion contingent, they were still finishing preparation for their "withdrawal to more secure positions," as the major had put it. The men had slept in abandoned buildings in the border town that night. They studiously ignored the foreign officers who were watching them. They had contented themselves with a good scrub in nearby streams and made a valiant effort with dull razors and sharp bush knives to shave off accumulated stubble amidst prolific swearing in several languages.

"We've arrived just in time, gentlemen. The unit commander will first inspect his command and them lead them across. I wanted you to see this. You couldn't have come at a better time." The major pointed to a ramrod straight officer heading in the direction of the bivouac area.

"That's him. They say he's a member of the Russian royal family. Who knows? I've served with him for four years and never had a single personal exchange with him. He's been wounded a couple of times, but that's all I know. I was told the General wanted to promote him to colonel, but he requested to remain at his rank to be closer to the troops. Who knows? Maybe it's just a rumor. You know the army."

The three officers stood on a slight rise above a small stream that separated them from the Legion unit. The unit formed up quickly for inspection the moment their commander arrived on the scene. Their uniforms were torn and still dirty despite their best efforts, but their weapons gleamed in the sharp sunlight of an unusually clear Yunnan day. The major explained that it was most likely the first formal roll call and inspection that the unit had undergone since they left Dien Bien Phu. It was sort of a joke, he said.

The commander strolled the lines calling out the unacceptable condition of each Legionnaire just as he would have on parade. A sergeant followed pretending he was taking notes. The company bravely attempted to contain their laughter. Their part in the charade was to look stern and military, and they did. After touring the ten lines of ten, the commanding officer took his place in front of the column with his small coterie of officers and gave the order to move out.

The man must have been well over six feet tall and extremely well built. He was now rather thin, but the major said that he started out much heavier. "We all did," he laughed. It was hard to tell how old the unit commander was with his lined, tanned face. The scars of past campaigns caused him to walk with a shuffling gait that apparently hid a limp. He was armed with a German Luger that could be seen nestled in an open holster. He carried a riding crop under his left arm.

Referring to the crop, the major said, "He's got a hidden sword made of an old bayonet inside that crop. I saw him once use it to kill a snake. I imagine he was quite a duelist in his day."

Sergeants repeated shouted commands that re-formed the column into five men abreast as the entire unit broke into squads. In the slow cadence peculiar to the Foreign Legion the unit marched silently. No cadence was called. John and Edouard followed the unit as it marched this way, with no drums to give the beat, just the rhythm of the boots on the earth. Their escort officer led the two OSS officers up and over a knoll that brought them to a position on the road ahead of the column. By the side of the dirt road were the squalid encampments they had observed earlier. Filthy *poilus* embarrassed at their own degradation shouted obscenities at the passing parade of Legionnaires each staring blankly ahead. John and Edouard, entranced by the performance, watched as the extended column, looking like a much larger unit than they were, headed toward the Americans standing on a raised mound, for better viewing. Unconsciously, both drew themselves to attention as the Legionnaires neared. Within ten paces of where they stood the grizzled leader boomed the command, "Eyes Right!" and snapped off a salute directed at the American officers which he held as they returned the greeting just as sharply. Major John Guthrie and Captain Edouard Parnell, officers of the US Army, held their salute until the last of the "centurions," with their rifles at shoulder arms and heads swiveled acutely toward them, passed by. There was no political question here. These were soldiers, fighting men to be honored. La Légion Étrangère had arrived in China.

Lost in the theater of the moment, neither John nor Edouard noticed that their escort was no longer with them. They looked around but could not find him. The major had disappeared. They started back toward Alessandri's command post, arriving there just as an afternoon rain came pelting down. They could see Tony and Sainteny sitting on one side of a field desk with the general on the other side, still engrossed in animated conversation. A tarp stretched outward from the entrance to the tent providing some shelter for the two. John and Edouard hesitated from interrupting the meeting going on yet were worried about what had happened to the Legion major. They were about to enter the command tent when the same two Legionnaires who had been on the vegetable detail before, and had been sent to find Castelli and Sainteny, arrived with their cart containing their prostrate major.

As best as Edouard could gather from the excited Legionnaires was that they had found the major out cold on the ground at a point that must have been close to where John and Edouard had been occupied with the passing formation. In a thick Corsican accent one of the soldiers explained breathlessly:

"We'd just dropped off another load and there he was. So we picked him up and took him into a nearby house… you know just to put him in the shade and maybe give him some water.…"

Edouard looked to John, wordlessly agreeing that that was why they hadn't found the man themselves. He most likely had seen his men in the distance and collapsed as he moved toward them.

The commotion caught the attention of the group inside the tent and they all rushed out. Edouard unbuttoned the major's shirt and felt for his pulse. The man's face was ashen, but Edouard announced the heart was pumping well. Alessandri sent one of the sentries on duty scurrying after their medical officer.

"It's either malaria or jaundice or some combination," the general said matter of factly. "He's a good boy, but he's already collapsed several times before. That's why he was on that procurement detail."

There was no emotion in the general's voice. Whatever he might have felt about one of his officers lying unconscious in a vegetable cart was impossible to discern. John was the one who was disturbed.

"Try to give him some water from your canteen, Edouard. I've got some malaria pills in this aid packet." He fished out the small packet from his webbing and searched through it. There wasn't much he could do. He hated this feeling of helplessness and was instantly annoyed at the lack of reaction from Alessandri for one of his officers. Edouard kneeled next to the officer who had now been dragged beneath the protective tarp as the rain poured down. Edouard alternatively attempted to wet the man's lips with water and wipe down his sweat-soaked face.

"We need a blanket, or something. Get a blanket," Edouard ordered, first in English then in French. The general motioned with his head toward inside the tent and one of the Legionnaires dashed in to retrieve whatever he could find. He returned with a large piece of cloth of indeterminate origin. It was the closest thing to a blanket available. Doubling the cloth over, John helped Edouard wrap the major securely just as the medical officer arrived. He ordered the man be brought into the general's tent and placed on the general's cot. He didn't ask anyone's permission, and soon kicked the entire group, including the general, out of the tent. They all stood under the tarp peering in at the doctor and his patient as torrents of rain cascaded down the edges of the canvas overhead.

No one spoke until the doctor turned toward them.

"So?" was all Alessandri said. It was an order not a question.

"Well, sir, it is as I told you the last time. He must be taken to some place where he can receive adequate medical treatment. I can do little here… for him or the others lying in my medical tent." The tone of the doctor was defiant as if he dared the general to say anything.

Tony Castelli, whose immaculate uniform now was half soaked with rain, shouted above the roar of the crashing rainstorm.

"We'll take him back to Kunming in the plane, General. And as many others as we can fit in. That is if this mess stops."

As if on cue the deluge began to slow down and soon stopped. A typical Yunnan springtime rain.

"We have far too many who need attention for your one flight, Captain. We accept your offer, nonetheless. Doctor, prepare your worst cases for departure. Major Sainteny, would you please assume responsibility for these men. I do not want any of them to fall into administrative limbo just because these American friends are kind enough to come to our aid."

There was an undisguised edge to Alessandri's tone toward Sainteny. John could only wonder what had precipitated the manner. He looked toward Castelli who rolled his eyes upward to signify he would explain it all later. Sainteny set his jaw and replied with a strong affirmative as if he had just been spanked—which perhaps he had.

The sun came out again hot and sticky. The two Legionnaires volunteered to take the major in their cart back to the airstrip. Sainteny suggested that if more carts were available, the other patients be similarly transported. It was the first time he had shown any initiative and he did it in a manner bordering on arrogance. John and Edouard both sought to say something to moderate the atmosphere, the derivation of which they did not understand. In the end John settled for a polite leave, thanking Alessandri for his hospitality, and the general in return was fulsome in his gratitude for "this emergency assistance from the officers of the American Army who are so kind as to make this trip to greet my beleaguered command."

Castelli didn't attempt to save his dress shoes. It would have been useless if he had. The previously dusty, dry dirt road they had traversed earlier had turned into a wide path of mud and gravel. The cart pullers did the best they could, maneuvering to avoid the deepest ruts. By the time the Americans and Jean Sainteny arrived at the airstrip they were all speckled in mud though Tony and Sainteny were much the worse off in their formerly immaculate uniforms. The chosen patients arrived in carts drawn by Chinese coolies eager to take advantage of the unexpected windfall of paid employment. The chance to make hard cash, even in small amounts, came rarely in this backwater of southwest China, and they happily struggled through the glutinous muck with their charges. Several Legionnaires had been detailed to accompany their comrades, though the original two refused to allow any help in their own efforts to bring their major to the plane.

Only six patients, including the major, could be fitted into the C-45. Several others had to be returned to the medical tent. John took it upon himself to promise the medical officer that he would arrange for a follow-up flight to evacuate the rest of his sick and injured as well as deliver a broad range of medical supplies. The doctor profusely thanked him. John sought to include Sainteny in these departure formalities, but the M.5 officer seemed bent on assuming the role of injured party.

"He's pissed off you didn't allow him the gesture of sending a relief plane," Edouard whispered to John.

"They don't have any damn planes. They'd have to get them from us," John replied after looking around to see if Sainteny was nearby.

"Well, we're not the reason Alessandri treated him like a red-haired stepchild," John added.

"Red-haired stepchild. I never heard that one before?"

"It's an old Hoosier saying. It's in place of saying they treated him like crap. We're very diplomatic in the Midwest, didn't you know?"

John distributed some Chinese coins he had in his pocket to the coolies even though he knew they were also being paid by the French medical officer. The coolies, wrapped in the rags that passed as clothes, were overjoyed at their windfall. They left shouting and laughing at their good fortune. These "long noses" were not as bad as their elders had warned them. In fact, they were very generous. The arrival of these soldiers could turn out to be a very good thing.

John wanted to exchange information with Castelli on the way back, but Tony indicated he wanted to wait by motioning toward Sainteny who was sitting forward wrapped in a blanket. Sainteny should have been talking to the soldiers they were transporting, giving them encouragement as the Americans were doing. Instead, he remained perversely wrapped in his blanket as if he had been the victim of some grand conspiracy. Tony made an effort to be friendly by bringing him a cup of coffee that the pilot had offered from his own thermos. Sainteny accepted the tin cup with unexpected grace and fell into conversation with Castelli. Edouard caught John's attention and motioned toward the two new best friends. John just shook his head, content to wait until later on and the promised revelations from Tony Castelli.

The pilot radioed ahead, and they were met at the airfield outside of Kunming by several ambulances from the 14th Air Force General Hospital. John and Edouard accompanied the men to the hospital doing the translations as needed. Sainteny had thanked them both for the interest they had shown in the Vichy soldiers but declined their offer to have him go along with them to the hospital. To John the entire circumstance was mystifying. Castelli decided to stick with Jean Sainteny but promised to send a jeep to pick up the other two. Edouard was as confused as John.

"I've been through some weird episodes in my time, but this takes the cake. Okay, I figure Tony is still working on Sainteny, but you'd think the Frenchman would want to hang around while we arrange this hospital thing. I mean they're Vichy and all that, but I thought he wanted to be the big shot. Tell me, have I missed something?"

"Not that I've seen. This Sainteny has a whole set of games he's playing. I say screw'im. We got what we came for far better than I thought we possibly could in such a brief trip. That's what counts."

* * *

The experience at Lao Cai became the primary topic of conversation at the "watering-down" party celebrating Bob Simpson's promotion to Lt. Colonel.

"This political stuff is a bit out of my range, folks," said Simpson, squinting through his new metal-rimmed GI eyeglasses at John and Edouard.

"It's as simple as pie," slurred John. "The French won't fight 'cept each other, 'n the Viet guys—the Minh people—want us to get 'em a country. It's all too much—much too much."

"Too much…" agreed a barely standing Edouard.

Chapter Six

Acting Corporal Thanh also had watched as the centurions of the Foreign Legion slow marched their way across the border into China. Unlike the other ordinary soldiers around him, Thanh held no disrespect for these elite soldiers. Quite on the contrary. He understood what brought them together as a fighting force and he knew that spirit had been drilled into them till it became part of their individual and collective soul. At the same time, Thanh regarded their motivation as empty and artificial compared to what he would expect from a future combat cadre of the Party. Now that he was safely beyond the dangers of the long escape—for that's what it was—he could once again concern himself about a future beyond this valley, that hill, the next rise. He thought about his comrades in the *to dang* back in Hanoi and about his real mission, his real self. He still had his old commitment, and was as proud of that as the Legionnaires were of theirs. Someday... he thought.

At the same time, Thanh had not been forgotten. The word had gone forward to Party members in Kunming to search the ranks of the arriving Vietnamese colonial units for Thanh and other Party members and candidates who were known to be part of the retreating force. Their role in this ex-Vichy army was no longer as valuable to the Party's objective as would be their serving directly in the armed cadre of the Viet Minh under Vo Nguyen Giap. The Japanese had done the Party a great favor in pushing out the French, and it was time to take advantage. This would be where men like Thanh would prove most valuable. Augmenting the Viet Minh cadre with trained soldiers loyal to the cause of independence was essential. It was time for Thanh to return "home."

Contact with Party members in an army unit previously had always been done with maximum discretion. However, the decrepit state of the Vichy forces, with their mixed units and straggling personnel, actually provided a logical justification for inquiring after "lost brethren." The lack of facilities for the quartering of the newly arrived troops kept the entire force bunched in the Lao Cai reception area. This allowed the hunt for Thanh and his colleagues to proceed in a systematic fashion down the line from one bivouac to another. Thanh was found early on in the search.

The messenger who actually made contact was merely a teenage boy, but he had his duties well memorized. Thanh was happy to be sought out, but nonetheless he was initially trepidatious at the idea of leaving. Faced with the fact of departing from his unit, an organization of which he had been a part for over six years, was a wrenching experience, far greater than he had ever thought. He cared little for the fact of the desertion from the French Colonial Army. In a way, that army had died ignominiously on the trail from Son Tay. It was the desertion of his squad, of his comrades-in-arms… of those who hadn't made it. He would have liked to have discussed his feelings, his confusion, with someone, but that was impossible. It was nothing new, of course. There never had been such a sharing. Perhaps it was better that way, Thanh thought. Better that he keep these weak moments to himself. He was loyal to the Party, and that should be his only thought.

The inner struggle didn't last long. Thanh gained his composure and faced his next task. His instructions were to make his way to Kunming to join others who were being organized to return to Vietnam; where exactly he had no idea. How to get to Kunming was his only problem. On this he was given aid by the messenger. First, he must discard his uniform. He was given a small amount of money to buy some old civilian clothes. He was instructed to meet a produce truck at a certain time on the main road two days hence. As a recognition signal, he should buy a large melon and put it on the ground before him. The driver would ask him if he had any more to sell, and he would answer that he had cabbages also. If all went as planned, Thanh would then get into the truck and be headed for Kunming about 200 miles away.

It was lucky that the rendezvous date had been set two days ahead. What had seemed so simple when he had received his orders—for that's what they were—became far more difficult in the accomplishment. How does a French Army Vietnamese soldier buy a set of civilian clothes from civilians who speak only Chinese? And to do this without drawing too much attention to oneself. The answer is that it soon becomes clear that such a thing is impossible, at least the part about not drawing attention. The fact that he wanted to buy something, anything, immediately drew a large crowd the following day.

"Is there anyone here who knows where I can get some clothes?" Thanh asked in his most polite voice. The crowd responded by speaking louder in Chinese.

"I'm sorry, I do not speak Chinese." Thanh tried to get the point across, but with no success. The Chinese just rattled on. He extracted himself from this first group only to have the scene repeated twice more. Merchants pushed forward at every opportunity attempting to press some form of goods or produce on him. There were French soldiers sitting nearby, but they showed not a bit of interest. Thanh worried that some officer or non-com would arrive at any moment to demand what he was doing. One officer did indeed pass by, a lieutenant. He just ignored the whole display, quite befitting an officer of the French Army. For this Thanh was grateful. He had not the slightest idea of what he would have said if he had been asked to explain what he was about. Buying clothes was not really a satisfactory answer in military terms. Why are you buying clothes, soldier?

"Are you looking for some clothes?" a man asked in Vietnamese with a strong Chinese accent. He had been standing away from the others, a small man with thick glasses. He looked like a teacher. The man had a soiled coat slung over his arm, but his white shirt was clean. He had approached Thanh quietly from the side of the jabbering crowd. The teacher repeated his question.

"Yes. They don't understand me," Thanh said stating the obvious. "I want to buy a set of clothes." He felt he should give some explanation. "I need them—the clothes—for a friend, a civilian refugee who crossed with us. His are all torn. It was a terrible trip." Thanh was not used to this type of lying; it didn't come easily, and he was very bad at it. He felt very vulnerable.

"I can sell you some clothes. What size do you need?"

"About my size. He's about my size. I would go get him, but he's sick. That's why I'm doing this for him." Thanh knew he should stop explaining.

The teacher motioned to Thanh to follow him. They walked for about ten minutes down a muddy side road. Trying to avoid the major ruts in the road, Thanh dutifully followed the man he had mentally dubbed as a teacher. He realized it was only because the man wore glasses and carried a jacket just as a teacher of his own had once done. Small children peered out from the corners of dilapidated houses that lined the street. Every now and then a woman would throw a pailful of the day's wastewater into the trough that ran roadside. Thanh could feel their eyes as he walked past. He was beginning to wonder what he had walked into when the man stopped in front of a wooden door. The man called out and soon a wrinkled old lady hesitantly opened the door. Thanh could see her straining to see her visitor. At last she muttered something in recognition and looked over in Thanh's direction. The man spoke to her in a soft, even reverential, voice.

The old woman squinted toward Thanh as the elderly will do when they actually can see nothing but a blur but want to give the impression of perfect eyesight. The teacher continued his presentation as if he was selling a product. It was Thanh's impression that the man was having a difficult time getting the old lady to understand what he wanted. The woman abruptly turned around and went back in the doorway. The man motioned to Thanh to stay where he was and then he, too, went in the house. Thanh felt totally exposed standing in that street. He had just come from weeks in the forest with danger ever present and the old instincts remained. Thanh began to wonder how long he should wait when the man returned with an armful of clothes and a large smile.

The negotiations went rather quickly. Basically, Thanh paid what the teacher wanted.

"What will you pay in?" the man asked.

"I have this," said Thanh showing a portion of the money he'd been given by the messenger. The man sniffed at the Kuomintang paper dollars but proceeded to count the money offered. Thanh had no idea of the value of what he had put in the man's hand, but he dared not show it.

"I'll take half, and the other half is for her," said the man adjusting his spectacles in an authoritative manner while continuing to count the bills.

"If that is all right with her...."

"It is," the man replied with complete assurance. "This is just enough."

The man then transferred the clothes he carried to Thanh. A quick look at the pants sufficed to determine they were long enough. The man went back in the house presumably to give the old lady her share of the money. When he came out, he was smiling again.

"She is very happy, and she thanks you for your generosity. I told her you were pleased to help. She is an old lady and very poor. I try to help when I can. These clothes were her son's. He died. They are good clothes. He was always very careful with them. You'll see. They'll fit fine."

Thanh never did find out who the man was. Perhaps he was the teacher he had originally guessed, or perhaps a magistrate of some sort. It didn't matter. Thanh returned along the same rutted road to the market area from which he'd come. He knew he had to hide the clothes or come up with a story as to why he had them. He also had to get a large melon. This secret life was very difficult.

When Thanh had finally made his way back to his bivouac area, he had worked out his story to explain the clothes. As it turned out no one was interested enough to ask. His collection of clothes wasn't even noticed. He simply stuffed them in his pack and that was that. His fellow troopers never even asked where he had been.

The big topic of conversation was the rumor that Vogel had been transferred out of the unit. A small pile of clothes was no competition for that juicy subject. Some said that Thanh would be made permanent corporal and maybe he would take over the platoon. Others said he'd have to be made sergeant for that. It was a hot topic that had the entire unit abuzz. For Thanh it was merely an unnecessary complication. It was easy to pretend disinterest because that was the way he should have acted. The truth was that he was flattered at the possibility, even though a moment's thought took that possibility out of the realm of reason. He had been instructed by the Party to leave the Army, and that was all there was. He had his civilian clothes and now all he needed was to procure his melon. This secret life had both irony and humor.

The following morning began very early. Thanh sneaked out while it was still dark carrying his bundle of new clothes. He had to leave everything else behind. It would be as if he just disappeared. Perhaps they would think he went for a swim in the river and drowned. That was always possible. The *Song Hong* was known to be very dangerous and he had purposely mentioned the fun of swimming the night before. It was a clever ruse and Thanh was pleased at himself for thinking of it. He would have to do more of that in his new civilian identity, he was sure. He would have to ask about identity papers when he got to Kunming. He realized that if he was stopped the clothes would not help much.

Surprisingly, the purchase of the melon and the wait for the produce truck went off without a hitch. Although Thanh felt conspicuous in his civilian shirt and pants, that was nothing compared to standing behind the melon. He was sure everyone was looking at the stupid man with a melon at his feet. He also had a jacket that came with the pants, but he decided it would be better if he carried it. He had kept his boots even though he knew they were unusual for a civilian to wear. His pants were a little long and they covered the tops completely. Otherwise, Thanh was convinced he looked like a real civilian even though he didn't think of himself as one. The truck came along close to the appointed hour, and after an exchange of the recognition signals, Thanh, the civilian, was on the road to Kunming.

Thanh had plenty of time to think on the drive to Kunming. The driver was Chinese and thought his passenger understood what he said when he spoke in his broken Vietnamese. It didn't matter because the driver talked incessantly and there would have been no point in Thanh saying anything if he had understood him. It took several hours of hard driving and non-stop talking for the Chinese to realize Thanh didn't understand him. Thanh's periodic polite grunts had apparently served as an effective camouflage of linguistic shortcoming. Once the driver became aware that his travelling companion really didn't understand his monologue, the driver went silent except for an occasional attempt to point out some local sight. Thanh was worried about his reception in Kunming. His lack of Chinese language ability could create a major problem. He encouraged the driver to repeat the names of objects in Chinese as they passed by. Thanh was suitably appreciative for the information regarding dogs, pigs, men, women, water, and other staple signs of road travel. By the end of the day they had moved tentatively into various verbs. The driver shared some of his food and water with Thanh as well as his erudition, and the otherwise hard trip passed amazingly quickly.

They arrived in Kunming in early evening on a first-name basis. Thanh had made his transition to civilian life.

The truck pulled up to what appeared to be a warehouse, and Thanh's first thought was that they would be unloading the cargo of fruits and vegetables. However, the driver motioned to Thanh that he should get out. After a moment's hesitation the ex-soldier opened the truck door and stepped down, clinging to his only possession, his second-hand jacket. A figure materialized from the shadows and greeted Thanh in Vietnamese.

"Hello, comrade corporal. Welcome to Kunming."

Thanh waved goodbye to the swiftly departing truck and turned to the welcome Vietnamese voice.

"My name is Li. You may call me Li. I will call you Thanh. We most likely will give you another name, but for the moment you'll remain Thanh."

"Thank you, comrade Li. Thank you for meeting me. I thought I..."

"No more 'comrade.' Just Li."

"Fine... Li. By the way, I wasn't yet a corporal, just an acting one, not that it matters."

"I know. I just thought it was nice. I could have said sergeant. As you say, it doesn't matter anymore. Just no comrade. It's too obvious, if you know what I mean. We have to be careful, I'm sure you realize. I used it in first addressing you just as a gesture of greeting for a returning veteran of the struggle."

"And I appreciated it, uh, Li. I understand."

"You must be hungry. I'll take you to some food and a place to sleep. I'm sure you have some questions."

* * *

The next few weeks began Thanh's new life. Li had arranged a room for him in a small home of a Vietnamese couple. It was explained that this old man and his wife could be trusted. Thanh asked no further questions, assuming they were Party members. It was enough in any case that Li had said to trust them. The old couple were quietly hospitable and solicitous of Thanh's health and comfort. It had been only several days, less than a week, since Thanh and his men had burst out of the gruelling mountainous forest that is upper Tonkin. He had stepped from one strange world he was just coming to know into another totally different world just as obscure as the other originally had been. Outside of this very modest house were people he did not understand in a city completely foreign. Even his own identity was clouded in shadow. For a less secure man the circumstance would have been unbearable. But the Party had brought him to this place and that was enough for Thanh. In his heart he was a soldier of the Party and his nation, Vietnam. For him, the two were indivisible. Allegiance, discipline, and a commitment to maximum effort were what the Party demanded, and he gave full measure. This, Li explained, was why he had been chosen.

The special training for which Thanh had been picked, Li explained, would all be given in Kunming. There already were many Vietnamese refugees in the city and their presence gave ample cover for the various activities of the Party, which since the Japanese takeover had taken on a greater importance. Kunming was a center of information, finance, and supply. Thanh learned that an army, a real army, was in the process of formation and trained soldiers such as he were the necessary cadre around which the army would be built. But, as Li emphasized, the training would not be military; it would be political. Thanh listened with increasing excitement as his tutor explained that the time had come for him to assume a greater role for the Party. The way the Indochinese Communist Party saw it, the French Army had been defeated, and it was now time for the liberation of Vietnam to begin with its own liberation army. Thanh and others like him would be in the vanguard just as he had always hoped.

These first lessons were held right in the home of the old couple. Li sat on the one comfortable chair and Thanh sat on a small wooden chair by an equally small table. The couple left the house as soon as Li arrived. The first thing Li did was to explain that he did not normally become involved directly in any training. The man whose responsibility this was had been sent off to organize the others from the fleeing Colonial Army just as Thanh had been. The difference was that these others had not been designated for a leadership role in the people's army. After slipping away from their units, these soldiers would be transported eastward to Kwangsi Province and eventually back into Vietnam. It was a risky business, Li said, but the Party didn't want to lose these well-trained soldiers, even if there were only a score or so considered reliable enough to approach at this time.

"You see, I am being very open with you, Thanh. I'm treating you as a Party member of status. We are expecting important things from you."

"I am honored, com… Li. Sorry."

"There is so much you have to learn, but I will endeavor to do my best. Let us begin with what is always the most sensitive of subjects—security. This is just an introduction, something of which you should be aware but not dwell on."

Thanh nodded expectantly. Every fiber of his being was attuned to each and every syllable of information Li imparted to him. His normally disciplined self had drained away to be replaced by an excited schoolboy's eagerness. Li pretended not to notice but was inwardly pleased.

"I will explain to you first about the Chinese security services because they are simply a good example of security organizations in general, and therefore make a good example—as well as being important to us in themselves. There are, in fact, several services within the overall structure of Chinese security. You understand that?"

"Yes, sir, uh, Li."

"Each of these services, local police, national police, local and national intelligence, Kuomintang Party security—all of them are tied together but at the same time are independent of each other. You understand the Kuomintang is the political party of Chiang Kai-shek, who is the leader. But that part is unimportant. What is important is that each of these services have their own private businesses besides their security activities."

"You mean private businesses like farms and shops and things like that?"

"That and much more. That is how we have been able to set up various areas of mutual interest with these different organizations. They are also tied into almost all of the black market operations that they are supposed to be controlling. This is typical capitalist government criminal activity. It's important to know for us because it's a way we can exploit their greed to our benefit. As I said when I first started, this is just for background to give you an idea what the world is like, really like, and what we in the Party have to learn to deal with and, if possible, exploit."

There were a thousand questions Thanh could have asked but he refrained from a single one. Li's tone and manner brooked no foolish questions and Thanh was not about to take the chance of upsetting him. Li had an accent in his language that was unknown to Thanh. It was obvious that the man was of mixed blood but his Vietnamese—though spoken with something other than a Tonkin accent—was correct, showing a good education or maybe travel. The ability to study another individual was not something Thanh had to be taught.

The schooling continued on for about six hours a day for several days. As excited as Thanh originally was, after a rigorous physical life in the mountains, the sedentary existence inside the small house became near suffocating. The food was ample and good after many weeks of rough living; and he certainly was safe. But the most difficult part of his existence was the absence of any companions. It was as if he was in jail. He said this quite innocently to Li, who responded with surprising vehemence.

"You are a foolish person. This is great luxury. What do you know of jail? What a foolish thing to say. These people give you part of their house. You are living like a little king. You should be grateful."

Li went on in the same vein for what seemed to Thanh to be forever. He had hit a very raw nerve and deeply regretted his comment. But Li's eruption ended as abruptly as it began, and he returned to his usual tight self-control. He did not apologize, nor did he appear to encourage Thanh to do so. The matter was not spoken of again. The lesson had been administered and learned. This was not the army. There was no room for personal griping. All was for a larger purpose, and inconveniences were merely that and no more. One must devote their whole being to the task at hand. It was something that struck the embarrassed Thanh deeply. He would carry it with him always. The rest that he would learn was important, much even useful, but none of it would approach the significance of this basic lesson. He would never realize that the wily and wise Li had waited for the first opportune moment to administer this essential instruction. It was the equivalent of what most armies refer to as "getting the donkey's attention."

Thanh spent a great deal of time reading and then being quizzed by Li as to what he read. Even though the pamphlets were in the Romanized Vietnamese script known as *quoc ngu*, it was hard for Thanh to fully comprehend the meaning of the writing of two Europeans called Marx and Lenin whom Li spoke of with respect. Thanh remembered hearing their names during the lectures at the *chi bo*, but he never had been told of their importance other than as European communist leaders. The pages of the papers were frail with use and that, in itself, held meaning for Thanh. But these were not the documents on which Li placed the principal emphasis.

"I now place in your hands a manual which you must learn by heart. You must know every word and—most important—understand what you read. It is called *The Revolutionary Path (Duong Cach Minh)*. It was written 20 years ago by a man, a Vietnamese patriot, when he travelled to Guangzhou, China, to secretly train other Vietnamese in our communist ideology, history, and revolutionary techniques. This training manual was the basis of his course and you must now consider it yours. We call this man, Ho Chi Minh."

"I believe I've heard the name, but I was unaware of his importance," said Thanh in utmost innocence.

"It is not a name we often speak of, but he is a real man. I have had the honor of meeting him. He has gone by many other names, but it makes him no less important. He is a world traveler, speaks many languages, and is the first among us. He has dedicated his life to us—you and me, the people—and the Party. He is the greatest of all Vietnamese, alive or dead. That is my opinion, but it is also a fact."

In speaking of the man he would call Uncle Ho, Li became reverential, as if he was speaking of a living deity. It was not difficult for Thanh to accept this veneration, for he had the gift of faith of which catholic priests had spoken so often in a different context when he was in school. The Party required all true believers to be so endowed; it was not an alien concept.

It was nearly two weeks before Thanh remembered he had information to impart from his own experiences on the long flight from Son Tay. It took that long for him to feel comfortable enough with his mentor to share with him the intelligence that had seemed so important at the time. The story of the Americans and the montagnards drew unexpected interest from Li.

"You say there were only five, but they had a force of montagnards? Do you know what tribe they were? Were they well-armed? How do you know the Europeans were Americans?

These and other questions were fired at Thanh like an automatic weapon. He responded as best he could. He only knew that the people he had seen on patrol with Sgt. Vogel were Americans because he heard the Legionnaire in his loud voice announce this fact to the first officer they met when they returned from patrol. Li explained his interest in the Americans.

"The Americans may become very important to us. We have cooperated with them in helping to rescue their pilots that the Japanese shoot down. They can be a very big help to us, with weapons and also politically. They're capitalists, but they are against colonialism. They don't want the French to take back Indochina after the war. At least that's what has been said. I've been told Uncle likes them. He is very experienced and knows a great deal about them, so I hear. I have met some myself and know that we can work with them."

This was the most enthusiastic Li had been since the lessons had begun. He liked to talk about the Americans, and he seemed to know them well. It was a chance for Thanh to show an interest in something of apparent importance to Li. An apple for his teacher....

"The ones we saw on patrol looked much the same as Frenchmen, although maybe a little taller. One was a very big man," Thanh offered in reference to the Americans. "He had what looked like an automatic rifle, but it was shorter than a rifle. I've never seen a gun like that. The others had short rifles. Vogel, our sergeant, said they were called carbines. They must be quite light, though I am not sure how accurate they are. These Americans certainly seemed well equipped, and as I said before, they seemed to be working closely with the tribesmen."

"If you ever get to meet them, you'll find they have a great many childlike mannerisms. They are very different than the French. They can be very loud, the Americans that is, but they are also quite generous. A very interesting people," Li said.

The American interlude passed, and the lessons began to focus more on political military matters. Thanh listened to this segment with great care because even though he was allowed to take notes, they would have to be destroyed later. Unlike the early part of the instructions, this was a topic on which Li seemed to have everything carefully memorized. It was more holy writ than political lecture. Even Li's voice took on a dogmatic intonation.

"It is essential to accept the fact that our Party controls our military. We do this through our organization and motivation of our personnel. The aim is to keep our soldiers focused on our ideological goals, and these you've been reading about. We accomplish this by keeping close track of behavior. We then guide this behavior, hopefully by positive influence, or if necessary, by more strict actions. There are three basic instruments for attaining this goal."

Li paused, perhaps for emphasis, perhaps to determine if his student was listening as carefully as he desired. Satisfied with Thanh's attentive demeanor, Li took a deep breath as lecturers do, and continued.

"The first is the easiest. Group meetings are regularly held where all aspects of current activities are discussed and lectures on various subjects are given. All this is under the guidance of political officers who are also responsible for explaining old and new Party guidelines. If you are competent, you perhaps will get to be one of these political officers."

This was the first inkling that Thanh had received as to the reason for his separation from the rest of those who had been sought out at Lao Cai. Li continued on, punching home each point with intensity.

"The second is *kien thao*, self-criticism. In *kien thao* there is a twofold purpose. One is, of course, to allow the soldier the chance to admit to failure without punishment other than the possible pressure from his fellow soldiers to do better. This pressure from the ranks is very important and effective in maintaining control. The political officer is particularly key in the second purpose which is to ferret out trouble spots and troublemakers. Naturally, all stressful situations require a method for troops to 'let off steam' and this is it—but under control, mind you."

Thanh was listening but little penetrated. All he could think of was the immensity of the honor that had been bestowed on him. To be a political officer in the new liberation army....

"And the third point of exceeding norms is very important in that..."

Thanh heard Li saying something about keeping production up, weapons and tools clean, and catching spies. It made no sense, but Thanh was sure he'd figure out what was meant later on. He kept his eyes on Li while hoping the fact that his mind had gone blank didn't show through.

Li finished his recitation and slumped back in his comfortable chair. He lit a cigarette and inhaled deeply, letting the smoke come through his nose. Li didn't smoke much, but when he did, he enjoyed every acrid moment. He sat allowing the cigarette smoke to curl slowly from his mouth as he scrutinized Thanh upright in his wooden chair.

"All these things are supervised by the political officer. He's the glue that holds each unit together. You understand how important this role is?"

Thanh nodded even though he knew it was less a question than a statement of fact. He struggled to overcome the fog of happiness in which he was enveloped. He'd taken notes but was barely able to remember what he'd written. His body was covered in perspiration even though he felt cool. To be selected to hold this exalted rank... the responsibility of it all was overwhelming. He sat unmoving, silent, dumbfounded.

Li watched his student carefully, sternly. The smoke from his cigarette filled the small room.

"I take it that you are overcome with excitement. Otherwise you just look stupid. What did you think we went to all this trouble for? Perhaps we made a mistake and you are too foolish for the job."

"Oh, no, Mr. Li, sir. I, uh…."

Thanh stopped himself from further blathering. He was acutely aware of the danger of sounding hesitant or even falsely modest. Best to assume his most soldierly manner. He sat straight in his chair with shoulders back and looked directly into Li's eyes while keeping his own face as impassive as he could. Li sucked in a deep breath and burst into laughter.

"What an expression. You are the most perfect, Thanh. The Party has exceeded itself. Where did they find you? If I was a religious man, I would think you were sent by the heavens. Relax, you make me nervous just looking at you!"

The next few days sped by. Li's manner changed to a more jovial tone and Thanh's own sense of security rose accordingly. Realizing that his young charge was used to regular physical activity, Li took Thanh to the university to run around the track. He also took him to the warehouse where he had first been dropped off. Inside, to the young soldier's amazement, were stacks of everything from foodstuffs to automobile spare parts. Li explained that these were all American shipments that had come up something called the Burma Road to Kunming.

"Half of everything that is shipped up that route is diverted by the Chinese, generals and politicians, when it should be going to the people and the Allied armies. It's well known, of course. Some of it ends up here in this warehouse," Li explained conspiratorially.

Thanh did not ask any questions. He accepted that this was high-level Party business and none of his concern. A truck arrived while he was at the warehouse and he helped unload it. The strain of the heavy weights was a relief from all his previous studying. Li looked on approvingly. What a rarity, he thought. Comrade Van will be delighted.

When the time came to move on, Thanh felt an unexpected sadness. The old couple who had been his caring hosts had become like an aunt and uncle, and their home a sanctuary. Li, the all-knowing, had been his guide, his mentor, his protector. Thanh would return now to the real world, the world of perpetual conflict. It was a return to combat just as many other soldiers had done throughout time. Thanh understood this. A return to the unknown yet still familiar. He wanted to leave the old couple a gift, but he had nothing to give. Li said he would take care to find something they needed. The morning came for his departure in a truck loaded with goods from the warehouse. This time the driver was a Vietnamese refugee who worked for Li. It would be a long trip eastward to Ch'ing-hsi thence to Pac Bo, but Thanh set off with a happy wave for his return home.

Li remained at the warehouse most of the morning checking inventory. He knew that it was time for him to return to his so-called normal life. This interval with the officer candidate had been annoying and a burden at first with all his other duties and activities. He knew now, though, that he would miss Thanh's eagerness and innocence. Li thought about the past weeks with his protege as he sat back in his rickshaw returning to his other business. Li had his own rickshaw driver as befits a man of his commercial substance. He had thought of obtaining a small automobile from one of his Chinese military contacts, but that would have been too ostentatious. As things were, he was painfully aware of his bourgeois lifestyle, though he had been urged repeatedly by his Party superiors to further develop his commercial links. With high-level Party officials now visiting Kunming and working with the Americans, he had received a commendation for his successful commercial cover and connections useful to the covert activities of the Indochina Communist Party. There was nothing wrong in enjoying some of the benefits.

The rickshaw stopped in front of a small building and Li stepped on to the street. He went to the front door and opened the ornate lock with a key. Inside he flipped over a sign in Chinese and French: "Restaurant Deux Chapeaux—Open for Business—Liu Chi Roget, Owner."

Chapter Seven

John and Edouard had spent a brief four days with the AGAS command in Ch'ing-hsi and had returned to Kunming buoyed by the chance to link up with the rescue net already in operation in Tonkin. This meant that their own plans for a campaign including the Viet Minh could pick up pace. Their ambitious scheme ran into an immediate roadblock from a totally unexpected direction.

"Hallstrom got orders to report immediately to Southeast Asia Command in India—kicked upstairs," Paul Schreymann explained. "He dropped everything, left Horse in command and that was it. Lord Edgar's Chinese business buddies who ran the mess and everything else around here decided their joy ride was over, and they left the next day—taking everything that wasn't tied down. That's it. What a disaster!"

"Did you call the MPs?" asked John.

"They said they had no way of dealing with Chinese crooks—just GIs."

"Well, we've got to get back to Ch'ing-hsi anyhow to get moving on the Viet Minh thing," Edouard said.

"Not right now, I think. Our new CO has different ideas."

Paul led the two into Hallstrom's old office now occupied by Bob Simpson in the process of going through files and talking on the phone at the same time. Impatiently, he waited for someone on the other end of the telephone line but immediately dropped the receiver when John and Edouard came in.

"Good. You guys are back. Paul filled you in, right? I've got a job for you. You were a D.A. in Chicago, huh John?"

"Labor lawyer."

"Close enough. I want you to take Eddy and anyone else you need and nail those bastards. Go find 'em. Get our stuff back. And Eddy, you're the gourmet, go find a new crowd to run our mess. I've got GIs cooking stuff nobody can eat. Chop, chop. This is an emergency."

Simpson returned to his phone waving his two SO officers away. Paul was waiting for them outside the office.

"Old Horse has the bit in his teeth, doesn't he?" he said.

"Paul, what have you got on these guys, the old man and his son?" John asked.

"Nothing, John, nothing. Tony doesn't either. We're tearing the place apart to find something, anything. Lord Edgar wasn't much on paperwork—or anything else for that matter."

"Has Horse lost his mind? We've got a war to fight. What the hell is he doing? So what if the food's lousy. Just turn over this whole business to the Chinese police and be rid of it."

"He thinks it's his responsibility as the new CO to clean up after Edgar. What can I tell you? Horse is a great guy, but when he gets an idea in his head—that's it. He still thinks the same way he did back when we were doing our Gorilla thing. I told him you weren't a D.A., but it didn't matter. I think he saw a movie sometime with a crusading district attorney, and he's cast you in that role. He figures the Viet Minh can wait."

Edouard joined in with a suggestion.

"Let's get cracking on the mess business first. We should start with that guy Chi-chi at the Deux Chapeaux. His food is good. He seems pretty smart. If we agree to pay him in US dollars, I'm sure he'll fix us up."

"By the way, Tony got his promotion to major and will be taking over as head of the SI section. He's also running around with his head cut off. I'm supposed to be the new adjutant, so you, John, can also expect a whole new job title," added Paul.

"What the hell does that mean?"

"Sworn to secrecy, sorry."

"Bullshit!"

"Exactly, but my boss said I should keep my mouth shut. Don't worry, it's good not bad."

"I don't like surprises."

"Well, Horse has his little peculiarities and he's the boss now."

"Let's get on with the mess problem. At least we have a place to start with that one."

Edouard's suggestion about the owner of the Deux Chapeaux turned out to be a winner. Chi-chi couldn't have been more eager to take over the entire concession of the 5329 AGFRTS. He even promised to improve his English. In the meantime, he would report directly to Paul Schreymann, who was equally delighted to have someone with whom to converse in French. Liu Chi Roget moved into the OSS compound mess and purchasing operations with barely a ripple. There was an additional benefit to Chi-chi's employment. He offered to assist his new employers in locating their lost supplies and equipment—and perhaps even to find the dastardly Chinese pair who had been responsible for the thievery. Everyone agreed Chi-chi was going to be a very valuable asset. In one fell swoop, OSS/Kunming had ensured its own penetration by the Viet Minh.

There was no hesitancy on John's part to accept the assistance of their new good friend, Chi-chi, in meeting with a man referred to as "an important member of the Chinese business community." Tony Castelli had gotten nowhere in his efforts at gaining cooperation from the Chinese security people. They weren't interested in getting involved in "petty thefts" as they called it.

"I wouldn't be at all surprised to find that they were sharing in a piece of our mess action. They get a kickback on every scam in town. They'd never help us go after their own," Castelli suggested.

"We're not unacquainted with that in Chicago," John had replied.

The first meeting arranged by Chi-chi was with a small, thin, waspish individual who smelled curiously like a bar of laundry soap. It turned out that this character had such a cleanliness fetish that he stopped in the middle of talking with John to wash his hands in a brass bowl set by his chair. The one advantage was that he spoke passable English.

"Oh sirs, you have good fortune coming to my very humble abode. Our friend Mr. Chi has told me of your needs and the unfortunate situation."

After a further lengthy preamble and yet again another washing of his water-wrinkled hands, the man admitted that he had no immediate information regarding the stolen goods and equipment nor the whereabouts of the vanished concessionaire. He did make one suggestion that intrigued John and which was later confirmed by Chi-chi to be a valuable step forward. A meeting could be arranged with someone who was referred to as a powerful behind-the-scenes member of the Chinese Nationalist Party, the Kuomintang.

"In other words, a fixer," John said afterwards to Edouard.

It took a few days but a meeting was arranged. At first, there was an insistence that only one person would be allowed to visit with the great man, but John was adamant about Edouard attending.

"Rule number one when you visit the North Side: never go alone. If it was good enough for Capone, it's good enough for me," John said in earnest.

An arrangement was made to meet and follow a man with a rickshaw. With their jeep slowly tailing behind an amazingly swift rickshaw puller, Edouard drove carefully down numerous pitted and winding streets in a part of Kunming they had never visited. It was doubtful many Westerners ever had. The people on the street studiously ignored them, except for an occasional child who shouted something in Chinese that seemed to be a friendly greeting of some sort. John wasn't that sure.

"He could be calling us something filthy. The French kids did that to the Germans, remember. Then they'd run away. The Germans never caught on either. It was just before someone tossed a grenade. Surprise, surprise. We don't know what the hell we're getting into here."

"You really think there might be some trouble?" asked Edouard just before he swerved hard to avoid an oncoming man-drawn cart.

"I think this place is no different from anywhere else that we've never been to before. This is a town that lives on thievery—of all kinds. Big, small, political, whatever. Frankly, this jeep alone is worth killing us." John knew that Edouard didn't understand his perspective. It was a basic difference in their upbringing.

Eventually the rickshaw stopped and the man went inside what appeared to be a vegetable stall with a door behind it—one of many on a very crowded street. There was no way the two OSS officers could ever find this place again. After a moment, the man came out and motioned to them to follow him. This meant that the jeep would be left unattended in the narrow, rutted roadway. There was nothing else they could do.

Passing behind the stall through the door and into a small courtyard was like entering another world. The modest courtyard led to a larger one hidden behind drapes of carefully tended ivy. The rickshaw driver disappeared, leaving the two Americans standing in the middle of a raked pebble yard with stone statues about waist high spread around as if they were guests at a party. The sound of Chinese music could be heard indistinctly coming from what must have been one of the rooms on the side of the courtyard. Other than that, there was no other sign of life. Out of nowhere flew a pair of lovebirds and the eerie emptiness was filled by the sound of their fluttering. John and Edouard exchanged glances but said nothing.

A silk-clad servant appeared from the recesses behind the ivy and gestured to them toward what turned out to be yet again another courtyard—this one leading to an inner room of lacquered teak flooring and tapestry-covered walls. Pillows were spread on the floor, apparently for sitting. Neither John nor Edouard made any move to take advantage of them. The two stood stiffly waiting for the arrival of their host. In less than five minutes a dumpy figure in a traditional Chinese silk gown with a high collar came in and without ceremony plopped himself onto one of the pillows. The servant who had originally guided them returned to stand by his master. Not a word was said. John gestured to Edouard to sit down and they both occupied a cushion. John didn't know whether he should start talking or wait for some signal. The master, or whatever he was, gazed intently at both of his guests, his eyes moving from John to Edouard and back. Still not a word was uttered. Just when John had decided that they were waiting for him to begin, the servant spoke. In halting English, he said, "We honored by your visit. We wish you know you under our protection."

What protection, and why? John exchanged glances with Edouard, who tilted his head slightly indicating that he also thought it was an odd thing to say. John replied graciously.

"We are delighted to have the occasion to visit you. I take it you are acquainted with the reason we are here."

This brought nothing but a confused look from the servant while the master sat without any reaction. It wasn't clear that either of them understood what John said. The servant leaned over to his master and whispered something, to which the other man replied in a sing-song Chinese voice. The servant gathered himself together for what was an obviously difficult task.

"We happy you here. How we help?"

Relieved that he had been able to put together his reply, the servant smiled and turned to his master who also smiled. John and Edouard both smiled in return. John decided to jump ahead, but hesitated when the master sneezed and the servant rushed to supply him with a large silk handkerchief. The important man's round face was flushed when he finished sneezing. He smiled at John and said something in Chinese. It was a surprisingly feminine voice.

"We say excuse," said the servant.

"Yes, of course," said John. "We are here to get your help." John realized it was best to keep his English as simple as possible. "We have had some things stolen from us. We have been told you may be able to get them back."

The servant/translator again spoke in a low tone with his master who quickly replied in his high-pitched voice.

"We not take anything," translated the servant.

"No, no, please don't misunderstand. Of course you didn't. We know that. It is that we need your help to find the men who did and get back what they took." John could see the entire interview slipping down the drain. He looked over at Edouard who could offer nothing more than a shrug.

More exchanges between the translator and his master produced much nodding of heads and rapid talk back and forth. Finally, the servant spoke again in his labored English.

"What stolen?"

Again John looked over at Edouard who once more shrugged. They had no list of items that had been taken. They hadn't thought they would get that far. It was very embarrassing. John tried to improvise.

"Many things were stolen. Food, equipment, many things. If you can help, we will get a list."

"List?" asked the translator.

"I mean we will tell you exactly what was stolen, if you can help us."

More palaver between the two silk-clad gentlemen and it was agreed that they would help if John could return with a list—in Chinese.

John and Edouard returned outside to find the jeep exactly where they had parked it. The rickshaw driver was leaning proprietarily against the hood. A small group of children surrounded the vehicle and one adventurously was turning the steering wheel while standing by the driver's side. The children fled and the rickshaw driver snapped to attention when the two Americans came through the stall. The driver waved to them signifying he'd lead them out of the warren of alleys into which he had brought them.

When they finally returned to the OSS compound, they found Chi-chi hard at work checking off items being unloaded from a large delivery truck. He spoke in French to John.

"You had success? Was everyone helpful?"

"Yes, quite helpful, but we have to have a list in Chinese of all the stolen items. Who are these people, Chi-chi?"

"As I said, they are important. Most likely also a tong member. They make things happen. Legal, illegal, tong people behind it all. Always a good idea to be friends with the tongs. The Kuomintang and tongs are very close. Each help the other. Tongs are very secret societies. They'll get your stuff back. What are you going to give them as a gift?"

"I never thought of that. What do you suggest? Money? Do they want money for helping us?

"They'll tell you. You must show you want to give them something. That is their way."

"What do tongs do?" asked Edouard.

"Oh, they make sure everything works. They kill some people too. Everyone is quite afraid of them. Of course they have fights among themselves, but that's just the way it is."

Chi-chi's matter-of-fact manner belied the harsh criminal character of the organization he described.

"I don't think Horse has the faintest idea what he's asked us to do," John said to Edouard in English. This is nuts. Why the hell are we wasting our time dashing around after stolen groceries and goddamn typewriters or whatever? I say we can this whole thing and get back to what we're here for."

Liu Chi Roget could not understand what John had said, but the meaning was quite clear. This Major John was not a person to send off on unimportant missions. He seemed to be driven by something. Always on the edge of anger yet holding himself tightly in control. If he'd been Vietnamese, he would have been a fine recruit for the Party. That assessment would look good in Chi's next report to Uncle.

Obtaining the contract as the new concessionaire for the OSS unit was not without its complications for Liu Chi Roget. He had received a polite but definitive invitation to a meeting at the headquarters of Chinese security. It was not unexpected.

"We are pleased to have you visit us today, Mr. Liu," said the CISB (Central Investigation and Statistics Bureau (Chinese Intelligence/Security)) captain, choosing to use the Chinese portion of Chi-chi's name.

"It is I who am honored by your invitation," replied the restaurant owner in his best Cantonese.

"We were delighted to hear of your good fortune in obtaining the contract for catering services with the American detachment," said the captain, getting directly to the point as security officials do when it suits them.

"I shall of course keep in mind my patriotic duty which I hope has continued to be satisfactory," said Chi-chi, exquisitely phrasing his role as an informant.

"Of that we are quite sure, Mr. Liu. What we have to discuss today is the lamentable circumstance in which my organization now finds itself. It is a matter of rice bowls in which my hard-working organization seems to have given up its natural share while your bowl is enhanced even more. Quick as you were to take advantage of the departure of your predecessor, just as swiftly did our bowl diminish."

The captain paused to shuffle meaninglessly among some papers on his desk, as if they contained evidence of the unfortunate circumstance to which he had just referred. Chi-chi, the old operator, approved of the professional manner of the officer.

"It is indeed unfortunate that to fill one's glass of water some from the other glass is lost. Perhaps if I would be allowed to make a monthly donation to the CISB family glass, it would somehow ease the transition. As I do not know all the members of that illustrious family, perhaps you would assist me by acting as intermediary, sir. It would be such a great help to me. I would deeply appreciate it if I simply could have the money delivered to you each month, and then you could pass it on to your family. Would you think $500 KMT would be adequate?"

"I think $600 might be more appropriate. It's a small but important difference."

"Then it shall be $600 KMT delivered to you monthly to assist the excellent security family that protects us all in time of need. I consider it a privilege to help, and am doubly honored that you, Captain, would bring this matter to my attention. Naturally, we shall continue to stay in close touch on matters of patriotic concern."

As annoying as the payoff was, it served a dual purpose. It got the bothersome CISB off his back and at the same time provided a reward to the captain that could only work toward Chi-chi's benefit in the future. Everyone's rice bowl had been protected and Liu Chi Roget had gained another layer of cover for his Party allegiance and activity.

Bob Simpson could not be dissuaded from pursuing his quest for the recovery of the items stolen from his new command. As a result, John had no choice but to have a list drawn up—and translated—of all items known to have been stolen and those that were suspected of having been stolen. The latter consisted of the entire store of foodstuffs as well as a substantial supply of liquor for the officers' club. The problem was that the departed concessionaires were the ones whom Hallstrom had entrusted to keep the inventory.

"John, am I missing something here?" asked Edouard as the two headed for their jeep and the return trip to the inner city. "We're supposed to get this guy—this tong leader—to go out and recover our stolen equipment and groceries, right?"

"Don't forget the booze."

"Never. Also the booze. He's not going to do this for nothing, so we have to pay him, right?"

"Right."

"So why don't we just buy the groceries wherever we can and pick up whatever equipment we lost on the black market—or simply put in a requisition for more stuff?"

"I said that to Horse already."

"And?"

"He believes we have to make an effort to recover what was stolen. He considers it a—what did he call it—'a blight on the reputation of our unit.'"

"But we don't have any reputation. This is OSS. For most people we don't even exist."

"He thinks that it's very embarrassing for a hot-shot intelligence outfit to have their pocket picked by some local yokels."

"I'm not embarrassed."

"And I'm not either, but he's hooked on starting off on the right foot as CO. Horse is great guy but a wee bit dense."

With Chi-chi's help they went through the same process as before, including making contact with the same rickshaw guide. This time they were armed with $1,000 KMT as a gift for the fat tong boss. They searched for landmarks during the trip in order to get some idea of the route they were taking. Some things were familiar, and others seemed totally new. It was impossible even to figure direction as they followed the rickshaw in and out of Kunming's dark streets and alleyways. When they arrived at the stall that they had parked in front of before, it was as if they had never been there. The streets and stalls all looked so much alike it was a surprise when the guide in front of their jeep stopped.

However, the inside courtyards and formal sitting room were immediately familiar. Again, the guide left as the servant/translator led them in and pointed to the cushions. This time John and Edouard sat down and awaited their tubby host. He arrived unsmiling and took his seat on his large cushion. Everything was the same as before except that out of the rear of the room stepped two enormous beefy Chinese men with pigtails and American Army carbines.

John ignored the ostentatious presence of the two thugs and smilingly offered the list of stolen items to the translator who looked them over before passing them to his master. The tong chieftain barely glanced at the list and looked up expectantly. John responded by passing over the envelope with the Chinese dollars. To that point not one word had been exchanged. John broke the silence:

"It is our honor to present this small token of esteem."

The translator responded with a blank stare. John tried again.

"It's a gift, a present. For your master...."

At that point Edouard made the mistake of attempting to change positions on his cushion. He rose slightly in an attempt to cross his legs. The rotund tong boss fell backward in expectation of some form of attack and the two gunmen jumped forward with their weapons pointed at the two Americans. Edouard held up his hands palm forward and finished moving into a semi lotus position—all the while with a big grin plastered on his face. The tong chief regained his own seat and in his soprano voice ordered the two gunmen back. The servant stood frozen.

John pointed to the envelope of money and repeated that it was intended as a gift. The servant looked at the money and passed it to his master who disdainfully waved it off. The servant counted the money and appeared to report its amount to the seated fat man. The tong leader furrowed his brow and whispered something to the servant.

"My master thanks you and excuses you because you are foreign devils and do not understand our ways. This is far too little for a man of his importance but not so little as make insult. He says we take your list and try and find your stolen things. We will show you what is proper gift."

With that the interview was over. The two thugs and their boss left the room. John and Edouard rose and followed the servant as he shuffled through the courtyards. He stopped for a moment and spoke to John directly.

"We fill your list and then we give you list of payment."

This wasn't a negotiation. This was how it would be. John smiled and said that it seemed a reasonable procedure. The servant smiled in return at both Americans and continued on through to the stall. He bowed to John and Edouard and returned inside. The Americans passed through the stall to the street. The jeep was not there. The rickshaw was parked in its place with its owner leaning against one of its wheels.

"Jesus Christ the jeep's been stolen," shouted John.

"I don't think so, John," said Edouard. "I think they just showed us what the proper gift was."

John wanted to go back in and take apart the place when Edouard reminded him that there were most likely more guys with pigtails than just the ones they had seen.

"Face it, John, they aced us. But hell, we've got the rickshaw."

A swearing John Guthrie ranted all the way back to the compound. At first, he was going to come back with a team and "clean out the whole damn place." After he had calmed down with Edouard's assistance, he decided that this was just another part of Asia he had to learn. They had taken him fair and square, even if they had been playing poker by their unique Chinese rules. By the time the rickshaw reached the OSS compound, John and Edouard were convulsed in laughter over the scene in which they had just been played the fool.

It took only two days before the rest of the game was played out. Lt. Colonel Robert Simpson, Commanding Officer of 5329 AGFRTS, had not been overly pleased with the loss of a jeep, but was surprisingly fatalistic over what had happened. The absurdity of the whole experience was mirrored by Simpson's reaction.

"It's not your fault, John. I ordered you into the operation. I'm sure you would have done much better in Chicago."

"What the hell did he mean by that remark?" John asked Edouard afterward.

"He's still hooked on you being a D.A. in Chicago. I think Horse has seen too many Jimmy Cagney films. The battling district attorney sort of thing."

"This place is getting too weird for me. I've got to get back to our nice, sane war," replied John shaking his head.

The following day, Edouard was crossing the compound to HQ when their stolen jeep came rolling in followed by two large, dilapidated trucks. He recognized the tong chief's servant as the passenger in the jeep.

"We have list here," shouted the servant, having become completely confused over the meaning of "list."

Edouard ran to get John as people began to spill out of the trucks followed by enormous amounts of foodstuff, crates of liquor, and an occasional piece of kitchen or office equipment. Soon neat piles had been set down in the dirt square. Chi-chi came running out of a storeroom and greeted the servant as if he were an old friend. The entire headquarters staff stood around watching the industrious tong members unload their cargo. Edouard returned with John who was immediately collared by the servant.

"Here your list. Here our list. This how much."

John handed the neatly recorded inventory, in Chinese, to Chi-chi, who ran his finger down the calculations mumbling to himself.

"*Tout va bien, patron*," he said handing the paper back to John.

"*Cinq mille de dollars KMT. Pas mal*," said Chi-chi smiling at the servant.

"I want the jeep back," said John heading for the vehicle. Both Edouard and the servant ran after him as he was about to drag the driver from his seat.

"Gift. That is gift. You say you give gift. This gift. We say we show you what gift. This gift," the servant pleaded. "You pay, please."

With that he shouted to the assembled laborers who came running over. There must have been 12 in all counting the truck drivers. They were a pretty ugly group. Horse Simpson burst out of his office on to the scene. His deep baritone voice boomed across the compound.

"Holy Mother of God. You did it. Great work, team. Great work."

"They want $5,000 KMT, Colonel. But John wants the jeep back. We've got a standoff here, sir," said Edouard.

"We already wrote the jeep off. Didn't we, Paul? Where's Paul?" said Horse looking for his adjutant. "Let's not have an international incident about this thing. Pay them the money. Let 'em have the jeep. Where's Paul? This is great. All our stuff back. There's much more than $5,000 KMT worth there. It's a good trade."

It took a while, but John was eventually dissuaded from repossessing the jeep. Paul Schreymann arrived to support his boss's thesis that the jeep having been written off would be much harder to write back in. At any rate, the logic was upheld and the servant with his small army of laborers sped off after Chi-chi swore that the goods delivered were worth many times the Chinese dollars that had been asked.

A disgruntled John Guthrie tried to get under control in a situation that he saw as an example of a total disregard of government property. Maybe he was a D.A. at heart. Whatever the case, he certainly wasn't cut out for the life of a staff officer of 5329 AGFRTS. Therefore, when Bob Simpson asked John and Edouard to follow him back to his office, John already had made up his mind that he wouldn't be interested in any new assignment that required staying in Kunming.

"Whaddya mean no? I haven't even told you what it is," Simpson exclaimed.

"If it's a staff position, I don't want it. That's all I'm trying to say, Horse."

"Dammit John. I want you to be my Exec and also take over as Chief/SO. It's a great job. I thought you'd love it. You'd be the big honcho. It's a light colonel slot, too."

"Sorry, Horse, it's the perfect spot, but not for me. I thank you for offering it, but I'm serious when I say I would fail miserably."

Edouard joined John in arguing that they both should return to Ch'ing-hsi to work with AGAS on the Viet Minh project.

Paul Schreymann unexpectedly jumped into the conversation with his hardnosed Alsatian logic.

"Sir, we're going to have a hard time to put anyone else in the field who has combat experience and also knows Dr. Ho. If John and Edouard continue on with that mission until the training phase is completed, they can then come back here and take over the SO section. What'll it take? Maybe four months?"

"Somewhere around the beginning of September then. Okay with me. Paul's right. It looks like the game in Europe is about over, so the timing looks good," said Simpson. "We got a deal?"

"Horse, in a few months you'll have made bird colonel and we'll all have to genuflect," said John, pleased to have had a way created for him to wriggle out.

Ch'ing-hsi was a Chinese military operations center strategically close to Tonkin's northern border with China and the limestone caves of Pac Bo; these had served as the headquarters of the Viet Minh during the early days. The caves now provided sanctuary and storage areas for the activities of the Vietnamese liberation movement. The proximity to Ch'ing-hsi made the area key to AGAS' aircrew recovery operations as well as Chinese, French and American intelligence missions. As exotic as all these activities may have been, Ch'ing-his was a dump. A large and bustling dump, but a dump nonetheless.

What had once been a small provincial town had become a well-stocked city in which every form of black market goods could be obtained—for a price. Similarly, all basic services of cooking, cleaning, and carpentry could be arranged through a ubiquitous system of compradores who provided whatever was needed. It was with the help of one of these "facilitators" that the two OSS officers had been able to secure a rather large section of a Quonset hut that had been divided into cubicles which simulated office space. The most important feature of the quarters was a large exhaust fan. When the electricity worked, the fan provided a pleasant breeze of Ch'ing-hsi air.

Sitting atop the regional mini-kingdom of AGAS was its chief, perhaps the top wheeler-dealer among the many in Ch'ing-hsi. It was through him that the OSS presence represented by John and Edouard was to gain its operational support for its intended mission with the Viet Minh. The Vietnamese liberation group had become an essential ingredient in the AGAS recovery net. The fear was OSS would foul up all its hard work.

"We got ourselves E&E nets all over Tonkin tryin' to draw as little attention to themselves as possible. I'm damn sure I don't want any OSS hotshots running around drawing fire from the Japs. No way," said the AGAS lieutenant colonel.

John had to use all his argumentative skills, explaining the need to tie up as many Japanese units as possible through resistance operations in case of a possible American landing in the south around Saigon.

"So you see, colonel, your AGAS people are going to be even more essential in the future. What we'll be doing isn't going to interfere. We'll be working hand-in-glove."

It was like being back home again negotiating with managers who had everything, and from whom the trick was to wheedle a few key concessions for the rank and file. John was good at it.

"You say this all comes straight from the War Department?" said the AGAS "manager."

"We got it on paper back in Kunming," lied Edouard, neatly getting into the act.

In the end, the AGAS colonel reluctantly had given his approval of cooperation with the OSS mission. Now ensconced in Ch'ing-hsi, the nuts and bolts aspects of their mission became their principal focus. From their AGAS contacts they had learned a considerable amount about the Viet Minh who clearly were not going to be that easily dealt with. An invaluable step forward was taken when the AGAS chief offered to introduce John and Edouard to the commander of the French M.5 unit at Ch'ing-hsi.

"They're pretty cooperative here, not like what I hear it is up in Kunming. We get along real good, but you've got to remember, gentlemen, that neither the Chinese nor the French are particularly eager to see us develop contacts in Tonkin."

"But the local M.5 are a decent bunch, right, sir?" Edouard said in his boyish manner.

"They are, son, but that has nothing to do with what I'm talking about. We're talking larger issues here. This is upper-level politics. Lotta stuff we have to dance around."

John repressed a smile at Edouard's play of innocence at receiving a political lecture from the AGAS chief. He was always amazed how effective his friend was working the dumb act.

As advertised, the M.5 office in Ch'ing-hsi turned out to be exceedingly friendly to the newly arrived OSS officers. It was a true field office working in direct support of real, if limited, operations against the Japanese—unlike the preoccupation of its headquarters in Kunming with internal Allied political machinations. John and Edouard met and immediately liked the ranking M.5 officer, Commandant Jacques de Laborde de Monpezat.

"A double 'de,'" remarked Edouard. "Very, very white shoe, French style."

It was not that Major Jacques, as he was known, was ever around long enough to develop a social life. He was charged with running a net, and, as he explained, *grâce à Dieu* that's what he did. He and his worthy collection of cutthroats were usually somewhere in the bush driving the Japanese crazy. According to AGAS, Major Jacques never asked for, nor did he get, assistance from the Viet Minh—but there was a mutual respect, albeit a wary one. Jacques de Laborde had been quite open about the fact that his small unit and a similar one operating from Laos were just about the only unilateral French activities against the Japanese in Indochina.

"That's not what Jean Sainteny says. He says Free French forces are fighting all over," said John with a smile.

"What would he know? He's never fought anywhere," Major Jacques replied with unexpected candor.

Jacques had not been seen for a couple of weeks when John was pleasantly surprised with a request for a meeting. The formality of the note was inconsistent with the usual relaxed courtesies of Ch'ing-hsi, but then Major Jacques was of the old school. John sent word back that the esteemed Commandant was always welcome and indicated that the following morning would be very convenient. Some real coffee was rounded up along with a platter of Edouard's favorite rice cakes and a large bowl of fruit. Their office was rough, but their hospitality need not be the same.

Major Jacques arrived exactly on time. He was dressed in a bush jacket that looked like it had been made by the best Parisian tailor—and most likely was. He had on American jump boots and his khaki pants were bloused to perfection. Major Jacques would have done Jean Gabin proud, except that the good-looking commandant was the real article and not an actor playing a role. John and Edouard greeted their guest and immediately sat down in their section of the "air-conditioned" Quonset hut to their coffee and cakes. Though Jacques de Laborde knew both Americans spoke French, he chose to speak English as a courtesy to the office of which he was about to ask a favor. His French accent was strong but grammar was impeccable, befitting his socially correct education.

"Ah, this coffee is magnificent," he said making the "is" sound as "eez." "I congratulate you on your excellent choice. With this coffee I most likely could purchase anything I wanted on the black market."

They all laughed at the Frenchman's reference to the notorious system which dominated life in Ch'ing-hsi. John originally had been vehement in condemnation of the practice, but eventually came to accept what was an economic inevitability.

"I will come right to the point, as you would say. I have—I mean there are—a group of French citizens being held by the sons of Nippon in a terrible camp at Tam Dao. This is located in the Cho Chu-Ding Hao sector about halfway between Son Tay and Thai Nguyen. In other words, right in the middle of the Viet Minh guerrilla country. I would like to go in there and gain the release of these unfortunate civilians. There are men, women, and children, but *malheureusement* there are two problems. The first is the distance. It is too far to walk in with a force sizeable enough to take the camp. And the second is the fact that I do not have a particularly good relation—relationship, right—with this Viet Minh. I have been informed they are all communists or something like that, which does not bother me, but it can be a problem, *d'accord*? The most important thing is that they do not like us, the French.

I have tried not to bother them with my own little group, and they have not bothered us. It has been *très aimable* in a fashion, *sans ardeur*, I would say."

"We would say, cool. You have a cool relationship," Edouard offered.

"Excellent. Cool, *très* cool. At least they do not kill me—yet."

"So, how can we help you?" John asked.

"You have good relations, better than cool, *n'est-ce pas?* At least that is what we have been told by Kunming. It bothers them, but not me. You are doing their job for them, M.5/Kunming that is. They should have good relations with everyone, but they don't. They are very *limité*, limited in their *point de vue*. I would like you to talk to the Viet Minh, if you can, and suggest to them to save the poor people who are being held by the Japanese bastards at Tam Dao."

"I don't think they'll do something just because we ask them. They'll want something in return, don't you think?" John replied.

"*Bien sûr*. They will definitely want something, but they also want to be your friend. They are smart. If they do this, they will think you will like them more. But you must go along on the mission so they do it right. I would be happy to go—I should go—but they would not want a Frenchman helping them. They would let you help them, though."

"You are suggesting that we get the Viet Minh guerrillas to attack a Jap prison camp to free some French civilians—only we're also going to tell them that we will tell them how to do it?" John asked incredulously.

"*Précisement!*" replied the smiling de Laborde as if the American major had just cracked a complicated code. The Frenchman continued his broad smile while John exaggeratedly rolled his eyes upward. Edouard unsuccessfully stifled a laugh.

"You are nuttier than a fruitcake," said John.

"What is this fruitcake? Do you have some? I think it would go very well with this wonderful coffee," said Jacques de Laborde being purposely and charmingly obtuse.

John went through all the reasons why such an idea was impossible. He explained that he doubted he ever could get clearance; that the Viet Minh guerrillas would never agree; that the prisoners would all be killed; that even if they were rescued alive there was no way to get them out of Tonkin. Jacques de Laborde had an answer for everything, and when he didn't, he would toss it off with his expert Gallic shrug. He was the best that France offered—courageous, charming, smart as a whip, and above all, a decent guy. John and Edouard never had a chance.

In a way, this proposed operation solved a great many problems in initiating a joint American/Viet Minh mission. The French could not object and the Chinese certainly were left without a political argument. M.5 in Ch'ing-hsi was a help not a hindrance, and the ambitious anti-American Jean Sainteny wouldn't be breathing down their necks. John and Edouard huddled after Major Jacques left, warning them that time was of the essence because he couldn't be sure the Japanese would not try to move the prisoners—or worse.

"Well, there it is, Edouard—the perfect scheme. The only problem is that we haven't got a team together to go do the job. We're still waiting for Horse's promised reinforcements."

"So we don't wait. I can drop in to say hello to Dr. Ho and organize the operation. We'll stay in touch via AGAS' vaunted radio net. *Pas de problem.*"

"First thing we have to do is get clearance from Bob Simpson and then from the big brass in Chungking for the objective. After that is accomplished, we've got to have an ops plan okayed. Somewhere in there we've got to get in contact with Dr. Ho and his people to see if they'll buy into this little number. There are a lot of steps here, so don't go off with your 'I'll just jump in' business. I figure we can push Simpson to push Chungking on approving the objective, but before we go any further, we've got to be able to say we have an agreement with the Viet Minh to proceed. We can tell de Laborde that we're working on it, but that's all."

Obtaining clearance for the operation was amazingly swift. Coded signals flew back and forth to Kunming and thence to Chungking. Everyone thought the chance to pull off a humanitarian mission involving French civilians had all the attributes of a political winner. Sliding the Viet Minh in through this mission would look really good in dispatches to Washington. The next step was to get in touch with Dr. Ho's crowd down in Tonkin. AGAS and its chief had to be brought into the loop.

"And what can I do for you gentlemen today?" the AGAS colonel inquired of the two OSS officers in front of him. It was the standard greeting he had learned at his uncle's general store—polite, interested, and removed. It was an excellent bargaining stance for whatever might arise.

"We have an interesting situation that we thought you might just be the one to assist in. In other words, we need your help, Colonel."

John explained the situation, carefully leaving out Jacques de Laborde's name. No need to expose that connection. It was a small thing, but there was proper security procedure, and then there was the usual way. John chose the "a friend told us…." explanation. "So you see we have to make contact with these Viet Minh people on a level that counts. The problem being that our HQ will want a clear idea beforehand as to what they're prepared to do… the Viet Minh, that is.

"And you figure we can just ring them up and we have a nice old meeting at a local bar, right?" The AGAS colonel smiled as he delivered his sarcastic response. It tended to soften his remark just enough without losing the bite.

Edouard took one look at his partner's face and could see John's jaw muscles working. A bad sign. John didn't like to ask favors of anyone, about anything.

Edouard knew his friend well and realized it was a good time to intervene in spite of his junior position.

"Whatever goes on in that area is AGAS business as far as we're concerned, sir. We're the new boys on the block. You've worked hard to get your operation going and we don't want to screw anything up. Major Guthrie was just saying that to me before we came in. You know the Viet chaps far better than we do."

It was the "chaps" that got to the burly Lt. Colonel. "Chaps," he roared. "Viet chaps? That's great. Are you a Brit? He's not a Brit is he?"

The question was directed at John who had used the interval to shake off his reaction to the heavy sarcasm. Edouard's glibness had made that possible. John tried to camouflage his own response with a try at flippancy.

"No, he's part froggie and part mick. He's a mutt, but he's rich as hell and talks funny. We use him to get girls for us."

It was a small bridge, but one that was in just the right place. It happens that way sometimes. One remark, a gesture, can turn around an awkward situation. Up to now the AGAS chief had been hospitable and helpful, but he sensed the writing on the wall. He wanted to make sure these two OSS officers, who certainly were the forward echelon of a powerful intelligence presence, remained aware of who and what had been there first. He hadn't missed the flash in John's eyes when he had delivered his needle. A hard nose, for sure. He respected that. And the other guy, the smooth talker, he protected his boss. Good work. Good guys.

"I can arrange something, of course. One of my men is down there in Dr. Ho's camp—actually nearby with his radioman. We're in regular touch. He knows them all. Jimmy, Jimmy Tau, used to be in the oil business in Haiphong but he's originally from Boston. He'll be able to feel out the situation for you."

"And he can keep his eye on us when we get down there?" John couldn't resist.

"Oh, yes, that also. We don't want you... chaps... messing up our little garden. No offense."

"And none taken. But you understand this has to be an OSS/SO show," John answered. The terms of the relationship would be set in these very early moments, and it was best that it was made clear.

"No problem there, Major. It's not the sort of thing we get directly involved in. We are delicate little boy scouts. We just go around looking for our little sparrows. Wholescale prison breakouts are for you boys... chaps. I love that."

The next step was to brief Jacques de Laborde on the developments. As usual the jaunty Frenchman was off with his merry band creating mischief in the upper Tonkin. When he did arrive back, he was in a deeply black mood. He had just lost several of his men in an ambush. He wouldn't discuss the details, but it was obvious that he was livid with the M.5 office in Kunming.

"I will never again trust those bastards," he said to Edouard after a few days of calming down.

"They, the Kunming crowd—you know whom I mean—gave us information that was supposed to be absolutely correct. All we had to do was follow exact instructions. We did just that and my boys were killed as a result. It was supposed to be a group of Vichy Army survivors, and it turned out to be lousy Japs. Those idiots in Kunming were completely taken in and we paid the price. They are so stupid. All they want is to have a big army show and have Le Grand Charles in Paris pat them on the head and say 'good boy.'"

He never mentioned anyone by name, but it was obvious that he was talking about M.5 command in Kunming, specifically Commandant Jean Sainteny. Major Jacques was at ease talking French with Edouard who responded to him accordingly. They both had the same aristocratic accent. It was a special bond for Frenchmen of that background as much as it would be for any speaking in the *patois* of their geographical region or social group. That Edouard Parnell was American was lost in the flush of the shared language and accent. Other languages may have elements of similar clubbiness, but the upper-class French have a language of particular exclusivity, and they know it.

Leaving aside Sainteny's predilection for coloring information to suit his particular needs of the moment, the fact was that the M.5 office for which he was responsible was incompetent to vet the intelligence they passed down the line. What made it worse was Sainteny's unwillingness to admit his unit's shortcoming, and he would always shift blame to the people in the field. Although he was of equal rank with Sainteny in Kunming, Jacques de Laborde was junior in the overall command structure and this required a deference that frustrated and annoyed him at every turn. This latest incident had gone beyond the usual absurdity and Commandant Jacques de Laborde de Monpezat had no intention of allowing the matter to drop.

From the outset, the information regarding the French civilians held at Tam Dao had been restricted to de Laborde's own net. He hadn't passed any of it on to Kunming purposely. It had been his idea to involve the Americans and he wasn't about to have something knocked down by Sainteny just because Kunming hadn't thought of it. Furthermore, nothing had yet been agreed on after his first talk with John, who still had to get his own approvals lined up. Until then, Jacques had decided he had no command obligation to pass the plan up the line to Kunming. After the recent debacle he had no intention of sharing anything with Sainteny. Let it be a complete American OSS show. Whatever was done or not done was their business. There was no way that his small team—now even smaller—could do anything on their own or with the Viet Minh for that matter. He was happy to hear that John had made no mention of exactly how he had learned of the prisoners' plight when the

AGAS chief was briefed. The Americans would do a good job. They were the only ones who even had a chance to do so.

The AGAS radio confirmed approval from Dr. Ho personally for the operation, and stated he looked forward to meeting again with his American friends who had been his hosts in Kunming. Even in radio traffic the Vietnamese leader contrived to be courteous. While waiting for the response from the Viet Minh, John and Edouard had prepared an ops plan which called for a six-man team for this initial mission to be followed later by another six. The reply came in from Chungking via Bob Simpson. None of these personnel were available at this time. It was suggested that the entire operation be delayed for a month until the expected new personnel would be in place. John could be heard shouting and swearing from quite a distance outside the Quonset hut.

John flew up to Kunming to plead his case directly with Simpson.

"This is the perfect introduction, Bob. Right from the outset we've wanted to involve this Viet Minh in resistance ops against the Japs. That's been the entire point of SO/Indochina. Okay, maybe I'm overstating it, but our job was, is, to get something going against the Nips in Tonkin. And Dr. Ho with his Viet Minh are the logical locals because they're already doing a good job for AGAS. They've agreed with this civilian prisoner mission and now we're not ready. That really makes us look like a bunch of incompetent asses."

"John, we just don't have anybody. 101 Detachment grabbed off the first bunch. We were supposed to get some, but it never happened."

"Edouard wants to go on his own."

"We can't do that, John. He's a good kid and smart, but I couldn't send him alone, and I'm not about to send both of you. We'll have some EMs ready in a few days for you and they need training. I'm thinking of giving you Applegate."

"I realize our original plan called for Edouard and me to train up a team. But the opportunity is here now. We could be saving some innocent civilians here. Jesus, Bob, what the hell are we out here for?"

John heard himself say it, but the full meaning didn't hit him until ten seconds later. Civilians, women, and children, just ordinary people. His father would have said, "The ordinary people, John. The working stiff. They're the ones we do this for. Who else's gonna do it, John? That's what we Guthries do. Since going back all the way to Scotland. Remember that's what we Guthries do."

Big Jack had said that to him just before he went off to law school. Of course, he was talking about John's obligation to the union, but even then John had seen it in broader political terms. These were the depression days, the days of Franklin Delano Roosevelt and the New Deal. Young people thought like that then. They went off to war thinking like that.

However, it was without thought that John next spoke.

"I'll go, Bob. I'm the mission commander, or at least I will be when we get enough people for a mission. I've got to have a look at what we're getting into. It's only logical. They're all friendlies down there with Dr. Ho, aren't they? A little pre-op reconnoitering. I'll also get a chance to meet the AGAS radio team. Whatever happens while I'm there is just, well, the fortunes of war. If you want... we never had this conversation."

"You know I wouldn't want it that way," Bob responded immediately. After only a moment's hesitation he said, "Remember, it's just a scrimmage, full pads but just a scrimmage. I'll make sure it's down in the record that way. Go there and find out what the score is. If a mercy mission pops up, well...."

John wasn't prepared either for his own suggestion or Bob Simpson's quick agreement. Horse Simpson was totally bereft of guile, so his response was as much a matter of reflex as John's offer had been. It was typical that the SO chief saw the operation in football terms. That's how he judged most of life and the war. He wasn't a hesitant player in either. For John, who considered himself a careful lawyer calculating every move, he found his recent turn toward emotionally influenced decisions to be completely contrary to a self-perception on which he had based most of his life. To further complicate matters, he wasn't sure which personality trait brought him more satisfaction—the security of his old protective self, or the new, more open and spontaneous one. One characteristic remained stable, though. Having taken a course, he had no interest in questioning the action, even if he himself was surprised at what he had just done.

It was agreed between John and Simpson that the Tam Dao operation would not be discussed with either Paul Schreymann or Tony Castelli, though it was recognized that the wily new chief of SI/Kunming would get wind that something was bubbling from his own network. The important thing was to keep details tightly held. Once John arrived at Ho's place he'd be free to deal with all matters with the prerogative of an officer in the field. Nonetheless, there still were issues of logistics and operational planning that needed to be discussed with AGAS and Jacques de Laborde—to say nothing of the delicate issue of informing Edouard he would have to stay back.

"I brought your name up and Horse turned the suggestion down flat."

"Why? Did he say why?"

"He said he couldn't send down one guy to deal with Ho and his team—you know how he talks—and then have that guy effectively replaced in the pecking order when the full team arrives later."

"Meaning what? I don't get it."

"Meaning, quite simply, you go down there and I arrive afterwards and your whole status is undercut. Look, he said it's the same as having one guy as the practice quarterback, but he just sits on the bench when the first-string guy gets ready to play the game. Now if you don't like that metaphor take it up with him. Basically, he didn't want us to be involved at all. This was the best I could do."

"So I sit around on my ass waiting for some more team members. That's real great. The war will be over by the time I get down there."

"I hope it is, and so should you. Don't worry, nothing's going to happen that quickly. The truth is that I would like to have a look around this whole Viet Minh thing so when you bring the team in, I'll know where the strengths and weaknesses are. I'd prefer having you along, but somebody's got to stay here and organize the show. You're it, Edouard. End of story."

"When does Applegate get here? You realize that's a mixed blessing, don't you?"

"He could be invaluable if they send us green guys. Sure, I know he can be a pain, but he's a damn good man to have in the field as well as being the core of a tough training cadre. We'll need that in handling the Viets. Oh, I forgot. We've got a name for the mission. We don't have anything else, but we've got the name. Paul showed it to me. Chungking sent it down."

"I can't wait."

"Moose. Moose Mission. That's it. They have a list of animals and we'll be Moose."

"What's that make us? Mice? Or maybe Mooses. I hate it."

"I thought you would. There is no plural. Everybody's a Moose. Moose Mission. It's not so bad."

"Tiger Mission. That would have been better. But dumb old Moose?"

"Edouard, my friend, the name is the least of our troubles. You'll have your hands full while I'm down there, but in the meantime, we've got to get me there and that means rounding up the GAS guys and our man, Jacques."

The AGAS chief proved a capable ally. He didn't want to know more than he needed and was quick to offer aid of any type. He'd heard from his officer in Kim Lung there was a serious need for medicines, so along with dropping John in they would parachute these and other needed supplies for the AGAS team. In addition, some boxes of arms and ammunition would be dropped as gifts to Dr. Ho and his people from AGAS. In this way John's reconnaissance trip on paper was unrelated to the AGAS supply mission to its team. What happened with the AGAS supplies afterward would be out of John's hands. The colonel had the instinct of a Chicago ward healer—and he loved the game.

Major Jacques, John, and Edouard worked on a plan based on the information already gathered by the Frenchman's own sources regarding the Tam Dao camp facilities. He must have had good intelligence because the details were extensive. He promised that none of the information came from Kunming M.5. It was all taken from his own net. He trusted the information, he said, and so should John.

"There aren't that many guards. After all, there are only 20 to 30 prisoners. I have nothing more specific. The men are separated from the women. I would say it is more a holding facility than a real prison camp, but I am worried about timing. They could be moved at any time."

"To begin with," said Edouard who had finally reconciled himself to staying behind, "French speakers, preferably females, will have to be found among the guerrillas to handle the women internees. In that same regard, the women and children have to be freed first. If there's any screw up—*bousiller*, Jacques—they have to be first priority."

"*D'accord*! But it is also *très, très important* to remember, John, that while the guards on duty have to be taken care of, you also have to eliminate those who are off duty. I would suggest the operation should begin after the evening meal when they will be most relaxed but there still will be light."

John listened carefully and took notes. They repeatedly went over variations of the plan and things to be alert to. The three of them had all had their own experiences in combat and respected each other's views, but in the end it would have to be John who carried the load. He was adamant that the camp commander had to be singled out for the initial strike.

"The rest of them will be turning to whomever is in command to give them orders when something like this happens. If we handle it right, they'll be completely surprised. If we take out the commander, first thing, that's going to give us that brief extra moment."

They went over the tactical plan several times just to try to dig out areas of weakness or error, but as John said on the final evening of preparation, "I could get down there and find there's no way I can control these Viet guys. They can have their own way of doing things and that'll be it. We just have to hope these people are willing to accept a little advice. In a way it's better that I'll be alone because that way they won't be competing with a team of us. The truth is that it'll be their show with me going along for the ride."

The actual send-off was more like the launching of a favorite son on his way to school. By the time John was ready to depart, Applegate had arrived from Kunming with best wishes from "the old man," as the sergeant called Simpson. A cortege of jeeps headed to Tepao airfield. The AGAS CO was in the lead jeep with his driver. Jacques de Laborde followed him in another jeep sporting his guidon of blue, white, and red, the French *tricolore*. Edouard and John came third followed by a truck carrying all the supplies to be dropped with John. At the tail end of the convoy came the AGAS air crew in another jeep. This had all been preceded by an evening of revelry hosted by Commandant Jacques during which an inordinate amount of very good French wine was consumed. It was amazing that anyone could drive, much less, as in John's case, plan to jump into the Vietnamese jungle.

The weapons and ammunition had all been loaded into their containers as had the rest of the supplies. Three riggers shifted the special cylinders into the plane and hooked up the chutes. It took about an hour to get everything settled in during which the ever thoughtful de Laborde produced a large thermos of hot coffee laced with some brandy to ward off the effects of the previous evening. A final toast of "*Merde*" accompanied John as he swung up into the Dakota. The plane revved up and taxied forward till its motors reached full speed, then roared down the field, lifted up, and gently banked southward toward Tonkin. Edouard watched until the plane disappeared. "Lucky bastard," he murmured to himself as he slid into the jeep.

Chapter Eight

Since Thanh's arrival in Kim Lung, he had found himself called upon to assume a role which was quite unexpected. He had been at the headquarters encampment for only several weeks and already he was treated by most around him as a veteran officer. He considered himself strictly a newcomer, but the others in the camp acted as if he was of a Party rank higher than his own view of himself. At the outset it was a bit disconcerting, but he came to realize there were few who had his Party and military combat experience.

Thanh had walked well over a hundred miles from Pac Bo with a small group of porters heavily laden with supplies for the Viet Minh camp. They were accompanied by a team of armed guards protecting them from bandits and Japanese security forces—both with similar larcenous intentions. The truck ride from Kunming had ended at a village on the Chinese side of the border a half day's hike to the caves at Pac Bo. The eight days that it took in total to get from Kunming to Kim Lung were seen by Thanh as a return to the real world, a return home.

A man in a clean but rumpled white suit introduced himself shortly after Thanh's arrival. He said he was Comrade Van. That Vo Nguyen Giap personally would greet him did not merely surprise Thanh, it left him nearly speechless. Comrade Van spoke of how he had received glowing reports from Kunming regarding both Thanh's training as well as his military and Party background.

"You are prepared to work hard, Comrade Thanh?" Giap presented the question.

"Yes, I am ready, comrade," said Thanh, holding himself in a stiff military brace.

"There is no question you are a soldier, comrade. I can see that right away. We shall want you to transfer some of that to our other comrades who have not had your experience and training."

It was a formal greeting consistent with the man's personality, but it was also a clear statement of truth. Thanh had been highly praised by his teacher and was seen as an especially valuable addition to the fighting brigade that Giap envisioned. Thanh would be one of the very first veteran Party cadre who also had formal combat experience and military training.

"Uncle Ho sends you his enthusiastic welcome and regrets his ill health prevents a personal meeting at this moment," Giap added.

Thanh barely comprehended what had been said. He was in such a state of excitement that only later did he realize that the man who led all the Indochina Communist Party, his Party, had sent word regretting not meeting him. For Thanh, a whole new life had begun. The hundreds of miles he had trekked in these last months had all led to this, this wonderful world of comrades. It had been his dream, and now he would live his dream. At barely 25, Bui Dac Thanh would be one of the first officers of the new liberation army.

* * *

The drop went off without a hitch. John jumped last after all the equipment cylinders had been pushed out. It was safer that way. The transport plane circled about and aimed John right at the drop zone. As he drifted down, John could see a clutch of people waving at him from below. When he landed, a happy Jimmy Tau raced over to help control the still-billowing canopy.

"Lt. James A. Tau, at your service, sir. Welcome to Kim Lung Station of the Air Ground Aid Section," said a grinning Tau. For the Chinese American from Boston and parts east, the arrival of Major John Guthrie was a very welcome occasion. There was another young officer located 50 miles to the northeast, but Jimmy hadn't seen him for two months. The new arrival would be someone to talk to about home, the war and maybe, if he was lucky, the Red Sox. The parachuting of the supplies would be important in local relations; it would show that the Americans were behind their Vietnamese friends just as Jimmy had been saying for weeks. It was an important recognition of US support for Dr. Ho in the continuing internal struggle within the Viet Minh leadership between the communist-led forces and the other nationalist groups.

Jimmy Tau led John to the edge of the campsite where a newly constructed wood cabin set on bamboo stilts had been built especially for the new arrival. The little encampment at Kim Lung had become a bit crowded, Jimmy explained.

"It was never intended as a major headquarters that it's become. Dr. Ho, by the way, is having one of his bouts with fever and hopes you'll understand him not formally greeting you. I gather you met him during his trip to Kunming."

John stretched out on the floor of the cabin happy finally to be at his destination. The only furniture was a bamboo table and chair.

"I hope it's nothing serious. He didn't look that strong when we met him."

"Who can tell? Even when he's well, he doesn't look that great. It's hard to say about Uncle. That's what we call him, Uncle. Everybody does."

Jimmy Tau continued on about the health problems of the Vietnamese leader. It was a matter of concern to Tau who wondered aloud if any of the medicines that had been dropped along with the other supplies would be of value for Ho's condition. John said that he had no idea what the medicine boxes contained.

"I thought you were the one who requested the medical supplies. I thought they were for you. What's the old man got, anyhow?" John asked.

"I just asked for a lot of stuff. You know, sulfa, malaria stuff, anything they got for dysentery. All sorts of stuff. I'm no doctor. They really need a doctor here. No one seems to have much idea of things medical. I certainly don't. Dr. Ho's got a nurse here, but I don't know if she's a real nurse or what."

"I had a survival course that included basic surgery and the usual combat injuries, but that's it," John admitted.

Jimmy explained in his eager manner how his day was filled with gathering all sorts of information to send on to Ch'ing-hsi—weather reports, troop movements, anything that might be useful to 14th Air Force.

"Mac's off fishing. Mac Soo that is. He's my radioman. He loves to fish. As you can see, we have plenty of water. Mac's Chinese, but as loyal as they come. I mean he's Chinese-Chinese, not like me. I'm MIT Chinese. Petroleum engineering. I came out here to make my fortune with Texaco. I barely got started in Haiphong when Pearl Harbor came along. I took off, but when I got to Chungking, they grabbed me, gave me a commission and eventually I ended up with AGAS in Ch'ing-hsi. What a character that colonel is."

Jimmy Tau was a non-stop talker. In barely a half hour of acquaintance John learned that Jimmy had been born in Boston, grew up in Boston, was a wild baseball fan, and had a girlfriend whom he didn't trust to wait for him. He also received a detailed report on the weather.

"I'm sorry about it, Major, but this rain we got is going to be pretty steady from here on in. We're sort of in the foothills here so we don't get as much as in the delta, you know the Red River, Song Hong. It sort of drizzles, then comes a short dry spell, and then maybe some big storms. It's that time of year."

John was tired enough after the previous night of heavy celebration and was quite content to spend the rest of the day pulling his stuff in from the rain and organizing his cabin. He sent a signal with the aid of the returned Mac Soo indicating his safe arrival, had an early dinner of the fish the radioman had caught, and slid off into a sound sleep under some hastily rigged mosquito netting over his sleeping bag.

The following day, John was surprised to find there was very little interest on the part of the rest of the camp in his presence. There had been the group of welcoming villagers at the drop zone, but other than that no official greeting committee. It was as if the house guest had arrived and he was expected to amuse himself while the rest of the household went about their everyday business. John brought the matter up with Jimmy.

"I figure that they think you're connected to Mac and me, and it's none of their business. They're waiting for you to take the initiative. With Uncle Ho sick, well, the others are waiting for you, like I said, to take the initiative."

"What initiative? I can't do anything without them. I thought all this was gone over by radio. They know what I'm here for. That's why we dropped all the armament and ammo. I know I've just arrived, but no one has even come to set up a meeting. Am I missing something?"

"Hell, Major, I don't savvy it at all. Maybe they're waiting for you to speak with Dr. Ho. But he's sick, and furthermore he already gave his okay to the whole thing. I just think they're expecting you to get them to do something. After all, it's your project, this Tam Dao thing. They figure, maybe, it's your move. They can be sort of precious, if you know what I mean."

"So who's the guy I do this with, set up a meeting?"

"Right, that's a good question. I guess if it comes right down to that, well, it would have to be Giap, Vo Nguyen Giap, Comrade Van. He's the guy. He's the military boss, I think. I've dealt mostly with Dr. Ho, himself. He speaks English and my French is only so-so. How's your French?"

"It works, but it's no thing of beauty."

"Me, too. I've spoken with Giap some, of course, but not what you'd call real complicated discussions. He's a very formal person, dresses like a colonial administrator, white suit and everything. But sharp as a tack. There's a new guy just arrived, much younger but very GI. You know, looks very military. But new. I don't know him. It's a small place here, but he keeps to himself."

Jimmy Tau might prefer to explain away the lack of enthusiasm with which John was faced, but he decided it had a far deeper meaning. It was a hell of a time to be starting to learn the idiosyncrasies of people with whom you're supposed to go into combat. As the morning wore on, John found himself digging an ever-increasing emotional ditch into which he plunged himself. Jimmy had to go off with Mac Soo to perform their ritual radio contacts with their spotters and that left John alone. He decided to drag out and empty the supply cylinders to make a checklist of the contents. He knew what was supposed to be in the containers, but it was best to make an inventory. Anyhow, it was something to do while waiting for some inspiration with respect to his next move. This was not how he had envisaged his first day in Kim Lung.

One happy surprise occurred as the sun broke through the drizzle. The bright and drying sun helped John with the heavy work of unpacking. He had worked up a satisfying sweat and begun to feel better mentally when a most unusual sight greeted him. A man in a white suit walked up. He was round faced, wore a white shirt and dark tie along with a battered black fedora. John recognized the costume immediately and realized that the impression that he made in his now sweaty fatigues was hardly the uniform he would have chosen for his first meeting with the Viet Minh's top military man. Giap stretched out his hand in a smiling greeting.

"*Bonjour, je m'appelle Van. Je suis très content de faire votre connaissance.*"

John replied with equal friendliness and formality but showed his dirty hands rather than shaking the other man's. Instead, John placed his palms together in front of him in the traditional manner. Giap smiled again and returned the gesture.

"I believe I have the advantage, Major Guthrie," the man in the white suit said in his perfect though slightly accented French. He clearly spoke the language far better than the American.

"Oh, I have heard of you, Monsieur Van. In fact, I was hoping to have a meeting so we can move ahead with this Tam Dao project."

It perhaps wasn't the politest thing to do, but John was not in much of a mood to indulge in the usual small talk of a first meeting. In any case, it didn't seem to bother the other man at all.

"I have spoken to Uncle Ho. He regrets he is still ill, but he will soon be better. He asked me to speak to you just about that very thing. I apologize for not being here when you arrived yesterday, but I was detained at a meeting."

It was as if he was an executive explaining his absence from the office rather than a guerrilla leader talking to a foreign officer in the middle of a muddy encampment surrounded by piles of military weapons and supplies. Looking over the neat stacks John had arranged, Giap continued:

"First we want to thank you formally for the extremely useful supplies you have brought with you. I see that you are now taking inventory. Excellent. I appreciate your care. It is a large responsibility to bring these things to us. Again, we thank you. Uncle will thank you personally when he feels better. Again, he deeply apologizes for his absence."

The apology for not greeting John when he arrived and the fulsome appreciation of the weapons and other supplies that had been dropped mollified John's initial reaction. He reminded himself he was a guest of these people as well as badly needing their cooperation.

"I hope you will excuse my preoccupation with my mission, freeing those poor people at Tam Dao. I have been informed that time is a factor and I've been hoping to get started as soon as possible."

John was treated to what he would soon learn was a rarity, a smile from Comrade Van.

"That was exactly what Uncle Ho said to me. He said that you are an American and that means you will want to get started immediately. He has travelled to your country. Did you know that?"

"Yes, Monsieur Van, he told us that. I met him in Kunming. I hope his illness is not serious."

"No, not at all. He will be better very soon. Lt. Tau said you might be bringing some medicines with you. That would be a help."

"Yes, I hope they are useful. We had no idea of Dr. Ho's actual problem, so I believe Jimmy just asked for a general list of things. But it is nonetheless extensive. Perhaps you have someone who can look them over?"

"Yes, we'll do that. Actually, Uncle knows a great deal about these things himself. But then we ask him about everything. He is very wise."

It was obvious that Ho was a demigod in the eyes of Giap and most likely the rest of his inner circle. John catalogued that information for future reference. In the meantime, though, it was important to press forward with his principal objective, getting the Tam Dao mission off the ground. He inquired if a team had been organized to carry on the rescue operation and was informed that arrangements would be made for John to meet with the team leaders.

"I am sure they also wish to see your wonderful gifts," Giap said pointing to the piles of weapons and ammunition. It was all theirs now and there was no sense in John pretending he had any control over what he had brought with him. In fact, John began to wonder just how much control he was going to have over the Tam Dao operation at all. Giap politely suggested that John might perhaps find it convenient to meet with some of Giap's people when he finished his inventory. In other words, Giap and the team were all waiting for John—just as Jimmy had suggested.

John decided it was best that he got out of his sweat-soaked fatigues, have a wash, and get a bit tidied up so he presented a slightly more military manner. He went down to a small stream which ran by the encampment. The site for the camp was completely hidden from view by heavy forest cover. A small area had been carved out in which six huts, all sitting four-foot high on bamboo pole foundations were placed. The largest were communal sleeping quarters, and the three smaller ones were occupied by himself, Jimmy Tau and Dr. Ho. Modest was far too elegant a word for the spartan facilities, John decided as he splashed water on himself while standing in the stream in his shorts. He hadn't expected much, but he had envisioned a far more permanent community, something larger with more people. This was the headquarters of the entire Viet Minh? He'd have to question Jimmy on that one.

John was lacing up his jump boots when a small boy standing below the floor of the cabin called to him in Vietnamese. The boy indicated by sign language that John was to come with him to one of the communal huts. A light rain had begun again as John ran over to the hut while carrying a poncho over his head and shoulders so as to attempt to keep somewhat dry. Comrade Van was waiting for him along with three other Vietnamese. One of these men stood out from the others because he was at something approximating parade rest. Taller than the others, Thanh wanted to, and did, project the image of a soldier. Comrade Van had encouraged him to retain his French-trained military demeanor. Giap was building an army and he wanted his officers to carry themselves as professionals. Soon there would be hundreds, maybe thousands, like Thanh. The Peoples Liberation Army of Vietnam would someday be as distinguished as the best French units, he had said to his new fine young officer. It was what Thanh had dreamed of. In the meantime, they would carry on their task as a guerrilla force.

The first major disappointment with John Guthrie came when Comrade Van's handpicked attack team cadre learned that their great American expert did not have the faintest idea how to field strip the two .30 caliber light machine guns that had been included in the collection of weapons they had seen being so carefully inventoried that morning. John admitted he didn't even know how to load and fire the weapon. Comrade Van did not stay around to hear any more of the American officer's inadequacy. Thanh was introduced as the man who would be the team leader for the Tam Dao operation. He was also the only one of the several guerrillas in the kerosene-lit hut who spoke French. Thanh's knowledge of the language was about the same as John's and that placed them on an equal footing in that regard. John was happy for small favors after the embarrassment of the machine gun. It was obvious that his standing in military terms had taken a severe blow when he looked at the faces of the Viet fighters standing next to Thanh. No impassive orientalism here, John thought. Thanh, however, showed nothing at all, but thought it was obvious John as an officer never should be expected to be able to dismantle a machine gun anyhow—at least in a French army.

For John's part, the most important issue of the moment was the actual attack plans. If they couldn't use the machine guns, it was too damn bad. As he began to review the scheme that de Laborde, Edouard, and himself had so carefully worked over, John noticed the tall Vietnamese watching him closely. Thanh said nothing, but he had suddenly realized that this was the same American he had seen during that patrol with Sgt. Vogel. This was the one with the montagnards. He thought of telling John that he had been with Vogel and then decided against it. He would speak first to Comrade Van. There might be some political element involved and it would be best to clear it with his superior. At the moment, what was important to know was that this American officer was experienced in the field. That was a good mark.

Regarding the attack plans, John was pleased to find that there were no serious objections from the guerrillas. Their team leader, Thanh, appeared to know his stuff, and aside from a few minor adjustments and suggestions, the planning session went well. Thanh seemed to know the layout of the camp where the French civilians were held, and that was key. He told John that they had made a reconnaissance of the area immediately upon being told of the assignment. They even noted there had been an alteration of the guard shifts. John realized that at least as far as this Thanh was concerned, he had a capable team leader along on the mission.

They did have a problem with the availability of French-speaking females to assist in handling the French women internees. John discussed this at length with Thanh who, in turn, translated to the others. John was impressed with the way the tall man maintained command yet at the same time was careful to include his men in all the conversation and, presumably, decision making. They decided that they would keep trying to find French speakers, but if none were produced, they all agreed they would have to go ahead without them. John was not about to be deterred over that shortfall. The most important factor was that they all seemed to get along well—after the disappointment over the machine guns. John did not know it, but Thanh had told his companions that John was a famous American soldier. That little bit of military morale support came right out of Comrade Li's instructions on pre-operational motivation. Thanh was not one to overlook a good lesson.

With the help of Thanh and his two companions, John completed the sorting out of the weapons and supplies as well as constructing a canvas shelter for the collection. Each of the Vietnamese guerrillas took turns checking out the armament. Jimmy Tau returned later in the afternoon as they were finishing up getting the materiel under cover. He was eager to learn how the meeting had turned out. Speaking in English, John mentioned their disappointment over his lack of ordnance knowledge. Jimmy laughed and said something to the three Vietnamese in their language. They all laughed in return, saluted John, and headed off still laughing.

"What the hell did you say to them? I didn't know you could speak Vietnamese."

"I don't really—just a few phrases and enough to get my shirts washed. I told them you were a very old man and used to fighting with swords not machine guns. At least that's what I think I said. I don't know what the word is for sword so I said 'long knives.' As you could see, I just pointed to the guns because I don't know what that is either."

"You could have said anything, then," John said, not very amused.

"I think they got my meaning. They laughed, didn't they? The important thing is that you seemed to get along. Don't worry about the machine-gun thing. They'll figure it out. When it comes to any sort of gun, they're naturals. I told you they were waiting for you to make the first move."

"Well, actually your Mr. Giap came up to me. He was wearing the suit you spoke about. He certainly seemed out of place. He introduced himself as Van and later he sent a kid to come get me. He seemed like a decent enough sort. Speaks extremely good French—far better than mine. Very polite."

"That's great that he and you got along. He's the key guy for you around here. Uncle Ho's the boss, of course, but when it comes to military and security matters, Comrade Van's your boy."

"So which do I call him—Giap or Van? He introduced himself as Van."

"I've always called him Van or Comrade Van. He knows we all know his name, so it isn't a big secret. In a way he's better known than Dr. Ho because Vo Nguyen Giap is his real name. Come to think of it, I often call him Giap if I'm talking or writing about him officially. I use Van around here because everyone else refers to him that way to me. I never had to think about it before. I'll tell you more about him over dinner."

Later on, they had an excellent meal of noodles and fish prepared by the multitalented Mac Soo, who had caught his daily quota. He had turned over a portion of the catch to the camp mess for everyone to enjoy. Usually they all ate in a communal mess which doubled as the housing for the many visitors who came and went. That night they ate in John's cabin in order to talk more freely of his meeting earlier in the day. John went over the principal points of the attack plan, mentioning the fact that Thanh had impressed him with his military manner and operational know-how.

"He definitely looks like somebody they've got big plans for. I wish we knew more about him, but it's impossible to inquire without seeming nosy. I get along here by not asking too many questions. Eventually stuff just seeps out, but you gotta wait," Jimmy said.

Mac Soo didn't talk much, but he seemed to listen carefully. John didn't know whether the radioman was really interested or just being polite. John was hesitant to ask about Mac's background for fear that it would appear to show a lack of trust. For the present he decided that it was best just to go along with Jimmy Tau's obvious approval of the guy. Jimmy went on at some length in front of Mac to extol his capabilities as a radioman.

"Mac's the best there is. He can send by key and code, if necessary—and whatever he does he can do in English or Chinese. He's picked up some Vietnamese now, too. And best of all, if something needs repairing, he can handle whatever it is. We'd be lost if it wasn't for Mac."

Mac Soo, embarrassed but pleased, attempted to deflect the praise by refilling the tin teacups.

"Jimmy thinks anything technical is special. That's because he's an engineer. I've told him that it is far more difficult to catch fish than work the radio," Mac replied smiling. Mac Soo spoke English well, if with a strong Chinese accent.

Jimmy Tau, never at a loss for words, filled the after-dinner conversation with his own story of how he ended up in AGAS.

"So I headed across the border right after Pearl Harbor and met up with some other guys from Haiphong. We figured our contacts might be useful. And sort of freelanced it for a while with Chinese Army support. We had quite a good thing going and then AGAS came along and wanted me to help with their setup, which is how I ended up here with my commission."

As much as Jimmy seemed to like to talk, John realized he also used his apparent openness to guard what he didn't want to discuss. There was clearly a big gap between the "freelance" days and AGAS, but Jimmy was not about to fill in the blanks. The one thing that was clear was that Jimmy Tau had a good deal of information at his fingertips.

"Tell me more about this guy, Giap," John said, not wanting the conversation to lean too heavily on personal history which might oblige him to reciprocate.

"Sure. Most of my info is pretty generally known—at least among those people who want to know these things. The French were always after him along with other… political criminals they called them. I think he was a college professor or something in teaching. At any rate, somewhere around 1940, I guess, he must have escaped arrest and fled to China. The next year, and this was before Pearl Harbor, apparently the *Sûreté*… now under Vichy control… grabbed up his wife and sister-in-law. She, the sister-in-law, supposedly was brutally interrogated and eventually hanged or guillotined by the French. The wife also died in prison in Hanoi, but I think that was from illness or maltreatment, although maybe the French executed her also. As you can imagine, this is not something that Giap talks about much. It doesn't take much of a brain to figure out the guy's state of mind, though. He's got to have a really big hate on for the French."

"How could he be otherwise? What about his politics? What started him off?"

"Oh, he's a communist, of course… just like Dr. Ho. But who the hell knows what that means here. They're all Vietnamese and that's a special breed. I guess you figured that out by now."

John shifted the conversation to the local scene, asking about the little community of which they were now a part.

"There's a village a few miles away, Kim Lung. This place is strictly Uncle Ho country. They are the eyes and ears for the headquarters here where we are. Damn good security, Major. Only the inner circle are welcome here at this camp," Jimmy Tau recounted.

"So where will my Tam Dao team come from, aside from the three I've already met?"

"Oh, they've got security patrols roaming all over. They can draw people, fighters, in from all over. In their own way they're very organized and disciplined. Not what we'd think was so great, but it works for them."

"So you think we can do the job?"

"If I didn't, with all respect, sir. I would have said so when we first got the message."

It was the first time that Jimmy Tau had exhibited annoyance and even then, it was with a smile. Although he was always careful to acknowledge John's higher military rank, it was clear that in certain areas he considered his professional judgement not to be questioned. Yes, John thought, this is a man who is used to running his own show. The clever AGAS colonel wouldn't have stuck him down here in this key spot if that hadn't been the case. Smiling Jimmy Tau was no neophyte.

"Okay, of course you would have, Jimmy. I asked the question because I got the sense from my talk with Thanh and the two others that they expected me to lead them in the operation. I just got here. I don't know the terrain or the personnel. How the hell can I lead them?" John asked, skillfully getting around Tau's earlier indication of pique.

"They do not want you to lead them," Mac Soo broke in unexpectedly. "They want you to tell them that you have confidence in them… that they can do the job, as you say. That's all they want or maybe need… uh, Major, sir."

"That's very good to hear, Mac," said John having learned much more from his two companions than he had expected, or they quite realized. It was one of the reasons John liked to work alone.

Mac Soo was right. The next day John reviewed the attack plans once more with Thanh. Afterwards he very formally asked the young Vietnamese to take over as leader of the operation. Solemnly, Thanh agreed. The first rule of union organization had been observed: let the locals run the show, if they can. John was happy to play the role of observer, advisor, and cheerleader. Mac Soo knew more than just radios when it came to dealing with the Viet Minh.

The attack on Tam Dao was set to begin in 48 hours. One French-speaking woman had been found, but she was Dr. Ho's personal nurse. When Jimmy Tau heard about this, he became uncharacteristically, and quite visibly, upset. John finally got the story after considerable effort. It appeared that Jimmy Tau had had his eye on this young lady ever since his arrival—but to no avail. Jimmy had visions of his little beauty—a proprietary sense totally without justification—being killed or otherwise injured in the attack. The fact that this amour was strictly one-sided mattered not at all to the smitten engineer from MIT. He insisted on accompanying John who had been invited to visit with a now much healthier Dr. Ho, eager to meet with the American major before the politically important mission.

Jimmy Tau wanted to put in a final plea directly to Uncle for his heartthrob to be dropped from the team. Unfortunately, the young lady, Truyen, was by Ho's side when they arrived. This was embarrassing for Jimmy who had not expected her to be present during his well-rehearsed speech, even though John had warned him this might be the case. In the end Uncle Ho saved the situation.

"Ah, Jimmy, we are all so proud of our brave little rose who will be taking care of those unfortunate women and children in the Tam Dao camp."

Jimmy's planned eloquent speech was ruined by that single sentence of the wily old man. Ho knew all about Jimmy's unrequited love, for he was the one who originally encouraged him. Truyen was of another mind, however, and the young Chinese American officer was left out on a limb. Jimmy Tau just stood by Ho's bedside looking forlorn. John was torn between feeling sorry for his colleague and bursting out in laughter at the absurdity of it all. He really didn't see a big risk for the girl in rounding up the women and children. Again, Dr. Ho came to the rescue by quickly moving the conversation along.

"Finally I get to greet you, Major Guthrie, and welcome you to our luxurious surroundings. I apologize for not being able to see you earlier. You see this dear Truyen may be pretty, but she is also very strict. What is that word in English you use?"

"Bossy? Is that the word you're looking for, sir?" John replied.

"Exactly the word, Major. She's very bossy."

Ho had spoken in English, but then translated what he had just said into French for his nurse. She giggled demurely and made no effort to contradict him. It was an enormous responsibility to be the old man's sole caregiver. She wasn't really a trained nurse, merely a former hospital orderly, yet she had to minister to the health of this great man who was far from being an easy patient. Ho had lost a considerable amount of weight since John had met him in Kunming and in addition his skin was jaundiced. John was not prepared for the gaunt sickly figure propped up before him. But the voice was the same Ho Chi Minh of before. In spite of his enfeebled state, the presence was still commanding. This is one tough old bird, John thought.

"It is my pleasure to meet with you again, sir. I bring greetings from all your friends at AGAS in Ch'ing-hsi, Gen. Chennault, and of course my colleague Capt. Edouard Parnell who I hope may soon join us here. The AGAS people told me I should ask if there is anything that you need. They will arrange for it to be dropped by parachute."

"It is nice to have good friends," said Ho. "I have no needs myself. This little fever is merely an inconvenience. I look forward to the arrival of Captain Parnell and his very excellent French. I like to keep in practice with my languages. By the way, Major, did you know that Parnell is the name of an important Irish nationalist. Do you know anything about the Irish fight for freedom against the English?"

"No, sir. In my family we've always been more interested in Scots nationalism."

"Yes, of course. Guthrie is a Scottish name. Do you have a kilt, Major?"

"No, but my father does."

"I should know more about Scottish history. If you know of a good book I could read, I would be most grateful."

"I shall send a signal to my Irish colleague to see what can be done. I think a request to provide a great Vietnamese leader with a book on Scots history should really bring us some attention."

"You have a devilish sense of humor, Major John Guthrie."

"And you, sir, understand it far too well, I might say with the utmost respect."

Ho Chi Minh laughed until his coughing forced him to stop. It had been an excellent exchange between the two men. The laughter coming from the wooden hut was heard about the camp and duly noted. More than even the arrival of the weapons, this signified a special status for the very tall foreigner. In the tight environment of the Kim Lung camp the news of the man who made Uncle laugh would spread immediately and ensure respect for John's presence.

Jimmy naturally heard the exchange but could barely muster a smile. He was far too involved with drinking in every essence of the angel-faced Miss Truyen, who steadfastly kept her eyes focused downward. Ho tired fast after his coughing siege and John offered his goodbye. Ho made an effort to recover and wished John the best of luck in the Tam Dao operation. The American major turned to go but had to tug on Jimmy's arm to awake him from his reverie. They left the cabin that way with John navigating Jimmy through the doorway tightly holding on to Tau's elbow. Only then did Truyen lift her eyes.

The plan John and Thanh had agreed upon was for the American to accompany the guerrilla team, numbering close to 50, to a point where John could observe most of the action although not actually participate in the initial assault. Thanh made it clear he did not want to accept responsibility for getting an honored guest shot. There was little John could do in practical terms with his lack of Vietnamese language or knowledge of the personnel. He had already exerted the maximum control he could in the tactical planning phase and was satisfied at this stage to go along "for the ride."

The idea of cleaning up the light machine guns for use in the attack was abandoned. They were heavily coated with cosmoline grease and wrapped in waterproofed tar paper. The weapons would have had to have been perfectly cleaned after field stripping, and that would have taken too long to be useful for this mission. John was impressed with the way Thanh seemed to be in perpetual motion, giving instructions to one group, helping another by inspecting their weapons. He was everywhere.

The worried "godfathers" back in Ch'ing-hsi had burned up the airwaves with radio signals querying the status of the mission, Ho's health, John's health, the weather, and just about everything else that might remotely affect the Tam Dao strike. John was happy to get out of radio range and on his way.

The earlier reconnaissance had confirmed the laxness of the guards, but it also had been reported that the internees were not in good shape. There apparently was a good deal of illness, though it couldn't be determined what exactly was the problem. It was clear, however, that quite a few of the French men and women were in a very debilitated state. The problem of caring for these people afterwards was going to be considerable. Truyen had pulled together several helpers to handle the women, but now a small cadre of men had to be added to assist with any ill and enfeebled males. There was no information on any children.

The expedition had ballooned to over 60, what with the extra "medical" personnel and a small team of porters carrying everything from food for the internees to ammunition and the newly arrived medical supplies. Thanh explained that normally they would have simply eaten and drunk whatever was available along the route, but with a group this large they had to be considerate of the poor country people from whom they would have to requisition these supplies. John was struck by the political discipline of this rag-tag group of fighters.

Jimmy Tau had wanted to come along, but John was adamant in his denial. He gave several excellent-sounding reasons to do with AGAS priorities. However, the real reason was that he knew that Jimmy wanted just to look after Truyen—who obviously did not need any looking after. John did accept a battery-run radio that had a radius just far enough to have a chance to communicate directly with Mac Soo and what would be the anxious Jimmy Tau. A simple code was agreed upon for this vital communication. The extra porters made it possible to transport the heavy battery ensemble as the stretched-out column snaked its way via back trails. With an overnight stop near a known friendly village, the march took most of a long day and a half. By mid-afternoon, the various elements were gathered together at the appointed jump-off site.

John held a final meeting with Thanh and his squad leaders. Scouts were dispatched to ascertain any late changes in the camp's physical set up or the presence of any unexpected Japanese relief units. The several hours before the early evening zero hour were used by John to go over, for the last time, Thanh's tactical strike plan and the after-action arrangement for the gathering and removal of the internees. Some trusted local people in the Tam Dao area had been recruited to assist in providing immediate shelter if any was needed. John was more than satisfied with the organization of the operation.

Thanh mentioned that, as far as he knew, this was the largest and most complex effort in which Viet Minh forces had been involved. He said it matter-of-factly as if he was a manager judging a sports team. It occurred to John that Horse Simpson would have loved young Thanh who, coolly professional, showed not one sign of trepidation. John, on the other hand, was more than a little anxious. Up to this point everything concerned with the mission had been future oriented. The future had now arrived and there was no time left for plan alterations. What they had there at that moment, about a mile and a half from the prison camp, was all they were going to have. His motley-dressed and armed companions ate and rested, seemingly oblivious to what would occur in the next few hours, while John concentrated on stripping and cleaning his carbine and .45 automatic as a distraction.

Thanh dropped by and reminded John that he would move John with Truyen's group to a spot closer to the camp about a half hour before the strike was launched. As if they hadn't already discussed the matter several times before, it was reiterated that John's group would remain there until sent for after the area had been secured. It had been agreed that if anything went wrong, John was to take the entire support group, including Truyen with her people and the porters, and head as fast as they could back up the trail they had just come down. Each agreed with the other that it was just a precaution and that no such problem was expected. By that time, John and Thanh had grown confident of each other's ability to do their job.

The fighters had all moved into their positions before John and the support group arrived at their forward site. John had hoped for a vantage point from which he could observe the action, but that was impossible whilst also staying hidden with his group in the heavy foliage surrounding the camp and its barbed-wire perimeter. The wire was separated from the surrounding forest by about 30 to 50 yards of cleared land. John's group held back an additional hundred yards, though the fighters had crawled right up to the edge of the dense tree line. The better shots among Thanh's men had been designated as snipers with the on-duty guards as their individual targets.

The tactical plan called for Thanh and two guerrillas to head directly for the wire which they would cut before a steady stream of covering fire was laid down by the fighters at the tree edge. Another wire-cutting team would hit the perimeter at the same time on the other side of the camp similarly covered. Thanh and his team would burst through, followed closely by two five-man squads, from the trees, as would the group on the other side of the camp. Thanh was then supposed to head to the camp commandant's shack and grenade it. The rest of the attack team would remain at the tree edge pouring careful fire into the Japanese barracks until they received the whistle signal to follow in a second wave. It was textbook assault tactics.

The only surprise was that everything went off exactly as planned—a rare occurrence in military operations. The snipers all hit their targets. The wire was cut, and the initial teams were through within 30 seconds of the commencement of the cover fire. Thanh never had to grenade the commandant's quarters because the astonished officer ran out into a hail of bullets. Most of the rest of the guards died in a similar way, though their barracks were grenaded for good measure. Several who were wounded were dispatched with shots to the head. Not a single guerrilla was wounded, even though two suffered severe gashes as they rushed too eagerly through the cut wire. The entire operation was over in what Thanh triumphantly calculated was seven minutes, maybe eight. He had taken up a position in a chair on the porch of the former commandant's quarters and was smoking a cigarette when John and the entire support group arrived to care for the babbling and weeping internees.

"An excellent job, *bien fait, chef*," John congratulated Thanh.

"*Merci, mon Commandant*," replied Thanh. "I think you should get your radio going now, Major." It was the first time John had seen the young Vietnamese officer look happy. It didn't last long for he was quickly back to business while John sought out the porters with the radio equipment.

As calculatedly successful as the attack had been, the securing of the internees was near chaotic. The French civilians were convinced the Vietnamese had attacked the camp in order to get at them and kill them. The situation was not helped by the guerrillas setting about systematically to rifle through the dead soldiers' possessions and collect all their weapons. As John and Thanh had previously agreed, the Viet Minh fighters were ordered to search all the bodies for anything of intelligence value such as ID papers and official documentation. Naturally, they also took anything else they deemed valuable. This included bits of uniform that a guerrilla might wish to have as a souvenir of his conquest.

Lining up the dead guards in a neat row while wearing a stolen Japanese cap and a newly acquired leather uniform belt created a fearful picture for the already traumatized civilians. They were convinced they were about to pay the price for the decades of colonial oppression that France had heaped upon a population they disparagingly referred to as Annamites. The women's wailing melded in an unhappy chorus with children crying and men shouting as the guerrillas joked among themselves and Truyen tried valiantly to quiet the hysterical former prisoners. It did not help that the swiftly encroaching darkness added an eerie half-light to the macabre scene. The one positive element was that it wasn't raining.

Truyen patiently explained repeatedly to adults and children, to men and women that the guerrillas were there to rescue them, not harm them. Meanwhile John had set up the radio and sent out the coded signal of operational success. Thanh went over to John to ask whether he thought it a good idea to bury the dead Japanese.

"I never thought of that, Thanh. Why would we want to do that?"

"I was just asking your opinion, Major."

"Well, chief, my opinion is that there are too many of them to bury without putting your men to a lot of hard work. Why don't you try and find some canvas tarps or something and just cover them up? It might quiet down these civilians if they don't have to look at the dead Japs."

At that point Truyen came over and insisted John come with her to the women's compound that was now crowded also with their men. She wanted him to speak to the French and quiet them down. It was less a request than it was an order, not unlike the manner Dr. Ho had referred to as "bossy." Thanh gave him a knowing smile as the tall American was led over by the diminutive Vietnamese doll who occasionally would prod him to move a bit faster.

John did his best to talk some sense to the frightened collection before him. He didn't have the vocabulary adequate to quell their fears nor the answers to the many questions shouted at him that he barely understood. Finally, as he clearly was having no impact, Truyen edged John aside and screeched at the throng to be quiet. As nurses sometimes do, she had arrived at the point where the caring bedside manner gave way to a demand for attention and response.

"This man is an American. He is trying to tell you that you have nothing to fear. We are here to help you and free you from the Japanese. He is Major John of the American Army. He has come a long way just to help you. We are helping him, don't you understand? We are the Viet Minh. We are not your enemy. I am a nurse and I want to care for your sick."

While her high-pitched voice tended to work against her command manner, the combination of the two ultimately quieted the crowd. John watched in amusement as this young pretty girl, dark eyes concentrating on particular individuals as an experienced lawyer does in attempting to control a jury, slowly brought calm. Having their attention, she now brought them around to helping themselves.

"You need to have someone to speak for you so that my staff and I can properly respond to your needs. We cannot do anything for you if you are all shouting at once."

An older woman stood up and said she had been elected to be the women's representative while the Japanese were running the camp, and if they wanted, she would carry on in the same manner. Then a man stood up saying more or less the same thing. John didn't like the implication that the situation hadn't changed but admitted to himself it was the best way to deal with a difficult circumstance. As soon as the crowd of internees lost their fears, it was amazing how quickly they reverted from weeping supplicants to determined colonists demanding care. Truyen appeared to ignore the change in manner and concentrated on directing her meager "staff" to assist those truly in need. John was far less understanding and soon left the scene of people who should have been grateful for their freedom, but instead seemed all too willing to treat their rescuers as servants.

The original intention—which now seemed quite absurd to John—was to move the freed French about five miles up the road where they could be bedded down in a small village for the night. To move this demanding and argumentative menagerie in the dark was impossible. It was best to stay right where they were till first light. This would give Truyen and her people a chance to assess and treat any with serious problems. John helped in the triage and then went to find Thanh and organize some cooking fires to prepare the food they had brought along. Thanh had already turned to that task but had discovered also a large stock of foodstuff which he was in the process of having his men separate out for immediate consumption and the rest for transporting back to Kim Lung.

Here and there cooking fires sprung up, providing light about the area. Men darted around on errands ordered by Thanh. There was nothing for John to do without getting in the way. Truyen and her medical helpers were working directly with the former internees who needed care. John decided to sit on the porch of the dead camp commander's shack where he had found Thanh immediately after the raid. The chair was still there but John decided that it was not his to occupy. Thanh had earned that throne; John had done nothing but followed along. He sat on the porch floor, legs dangling over the edge, and watched as the substantial team of Viet Minh fighters went about their tasks with order and discipline. John marveled at the previously bloodthirsty guerrillas now so quickly restoring what they had so recently devastated. The dead soldiers had been carefully laid out as in formation on the side of the camp near the wire. Their bodies were neatly covered with tent canvas. No one went near that parade of the dead as darkness provided an additional blanket of cover for the makeshift cemetery.

It had been an extraordinary experience for John. An entire contingent of Japs wiped out and he hadn't fired a single shot. In fact, he never came near to firing his weapon. He had given no direct orders, shot at nothing, and basically stayed behind with the women and old men of Truyen's troop. How many more were there in the Viet Minh like Thanh? They certainly didn't need much other than supplies. They could be trained to use more advanced weapons, but even that could be overcome if necessary, by their own ability to learn on their own. Did they know they had that all in their own hands? Did Ho know that? Was it all a pretense, this supposed need for American assistance?

The fires flickered in the night, mesmerizing John. Just a year before he'd been in the Vosges, running to and fro with his *maquisards,* avoiding and ambushing German patrols. Another world, another era. So far away. And here now a new world, a surreal world of doll-like women and fresh-faced young men who can care for the ill and emotionlessly kill. And yet John felt surprisingly at home, at home in an entirely alien environment. There had been stress aplenty, but he had come through with no pain in his gut. In a sense he was totally at the mercy of the little Vietnamese all around him, yet he felt perfectly secure. He did not speak their language, but nonetheless he was one of them. They smiled at him, they saluted him. He knew they would give or get him whatever he wanted; if he was hurt or sick they would care for him. Jimmy Tau had said it: a different breed he'd called them. An amazing breed that certainly could be a deadly enemy—but also perhaps a loyal friend. Time would tell, he thought. Meanwhile he would enjoy the experience. Just weeks before in the mountains with the Gorilla Mission his view of the country was totally different. Had he changed that much? What was it?

Deep in thought, entranced by the yellow light from the cooking fires, John was surprised by Thanh's arrival.

"You should come, Major. Truyen asks you to listen to the story these French are telling."

John slipped off the porch, regretfully, and hurried over to where Truyen had set up her infirmary. The man who had introduced himself as the men's representative was regaling Truyen with the group's history. He stopped when John arrived.

"Monsieur, here, was telling us of how they all got here. I thought it was important that you hear him, Major. Please, monsieur, repeat briefly what you've just told me."

Quickly, the spokesman explained that they were all refugees from the floods in the Red River delta. They had been thrown together in Hanoi where the municipal government had temporarily housed them in a small hotel. Most of the people had never known each other before. This had all happened before the March 9 Japanese takeover. They had been moved to a government rest house in Son Tay just that week when the word spread that French Colonial Army units were moving north. This group of refugees decided to follow them, but their carts and wagons just couldn't keep up.

At this point the man hesitated. Truyen encouraged him to go on. This was the part she hadn't yet heard. Slowly, the Frenchman began again, clearly embarrassed at what he was about to reveal.

"We were stuck there. We didn't know whether to go forward or back. We were sure the Japanese would soon arrive to kill us. A column of Japanese soldiers did arrive and we knew our time had come. But this officer just had us move our carts to the side of the road to let his soldiers through. We were so happy. But here is what he said to us. He said that there were Vietnamese rebels rampaging around the countryside. I'm sorry, but that was what he told us. We had no way of knowing... I am so very sorry to tell you this, but I want to be completely truthful."

"Go on, continue with your story," Thanh said from behind John. It was obvious that Thanh was not happy with this version by the Frenchman.

"Well, we had no food or anything. I have to explain that. We didn't know which way to go when the Japanese officer returned the following morning in a staff car. I figure he must have been a colonel or something. He said we should proceed under his protection to Tam Dao where there was this small camp that had been designated as a supply site for his troops. He said we could stay there, here, where they, the Japanese, would give us food, shelter, and protection until something could be figured out. So we came here. The lieutenant in charge wanted us to keep separate from his troops who were there to guard their supplies, and that's why we are separated like this. He was a good friend to us. We weren't their prisoners. They were protecting us!"

The last sentence was delivered with hands stretched out, palms upward, imploring understanding. The man broke down and began to cry.

"I do not like this story or this man," Thanh whispered hoarsely to John.

John took the Viet Minh officer aside and asked him, "Do you think he's lying? Why would he lie?"

"I just don't like him. Even if he's telling the truth, he's saying that he likes the Japanese more than he does us, and I don't like that."

It was a sensitive situation that demanded a degree of diplomatic skill of which John felt woefully inadequate. Not only was it difficult for him to argue in French to the degree required by the circumstance, John wasn't sure what the reaction would be among the other guerrillas if Thanh shared with them his reaction to this story. He decided that the best course of action would be to declare victory and let it go at that. He took Thanh aside and spoke to him in as confidential tone as he could muster.

"My dear friend, I have no doubts that you are absolutely correct. However, nothing says we have to like these people. Our job, yours and mine, was to get them out of the hands of the Japanese. It was for a political reason and Uncle wants us to do it. It is not always easy to fully understand politics, but that is not our job. It is enough that Uncle and Comrade Van wanted it done. We have succeeded and that's all that is important."

Nothing else needed to be said. John had said the magic names and that was all that Thanh required.

"You are of course right, Major. It is best we don't discuss this with any of the others. They are happy with the idea we have freed prisoners. Sometimes it is best not to explain too much to the... ordinary soldier. I shall mention this to Truyen, though."

John nodded with as much gravity as he could muster—and not an inconsiderable sense of relief.

The post-action plan called for the entire group of French civilians to be transported to the Tuyen Quang region about 20 miles from Kim Lung, well within the Viet Minh controlled area. The job had been made much easier by the availability of two Japanese Army trucks at the camp. The previous intention of commandeering wagons from nearby farmers thankfully could be abandoned. One truck held all 20 civilians and the second truck contained the food plus Thanh and some guerrillas as a protective force. There was no trouble expected heading north into strong Viet Minh territory, but it was prudent nonetheless. Truyen was to ride along with her helpers in the second truck with Thanh, but switched at the last minute to care for one of the children who was still ill from flu and quite dehydrated.

Truyen was very much in charge now that the mission had moved on to the second phase of strictly caring for the refugees. Thanh was happy to turn over the job of wet nursing the civilians, even if doing so carried with it a certain loss of authority. The American major had seen what a fine job they had done and would certainly tell Comrade Van about the action. The Viet Minh guerrilla team had done everything that had been asked of them, and with no real casualties. What's more, they now had two excellent trucks. It had been a very successful raid. Comrade Van had to be pleased.

John marched back to the Kim Lung headquarters with the rest of the attack force. There was no one with which to talk French in the group, though one of the original team leaders he had first met with Thanh did have a few words adequate to explain important functions such as, eat, rest, stop, go. The rest of the happy group just strolled along chatting and laughing as if they had just come from a picnic. John decided that they must have been rather sure no Jap soldiers were in the region. It was a good time for him to reflect on the fact that the Japanese were protecting the civilians rather than interning them. It made the wiping out of the Japanese guards less than the heroic action it otherwise would have been nor the political *coup de maître* that had been the sales point for Ho. After the initial surprise, the situation did not appear to bother either Thanh or even the angelic Truyen. John had no feelings for the Japanese; they were his enemies and he should have no qualms about the how or why of their deaths, but it nonetheless bothered him. He wasn't new to this business of war, yet he was still perplexed by his concern. Push it out of your mind, he told himself. Enjoy the win, Horse Simpson would say. It was a nice early summer day in Tonkin as a shower periodically floated down, cooling the perfumed air. It was a day to enjoy… one day in a long war.

Chapter Nine

"It is inconceivable to me how they can be so stupid. They have no knowledge of the region. They have hardly anyone who can speak local languages. They have no experience with the Annamites, at all. They have a child's conception of the problems here and also a puerile view of colonialism. They have their colonies: Hawaii, Alaska, Puerto Rico, others, but we're not supposed to have ours. It's so sanctimonious… as if we should ignore their double faces. And this Philippines independence charade is, well, just that, a charade. I tell you………"

Commandant Jean Sainteny had been ranting on and off since his arrival that morning at his M.5 office in Kunming. His adjutant listened patiently, nodding every now and then to agree with his superior's view. He had heard the theme before, but this morning's tirade was longer and harsher.

"I have reached the end of my tether, the end of my patience with this business. I get no guidance from Calcutta and no response to my questions from Paris. They want us to perform miracles. *Mon Dieu*, the fact that I haven't shot that Castelli yet is a miracle."

The adjutant smiled broadly hoping to mollify Sainteny. The commandant acknowledged his own little joke with an exaggerated head shake.

"Yes, certainly it is a bit funny, without doubt, but that man Castelli, that shrimp, is a troublemaker. He thinks I am taken in by his artificial friendliness. I am never quite sure whether the things that go on are American policy or if it is just some brainstorm of that little Italian. It was bad enough I had to stand for the embarrassing treatment by Alessandri, that Vichy toady, without having to listen to the phony sympathies of *le nouveau Commandant* Castelli. You remember that incident?"

"Oui, mon Commandant."

"I wish I could blame it all on him, but I'm sure he's getting his marching orders from Washington. I'm worried about Chungking also. It smells as

157

if there's a business deal in progress here between the Ami's and Chiang Kai-shek. I can't figure out what the Americans get in exchange for handing over Indochina—or at least most of it—to the Chinese. Or does Washington want it all for themselves? And of course we are getting absolutely no help from Paris one way or the other. We've got to take a firm line. We must do it now. What do you think, lieutenant?"

Jean Sainteny was not really looking for an answer from his adjutant. The lieutenant read the signs he had seen before. Sainteny was about to take some action. Best to keep one's mouth shut. He knew how to remain silent when policy might be made for which he would be asked to share in the blame if things went wrong. On the other hand, if everything progressed well, he was, after all, still close enough to gain some reflected credit. The young adjutant did allow himself one observation.

"I am not sure, sir, that American and Chinese interests in Indochina coincide. I think that perhaps Chungking would like it to appear that way, but they've had their eye on Indochina for a long time. No matter what the Americans may think, I believe that Chiang and the Kuomintang have their own ambitions, sir."

"Good comment. I believe I wrote something similar to that to Paris last month, remember?"

"Yes, sir. I was just reminding you," the adjutant said disingenuously.

"It is time to move authoritatively to protect France's interests, Maurice."

The lieutenant knew when Sainteny was about to make a big decision. The commandant would use his adjutant's first name. It was a psychological device linking the two of them in the action that was to follow.

"I want you to send a signal to our people halting forthwith all collaboration in joint operations—that includes training—with the OSS. And, yes, that includes the Hanoi rail and communications project."

Long before John had jumped into Kim Lung, Major Jacques de Laborde already had seconded a newly arrived M.5 senior lieutenant to work with the OSS team in Ch'ing-hsi. Lt. Guy Montfort had been on General Alessandri's Vichy staff while acting at the same time as a valued Free French agent—a fact to which John and Edouard had been sworn to secrecy. The English-speaking former Legion officer was now in training with Applegate and the other newly assigned Americans. Montfort's extensive field experience in Tonkin was expected to be of great aid to the Moose Mission, no matter their ultimate objectives. No one had asked for authorization for this. It was just one of those private arrangements arrived at by field officers with shared low opinions of military bureaucracy. Special Operations officers tended to have this attitude even more than most. Jacques de Laborde had always run his own show out of Ch'ing-his, and he reacted predictably to Sainteny's directive.

"I tell you, Edouard, this is the most absurd thing I've ever heard. I am certainly not going to cut off my plans with you and your team—especially when John is away and counting on our cooperation. This fool Sainteny has not the slightest comprehension of matters in the field. This makes me completely furious. What right does that commandant pig piss have to tell any of us what to do? Who the hell made him Napoleon's Marshal? He has never seen a day of combat in his life. He can shove this piece of dog shit up his rectum. Let that *bourgeois parvenu* come down here in person and tell me to break off my American contacts. I'll show that *pédale* what he can do with his orders."

The words were raw, even in his exquisite Parisian diction, but Jacques de Laborde's voice retained its most aristocratically controlled tone. Edouard marveled at the man's calculatedly vulgar use of language.

Jacques de Laborde was not the sort of man who allowed those above him in the line of command to rule his life. He carried with him the *droit du seigneur* as another might a hefty club. It was a weapon that was held quietly, appropriate to his own sense of class. He explained all this to Edouard.

"There are always ways for the imaginative to overcome the brainless, no matter the latter's perceived rank."

The two men sat stretched out on immense silk pillows placed on the heavily carpeted floor of Ch'ing-hsi's most exclusive club. This was the officers-only, very private bordello located in what had been the home of a rich merchant. The courtyard contained lovely hanging ivy and flowering plants providing a luxurious outdoor setting for drinking and dining when the weather permitted. Inside, private rooms each had their own maidservant to respond to all non-sexual needs of the visitors. The courtesans, as Jacques liked to refer to the high-priced prostitutes, came and went as the "club members" desired their services. It was all very civilized in a community where nothing else fit that term. It was Edouard's second visit as a guest of the French major. Just like any club back in New York or Boston, one had to have a sponsor before joining. Jacques de Laborde called it his office. Like the high-ranking Chinese officers who made up a large portion of the clientele, he often had his most confidential discussions in the seclusion of the house's private rooms.

"It is now our task, Edouard, to defeat the bourgeois mentality of that hotel concierge, Jean Sainteny, and I believe I have the method."

Consistent with the ambiance they were drinking cognac, real cognac, and speaking in French. It was, as Edouard would explain to John later, quite *comme il faut*.

"This doesn't involve assassination, does it, Jacques?" said Edouard sipping from his snifter.

Edouard had tried to treat his surroundings in the blasé manner he believed appropriate to men of the world. The other time he had been Jacques' guest at this establishment, he had been blind drunk and barely conscious. Afterwards he had to be told what a fine time he'd had. This time, nearly sober, he was totally insecure and nervous, though these were the last characteristics he wished to display. As a result, he found himself being flippant while de Laborde was dead serious. It was hard, Edouard thought, to be as serious as Jacques was in this environment of silk and exotic scents, to say nothing of the professionally smiling young ladies with their clinging satin dresses. In spite of these distractions, Edouard concentrated on the French officer's intent expression and apparent cool *savoir faire.*

"Don't think for a moment that I don't believe the death of that man, Sainteny, wouldn't be in the best interests of all concerned. *Malheureusement* it is too risky to accomplish," Major Jacques replied with no softening smile.

Edouard didn't know how to react, so he simply took another sip of cognac and hoped he looked appropriately steely as his companion continued.

"What we're faced with here is a person well out of his depth in an army that is in the process of being reborn. The result is this person believes he can run everything. On top of that, this person is endowed neither with scruples nor intelligence—though I must say he is cunning."

Quite satisfied with himself, Jacques took a long, slow sip of the brandy. His brow knotted in contemplation of his next thought. Jacques de Laborde had begun to feel the effects of his third substantial cognac.

"We must assist our friend, John, to overcome the shortsightedness—and I might say, bad manners—of this Sainteny. Therefore, I suggest that Lt. Guy Montfort remain with you and your team. But, *ecoutez, mon vieux*, we shall add also a veteran French-speaking *indigène* from the Colonial Army to assist in translating when you get down there and you're trying to communicate with the Viet Minh fighters you're training. Just what John asked for, *d'accord*? This way we'll have French participation, but under temporary assignment to American command. And the two, Montfort and the Vietnamese, are there only to aid in communication with the local people—they technically will not be in a joint operation. They're merely providing a service. What do you think?"

"I think it's fine if you do. They'll all be in American uniforms anyhow. I'm sure John will agree. He's already said that Vietnamese language skills were what he needed for future training ops," said Edouard, wondering only if arrangements like this made on a stack of pillows in a high-class whore house had any legitimacy.

The following morning, Edouard vaguely remembered agreeing to accompany Jacques de Laborde on "*un peu de l'aventure*" to reconnoiter the northern sector of the rail and communication line that ran from Hanoi up into southeastern China. Just a pleasant walking tour; it would provide good information for Edouard to pass on to John when it came time to hit the railway. Less than a week in the field, Jacques had promised. It was perfectly safe. They'd jump into an area north of Hanoi near the rail line. This was a region de Laborde said he knew well and where he had already made contact with several villages that supposedly were eager to rid themselves of the Japanese invaders.

Edouard rationalized his dashing off on the "lark" by the fact that John's apparently well-established situation at Kim Lung no longer required daily radio contact, and the AGAS people would be covering that end anyhow. Furthermore, Applegate neither sought nor needed help with the training of the rest of the Moose team. The truth was, Edouard was bored being stuck in Ch'ing-hsi and this was a chance to get out of the rut. Jacques arranged for a Dakota to make the night flight and 48 hours later they parachuted into Tonkin.

The entire operation was supposed to be strictly an "in-and-out" activity. Jacques de Laborde had said he knew the area like the back of his hand. The plan was to be air dropped in, check things out, and then a brisk two-day, 40-mile walk would get them out. The problem was that he hadn't been there in a long time. The floods had turned what had been simply the usual Tonkin farm acreage into one large, if shallow, lake. A quick reconnaissance he had called it. Something to give them a better idea of what a larger force would face when they ironed out all that nonsense regarding the restriction on joint French–American special operations activities. It was Jacques de Laborde's way of defying his rival, Jean Sainteny. "A reconnaissance is not really an operation," he had explained to Edouard. "At least that's the position I'll take, if necessary. *Sacre bleu, quell erreur. Je m'excuse*."

There was no way they could have landed in a dry place. The water wasn't deep, but at waist high it was just deep enough to make moving extremely difficult. As soon as they landed, Edouard had second thoughts about this scouting venture. Splashing down in water rather than on dry land as expected does tend to change one's thinking. Edouard could see de Laborde struggling to pull in his parachute silk that had collapsed and was partially submerged. Edouard rolled up his own chute as best he could, but it weighed a ton dragging it through the water. The Frenchman waved he was okay and continued on with his chute struggle. Edouard looked around to see if he could find a place to stash the telltale cloth. It was too dark to see more than 200 or 300 yards with any clarity. Jacques de Laborde, who had landed further away than that, was just a dark shadow.

Edouard plunged his parachute under the water, trying to push the air out so it would be completely submerged. There was nothing else to do. They could spend the rest of the night dragging the sodden mess around looking for a place to hide it. Finally, he had the entire chute under water. He tried to pull some mud up from the bottom to weigh down the pile but wasn't too successful. Edouard could see the distant figure of de Laborde still battling. He decided he had done all he could do with the hiding of his own chute and pushed himself though the water toward his companion.

Major Jacques was having a very difficult time with the canopy that had trapped a large air bubble in it. Edouard clumsily reached out at the far end and between the two of them the entire chute was eventually dragged under water. It wasn't a neat pile, but at least it was submerged. Hopefully, the local peasants wouldn't be working in that section and would not see the drowned cloth. It was a good bet, though, that Japanese soldiers wouldn't be slogging through the paddy fields. Without speaking, the two officers headed off into the dark expecting eventually to stumble across some high ground. It took a solid 15 minutes before a raised dirt pathway loomed in front of them. They dragged themselves out of the muck, soaked from head to toe and covered with grime.

The dark night that had been so useful in covering their jump now made it impossible to get any bearings. There were no identifiable landmarks other than the seemingly endless grids of submerged paddies. Major Jacques' agents who were supposed to meet them were not there. And why should they when nobody expected the two officers to land in a lake of flooded fields?

"This was supposed to be all dry land right near the village. We must have been dropped in the wrong place," said de Laborde.

"Or the village has been just swept away," ventured Edouard.

"No, I had radio contact with them. They were expecting us. We've worked with them for a long time. They're very loyal."

Edouard and Major Jacques spoke in French. For Edouard it seemed the diplomatic thing to do. This, after all, was de Laborde's mission and his operational assets—if any were to be found.

"We've just been dropped in the wrong place. But what place? That's the question," the French major said.

There was nothing else to do but wait until daybreak when they might get a better idea of their situation. It was important, however, that they get some sort of bolt-hole to crawl into so they wouldn't be so conspicuous in the morning. There was no alternative to following the raised dirt path until they ran across some place they could hide. They knew that the security of the night would disappear in a few hours and that they would stand out as two conspicuous and filthy scarecrows. They trudged on, with Major Jacques going first along the narrow dike. They didn't speak; there wasn't anything to say. A small palm frond shed loomed in front as the dirt path expanded into what seemed to be a wood-fenced corral. There were no animals occupying the space at the moment, so they decided without much thought to take advantage of the accommodations.

"What should we be looking for when the light comes up?" Edouard asked.

"*Franchement, mon vieux*, the only thing we can look for is the rail line. We have to orient on that because it is the only landmark in all this flat country," Major Jacques answered.

"Any main power lines?" Edouard asked.

"Those will be along the rail lines," replied the French major.

A simple contact and recon mission had been transformed into another shambles—or at least potentially so. Both men were of far too optimistic personalities to dwell on the negative and griping over what couldn't be changed wasn't going to improve their situation.

"My agents will find us eventually, but we shall have to move around the community in order to get the word out. That of course carries its own risks, as I'm sure you are well aware," said Major Jacques.

Edouard shrugged. He had nothing else to offer. It was an annoying predicament they found themselves in, but he wasn't prepared to consider it more than that. Edouard retained a strong belief in the inevitability of life, and this resulted in an expectation that things always worked out. In that sense, privilege had left the same peculiar mark on both men. A principal concern they shared was the extremely uncomfortable feeling of sitting in dirt-grimed clothes sodden with water. The more important inconveniences would take care of themselves.

Edouard relaxed sitting with his back against the wall of the shed. He thought about how John would have reacted if he had been along with them. He certainly would have been steaming over the moronic pilot who missed the drop zone or the equally demented operations officers who hadn't calculated that the entire area would be flooded. John undoubtedly also would have been chastising himself for not anticipating the screw-up. The last thing on his mind would have been the personal discomfort of the filthy wet uniform.

"What makes you smile, *mon ami*?" Jacques asked.

"I was just thinking about John Guthrie. I don't think he would care for this little contretemps in which we now find ourselves."

"*Ah, cher John est—comme on dit en Anglais—*'tightly wound'?"

"Yes, he is a bit—but a splendid soldier," said Edouard, rushing to his friend's defense.

"*Vraiment un brave*," quickly added Jacques de Laborde not wanting his remark to be misunderstood. Even in the middle of the mess that surrounded them, the two officers maintained the politesse of their mutual social background. Two dismounted knights searching for a way out of the forest.

Dawn seemed to be delayed by the gray overcast that enveloped the first light. It wasn't raining, but it might have been with all the moisture heavy in the air. The two men peeked outside the shed to see if there was any life moving about. Some birds twitted about, but that was all. They sat munching on crackers and fruit bars from their K-rations, neither discussing the fact that they had little in the way of supplies other than the few ration cartons in their combat packs. The expectation had been that Jacques' friendly agents would feed them. Both officers sat at the opening of the shed watching the edges of the morning fog for signs of life. They agreed that the farmers should be out soon with their oxen to work the paddies. This was supposed to be "friendly" territory, Jacques continued to insist. He was still hopeful of making contact with any of the agents who might come from nearby farms and villages—all predicated on the belief that he and Edouard hadn't been dropped too far off course.

They waited with increasing impatience for someone to show up. The light became stronger even as the day remained extremely gray, but not a single person could be seen. By eight o'clock, the two began to contemplate striking off on their own in a northern direction. It would be impossible to set a true course because they would have to follow the raised dikes in order to stay out of the flooded rice paddies. It was eerily quiet for a place that should have had at least some sort of bustle of men and women farmers planting and plowing. It wasn't a good sign.

"Don't see any rice shoots. Shouldn't there be some rice shoots?" Edouard asked.

"Exactly. There doesn't seem to be anything growing in these paddies," said de Laborde. "This is all completely flooded. That's why no one's around. These may not even be rice paddies, just fields of something else—vegetables perhaps. And it's just all under water now, too deep to grow even rice. God knows where all the people have gone."

"The one good thing is that there's nothing for the Japs to patrol. I bet all roads leading in and out are impassable," said Edouard venturing outside the shed.

"The question is whether or not the rail lines will operate. Maybe our job has already been done for us," said de Laborde.

"It would only be temporary, don't you think, Jacques?"

"Yes, of course. I was making a small joke. The roadbeds for the trains are most likely set up five or six feet or more above the fields. They'd have to have a firm base to carry the weight of the trains—rock and gravel with dirt on top would be my guess. Although the floods have been particularly bad this year, it is something the engineers who built the line must have taken into consideration." Jacques de Laborde joined Edouard outside the shed surveying the horizon.

"I think we might as well get moving. Nothing much seems to be happening here," Edouard said.

"D'accord," replied de Laborde.

Without saying anything more, the two officers set off along what was a wider than usual dike. There wasn't much else to discuss. The day grew warmer but the humidity in no way diminished. Their own perspiration mixed with the wetness of their already-soaked clothes. They had trudged along for about two hours when Jacques, who was leading, spied an electric power pylon in the distance. They decided to shift direction and head for the pylon. An hour of some very circuitous walking along connecting perpendicular dikes brought them to the pylon and the nearby rail line. It was a great victory, except that they were just as alone as they had been earlier.

Edouard kneeled down and placed his ear on the rail but could hear nothing. They decided to follow along the rail line that appeared to take a northeastern path away from Hanoi that would be far to the south. It was too dangerous to walk totally exposed along the tracks themselves, so they trekked just above where the raised rail bed met the water. It was difficult footing at that angle and more than once one or the other slipped on the loose gravel, ending up very close to another soaking.

It was about noon when they heard an odd sound in the distance. It wasn't a locomotive, however it was something coming along the tracks. They hugged the side of the rail bed as they heard wheels rolling along the metal and loud voices yelling at each other in Japanese. As the noise disappeared down the line, they could see two Japanese soldiers working the handles of a "push-me-pull-me" handcar as it sped away. Obviously, they were enjoying their task of checking the line, or whatever was the purpose of their outing was.

"Well, that satisfies the question as to whether or not the rail line is operational," said Jacques.

Another hour of hard walking brought the two officers to a point where they could see a small village in the distance. It seemed that their problems might soon be coming to an end until they drew closer and saw what was clearly a Japanese encampment set up in the middle of this village of peasant huts surrounded by flooded fields. The higher ground of the village most likely had been taken over by the soldiers marooned by the rains. At least that was Edouard's opinion as both men huddled out of sight from the village about 200 yards away. They had been lucky not to be sighted as they approached.

"We'll have to wait here until dark and then slip by," said de Laborde, seemingly not deterred in the slightest by the danger that faced them a bare two football fields away.

"It would be better, Jacques, if we were on the other side of this embankment, don't you think?" said Edouard concerned about trying to remain invisible for the entire afternoon curled inconspicuously close to the water's edge.

"Yes, it would, but how do we get there? I don't think we can afford crawling up and over to the other side. Here at least we can keep an eye on their movements. I think we'll be just fine as long as we don't do anything that attracts attention," Jacques replied confidently.

They could see the Japanese soldiers and Vietnamese farm families mingling among the village's animals that had been gathered in the center of the little community. There was a surprising lack of discord in the gathering. They all seemed to be getting along and making the best of what undoubtedly was a difficult situation. The Japanese didn't seem to be ordering anyone about and the villagers seemed to be busy going about their daily tasks.

"I don't think I recognize this village," said Jacques. "My people were all further west."

"I hate to bring this up, old man, but are we just going to follow along this railroad till we get to China? Weren't we supposed to be led out of here by your agents—or whatever they are?"

Edouard tried to be as polite as possible, but the situation that had seemed so straightforward when they started out had become decidedly murky.

"We're not really that far from the border and the Chinese-held positions," responded Jacques as if they had just taken a wrong turn somewhere on the road to Versailles. "I can get us there. Really quite simple except for this flooding."

Edouard decided that if de Laborde wasn't worried, he wouldn't be either. It was as simple as that.

The afternoon dragged on, hot and humid. Sitting at the bottom of the rail embankment turned out to be a good way to soak through to the skin but there was nothing else to be done. They couldn't move higher away from the water for fear of being seen, so they were stuck with wet rear ends. Not exactly the image for two international dandies.

It was about four in the afternoon when they noticed that the soldiers had begun to form up in what clearly was preparatory to marching out of the village. The villagers waved and shouted goodbye as if they were sending off their dearest friends. The Japanese headed straight to the rail line—or as straight as they could with the limitation forced on them by the flooded fields. Jacques and Edouard watched carefully as the platoon of about 20 soldiers trooped across the dikes, eventually ending directly up the line from where the two officers crouched. They couldn't have been more than a hundred yards away at that point. With most of the soldiers remaining strung out along the dike, one of them climbed up the rail embankment in an apparent effort to look for a train coming down from the north. He put his ear to the rail and rose to give a signal to the rest of the group.

"Those Japs must have a radio," Edouard said. "How else could they know a train would be coming?"

In about ten minutes a train with a locomotive and four freight cars rumbled down the track and stopped in front of the Japanese platoon. The soldiers streamed off the dike path and up the embankment to haul themselves into one of the freight cars. Slowly the train moved on down the line passing the huddled Edouard and Jacques in a rolling crash of noise of its coal-fired boiler dragging the wooden cars.

"*Au revoir, mes amis,*" said Jacques, blowing a kiss in the direction of the departing Japanese. "Now the question is, my dear friend, Edouard, whether we make a visit to the village or pass it by. What do you think?"

"They were pretty friendly with the Jap soldiers, from what I saw," said Edouard.

"That could mean anything. These people are very smart. They're going to be very hospitable to an armed group of soldiers no matter what they really thought about them. However, I agree they seemed perhaps just a bit too enthusiastic. I suggest we take the chance of crawling over to the other side of the line and go on past without dropping in for an aperitif. Let's see what lies a bit further up."

Hugging the gravel embankment, the two wriggled across the rail lines and down the other side. For the first time in hours, they straightened up and resumed their trek north. It was good to get moving again. Jacques explained to Edouard that he had calculated they would have to turn back westward in about ten miles. Edouard didn't question the Frenchman's logic. He felt much better just believing that Jacques de Laborde knew what he was doing. By the time darkness fell, Jacques announced he reckoned the ten miles had been completed and they should bed down before they took off on the next leg of their journey back.

They had arrived at higher ground and the area between the rail line and the neighboring farmland was much drier. The two men stretched out in a grassy area and soon fell asleep, but both awoke again after only a few hours.

"We might as well get moving," said Jacques. "The moonlight is bright enough and it won't do us any good to just stay here."

Edouard agreed and stiffly dragged himself to his feet after eating what was left in one of his open K-rations. The going was far easier now that they were on flat ground and not walking on the angle of the rail embankment. They soon came upon a dirt track that easily could pass for a country road. Jacques decided he recognized this track as leading northwest—just where they wanted to go.

"Of course, I could be wrong," he said after they had confidently set off. For the first time Edouard began to have a slight hesitancy in his estimation of his companion's infallibility. He shouldn't have. The Frenchman's prediction that they should shortly run into a large village straddling the road proved to be correct. Edouard was more pleased than he let on. Jacques took the discovery in stride.

"*Excellent, mon vieux.* This is where things get, as you say, 'tricky.' That's the correct English, right, 'tricky'?"

"Why tricky?" Edouard asked in English.

"There should be a Japanese garrison somewhere around here—that is if we are where I think we are."

This not particularly good news hit Edouard about the same time as a sudden roiling in his lower gut signaled an emergency need for relief of his bowels. This was the way dysentery begins in tropical climes and nothing can restrain the demand. A quick dash to the roadside was as far as he could get in time to pull off his pants. Jacques nonchalantly took the occasion to stroll on ahead. He informed the squatting Edouard that he'd return in about ten minutes—time enough for the otherwise-engaged American to overcome his spasms. At that point Edouard hardly heard the Frenchman's advisory. His own concerns were concentratedly anal. There could have been an earthquake and he would have ignored the entire thing.

Jacques took longer than the ten minutes he had promised to return. It was just as well because Edouard needed the extra time to recover from his exertions. He was sitting by the side of the road, his pants once again belted, but bent over in fatigue and residual intestinal gripes. Jacques wasted no time on sympathy.

"Yes, there are Japanese up forward, just as I thought. Maybe just a small garrison, but they are a problem, nonetheless. How are you? Are you ready for a little running?"

Running was the last thing for which Edouard was ready. His response was limited to a grunted, "Huh?"

"I thought we might just walk on through the village and if anyone started shooting, we'd run away. Good plan?"

"Oh, Christ, a lousy plan," Edouard groaned.

"Perhaps you have the better plan?" Jacques replied in English apparently thinking the scene quite amusing.

"I say we stay here until I can think better."

"It seems to me, *mon vieux*, that you are thinking from the wrong end." Jacques thought his remark extremely funny and barely contained a laugh. "We can't stay here, old chap," he continued in a low voice, still in English.

"Can't we go around this place?" Edouard asked, still sitting and holding his arms around his stomach.

"We might try, but we might still alert people. I think we might just walk through. Faster, easier."

"Then we run?"

"Only if we have to."

Edouard struggled to his feet, adjusted his pants, and slowly walked down the road with Jacques muttering encouraging words. A dog barked in the dark and then one more, but nothing else happened. The village ran for about 150 yards along the road. There had been no sentries guarding the approaches from the southeast. But as they quietly and carefully edged through the town, they could see a soldier sitting on a box at the far end of the road. His head was bent over apparently in sleep, a rifle on his lap. They kept walking along the rutted dirt track until Jacques motioned Edouard to the side of the road. There was still about 20 yards to the soldier. Jacques covered the distance silently moving five steps at a time and stopping. The last few yards he traversed in a glide that took him to the back of the sleeping sentry who never woke up as his throat was slit. Carefully lowering the dead man to the ground, Jacques waved Edouard forward. At that instant, two befuddled Japanese guards who apparently had been sleeping by the side of the road rose with a loud cry and attempted to fire their weapons. One man was dropped by Edouard who saw them first as he quickly had responded to Jacques' wave. The other one, however, was able to get off a burst from his machine pistol, a slug of which spun de Laborde around with a shot through his upper arm. By that time Edouard had closed to within ten feet of the soldier and put three rounds into him before the man's dying finger released the trigger.

All the village dogs were now awake and barking madly in all directions. Japanese soldiers tumbled out of huts along with Vietnamese civilians screaming and dashing about. The soldiers were only partially dressed, and none seemed to know which way to go. Edouard grabbed the wounded Jacques de Laborde and did the only thing he could. He and Jacques ran down the road just as the Frenchman had said they should. Under the cover of darkness and a totally confused garrison of Japanese soldiers and petrified Vietnamese villagers, they didn't stop running until they no longer could hear the sounds of the chaos behind them.

Edouard tore off Jacques's sleeve, shook some sulfa powder on the wound, and tied off his arm with a bandage slowing the flow of blood. Jacques Laborde had a devilish smile on his face all the while Edouard tended to him.

"Looks like a flesh wound, Jacques. Does it hurt much?"

"Oh, yes, *mon ami*, very much, but they are the best kind. It is only when you can't feel them that is the big trouble."

"Who told you that, and why are you smiling? There, I'm all finished."

"A lovely nurse who knew all there was about male anatomy. She told me, and I believe every word she said. And for your second question—I'm smiling because you thought you couldn't run, but you see you did. There is nothing like a little excitement to tighten up the sphincter muscles. That I found out by myself at Dunkirk."

The next two days of alternated hiking and hiding ended with a thoroughly dehydrated and weak Edouard stumbling alongside a still vigorous, if feverish, Jacques de Laborde. They were intercepted by a Chinese patrol that luckily had seen them from a distance and had made an early determination that they weren't Japanese. In fact, the Chinese officer was quite disappointed to find out they weren't downed flyers. He would have then received a nice reward from AGAS. Jacques made up for the man's unhappiness by giving him two gold Louis he always carried with him "just in case." The end result was that they were transported back to Ch'ing-hsi in a Chinese Army staff car as a symbol of the great cooperation between the Allied armies.

The entire adventure had lasted less than a week. Jacques de Laborde had, in his own words, "shown my friend Edouard a bit of Tonkin," thumbed his nose at Jean Sainteny, and determined that a small force could indeed cut the Hanoi rail and power lines with not too much difficulty.

"It has definitely been a *bon marché*. One nicked arm and *un peu de la dysenterie*. We have definitely done well, *mon vieux*."

* * *

The newly promoted Master Sergeant Ted Applegate had welcomed the chance to join the Moose team and get back into the field. It was his job to take Montfort and his recently arrived Vietnamese sergeant, along with three OSS noncoms fresh from the US, and whip them into a cohesive special operations team. The Americans were eager even if Applegate constantly ragged them about their modest achievements on the range. Guy Montfort was a natural parachutist even though he never jumped before. He completed his required six jumps with amazing ease and won the approval of Ted Applegate.

One of the Americans was Len Sorenson, designated as the team's medic. He had left his pre-med college studies to enlist in the paratroopers but was waylaid by OSS recruiters who got him his jump training and also a very intensive combat medical course. From the beginning it had been Edouard's idea to use Sorenson to provide medical assistance to the Viet Minh as well as care for the mission members. It wasn't a revolutionary idea but certainly was a new element in OSS operations. Quiet but committed, Sorenson also scored well on the Applegate combat scale.

The one who fared not at all well in the top sergeant's eyes was the Vietnamese, Sgt. Phac. From the outset the Alabaman was down on the French Colonial soldier.

"Ah'll tell ya Cap'n this here's gonna be trouble," he said to Edouard. "This guy is all Frenchified and on top of that he's a local which makes 'im double bad from where ah stand. Ya'll gonna take a big chance bringin' him along. Ah figured the officer was maybe okay cause he spoke English 'n we could say he was one of us. But this other one… It ain't no way smart, sir."

Edouard knew that Ted Applegate was very serious. The man was too good a soldier to openly question something like this.

"You don't like him because he's, uh, local as you say?" asked Edouard.

"Hell, no Captain. He jes' ain't the right local. He's a French local, if you get mah meanin'. We're goin' into some territory like if yuh jumped into the hill country of 'Barra with some guy you figgered was a good ole boy. 'Cept he's not the same local ole boy, so it jes' means he's still a furriner. It don't do no good t'bring 'um along. He jes' won't mix—t'say nuthin' 'bout his attitude which ain't good."

The uncharacteristically long-winded point made by Applegate reinforced second thoughts that Edouard had been having on his own soon after Phac had arrived. Edouard had noticed that the Vietnamese seemed very hesitant over the jump training that was an essential part of participating in the mission. Additionally, it was not too long after Applegate's objection that the usually reserved Len Sorenson, the medic, also brought up the behavior of Sgt. Phac, whom the other GIs had begun to refer to derogatorily as "The General."

"I can't explain why, Captain, but this fellow acts as if we're all sort of beneath him. I'm not saying he doesn't know his stuff or try hard. He's okay that way, even if he is a bit windy about the jump training. But as a person he acts as if he's doing all of us a favor by being here. Lt. Guy told me Phac was part French, so I figured he had a chip on his shoulder. I thought I better bring this to your attention, sir."

"Thanks, Len. I'll keep my eye on him. Sometimes these things work themselves out, as I'm sure you know. I'll mention it to Guy Montfort. In the meantime, just don't react—and tell the other guys that's what I said. That's the best way to handle it. Any other problems?"

"No, sir, everybody's in great physical shape, and mentally we're just all eager to get on our way."

Edouard decided not to say anything to Montfort. There wasn't anything he could do about the man, and there was no sense in adding an additional disruptive element into the situation. What was required was the exercise of command for which Edouard had neither the experience nor inclination. John could sort it all out when they got to Kim Lung, he decided. For the moment, the best solution as far as Edouard was concerned was to do nothing.

The required training to qualify Montfort and Phac was completed and all that held up the mission was a series of unsatisfactory weather reports. Heavy cloud cover over the drop zone made the risk of missing the designated landing area too high. So far, all aspects of the training, including the night jumps, had gone off without incident. Edouard's attempts to emphasize the positive nature of this experience only brought from the more superstitious Applegate the statement that they would pay a penalty later. In spite of the annoying delay, all the team members, except Sgt. Phac, remained in an upbeat mood. The Vietnamese turned increasingly morose and uncommunicative as time wore on.

The commanding officer of AGAS in Ch'ing-hsi had become the benefactor of the Moose Mission. The fact was that without the help of AGAS the OSS operation could never have been launched as speedily as it was. The little personal empire of the lieutenant colonel had made it all possible. It also gave him the right to ask a lot of questions about matters that weren't necessarily in his "need-to-know."

"What are you going to say to your people in Kunming?" he asked.

"Guy Montfort was part of the original plan before Sainteny pulled the rug from under us, and we say so was one Viet translator."

"You know that you and John are playing with some hot political fire here," the burly Air Corps officer said.

"It's not like I haven't been worrying about it, but what else can I do at this stage? As far as the Viet Minh are concerned, they should be satisfied by the fact that Montfort and Phac are in GI uniforms. I just wish the airstrip had been finished down there."

"Well, it looks like tomorrow morning is your new ETD. I've alerted my transport people. I just received the latest weather updates. Looks terrific."

"We're going in with a lot of stuff. I hope it's not too much."

"I don't think that's possible under the circumstances. The more supplies and equipment you arrive with, the more serious you look. Remember these Viet Minh have been living hand-to-mouth equipment-wise for a long time. You come in heavily laden with goodies to share and it's Christmas time with you being Saint Nick, or in this case Saint Eddy. Stop worrying."

"Pre-jumpitis, colonel. The other times I didn't have anything to worry about other than myself."

"Welcome to command, Eddy. It's a bitch, but you'll get used to it. Anyhow when you land, it all becomes John's worry again."

The word of the weather clearing was passed on to the others in the Moose team and the rest of the day was spent in last minute preparations. There wasn't much to do; they had all been ready for some time. Edouard tried to get hold of Jacques de Laborde for a final chat, but found he had departed somewhere. That was his usual style. It would have been nice, Edouard thought, to have an *au revoir* drink, though another session in the house of joy would have been too much happiness for the night before a jump.

Shortly after dawn, the entire Moose team was transported over to Tepao airfield. All of them were decked out in their jump gear. The AGAS colonel and some of his support staff were on hand to see them off. Nobody had slept much the night before. Ted Applegate had sat up till late with his three American sergeants sipping from a bottle of bourbon that the AGAS crew had sent around as a good luck going away gift. Edouard was over with the AGAS colonel until midnight exchanging radio messages with Jimmy Tau and John in Kim Lung ensuring timing of the reception team and other last-minute details. Weather checks and enemy activity reports were coordinated with 14th Air Force liaison. Everything that could be was checked for the hundredth time. Guy Montfort was left to babysit his Vietnamese with the aid of a few friends from the French M.5 office.

The business of waiting to load up was always difficult. Jokes kept things light, but all the old lines were quickly expended. All the alternatives of worst-case scenarios had been covered several times in the past few days both by radio with Kim Lung as well as with the AGAS support echelon. The members of the Moose team adjusted each other's packs. The Americans talked nervously among themselves while Phac stood to one side. Guy Montfort was the most relaxed of them all. He smoked a Gauloise and exchanged smart remarks with Edouard and the AGAS chief. Edouard repeatedly climbed in and out of the plane checking with the pilot and the jumpmaster. Finally, the pilot signaled they were ready for takeoff. The Moose team—all seven of them—clambered aboard the transport plane. The plane's motors sputtered at first and then caught full voice and roared down the Tepao strip with unexpected swiftness. After all the preparation, the actual departure was anti-climactic.

Chapter Ten

The jump itself went off without a hitch. The drop zone was well marked and, as the weather guys had predicted, the skies had only scattered cloud cover. The first problem came with the landing. Again, Edouard landed ungently in the trees, but this time he wasn't alone. Guy Montfort and Phac also were hung up and had to be cut down. The impressive arrival that had been planned was less than intended, but at least no one was injured beyond a few scrapes and bruises. The ignominious entrance really didn't matter because the nearly 200 Viet Minh guerrillas drawn up to greet the team were primed for disciplined enthusiasm. Vo Nguyen Giap, the redoubtable Comrade Van, was on site for the arrival of the American friends with their numerous supply containers that parachuted down.

Giap, dressed in his usual unpressed white suit and dark fedora, had intended to give a short speech but abandoned the idea in the excitement occasioned by the cutting down of three of the parachutists in the trees. He stood quietly aside as John and Jimmy vigorously directed the recovery and welcomed each of the newcomers. The two French Army participants were conspicuous in their new GI fatigues and jump boots. John tried to corral the OSS gang who were loudly enjoying their successful landing. As soon as all the Moose team had been gathered in, Giap began his welcoming speech. The guerrillas, assembled in neat ranks, each soldier armed with some sort of rifle, stood at an approximation of attention. Edouard drew his own small group into a line in acknowledgement of the formation and greeting by Giap. He saluted John and Giap in turn. It was a confused but proper military beginning.

Ted Applegate immediately noticed the antique nature of many of the firearms. Even without close inspection he could spot old Chinese, French, and some Japanese weapons. In the rear line he even saw some ancient shotguns. Most conspicuously, however, was the front rank of fighters proudly carrying the small number of carbines and Garand rifles that had arrived with John. Phac had chosen to stand aside hoping to be ignored. This Applegate also saw.

John suggested that all members of the team come forward to be personally introduced to General Giap, as he called him. The moment became a bit awkward as Giap, a fixed smile on his face, shook the hand of each team member until he came to the Moose Mission's single Vietnamese. Phac saluted Giap who returned the salute with a clenched fist held to the side of his hat. He kept his face pleasant, but he didn't smile. Phac remained defiantly erect and military. The unspoken exchange passed swiftly as Giap turned to his assembled troop to lead a cheer for the new arrivals.

Edouard had quickly seen that John seemed fit and very much at ease in his new environment. For his part, John Guthrie was delighted the waiting was over. The Moose team was finally in place and his friend Edouard available for moral support. The privacy for him of Kim Lung, though, was now lost along with his odd feeling of peace amidst war. Edouard chatted away with Jimmy Tau whom he had never met but with whom he had developed a friendship through their many radio exchanges. Ted Applegate took over attempting to organize the disposition of the supply canisters. Politely he interrupted the officers.

"Excuse me, sirs, but we gotta get us some transportation. There's too much stuff t'carry. Them canisters are damn heavy."

"The villagers will carry them for us. John caught a couple of trucks at Tam Dao, but they're not used much because of the fuel. There'll be some wagons along very soon," Jimmy responded in his usually optimistic way. Surprisingly, several ox-drawn carts happened on the scene just at that moment as if on cue.

Giap gave an order to one of his officers and a squad of guerrillas broke ranks to act as porters for the Moose team. They wouldn't allow the team members to carry even their own packs. Jimmy explained that they considered this an honor and not a burden. Nonetheless, the Americans attempted to share the loading of the heavy canisters into the ox carts. To his credit, Phac joined in, though it was clear that the guerrillas were a bit confused at his presence. There was no animosity, but there definitely was distance. Although he didn't understand the exchange, Applegate took it all in. He had been intent on keeping his eye on Phac ever since before they took off from Tepao.

Applegate's interest was not that subtle and Phac had become well aware of the top sergeant's scrutiny. Phac was happy therefore for the diversion when one of the guerrillas strode along with him as they began the march toward the encampment. The man was quite well spoken, a fact that Phac quickly noticed. The guerrilla must be an officer, he thought, as the man introduced himself with some formality. His name was Thanh.

The moment the Moose team had landed, Phac had become the unspoken object of attention. Comrade Van had caught Thanh's eye and nothing more needed to be said. Phac's Eurasian looks and standoffish manner had immediately set him apart. The conversation between the two Vietnamese during the 45-minute trek to the headquarters camp included seemingly casual questions from Thanh. Phac's responses followed the instructions he'd received regarding his cover story. He had been made available to the Americans by the French Army to supply added translation capability as well as a feeling for traditional Vietnamese sensitivities. Guy Montfort never came up, but if he had, Phac would have backed up the story he was an American officer of French heritage. Thanh's report to Giap was not very enlightening.

In addition to keeping his eye on Phac, Ted Applegate made it a point to use the march to the Viet Minh camp to continue to instruct the two OSS specialists who had been assigned to the Moose Mission. One, a former New Jersey State Policeman, was there to supplement Ted's own weapons background. The other was a bright-faced engineer who had finished the Vietnamese-language training program and had been rushed over from California. Both were eager but woefully lacking in field experience. Ted took every occasion to cram bits of knowledge into their heads.

"See how these here guys got no uniforms. That don't mean they can't fight. Can't judge these tribes the same way yuh judge reg'lar troops. None of the chicken shit stuff we jam down all you boys' throats back in Benning—though I personally would'na minded a little more snap in their formations."

Applegate was secretly looking forward to "shaping up" these Viet Minh guerrillas. Like a ballet master with a talented new class, his joy would be to turn the raw fighters into a trained military force—into professionals. To do that he'd have to get his own instructors to think the way he did.

"Remember they'll be watchin' us all like hawks, so you boys better be on the ball at all times. You are the US Army for them. No screw ups allowed. You people readin' me?"

"All the way, Top," said the ex-cop.

"They look pretty eager, Top," said the other.

In the back of Ted Applegate's mind was always his experience in the Philippines and the ambushes by the Moros still fighting in the south after 40 years of American occupation. If these damn Viets were half as good as his old Filipino Scouts, he thought, the Moose Mission would give the damn Japs a few surprises. So far, he was pleased with what he'd seen.

People seemed to materialize along the dirt road as the band of new arrivals trudged along, noisily accompanied by the guerrillas-turned-porters and the rest of the Viet Minh reception unit. Edouard walked up front with Giap and John. The Vietnamese leader in his usual very polite French questioned the OSS officer on his work before coming to China. Giap seemed intrigued by Edouard's account of his experiences in Belgium.

"So, Captain Parnell, like our Major Guthrie here you are quite experienced in—what is it you called it, Major John—partisan warfare. I have heard about his fighting with the French communist partisans in the Vosges Mountains Were your partisans communist also, Captain?"

"Honestly I never knew. I think some of them might have been, but we weren't an organized communist unit such as the Major's," Edouard replied after catching a quick glance of approval from John.

It was obvious to Edouard that his friend had used his contact with General Giap to establish a good basis for a sense of shared experience even to the point of showing previous friendly relationship with another communist fighting group—even if it was halfway around the world. The creation of rapport through apparent openness, Edouard recalled, was one of the first things taught in ops training. Just as Giap's expert elicitation was focused on gathering as much information as he could about the American officers without appearing to probe into their personal life. Edouard was amused at the thought of John and Giap going at it, each from their own strength. It was a question of the lawyer versus the professor, both quite well trained and naturally talented for their job. For Edouard, brought up with a lifetime of precious social exploration and obfuscation, it all came naturally.

Guy Montfort had followed close on the heels of Edouard, John, and the serious-faced man in the white suit and the improbable hat. So, this was the already well-known Vo Ngyuen Giap. It was interesting to listen as the clever little Vietnamese sought to gain tidbits of personal information from the American officers. Guy Montfort did not think of his American friends as naive, but he did retain the Frenchman's usual belief that they tended to lack a certain sophistication. He did not think of this as a deprecatory judgement, but rather merely realistic. He liked both Edouard and John and otherwise respected their country, but it was at times like this that he was amused by their national characteristic of ingenuousness.

Jimmy Tau and Len Sorenson walked together by Guy's side. They had discovered they shared both a New England upbringing and a Boston Red Sox baseball allegiance. Their incessant chatter made it impossible for Guy to track everything that was being said by the trio in front, so he eventually directed his attention to the two Americans at his side. Jimmy pointed out the villagers who had come to see the "visitors from the sky," a term the country folk had recently coined to explain the parachuting guests. Jimmy explained that the cleared area that had been designated as the drop zone was in the process of expansion long enough to evolve into a landing strip. As the architect of this enterprise, Jimmy quite rightly spoke with a good deal of pride.

The Vietnamese peasants shouted greetings to the Moose team from a respectful distance at the tree edge of the roadside. The air was heavy with humidity but amazingly mild. It had been a great boon to have had this interim of dry weather. The fortuitous occurrence was not lost on the always superstitious farmers. It made the occasion all the more momentous. It would start raining again soon, but these small things were an excellent sign of good omens brought by these newcomers. Rural Tonkin, even outside the tribal areas, was still rooted in the old ways. Jimmy explained all this to Guy and Len Sorenson.

Guy just smiled and nodded at the information. It was obvious that no one had yet told the AGAS officer that Guy wasn't an American. Jimmy's insight was correct, though, and Guy gave him full marks for that knowledge of the local scene. It was his own fascination with the Vietnamese culture that had made bearable his several undercover years with Vichy forces. Nonetheless, it was a surprise to find Jimmy still so enthusiastic after so much time in the bush. Guy Montfort was acutely aware of how the march from Son Tay had altered his own life. It was ironic after that grueling escape he was now back in Tonkin walking down a muddy dirt road on a delightful summer morning. Finally, he would be doing something of value. The long overdue captaincy would be soon in coming. *Vive les Américains.*

The encampment was all abustle. A cow had been slaughtered in honor of the arrival of the Americans. Choice cuts were being roasted slowly over several fires. The succulent aroma filled the air. The rest of the beef would be distributed among the soldiers, along with additional goat meat. It was truly a celebration for it was a rare time that the guerrillas would see such a feast of meat. Great care would have to be taken if the troops were not all to get sick from the unaccustomed richness of their diet. It was a special time. Uncle Ho's friends, the Americans, had arrived.

New bamboo huts with their intricately woven palm leaf roofs had been built on the usual stilts. The entire facility had been expanded to accommodate the Moose team. John had explained that they would arrive with their own tents, but somehow the word went out and the construction started. The first order of business after settling into their quarters was a series of introductions by Comrade Van of various important Viet Minh officials who had been invited to meet the Americans. Again, John had tried to head off what he saw as an unnecessary social event until he was told by Jimmy and Thanh that these were key political personalities.

The really important function was the courtesy call by John, Edouard, and Guy Montfort on Ho Chi Minh. John had not had a glimpse of the old man for at least a week and even then, it was only to tell him briefly of the expected Moose team arrival. Propped up on the floor of the hut, Ho welcomed John and his two officers.

"Uncle, you remember Edouard Parnell from Kunming, of course. And this is another of my officers, Lt. Guy Montfort."

Edouard was shocked at the emaciated figure before him. Ho's face was grey, hands wrinkled and bony, eyes yellow and dark. John had sent word that Ho was ill, but this was a very sick man. The room had the odor of ill health about it—human smells suffused with pungent ginger which was the all-purpose Vietnamese antiseptic and deodorant. Clearly Ho was in no shape for prolonged discussion.

"Please excuse me, Capt. Parnell. As you can see, I am a little under the weather. So nice to see you here. Lt. Montfort it is a pleasure." Ho apologized for his frailty and promised he would be in better condition the next day, as if informing them he had just given orders for his body to be in an improved state.

As they left, the angelic but ever tough Truyen came outside with the visitors. She had no idea what her patient had just said because he spoke in English, but she wanted to make sure he wasn't giving a false impression of his health. In French she said,

"Uncle is very sick. He insisted on seeing you, but he is unable to meet with the others. Do you have a doctor with you? He has already told me that he won't have anyone treat him, but maybe if I know you have an American doctor with you, I could get Uncle to let him look in."

"Would it help if I spoke to him?" John asked.

"No, he is embarrassed to be so ill. He insists he will get better on his own. You know Uncle can be very stubborn."

"We don't have a doctor, but we have a medical assistant," Edouard quickly replied.

"I was hoping you might have a real doctor."

"Give us all his symptoms and we will radio for advice. I'm sure we must have something that can help him. If he needs something else, we'll get our people to drop what he needs," John said. "We'll worry about getting him to take whatever it is afterwards. You should have spoken to me earlier, Truyen."

"Uncle forbid me. But he is getting worse and I'm worried." Her normal composure was strained. John could see that from the moisture in her dark eyes and tightness in her jaw muscles. The depth of her love for her patient was evident.

"Just write down his symptoms in detail as best you can and let us see what we can find out. If you have any trouble describing anything, you can speak to our medical assistant and maybe he can help you," John said then turning toward Edouard.

"Does our guy, what's his name, Sorenson, does he speak French? I don't remember."

"He has some. He's been working on it. He could talk with her."

"I have to go. Uncle will be sure I've been talking to you," Truyen said and dashed off.

Edouard began to talk about the scene they had just left, but John cut him off. He didn't want to discuss the matter anymore in front of Guy Montfort. Edouard didn't understand what was going on, but he dropped the issue in favor of the more pedestrian questions John was asking on the types of supplies they had brought with them. It was an easy transition and John hoped not noticed by the Frenchman. Later when the two Americans were alone in John's hut, Edouard asked what the motive was for the change in topic.

"I knew the old man was sick. He's been sick ever since I arrived. I hadn't realized things had gotten as bad as they have. Frankly, I've been so wrapped up working on plans for the training after the Tam Dao op that I really haven't thought about Dr. Ho. Seeing him in that state, though, puts a whole new complexion on why we're here."

"I don't understand, John. Everything seems to run pretty well around here without him as it is."

"But that's just it. They're not without him. He's still here. If he dies or is unable to adjudicate differences, this whole show changes. Everything here is much more complicated than it seems. The Viet Minh is held together by Uncle. He's got his guys—they're all ICP—but they aren't the only ones in the Viet Minh. Even among the communists there are plenty of rivalries. I've learned a hell of a lot more down here than we ever knew before. Jimmy knows the names of all the big players. You were just introduced to some of them; that's just a couple. There are other ones. These guys are loyal to Uncle, but if Uncle goes, they'll be pushing and shoving all over the place. That's to say nothing of good old Comrade Van, Giap, who runs their internal security as well as military ops."

"Oh, boy. We really stepped into it."

"It's not so bad as long as we can count on Dr. Ho being around. He's great. I also figure we can work with Giap, though he's not real easy to get along with. He's smart as hell. I've talked with him some and he knows one hell of a lot about military tactics—a lot more than I do, that's for sure. If you can get him talking about Napoleon's battles, you'll learn something."

"So what do we do?"

"First thing is to try and figure out what he's got, Ho that is. That we turn over to Sorenson. Hopefully, he'll eventually be able to take a look at the old man. After that we just do our job and a lot of praying. But this is all Top Secret. Not a word to anybody. Can we trust Sorenson to keep his mouth shut?"

"I think we can on any of the medical things with Dr. Ho. He's not a big blabber anyhow. I'll just remind him. I don't think we'll have any trouble there."

"I just don't want any of this talked about with our French friends. Guy is a good man, but I really want to have his full attention on the training aspect of our job and not any political sideshow. It's my fault. It never occurred to me that the state of Uncle's health would be where it is."

"You were pretty busy with the Tam Dao mission, John. Don't forget that. Afterwards it was all a matter of getting set up for our arrival."

"I asked how he was, and they always said he was doing well. I didn't want to seem too nosy. They're very private, these people. Thanks anyhow, Edouard. It's good to have you here. Now I've got someone to gripe to again."

After Edouard left to check on the status of his charges, John sat on the floor of his hut with his back against the bamboo wall. He'd found it a comfortable position in an otherwise spartan quarters. He began to think of how realistic his statement was of getting a long-distance diagnosis of Ho's condition. Things had been going well, it seemed. But then that was because he hadn't really been doing his job—at least not the way he should have. It just never occurred to him, he said again to himself. One can lose track of so many things when you're trying to focus on a distant task. It was the price of solitude.

The evening meal began earlier than expected with the various cooks arguing over the readiness of the roasting meat. Heaps of rice and bean sprouts were served with slices of the roasted beef on plates, real heavy porcelain china. There were only six of these and they were divided among the team members after some raucous bargaining. The other plates and bowls were wooden. No one would tell where the porcelain had come from even though Jimmy Tau—whose Vietnamese was now in full use—made jokes about it to the cooks. They decided the plates most likely came from the same place as the Japanese beer that miraculously appeared. The cooks burst into laughter when Jimmy chided them about the beer. He then explained to the newcomers that it was all captured booty, including the cow they were eating. He then told the cooks what he had told the team members and they howled even louder than before. So did the guerrillas who had joined in the feast. It was definitely a celebration, and those didn't happen very often in the austere environment of Ho Chi Minh's headquarters. Even the somber-faced females who could be found among the ranks of the Viet Minh fighters allowed themselves to flutter and giggle. Jimmy Tau called them "guerrilla girls" to distinguish them from the village women who performed the housekeeping chores in the encampment.

"The old man, Uncle Ho, tried to fix me up with one of the guerrilla girls," Jimmy explained between mouthfuls. "I was going on about not seeing my long-term girlfriend and how she's most likely gone on with someone else. He'd asked me if I was married. He said I should find a girlfriend among these guerrilla girls."

"So how did it work out? We need tips," Edouard—immediately alert to the possibilities—rushed to inquire.

"Nothing. I struck out every time. I think it's because I'm Chinese, you know, Chinese American. They like the American part but hate the Chinese. Right, Mac?"

Mac Soo, in his usual quiet manner, simply smiled enigmatically and continued eating.

"So, you're saying everyone else should do all right, eh?" Edouard pointed out with a lascivious grin.

John broke in with what he felt was a necessary caution.

"I want no problems from the locals here. We have a tough enough job as it is, so keep it in your pants. That means all you people. I'm not kidding. I don't give a damn if they come up to you with their pants off. No touch. Got it? You'll be on the trail back up to China so fast your little weenie won't know what hit it!"

John Guthrie had had quite a few beers, but no one doubted his statement. John never used his command voice unless he was being Major Guthrie and 100 per cent GI. This was a serious order that had been laid down. Len Sorenson broke the silence that followed John's pronouncement.

"We have a saying where I come from—I think—that covers this situation... but I forget what it is."

The resulting laughter returned everyone to the celebration, with the exception of Phac who clearly hadn't understood a word of the English. Guy Montfort realized his sergeant had no idea what was going on. He tried the best he could to translate the gist.

John had taken Jimmy Tau aside earlier to explain the situation regarding Guy.

"I meant to tell you about him before, but I was so involved with everything else.... I'm sorry, Jimmy. I think it can all work out, though. His English is adequate."

"It's none of my business, of course. It's your show, John, but these guys here are pretty sharp. They'll pick up any inconsistency. And Uncle speaks very good English, as you know. Eventually he'll want to speak to him in English and talk about America. He loves to try his English on new people and find out about them. He did it to me and you, didn't he? He'll ask where he's from in the States and all that stuff."

"It's one of those 'it seemed like a good thing at the time' deals. Maybe we should work on the idea that he's a recent immigrant from France or even a French Canadian?" said John unconvincingly. It occurred to him that the fact that Ho was sick might turn out to be an advantage.

By early the following morning, every shred of cover had been stripped. Thanh sought out John having a morning cup of tea with Edouard. With considerable solemnity, the tall Vietnamese guerrilla officer informed John that Guy Montfort had been recognized as a French officer by one of the recently arrived former members of the French colonial forces. The soldier had told Thanh that he was sure he had seen Montfort when he served on General Alessandri's staff.

"How could he be so sure of that?" John asked quickly in his natural defense lawyer manner.

"This man was a cook with the general's headquarters detachment. He saw all those officers."

What Thanh did not say was that all French officers were carefully observed by the Vietnamese colonial soldiers, for the French were the reigning aristocracy. The lowly *indigène* might never have a personal verbal exchange with an officer for the years of his service, but every move of each officer was always followed with great interest. There was no question in Thanh's mind that the new Viet Minh recruit was correct.

Thanh had passed the information directly to Giap who had authorized him to inform John so that the revelation could be handled as unofficially as possible. Giap knew that Ho would want a sensitive matter such as this treated in that manner. The official discussion would be held after the ill Uncle Ho could be briefed and the Viet Minh command decided what to do with the Frenchman.

"Comrade Van said that I was to tell you that he will be reporting to Uncle and then either he or Uncle will speak to you further. He said I should also mention to you that if at all possible, he preferred that you did not speak of this to Lt. Montfort until Uncle can be briefed. He asks this most respectfully."

True to his training, Thanh drew himself to attention, saluted and left the hut having completed his important and sensitive mission. Edouard exhaled loudly.

"Well, at least that shows they're leaving you an opening," he said.

"What opening?" John replied.

"The opening that allows you to say you didn't know anything about this. You can blame it all on me or higher ups that passed Montfort on to us without telling us who he really was."

"That's pretty farfetched, but you're right, the signs are there Giap is leaving this damn thing open for discussion and explanation—at least for the moment. We should keep our mouths shut till it plays out. I wonder if you were even supposed to be in on this."

"Right. He—the messenger—what's his name, Thanh, could have asked me to leave or taken you outside or something."

"That would have been rude. Maybe Giap told him not to worry about you. Who knows? At any rate the fat's in the fire now. There's nothing left but the truth or something close to it. We'll have to see how this plays out. I suspect it will move quickly. Meanwhile, you and I are clams."

"They wouldn't have asked me to leave because it was rude?"

"You got it. These are very polite people. I mean to a fault."

"But you sent us the report on the Tam Dao operation…. They killed every single Jap. Not too worried about politeness there!"

"I know it sounds a bit weird. But that's the way they are. One thing has nothing to do with another. An enemy is an enemy. A friend—and we're friends—is something quite different. Well, at least I'm a friend. They'll decide on you soon enough. As far as the Japs…. Hell, they had no care for the wounded."

"So it's not that you're an American and that makes you a friend?"

"Sort of. We're American friends of Uncle. That's what does it. Maybe you are a friend. Montfort sure as hell isn't—and that's for sure."

The two sat cross-legged on the floor of John's hut. Each still held on to their half empty tin cups of now quite lukewarm tea. John had acquired a larger table and chair, both made of bamboo, but it was still more comfortable sitting on his sleeping bag. It had started to rain again and there was a gentle patter on the palm frond roof. A large candle on the table provided all the light they needed. They sat quietly for a while, sipping their tea and thinking about what had just happened.

"Do you think this has screwed up the whole mission?" Edouard asked.

"I was about to ask you the same thing. I never thought they'd figure out he wasn't American right away. I always thought it was something they might come to suspect over a period of time—if at all. To answer your question… who the hell knows? Let's go over and find the rest of our gang."

With their ponchos over their head to keep out a quick rush of rain, John and Edouard made their way over to the communal mess which was nothing more than an extremely large lean-to made of the usual bamboo and palm fronds. Inside were the rest of the Moose team who had gathered shortly after first light with the intent to brew some tea and have breakfast with some of the rations they had brought down. Jimmy Tau was already there with Mac Soo who left shortly after John and Edouard arrived in order to make his regular morning contact. Jimmy, in his usual good humor, said that Mac would return shortly with any messages from Ch'ing-hsi. The other members of the team waved hello as they intently attacked the breakfast that already had been prepared for them.

The village women who handled such things had started their breakfast preparations before dawn in order to provide the visitors with a substantial meal with which to begin the day. Rice and a rich vegetable soup were accompanied by a steaming cup of fragrant tea similar to the cups supplied earlier to John and Edouard. Even in Kim Lung, rank had certain privileges and early tea in the hut was one of them. Len Sorenson, still stuffed from the previous night's feast, at first said he would stick to just a cup of tea. Shortly after finishing his it, however, he found his way to the soup pot and ended up happily putting away an enormous portion of rice with his large bowl of soup. He lit a cigarette and announced complete contentment.

They all sat around after breakfast smoking and gabbing about what they had seen and experienced since landing. Len Sorenson and Jimmy Tau immediately began reminiscences about past Red Sox exploits as Guy Montfort became involved with Ted Applegate in a discussion of leeches which abounded in the local environment. Even the taciturn Phac seemed finally to be at his ease and eager to get on with whatever tasks lay ahead. He and the rest of the team waited for instructions from their major for their first wet day in Tonkin. John rose to give what he had intended as an introductory briefing to the training cycle that they were supposed to begin with 20-man units of the Viet Minh fighting cadre. A small boy arrived with a request for Major Guthrie to follow him to a meeting. The boy spoke in Vietnamese, but the rank and name were clearly enunciated. The meaning was clear even if it hadn't been translated.

"Relax troops. I'll be right back, and we'll get on with the briefing. Edouard, why don't you make sure that everyone has all their stuff properly laid out and GI. We don't want these people here to think we're a bunch of slobs."

Ted Applegate, who had been quiet through breakfast, came alive with that instruction and gave an appropriate order for everyone to be ready for inspection. John shot a quick look in Edouard's direction and he responded with a nearly imperceptible nod.

The meeting, not unexpectedly, was in Ho's hut. Giap was there, but otherwise they were alone. The conversation was in French in order for Giap to participate. Dr. Ho was more alert than he had been the day before, a fact which John considered at least one good sign. Ho's eyes were still yellow, though far brighter than the previous day. His voice and expression were darkly serious.

"Comrade Van, here, has told me that he sent word to you regarding the problem we have. You understand, Major Guthrie, that this French officer—Montfort I believe he is called—cannot remain here."

"I would like to explain the situation first, Dr. Ho," John replied politely. Giap's face showed nothing, his brown eyes intense as usual never left John.

"I'm afraid that nothing you can say will change our mind, but I would be happy to listen," Ho replied with just the slightest condescension.

"Lt. Montfort has been seconded to my command in order to provide us with some knowledge of the local environment. France is an ally of the United States and it is quite normal for each country to provide the other with technical assistance."

"But Lt. Montfort is a former Vichy officer. Certainly, they were not your allies," Ho interrupted.

"No, sir, of course not, but Montfort had been working with the Free French all along."

"So he was a spy, then."

There was something in Ho's intonation that connoted a degree of mischievousness. John judged it to be an attempt to lighten the seriousness of the discussion. The lawyer that John was, sought to exploit any indication that Ho did not want this matter to interfere with the larger purpose of the OSS team's presence. John tried another tack:

"It seems to me that good relations between you, the Viet Minh, and the French might assist in your evolving Vietnamese independence. Working together against a mutual enemy, the Japanese, could contribute to a new relationship."

Uncharacteristically, Giap jumped in before Ho could respond. Giap, the teacher, lectured sharply as if to an opinionated student:

"Major, the French wish only to reestablish themselves as a colonial power. They have no interest in 'evolving' anything with us—certainly not independence. We are fighting for our liberation from them and anyone else, such as the Japanese, who want to rule Vietnam. We thought America was against colonial exploitation."

Before John could answer, Ho quickly took over. "How we decide to deal with the French will be determined by the people of our country, whom we of the league, the Viet Minh, represent and serve. At this time, we wish to work with your organization, the American OSS, not the French intelligence service. We do not wish Lt. Montfort to remain here, and we do not wish any other French in his place. It is our hope that your new president, Truman, will continue the great anti-colonial policy of your late President Roosevelt who died so unfortunately in April. We may seem to you to be a small political group in a not very large country, but we understand that all of us play a role in the world scene. I am sure that after you and your team are here for a while, you will come to learn more of the history of our land and thus our struggle to liberate ourselves from colonial oppression."

John was experienced enough as a negotiator to recognize a purposeful political speech when he heard it, and also that further comment on his part would be counterproductive. Uncle already had conceded the most important point of wanting to continue to work with the Moose Mission. That was all that was really important. The little man in the rumpled white suit, however, was another case. Giap was ready for a fight. He would not get one from John, but Comrade Van's controlled belligerence was palpable. This man really hated the French. He was a dangerous enemy for them—and anyone else who got in the way, John thought.

"And what about the enlisted man—the sergeant? He's Vietnamese. Can he stay? John asked as pleasantly as possible.

Ho replied that he doubted the French would allow that "under the circumstances." Giap leaned over and whispered something in Ho's ear in

Vietnamese. The old man nodded his head understandingly but didn't say anything.

"I shall have to work out the details of getting Lt. Montfort out of here," John said matter of factly.

"As soon as possible," added Giap without rancor. John could see that Vo Nguyen Giap knew how to win—and expected to. John wondered if the man played chess. It would be an interesting way to learn more about him. But then Comrade Van was too clever to be caught exposing more than necessary in the game within the game.

"One question, Major, if I might," asked Ho, still bundled up sitting on his straw mattress. The strain of the meeting had begun to show, and he started to perspire with a return of fever. "Did you know that Montfort was an M.5 officer?"

"I knew he worked with an M.5 unit, but not that he was an M.5 officer. Do you mean by M.5 that he is professionally an intelligence officer?"

"Yes, a professional. We think he is."

"No, I never thought that. To me he's just a French officer who knew Tonkin and was assigned accordingly. Does it matter?"

"I would think it would, to you," said Giap with only the barest wisp of a smile.

"I see your point. I'll have to think about it. I better go now and talk to Montfort. Then I'll have to figure out what we do with him. He must be protected, you realize."

"Have no fear regarding his safety. You have my personal guarantee," Ho replied earnestly, looking first at John then at Giap. The latter nodded affirmatively. Giap looked back toward John in confirmation and acceptance of the unspoken order he had received.

"This has been difficult for us both, John," said Uncle Ho in English. He reached forward and grasped John's hand in a firm shake.

"Yes, sir," the American major replied simply. He turned and left the hut, but not before he placed his palms together in the traditional manner and nodded goodbye to Giap. The man in the white suit gave a small polite smile and returned the gesture. Both men had taken the measure of each other, and that was not missed by Uncle.

John knew that it wasn't luck, bad luck, that had exposed Montfort. Even if he hadn't been recognized by that former colonial soldier, it would have been something else. Ho was too smart to be taken in by a lieutenant that spoke only passable English, and that with a French accent. The cover stories he'd discussed with Jimmy Tau to explain away those lapses were pretty damn useless now. As John had done many times after losing a case in court, or coming out on the short end of a negotiation, he went over why he'd approved of this incorrect move. He went directly to his bamboo hut to be alone and gather his thoughts before talking to Guy Montfort. He didn't want to pull Edouard away from the Moose team in order to confer. Everyone would get the idea that something was up. This was a matter that had to be handled by himself alone before the rest of the team was informed.

John did not take his losses well. The failure to accept his own shortcomings always had driven him to strive beyond the point where logic may have dictated. As he had done often before, he went over his thought processes in order to search out the intellectual failure which was at the root of his making the erroneous judgement. The rain beat its gentle tune on the palm frond roof as John sat in the corner of the hut for nearly a half hour going over each step in his original agreement to add Montfort to the team and then to keep him there in spite of the Sainteny directive. In the end, he decided to put the whole damn thing aside. He couldn't afford to devote any more time to himself. Maybe later when he could talk to Edouard, he'd work it out with him. It was a rare trust he had in Eddy Parnell. He had never allowed himself that luxury before, the luxury of trusting.

John went out into the rain and found Montfort going over a list of supplies they had brought in with them. Edouard was doing the same thing, but John waved him off. The fact that he was talking to the Frenchman told Edouard all he needed to know for the moment. Guy followed John back to his hut. John made no attempt to smooth the way into the matter at hand. Speaking carefully in French just to make sure there was no misunderstanding, John got right to the point.

"They know you're a French officer. One of their men recognized you from when he was with your Vichy forces. You have to leave, and quickly. Giap is very unhappy, to put it mildly. Uncle Ho's the same. I got you a guarantee of protection, effectively a *laisser passer* out of here. If it was up to Comrade Van, I'm sure he would have put you in prison, or worse. He's a tough bastard. I believe he really hates the French."

John said nothing about the comments on Guy being an intelligence officer. He didn't want to get involved in that. The implication that Montfort might have been introduced into the Moose Mission also to track what John and the OSS team were doing was all too obvious a secondary target, and perhaps even primary. The thought added to John's aggravation with himself. He pushed that out of his mind to concentrate on the immediate problem.

"Is there anything else I should know?" John asked, the defense lawyer's typical question.

"I don't know what you mean. You knew everything already. It was a chance and we took it," Guy answered in a tone no longer carrying the military deference of past demeanor. It was obvious he no longer considered himself under Major Guthrie's command. That was a mistake.

"Lieutenant, we shall get this straight right now. I have it in my power to turn you over to Giap's tender mercies if I'm so inclined. You will respond to my questions and satisfy me that there is no reason I should think you are part of some damned effort by M.5 to screw up an American special operations mission."

John's voice was low, controlled, and hard. He had made a very large error in accepting the French participation. He had been conned and didn't like it. But worse, he had overlooked the obvious implications. And now this smug Montfort would rub his nose in it. John's vow to himself just minutes before to put aside the emotional aspects of this debacle had fallen victim to Montfort's arrogant retort. John was livid, mostly at himself, but also at the overall situation. He knew he had to regain composure. Guy, himself stunned by the vehemence of John's reaction, rushed to repair the damage his response had caused.

"Sir, please excuse me. In no way did I wish to be evasive. More importantly, never was there any intent to hinder the Moose Mission."

Guy Montfort had been a French staff officer long enough to learn how to mollify an angry and embarrassed superior. The best way in this case was to tell the American major all that he knew.

"Sir, you know my story. I'm not an M.5 officer. It is just because I was considered a loyal Frenchman… because of my contacts with the Free French of General DeGaulle that I came to the attention of Commandant Laborde and his field operation. We have family ties. Yes, M.5 in Ch'ing-hsi knew about and approved of my joining your group, but that's all. They also agreed to have me continue after the other joint operations were cancelled. But that's it. It was not my idea to appear to be an American."

The entire discussion had degenerated into an attempt to recall who had said what to whom and when. This, combined with the fact that John's spoken French was about equal to Guy's spoken English made conversation at this level of intensity quite problematical. John tried, as carefully as he could, to frame a crucial question.

"So you're saying there is no M.5 alternative objective involved?"

Guy knew he would have to lie to avoid the answer to the question. It was not that he minded lying, but in this instance, John was in a position of control. The lie somehow might be exposed and here in the middle of the Viet Minh camp the American held all the cards. It was a quick but not difficult calculation that Guy made. His loyalty was to his country—something he had well proved—not to some ambitious intelligence unit. He had no choice but to trust John.

"This is completely confidential, sir. You can't share this with the Viet Minh—in fact, no one else, not even your own command. This is most secret…."

Montfort waited to hear John's reaction to this announcement, all the while rationalizing that what he was about to give away wasn't really important now that he, himself, had been effectively taken out of the action. The promise of secrecy he sought from John was worthless and Guy knew it: John said nothing but nodded his assent. Hesitantly, Guy continued in a lowered voice, nearly a whisper.

"It's Phac, sir. He's an intelligence officer. We, that is Jacques de Laborde and I, didn't find out about it until the last minute. He works for Commandant Sainteny, directly. Sainteny slipped him in without us knowing anything about it. I can assure you, sir, Jacques de Laborde would never have allowed this to happen. He was very mad. I know that just before we left, he flew up to Kunming to try and get the man removed. Phac's a lieutenant in M.5, sir. Jacques said he was prepared to take it over Sainteny's head, but I guess there wasn't enough time. I was never supposed to know. In fact, I don't officially know yet. So in a way, I have no obligation to protect Phac anyhow."

The last disclaimer was meant as much for Guy's own conscience as it was an explanation to John as to why he was giving up security information. John's reaction was controlled. He was in what he called his combat mode. What he really wanted to do was to use every four-letter word at his command.

"And what exactly is he here to do?" John asked while immediately thinking ahead to how he might have to sacrifice Phac in some way to Giap just to keep the Moose Mission operational.

"I'm not really sure. He was sent down by Kunming. I know that Jacques didn't know anything either. He said that Sainteny was trying to get back at him for having his independent command. There's something political there but I don't know what it is."

"I repeat my question. What do you think he's here for?"

"I, well… it's just a guess. He could be here to pave the way, perhaps, for a meeting between Commandant Sainteny and Dr. Ho. You know, take the temperature for a possible meeting, and then maybe lay the groundwork. I really don't know… I'm just guessing. But otherwise he seems decent enough—at least I think he is. I'm sorry, that's all I know about this. I didn't have much time to talk to Jacques about it. I'm sure he must have a better idea, certainly by now. I know he was very mad at himself also because he had opened the door by requesting a sergeant to accompany us."

There wasn't anything else that Guy Montfort could say. There was nothing else he knew. He was smart enough to stop talking. For John's part the revelation about Phac had added a new dimension to Montfort's situation. But then he would have never learned of Phac if he hadn't had the Montfort mess blow up in his face. He still didn't totally believe the Frenchman's explanation of his own role—especially the lack of mention of any part to be played as an intelligence penetration within the American mission. But now that was

John's fault. He was the one who should have been more protective of his own command. Back in Ch'ing-hsi he had become caught up in the camaraderie of the cooperation with the French.

John agreed not to mention the Phac case to anyone, and counselled Guy not to discuss any of their conversation with Phac. It was all an empty agreement at this stage, but at least the appearance of trust was maintained, even if the reality had succumbed to operational pressures. John said that he would brief his Americans on Guy's status as a result of the meeting with Ho and Giap. He asked the French lieutenant to get hold of Edouard and have him bring the team to John's hut. Guy snapped off a salute and a "*Oui, Mon Commandant!*" He didn't have to try to be American anymore but wanted to assure John he was still following his orders. John was too involved in his own thoughts to take notice of that subtlety.

The four American sergeants arrived with Edouard and Jimmy Tau. Seven people in the little hut was unworkable so they all trooped out again and went over to the now empty communal mess. They sat at the rough-hewn tables, faces expectant.

"Good we're all here. I know you must all be wondering what's going on, so I'll give it to you short and sweet."

John proceeded to explain as simply as he could results of the meeting about Guy Montfort with the Viet Minh leaders. He said nothing of Phac. Jimmy Tau spoke first, though Ted Applegate seemed about to say something. He really liked Montfort.

"Guy Montfort is maybe in some danger, right?" said Jimmy. "What about the Vietnamese sergeant?" he added.

"T'hell with 'im," said Ted. "The lieutenant's a good guy. We gotta make sure he gets taken care of."

"Dr. Ho has said that he was under their protection—meaning him and General Giap. And I guess that goes for Sergeant Phac also. I certainly don't want him now. I had no idea the antagonism ran this deep. Well, maybe I did, but I didn't value it properly. My fault!" said John.

"If Uncle Ho said he will protect Montfort, that's good enough. But how do we get them out? The airstrip won't be ready for a while," commented Jimmy Tau.

"You'll send a signal to your boss, Jimmy, and maybe he can come up with something. But we aren't going to do that right away. We have to take a little time to see how this thing plays out," John replied.

"Excuse me, uh, John," said Len following directions on the first name rule. "Why is this our problem? I may be a bit of a cold bastard here, but this is a French problem the way I see it. If I understood correctly, they wanted to come along. We didn't twist their arm or anything. Or am I wrong? I've been known to miss the point before."

"I guess you're right, Len. The French offered the help and we accepted, so technically you're right. But again, technically Guy is under my command, so he's my responsibility. I could have refused the offer to participate, but from a strict standpoint they, Guy and his boss, initiated the whole business of joining the Moose Mission. We agreed and thought it generous and useful. However, it's still for me a personal responsibility: One, because I made it all possible and two, because I'm here now and the guy in charge. I must make sure they all get out whole and breathing regularly."

Edouard hadn't said anything. He had known more or less what was coming and the best thing he could do was just keep his mouth shut and look supportive as a good second-in-command should do. Jimmy Tau was bothered and kept nudging him and making side remarks.

"Something not right with you, Jimmy?" John shot out.

"Okay, I'm not really a member of you Mooses, but I got to tell you that I've been around here for a while, which you know, and I don't like the feel of this thing at all. It's not that I don't trust Uncle's promise of protection for Guy and all that. It's just that I don't trust them when it comes to the colonial soldier. In the Viet Minh, especially those who are communists, it's strictly a 'if you're not with us you're against us' deal. I don't know that Uncle's protection can reach down to the basic level, or, in truth, whether he would want to. He's a guy who leads by delegating the tough stuff to his lieutenants like Giap and others. I'll make it simple. These are lovely people. They've been damn nice to me and Mac. That's fine, but it's not the whole picture. A guy comes down with you who's Vietnamese. They don't know who this guy really works for. He's got to have some connection with M.5 as far as they're concerned. It's only logical. One of these mornings we could find that he's just disappeared. It's happened, I guarantee you."

For all his boyish manner, Jimmy Tau was as old as John. He had spent the war years in and around China and Vietnam doing things that his AGAS boss only alluded to but never really explained. John respected his exceptional knowledge of the politics and personalities. This was the first time Jimmy had spoken up this way, and he was not to be ignored.

"By disappeared you mean killed?" John asked.

"If they thought he was working for the wrong people… most certainly. Aside from the M.5 he could be working for the Chinese—of several different colorations. Maybe even some other Vietnamese nationalist group—some have Japanese ties. It's crowded out there, my friend. Oh yeah, I forgot—any of these could have connections with the criminal tongs. Our hosts had to have the same suspicious reaction I did when he arrived with you. Why would any Vietnamese colonial noncom parachute into a Viet Minh area unless he had something else on his mind? There, that's it in a nutshell."

John was committed to his pretend ignorance. Jimmy had divined more of the truth than he realized. As the fragrance of jasmine mixed with leftover cooking smells, the Moose team sat quietly, contemplating. A gentle rain still fell outside the large lean-to.

"We got no choice but t'git on with our job 'n fergit this guy. It don't matter what he's connected to. Let these here locals make the decision. John thinks he got responsibility, but he don't."

Ted Applegate's proclamation ended the discussion and the meeting.

A not dissimilar discussion was underway at the exact same time at a meeting site just outside the Kim Lung encampment. Vo Nguyen Giap had gathered together several of his political officers, including Bui Dac Thanh who already had risen to the level of a military operations chief. Thanh had quickly shown himself to have the unusual combination of political skills and sound military experience. His handling of the Tam Dao raid and ability to get along with the American major clearly showed his potential. It was rare to find a Party member who had the combination of political and military capability. Thanh may have been young by ordinary standards, but as a Party member with actual army training and combat experience he was already a ranking Viet Minh officer. In the new liberation army Giap was forging, age had less consequence than demonstrated loyalty, personal courage, and talent.

This special security meeting had been occasioned by a report received via courier from Kunming some time before that the French M.5 chief, Sainteny, had met with a well-known pro-Japanese nationalist from Hanoi. The information had come from Liu Chi Roget's net and therefore was highly valued. While the fact of the M.5 meeting had an importance in general terms, the details of its arrangement were significant for the Kim Lung headquarters. The report stated that the meeting had been set up by an M.5 officer of French/Vietnamese birth who was known to be now working with the Americans at Ch'ing-hsi. When Phac turned up with the American team, and Montfort was exposed as a former Vichy officer and not the American he was presumed to be, the report from Kunming immediately took on new importance. The coincidence demanded investigation.

"It is a delicate matter," Giap began. "I would like to place this so-called sergeant in some form of detention so he can be interrogated. But that would be considered an insult to our American friends who Uncle believes are completely innocent of this duplicity. It is my instinct that careful questioning will prove who this one really is and what his intentions are. Have you any suggestions?"

"I understand, Comrade, that Uncle believes these Americans to be innocent, but what if they are not?" Thanh was not questioning the infallibility of Uncle Ho as he was the saintliness of the Americans. His dialectical training had stuck. Giap replied in his professorial tone:

"The Americans are not sophisticated people like the French. They are very straightforward. They are a very large and rich country that does not need colonies. Uncle has known them for a long time and has instructed me about them. It is a reasonable question you ask, but Uncle has made this matter quite clear."

The other political officers all nodded in agreement of the obvious. One of them offered an idea.

"Thank you for the instruction, Comrade. In that case I recommend that Comrade Thanh, who knows the French Army well, be assigned to elicit from this Phac what we need. And he already has made his acquaintance."

"This Phac is a talker," Thanh said. "As my comrade here knows, I spoke with the man when he first arrived. We walked back to the camp together as Comrade Van indicated I should." A bit annoyed at his colleague's remark, Thanh wanted to get straight how he had come to speak with Phac.

"As I said, this Phac likes to talk, but he appeared to me to be a bit fearful at being here. He didn't say anything, but I sensed that. I first thought it was that he had just parachuted in, which it would seem is a very exciting and scary thing to do. If he reacts to fear by talking, may I be allowed to place a little fear in his heart?"

They all laughed when Giap, in a rare display of humor, said, "Fear is good for the soul."

Contrary to his agreement with John, the French lieutenant had waited only a few hours to share the news with Phac. After reflection, Montfort decided that as a French officer it was incumbent upon him to alert his compatriot to the changed situation in spite of the American commander's contrary view. A few hours of stewing in contemplation of the dangers implicit in the changed circumstances had altered the justification for the previous agreement. By that time, Guy Montfort wasn't even completely sure as to what he had exactly agreed. Sometimes the mind creates convenient memories, or lack of memory altogether.

When Thanh found Phac that evening in the mess hut, it was shortly after the unfortunate news had been delivered by Guy. The revelation had been limited to the bare facts of Montfort's own exposure, but he had warned Phac that he was consequently vulnerable. Guy's commitment as a French officer had not been extended to the point of telling Phac that his cover had also been given away to John along with his rank and status. Nonetheless, Phac took badly even the limited disclosure. Fearful of the implications for his personal safety, Phac trembled with a full-scale attack of nerves. The arrival of the friendly Thanh became a valuable interruption at just the right moment.

Phac cradled a cup of hot tea as he sat alone in the semi-dark of the hut. A smiling Thanh sat down beside him.

"So, how's your first full day been? It's a bit rough living, not like China, I suspect."

"I've been better," responded Phac disconsolately.

Thanh had planned on a lengthy buildup of good will and clever maneuvering. Phac's obvious distress could not be overlooked and required a change in tactics. Thanh's mind raced as he shifted into his sympathetic colleague role.

"I'm really sorry to hear that. If there's anything I can do.... Remember we're all countrymen here. I can't tell you how delighted we've been that you are part of this American team. At least we know that they'll have somebody to explain things. It's a big help to us."

As far as Phac was concerned, it was like a life preserver thrown to a man in rushing water.

"Well, that's why I agreed to come along. We all want a liberated Vietnam, don't we? I think the Americans are well-meaning, but they don't really understand the complications. I thought if I came down... I thought maybe I could be a help... in general. I'd heard of the Viet Minh, of course, but I can see now how well organized you are. It's just what we need... here in Vietnam, that is."

The fear emanating from the man was easy to sense. Thanh had not expected such an obvious and swift breakdown—and with absolutely no pressure. This Phac had worked himself into complete capitulation even before he'd been asked to surrender. Not much of a soldier and certainly not what Thanh thought of as an intelligence officer. Of course, it all could be a guise to gain acceptance. But this man was petrified, ready for full-scale questioning. The trick, Thanh remembered from his lessons on the subject, was to keep the man in the proper mental state for interrogation. As Comrade Van had said, it was a delicate situation. The man must be encouraged to continue his own efforts at self-recruitment. Later that would be used as the vehicle to guide his willingness to talk into areas of interest to the questioners. It's all a matter of timing; this had been emphasized. So far Thanh had been lucky in that regard, but now he must use the moment to guide this Phac along a road of perceived safety.

By the time the two men parted it was close to midnight. Thanh had allowed himself to be enlisted by Phac in an effort to get him accepted as a true Vietnamese patriot whose only wish was to join the Viet Minh and fight the Japanese. Thanh reported the contact immediately to the "never sleeping" Comrade Van, who complimented him on his good work. Further interrogation of Phac in any manner at all had to be approved by Uncle, himself. Thanh would be informed the next day if and when he was needed. In the meantime, Thanh was instructed to attempt to stay close to Phac, but not in such a way that would seem suspicious, either to the target or the Americans.

The situation had worked out better than Giap had dared hope. Phac was on the verge of total cooperation without physical persuasion just as Uncle Ho preferred, though not necessarily what they were always able to accomplish. However, even with this advantageous turn of events, Giap could see no alternative to putting the already vulnerable Phac into some form of controlled environment in order to create the proper sense of isolation so important to any level of interrogation. How that could be accomplished without creating a break with the Americans was something on which Uncle would have to advise. Again, Vo Nguyen Giap was reminded, as he had been so often before, of the extraordinary importance his wise old mentor was to his personal, as well as political, existence.

Ho was not doing well and Truyen did not want even Giap to disturb him. The malaria that was surely part of his illness left Ho alternating with shivers of cold and downpours of fever-induced perspiration. In spite of his wracked condition, the ill man insisted on both his regular briefings and access to his principal aides. Nurse Truyen might try to dissuade Giap, but she would never go against explicit instructions from Uncle. She urged Giap to be as swift as possible in his visit in order to avoid overly stimulating her patient. It may have been simply the usual advice a nurse would give a visitor, but Giap knew she was justifiably worried about her charge.

The hut was kept immaculate by Truyen, who now made everyone who entered wear a white mask she had fashioned from gauze. The smell of peppermint mingled with the ginger emanating from strategically placed pots in the corners of the hut. Ho was bathed periodically in the refreshing peppermint oils to ease his fever. They had no quinine, though word had gone out earlier to nearby Viet Minh groups to be on the lookout for possible supplies. Ho had refused the medications that Jimmy had had parachuted in. The searches had been carried all the way to Hanoi in hopes that the scarce quinine could be obtained there. Truyen had already spoken to Giap about the need to get help from the Americans, but that was impossible without first getting permission from Uncle. Giap knelt by the figure wrapped in blankets against the fever chill.

"I have only a couple of questions on which I need your advice, Uncle. The first has to do with your health, I...."

"I'm doing much better than I look, comrade," Ho interrupted firmly.

"Yes, of course, but I was wondering if the Americans might have something to ease your illness—for the malaria for example."

"No, I do not want you to ask them for anything. Truyen has already told me about Lt. Tau's medicines. They must not know I'm this ill. It's just a bad cold, something like that. Tell them only that. Next question." Ho's voice was raspy and seemingly always on the edge of interruption by a coughing spasm. Truyen wiped his brow and cheeks with her peppermint-scented wash rag.

"As you wish, Uncle. My second question is a bit more complex. It has to do with the colonial soldier the Americans brought with them. Comrade Thanh—remember he is our new political officer who led the Tam Dao raid—has reported to me that the one we think is an M.5 officer is on the brink of defecting to us, or at the very least can be encouraged to give us all the details of his assignment."

"You have confidence in Comrade Thanh?" Ho coughed the question.

"Yes, Uncle. I have already promoted him to be a military operations commander. I see him as both militarily and politically capable. You remember he arrived with the highest recommendation from his training in Kunming."

"I remember quite well, comrade. My mind doesn't have a cold," said Ho in a rare display of sarcasm brought on by the ill health he was denying. "And you want to have permission to formally interrogate the potential defector?"

"Yes, Uncle, but I realize this might cause some problems with the Americans."

Ho tried to take a deep breath and began coughing again. He gained control and carefully began to speak, attempting to make the words clear.

"If you must question him... you should go directly to the American Major... Guthrie... Tell him what you intend to do and why... Then you must be careful not to injure your subject... All questioning by psychological persuasion... You know what I mean... This is the only way... The American knows we can't accept the Frenchman, so this now should not come as a big surprise... You must be clever in this... I know you can do it."

Ho's breathing was too labored to speak anymore. The extended instruction had worn him out, but the words were clear. It may not have been the *carte blanche* Giap had been hoping for, but he had asked for his marching orders and had received them. It was now up to Giap to figure out how to accomplish the task as laid out. He looked at Ho lying now with his eyes shut, chest rising and falling as he rushed air into his lungs. Truyen motioned for Giap to leave. He hesitated for a brief moment, turned quickly, and left. He knew it was her job as a nurse, but he didn't like being dismissed in that manner.

Wasting no time, Giap immediately searched around the camp for John. He found him at the radio shack with Mac Soo. In his usual extremely polite manner, Giap asked if John had a moment to speak with him. John suggested they go back to his hut. The small size of the Kim Lung encampment meant that the American major and the man in the white suit's meeting would be an instant news item. It certainly wasn't an environment conducive to clandestine sessions. The important part of the meeting was what was said, not the meeting itself. By the same token anyone hanging around to listen outside the hut would have been easily seen by everyone in the camp. The exchange between the two men therefore was kept quite confidential during the process. The entire camp knew of the meeting, but no one had an idea of what was said. Security sometimes takes on odd forms.

Some equipment and supplies had been moved into John's hut and the small space had become cramped. John apologized for the mess and moved some things so Giap could sit on the one chair. John assumed his usual position sitting cross-legged on the floor. He was conscious that this placed Giap above him, which John was aware might make him more at ease. It was a good idea, but one which mattered not at all to the supremely confident Giap. He would have been just as secure if the positions were reversed. However, the Vietnamese did take notice of the *politesse*.

It was hard to consider Giap as a soldier, but John had been well briefed by Jimmy Tau. He knew that this slight, unsmiling man in his uniform white suit was the operational chief of the entire Viet Minh guerrilla force as well as head of their security apparat. Why the man insisted on wearing clothes which better characterized a typical colonial functionary was a matter of conjecture. It certainly was impractical garb for the middle of the Tonkin jungle, and hardly could be a symbol of socialist egalitarianism. Then there was the battered blackish fedora. Jimmy Tau said that in his opinion, the whole outfit was left over from Giap's days as a schoolteacher, although he did admit the possibility existed that they might be worn in perpetual mourning for his dead wife. It was agreed, however, that Giap wore the suit as if it was a uniform, and that in itself held a significance—even if they didn't have a clue as to what it was.

Sitting with his hands clasped in front of him, Giap, in his carefully chosen French, launched into the reason he had asked for the meeting. He explained that they had received information indicating that a man of Phac's description was an M.5 officer working directly for Commandant Sainteny in Kunming, and that this man had been assigned to a special mission with the Americans in Ch'ing-hsi. He let the last bit of information sit without further comment and then continued:

"What is the most important part of this is that this same man was responsible for arranging a meeting between Commandant Sainteny and a person we know to hold himself out as a Vietnamese nationalist when he is in reality a Japanese puppet."

"You think this man is our Sgt. Phac?" It was a rhetorical question from John; he didn't expect an answer. "So what do you suggest we do?" he asked, this time meaning it.

Giap shifted a bit on the wooden chair, his hands relaxed.

"I think you should do nothing at all. It is best that we interrogate him. I am under very strict orders concerning this interrogation from Uncle. I assure you we will be very careful in our questioning. There will be no physical abuse. I give you my personal guarantee that no harm will befall this man. We understand he is under your command, and this is important. We recognize that."

The little man in the white suit may not have looked like a soldier, but John realized by that last statement that he had a full sense of military courtesy. When John had referred to Giap before as "General" it was simply a recognition of the man's titular role in the Viet Minh. But Major John Guthrie now understood he was now actually talking to General Vo Nguyen Giap, and he decided to respond accordingly.

"Sir, I appreciate your position as you appear to appreciate mine. I must admit that from the beginning we noted that this Sgt. Phac did not carry himself as the usual enlisted man does." John knew that Ted Applegate would give himself a large pat on the back on this one. "We have no way of knowing what all this is about. I must tell you, however, that I am personally convinced that Lt. Montfort was not intending anything that would bring injury to the Viet Minh."

"Major, there are so many possibilities it is best just to ignore them and concentrate on what this Phac can tell us. But I am sure you realize that this means we must somehow remove the two of them from... how shall I say this... harm's way?"

"Perhaps also... from temptation," John added with a smile.

"I see we are thinking along the same lines, Major. Excellent! We shall have to find a way eventually to return them to where they came from... but that is something for later."

Giap rose from the chair and John stood up. Their height difference was accentuated by the lowness of the roof of the hut which had been built for men of Vietnamese stature. Giap reached for John's hand and shook it. It was a firm handshake even though John's far larger hand engulfed Giap's. John was surprised to find the little man's hand was calloused, and he realized that this general did more than waltz around in a white suit.

As John and Giap climbed down from the elevated hut, gunfire at regular intervals sounded from the nearby forest.

"The training has begun, sir," John announced.

"I'm sure that under your men's apt tutelage our soldiers will become excellent marksmen," Giap commented. It was the sort of praise generals pass on to hard-working junior officers.

Applegate's two instructors had begun their promised target practice session with Thanh and a platoon of guerrillas. Thanh had already asked for instruction on the disassembly of the .30 cal. machine guns that they had received but never used. While both sergeants had fired the weapon back during their own training, neither had ever field-stripped the weapon. Ted Applegate took over that phase of the instruction himself. It was messy work because every working part was coated in cosmoline. Nonetheless, the crusty

199

top sergeant was in his element. With some effort and constant reference to his pocket dictionary, the one young noncom who had learned Vietnamese at the Army language school translated each step as Applegate broke down, cleaned, then reassembled the light machine gun. A selected group of eight guerrillas stood in a circle with Thanh around the demonstration. Meanwhile the former state trooper continued with the target practice and the other guerrillas by showing the correct shooting stance and firing procedure. He gave the instruction in English that the fighters dutifully pretended to understand. With careful attention, however, they studied his every move and replicated each exactly. It gave the impression of perfect comprehension.

John learned that Edouard had gone off to the main village of Kim Lung with Jimmy Tau to investigate the progress of the airstrip. Len Sorenson had proceeded to set up a small dispensary and was cataloguing and consolidating the medical supplies he had brought with him as well as the ones Jimmy already had on hand. John went back to his hut to prepare a written account of the security situation as it had evolved since the arrival of the Moose Mission. The lawyer in him dictated such care. It might become important in the future.

Chapter Eleven

The new information regarding Phac and his connection with Sainteny and the pro-Japanese Vietnamese was hardly a surprise to John. With as much as had already happened in the area of snafus, John had taken on the protection of a veneer of fatalism. The truth was that he really didn't care that Giap intended to use non-physical methods to get the supposed M.5 undercover officer to tell the whole story. John had already been through far too much in his war to be squeamish over the prospect of violent interrogation. Anyhow, he still was embarrassed over the fact that he had been taken in. He took it as an assault on himself, personally. In the streets of Gary, Indiana, assault of any kind is taken very seriously and responded to in kind. It was best that this matter be handled by the Viet Minh, because if it had been up to John, he knew he would've beaten the crap out of the guy.

The interrogation of Phac was less a matter of detailed questioning of the now-admitted M.5 lieutenant as it was slowing him down so that all the information pouring out could be assimilated and taken down. Phac's story was that he had been ordered by Sainteny to join Guy Montfort and the Moose Mission. He admitted that he had been assigned previously to work with the VNQDD, a rival nationalist organization to the Viet Minh. During the course of this enterprise he also met and developed the head of the pro-Japanese faction Dai Viet. This was the man Phac had introduced to Sainteny.

"So what was the reason that Commandant Sainteny wanted you to join the American team?" Giap, who was acting as principal interrogator, asked.

"Sainteny wants to have direct contact with the Viet Minh. I was to create that route. He also mentioned he'd like to meet Dr. Ho Chi Minh. So I said to myself that this was a great opportunity to come down and join the Viet Minh and fight with you. The Americans knew nothing, and as far as I know, Montfort didn't know that Sainteny had any interest."

Giap took note of the exoneration of the French officer, but that didn't change his opinion of Phac. Vo Nguyen Giap was both a student of history and human behavior. He long ago learned the tactic of "one truth to cover one lie." The truth regarding Lt. Guy Montfort, however, did not succeed in covering the lie of Phac's eagerness to join the Viet Minh—no matter the excellence of his performance. However, with the soft technique he was using, it was best not to challenge the man's story at this stage. Let him sit and mull over what he had said but keep him separated from all contact. There was plenty of time to deal with him.

With Phac held incommunicado and Montfort no longer treated as a welcome guest, the atmosphere of the camp tensed. John had to give explicit orders to the Moose team to treat Montfort in as normal manner as possible in order not to encourage the Viet Minh fighters to act even harsher. Guy was allowed to roam about the camp—to a point. He attempted once to accompany Mac Soo on one of the radioman's regular fishing trips but was stopped just outside the camp's boundaries. The control was loose, but effective. Several days went by without any final solution for the unwanted guests proposed by the Viet Minh side. It was Edouard's idea to have a session he called a war council. The hope was that the collective American brains would come up with some workable answer.

Jimmy Tau's hut was chosen for the meeting because it was a new one, nearly twice as large as any of the others. The AGAS officer had done his best to fit out his quarters with locally made furniture and assorted, colored, woven straw hangings he had purchased from village artisans. He had obtained one rattan chair that was amazingly comfortable. They had kidded him about "setting up house," but everyone enjoyed visiting—especially to have some of the delicious local wine he had mysteriously obtained. As he explained, he had all the comforts of home, if one didn't mind the occasional snake.

Jimmy Tau insisted that John take the rattan chair. "It befits your rank," he said. The others spread around the room that easily held all the Moose men and the one "Honorary Moose," as Jimmy was dubbed. In the past few days John had come to enjoy his little group. They had been supportive and helpful ever since the situation arose that they now called the "French flap." Their team leader was willing to take the burden completely on himself and they reacted by trying to ease that burden. John could tell that it had brought them all closer than they would have been, though he suspected it had been Edouard's deft guidance that had been behind the new *esprit*.

"The problem we have is one of time and space," said Edouard opening the meeting. "We've got to get two guys out of here as quickly as we can."

"But we can't just put them on the trail to Pac Bo and forget about them," Jimmy Tau added quickly.

"Why not?" replied the ever-practical Applegate.

"Because the Viet Minh don't seem to want to. And that's another question: Why don't they want to, as Ted is about to ask?" said Edouard.

"My impression is that they're arguing amongst themselves," Len Sorenson spoke up. "They know I can't speak their language, so they talk pretty freely around me. She's pretty closed mouth, but I can get Nurse Truyen to translate a bit every now and then. Obviously, this is the big topic around the camp, and everyone seems to have an opinion. Some want to outright shoot the two of them, but that's apparently been solidly vetoed from upstairs. At least that's the gist of what I've been able to put together from the bits and pieces."

Jimmy Tau, as the longest resident and a Vietnamese speaker, was generally accepted as the Moose Mission's authority on local matters. After Len's assessment everyone turned to Jimmy for his commentary.

"My impression is that we have two different groups of people around here, maybe more, but certainly two basic ones. On the one hand there are the loyal gung-ho fighters that just want to get out there and kill somebody. I'm not sure they care much who, just so it gets rid of any foreign government like the French, the Japs, whatever. The second is the village people, the ordinary farmer who is currently under the protection of the Viet Minh and is considered loyal to whatever they think that cause is. The fighters run the show, but they can't really exist without the support, food and so forth from the villagers."

"Are you saying one side controls the other and that accounts for the differences that Len referred to?" asked Edouard.

"I don't know. I think I mean that they don't know either. All this talk is going on around the camp as Len says… but how much say do any of them have?" Jimmy answered.

Back and forth the discussion went with each person adding a little something and bit by bit getting further away from the principal point of the meeting. John looked at Edouard who showed signs of fatigue at the others who didn't seem to be able to stay on track. Edouard raised his eyebrows as if to indicate that the good idea for a group discussion had run its course, aided perhaps by too much lubrication from the wine. In an attempt to get things back on point, John, who hadn't spoken at all, waved off the conversation.

"Look, we may not be able to get these people out—which was Edouard's opening issue. But what we don't know is clearer than what we do know. For instance, with all due credit to our friends, the Viet Minh, we really don't know enough about them. We have no idea how far an order from Dr. Ho goes when it comes to something like this. We don't know the extent of their discipline, though I grant it seems to me to be pretty damned strict. I want to believe Dr. Ho runs the show. It seems that way, but you can't really tell what happens under stress. In fact, Uncle seems like a great guy, but how much do we actually know about him? Very little. Giap seems pretty easy to read;

that, too, could all be part of the picture we're supposed to see. We all know what I'm talking about. Good cop and bad cop tandem."

"I don't think it's quite as clever as that—not that they aren't capable of that sort of thing," Jimmy Tau disagreed. "I've been pretty close to them for quite a while. Ho's deeply respected by all those I've met. As far as Comrade Van, and that goes for others on his level, maybe five or six top guys... he and they follow what the old man tells them to do. I don't think they go off on their own very much. He's sick now, of course, but even then... he gives them the line and they follow it."

John responded immediately:

"Don't get me wrong. I like Uncle Ho as a person. He's very smart and not prone to snap judgements. But that doesn't mean the same thing as trusting him or any of the others. They have their agenda and we have ours. They also have their way of doing things which might not necessarily be ours. Remember they're in a war, but it's not the same one as ours. We might have a mutual enemy today, the Japs. Tomorrow that could change. Their war is just what they've told us. Liberation is the word they use. That's their war. It's not ours. At least not until someone way up the totem pole tells us differently."

"Aren't we getting a bit off the subject?" Edouard broke in as diplomatically as he could. "I agree with both John and Jimmy. That's what makes dealing with these Viet Minh so difficult. Both you guys are right, but where does that leave us? We still have to arrange something for the two Frenchmen. Correction: One-and-a-half Frenchmen and only a half Vietnamese. I thought I'd say that before one of you ethnic experts chimed in."

Sensing that this was a good time to call for a break in what he considered a lot of unnecessary yammering, Ted Applegate loudly announced he was in need of a refill. Jimmy brought forward his large gourd filled with the local wine. Smaller gourds had been cut in half to serve as wine glasses. The wine had a sweet flowery flavor cut by what the connoisseur Applegate referred to as approximately 12 per cent alcohol content. He said he could determine this by his natural talent to determine the "kick" in all drinks. Whatever the actual alcohol level, the wine had a very quick impact on the unwary, and they all learned that a couple of "glasses" were quite sufficient to produce a buzz. The conversation detoured to the subject of reminiscences of exotic drinks—a topic that Applegate's Philippine experience clearly dominated. It was sometime before Edouard got the talk back to the original issue.

"When do you think the airstrip will be finished, Jimmy?" Edouard asked.

"Well, you saw it the other day. The answer is, I really don't know. They told us at that time it would be a couple of weeks. But like I told you then, I think they said that because you were there, and they wanted to make a good impression. Before you came, they told me a couple of months. Take your pick. I don't think they know. It's a question of when the labor is available from the village. Now, if we told Comrade Van we needed the strip in order to bring in a heavy load of weapons and equipment for them, they'd get it done in no time."

"So we can't wait until the strip is finished, but we've got to keep them someplace until it is. Can we do that? My impression is that the Viet Minh definitely don't want them here," said Edouard, stating the obvious.

"How about the Tam Dao people? John asked quietly, as the idea just dawned.

"Those people from Tam Dao are still sitting up at Tuyen Quang. We could suggest that our two be moved up there with them."

"And then what?" asked Len.

"And then when the airstrip is finished... take 'em all out. Right?" The ex-cop, having polished off his third or fourth gourd, was eager to participate.

"That is if our hosts agree with the plan," said John.

"What size plane do you expect to take them in, sir? We're talking about a helluva crowd, aren't we? It would have to be a pretty big plane," the other one of Applegate's instructors offered quite reasonably.

"They could make several trips," suggested Edouard.

"In any case," John said, "it's a place to put the two guys that's not here. It would be a situation that is under Viet Minh control yet separated from them. At the very least, it gets them off our necks, and it can be done right away."

"It sounds pretty good to me," Jimmy Tau said. "But you'll have to sell it to them, to Uncle Ho. And frankly, I think you better do it quickly before our Comrade Van comes up with a more drastic solution."

"A couple of them boys ah've seen could end this problem with some real quick knife work iffen they wanted to!" Applegate said, adding a conversation-ending exclamation point to Jimmy's comment.

* * *

John sought a meeting with Ho the following morning. A guard at the hut waved him in with his new carbine and a smile. Truyen was nowhere in sight. John politely knocked on the open bamboo door before entering. Surprisingly, Ho sat at a small desk dressed in his regulation shorts and shirt. It seemed he had recovered.

"You've come at a perfect time, Major John. My tormentor and protector, Nurse Truyen, has slipped away on an errand. She is an angel but very domineering, as you know. Domineering is the right word, I hope. I looked it up some time ago."

John continued to be amazed at Ho's grasp of English. He was sure that Ho must have a dictionary that he regularly studied, because the Viet Minh leader seemed to come up with a new word or phrase each time they met. John glanced around the dimly lit hut for the telltale signs of a Funk & Wagnall's or a Webster's dictionary. There was a pile of books by the straw mattress that was Ho's bed, and John decided that it must be among that collection. The single room was surprisingly fresh for a sick man's chamber. Nurse Truyen was indeed a valuable asset. Ho sat on the straw mattress and John sat cross-legged next to it. He could see the title of only one of the books; it was written in Cyrillic letters, a Russian book. Ho noticed John's gaze.

"Part of my little library," said Ho motioning toward the pile. "Do you read much?"

"I haven't had much time lately, Dr. Ho. But there was a time when I was younger when… well, shall we say all my adventures came from the books I read."

"Jack London. Have you read Jack London?"

"Yes, sir. He was one of my favorites."

"One of mine, too. I read his books when I worked aboard ship. I was always very busy, but there was always time to read. I learned a lot of English that way. It was hard to get history books then. I like to read history books. You must be careful with them, history books that is. It depends who writes them. They say the victor writes history. What do you think they will write about this war, John?"

"Which war, Dr. Ho?"

"Ah, yes, you are so right," replied Ho, laughing and coughing afterward. "You are a very smart man. It is very nice to have you here. You have something to ask me about today?"

John explained the idea to send Montfort and the troublesome Phac off to Tuyen Quang to remain with the refugees until they could be transported out. He could see from the beginning that Ho liked the idea; his head nodded up and down in agreement as John spoke.

"It's an excellent plan. Montfort can be put in charge of their welfare, all of them. The French should be very pleased with that. Also, they will then see we are not the monsters they think we are. Excellent idea. Comrade Van and I were just discussing what to do with our unwanted guests just last evening. This is perfect. Was this your idea, John.?"

"It was sort of a group idea, Uncle. I sat around with all my boys and we drank a lot of Jimmy Tau's wine last night and it just sort of came up."

"That sounds very communistic to me, John."

"I think it's just rather American, sir. It certainly isn't Regular Army."

"It is also very smart… to involve your whole small group. You have done good work here, Major John. The planning on the Tam Dao affair was well done, as I have told you before. It is not easy to just arrive in a new place as you did and work so well and closely with strangers."

"You are a great flatterer, Dr. Ho."

"Not at all. I tell the truth. It is obvious."

"May I change the subject for the moment?"

"Yes, of course."

"You seem to be in much better health. I take it you are feeling better?"

"Oh, yes, much better. It was just a bad cold, *la grippe, peut-être.*"

"In that case I would appreciate it if you would allow my medic, medical assistant, to take a look at you so that we can leave some things with Nurse Truyen in case of a relapse or something like that. He would also like to provide her with various medicines for other ailments as well as treat some of your people here. If they know that he has seen you, they will be more willing to allow him to treat them."

"I am feeling much better, but I appreciate your medical assistant's interest in helping the others. We definitely need medical help here. I'll see him, but he'll find I'm just fine."

At Ho's encouragement John stayed and talked till midmorning. Ho's eyes and overall manner were alert, much better than at their last meeting. But his skin was still jaundiced yellow and the persistent cough remained. John was struck by how old Uncle Ho looked even though he knew he was only in his fifties. The man was fascinating to talk with. His English was careful in his effort to be correct in his pronunciation and grammar. Ho's dark eyes would become illuminated with brightness as they moved from subject to subject. There was no doubt he loved to talk with someone from outside his immediate world. Maybe it was that any intellectual exchange was rare in the harsh environment of revolution and survival which was the life force of the encampment at Kim Lung. Ho allowed himself the luxury of letting his mind run free, unencumbered by the need to be the ever-prescient leader.

They spoke of Ho's days as a young man in France—of nearly getting to meet Woodrow Wilson to whom the young Ho sought to deliver an appeal for self-determination and constitutional government for Indochina. He explained that in those early years he had been careful not to speak of independence. That was 1919 and his political awakening, as he called it, was in its formative stage. Ho spoke as if of another man, a third party. John was entranced by the stories, but even more by the man telling them. Seemingly a stream of consciousness, the stories remained carefully structured, avoiding too great intimacy, too great exposure. Yet the sense of reality was there, the important details often hidden by the intricate gauze of the story telling itself. It was the self-portrait as the artist wished to be seen, close but never actually the real man.

For John's part he shared his early years in Gary and the tough times later on struggling to get his law degree. Ho was obviously impressed with John's working-class credentials, though he never played the political card that was offered by the disclosure. John was aware of this as he was spinning out his

207

tale. He saw himself as the bait, but the fish never snapped at the hook. In a way, John was disappointed for he enjoyed being clever, especially with an acknowledged master. He had expected some sort of recruitment pitch, some line to tie him more personally to Ho and his political beliefs and ambitions. It never came. Uncle was never that obvious. John was satisfied with establishing himself as a worthy, if lesser, adversary in the art of obfuscation.

* * *

The radio waves had been jammed with signals back and forth from Kim Lung and Ch'ing-hsi. With the disposition of Montfort and Phac now settled, a frantic M.5 could relax into its normal posture of Gallic paranoia. They certainly had no means to get their own people out. As much as they might deny it, they would have to rely on the Americans—as usual—to pull their two chestnuts out of the fire. Meanwhile the two men were trucked to Tuyen Quang in the vehicles taken during the Tam Dao raid. The attention of the Moose Mission was now focused on the training job they had been sent down to accomplish, and Len Sorenson was briefed by John on the political importance of his medical role.

John explained to his medic that he wanted him to give a thorough exam to Dr. Ho, whom he characterized as "the leader of this whole damn shebang." It was explained that Ho spoke English, which should help in the examination. John also told Sorenson of the repeated relapses that his patient had undergone. The pre-med student converted into a combat medic by the OSS was now expected to be a diagnostic specialist. John waved off Len's protestations of inadequacy by pointing out that he was by far the most medically trained and experienced person available this side of Hanoi—not exactly the healthiest place to seek treatment at the moment. Nonetheless, Len insisted on taking a couple of days to give time for AGAS in Ch'ing-hsi to contact someone at the 14th Air Force Hospital in Kunming who would be able to respond to Len's questions on symptoms and preferred treatment of various exotic diseases. Ho's problems were not a passing thing, and Len insisted that the time taken in his "research" by radio was well spent in such a situation. The fact was that the young medic was petrified at the responsibility of caring for such an obviously sick—and important—man.

John urged Len to get into his most "doctor-looking" outfit. "It's important that you look as professional as possible," he said.

Unfortunately, the white medical orderly uniform of which John was thinking was not part of Len's field kit. He did have a set of fresh fatigues and a red cross armband.

"Looks are everything," Edouard offered as his helpful comment as John and Len set out through a light drizzle to make it over to Ho's hut carrying a large duffel bag of medical supplies. Nurse Truyen met them at the door of the hut. She bowed politely with her hands pressed together in greeting. John introduced "Doctor" Len in French and she replied in the same language. John asked Len if he understood, and the medic answered that his college French was barely adequate, but enough for that exchange. Ho was propped up on his straw mattress as he had been previously. It was obvious to John that he'd had another relapse, a shock after seeing him so recently in good shape. John didn't want to say this to Len in front of the English-speaking Ho, but John was now fearful that the delay caused by contacting the Air Force hospital in Kunming might somehow contribute to the problem.

Ho welcomed the two Americans in English, his voice hoarse and clearly not strong. John presented Len, and Truyen interrupted immediately to advise her patient that the American doctor was there to examine him and that he should be cooperative. She said this in Vietnamese, but the meaning was self-evident by Ho's exaggerated response. He hadn't lost his sense of humor. He translated Truyen's instructions into English explaining to "Doctor" Len, as he did to everyone, that Truyen was a nag but a very good nurse. Len Sorenson smiled knowingly and turned to the young lady giving a slight bow as if he was acknowledging her professional assistance. Truyen giggled in response.

"She likes you, Doctor. Don't be alarmed," said Ho. "That's what Vietnamese girls do. They are not very sophisticated. What would you like me to do?"

Len opened his duffel bag and pulled out a typical black bag such as the ones doctors carry. He politely asked John to leave so that he could get on with his exam. Truyen beamed at the unfolding scene. Len allowed her to empty the rest of the duffel bag full of supplies. She immediately piled them along the bamboo wall. The doctor had arrived and her beloved Uncle would be cared for. The Americans were her friends.

Methodically, Len went through his procedures: temperature, blood pressure, and pulse were quickly checked. He listened to his patient's chest with his stethoscope. All the while Truyen smiled. Len removed the covers from Ho and was surprised to find him on a bedpan fashioned from beaten metal that once had been something else. Ho explained that he had to stay on the device because of his diarrhea. Truyen spoke quickly in French which Ho translated.

"She's trying to tell you that I have dysentery, but that she's had no drugs to treat it."

"*Merci, j'ai beaucoup des medicaments*," Len said directly to Truyen in his very American French. Again, the Vietnamese nurse beamed, this time nodding in approval. Len could do no wrong. Even his funny French became another asset as far as she was concerned. Len spoke in English to Ho.

"I have to tell you, sir, you are very ill. You must have malaria as well as this dysentery and I don't know what else. But I do have some excellent drugs and if you will take them as I tell you, I think they'll do the trick. I mean...."

"I know what you mean. 'Do the trick' means fix it up, right? You just tell Nurse Truyen and she will force whatever it is down me at the right time. I assure you of that, Doctor."

"I have something we call sulpha drugs. These will combat a broad spectrum of bacteriological infection. Sometimes these cause a side effect of nausea—your stomach will be upset—but otherwise they work very well. As I'm not sure of all the things you may have, this is, I think, the best way. Plus, I have some new anti-malaria medicine that I'll put you on. You'll have to take it as long as you're in.... Well, this is a place with much potential for malaria, especially this time of year. "

"Do you have something that can stop this diarrhea, Doctor? It is very difficult for me...."

"I have something that will stop you up very quickly, but the sulfa will work on the infection and that will take a little longer to clear up. In the meantime, you must drink a great deal of fluids. You are quite dehydrated. All the water you drink must be boiled—for 15 minutes to be sure. I'll pass all these instructions to your nurse here. And, of course, I shall be nearby to monitor—to keep an eye on you."

Len stepped away from an already exhausted Ho and carefully began in his limited French to give Truyen the schedule for the medications. Len turned back to the patient to administer the first course as Truyen wrote each item down on a small piece of paper she took from Ho's desk. They reviewed the instructions twice to make sure she had it all correct. Ho was so weak Truyen had to hold the cup for him to swallow the medicine. Len realized that his charge really needed a true physician—that and perhaps a couple of specialists. This was a hell of an assignment he had been stuck with. But the obvious sincerity of the old man's appreciation of his efforts touched the young medic. Len was acutely aware, though, that he would be the one blamed by all this old man's followers if things didn't go well. It was a confusing combination of emotions for the young man, so recently just another pre-med on campus.

Len packed up his medical bag and left the always-useful duffel bag behind. Truyen would finish arranging the supplies later. Len had made it clear what each packet was for and that they were for her sole use around the camp. He said goodbye in English to Ho, but the patient was already asleep. Truyen took Len's hand and spoke her gratitude with her eyes. Embarrassed, Len turned quickly and hurried back to the communal hut where he could see the Moose team had gathered.

The rain poured down and Len was soaked by the time he had crossed the 50 yards—but he never noticed it. His mind was still totally fixated on the scene he had just left in spite of the fact that his fatigues clung to him and the rainwater dripped down over his face from his plastered hair. This ancient man he had just cared for called him doctor and had placed his full faith in him. It was a responsibility for Len equal to any of the combat of which he'd heard so much.

Len sat down at the large table and then realized for the first time how exhausted he was, and how hungry. He was about to inquire when chow time was when a heaping bowl of steaming rice and vegetables was placed before him by a grinning mess helper. As the man rambled on in Vietnamese, Len poured some hot tea into a cracked porcelain mug. The mess man never stopped grinning. Jimmy Tau rushed to translate.

"He's telling you what a big and important man you are. He says you are the man that will make Uncle Ho Chi Minh well again. He said all Vietnamese will love you for that. At least I think that's what he said. It seems he already loves you, so you better watch out."

Like everything else in the small camp, the news of the man with the medicines visiting Uncle had been circulated instantaneously. The entire encampment had waited expectantly for the results of Len's ministerings. The assembled American team broke into applause for their new hero. Len wasn't sure what had just occurred, but the food was great, and he began to wolf down the meal. They let him get well along with his eating before further questioning. Eventually, John spoke first.

"So what's your diagnosis? Is Ho as sick as he looks?"

"Yes, he is, sir," Len replied, continuing to shovel in the rice.

"What is it? He was thin when we met in Kunming a few months ago, but now he's emaciated. And his skin is all grey..." said Edouard.

"To start with I think it's safe to say he has malaria and dysentery. He's jaundiced and most likely has other stuff too. That's what I needed from the hospital. There's a whole batch of things his symptoms can show. You got typhoid, cholera, dengue fever, hepatitis, God knows what. I can only treat the obvious symptoms. After a while I may be able to winnow out some of the possibilities. If he's got some exotic disease, like... whatever. I don't want to speculate. He could be tubercular. In which case this is not the place for him. I can't do anything about that. They think I'm a doctor, you know."

"I told them you weren't. They know. He knows," John explained, a bit defensively.

"Well, with all due respect, sir, they call me doctor and seem to expect the same results as if I were."

Edouard sought to lighten the scene.

"They call everyone doctor. They respect you and your judgement. They're very polite people. Anyhow you've got the armband. That means doctor to them. Frankly it does me, too. And you've got the black bag. Don't forget the bag."

"I just wish I had more expertise," Len said, now finished with his meal. The others were still drinking tea and having an after-meal smoke. He asked if he could have a refill, and the mess helper scurried back responding to a signal from Edouard that he should return with the large teapot. Attention was all on Len. It was as if he had been the first member of the Moose team to come under fire, only it was in combat against illness. Len found the attention disturbing.

"What is it? Why are you watching me?" he asked.

"Yur the first one other than the boss," said Applegate pointing to John, "who's done anythin' since we got here. Ah mean somethin' real positive. It's nice. We're real proud of yuh."

Completely embarrassed now, Len said, "I haven't done anything, really. I just gave him some medicine. I have to wait to see what happens. That's all I did."

It took several days, nearly a week before the full effect of the drugs that Len had given Ho made an impact on the patient. The recovery was amazingly swift after that. Ho Chi Minh's constitution was iron-like and with a minimum of decent medicinal aid he could fight off most everything. Like it or not, the former pre-med student became Doctor Len to everyone in the camp. He had no difficulty in organizing his treatment center for the local populace, both villagers and guerrillas. Truyen became his adoring assistant—much to the consternation of the rebuffed Jimmy Tau.

The treatment of the Vietnamese leader by Len Sorenson drew together the camp at Kim Lung in a manner that nothing else could. The Americans of the Moose Mission had become an integral part of the Viet Minh world. Even though most of them had little idea what an American was, every villager for miles around swiftly came to learn an American doctor was caring for their beloved leader. This was solid Viet Minh territory all the way to the Cao Bang region 100 miles to the northeast; and by the middle of the summer the dream of a liberation army began to draw closer.

The guerrillas passing through the camp took to saluting every American they came across. While this was a bit off-putting for the more informal-minded OSS troopers, their top kick, Ted Applegate, decided it was just the sort of army discipline needed by the unpracticed soldiery of the Viet Minh. He might not speak their language, but the Alabaman's fifteen-year experience in the Regular Army and near encyclopedic knowledge of weapons created an invaluable bridge to the Vietnamese fighters. For his part, Ted Applegate was pleased with the cooperation he'd been getting.

"That Thanh is a hell of a soldier," he'd reported to John. "He's got his boys real sharp."

Thanh was equally complimentary when he reported the progress of training to Giap.

"The sergeant they call Ted—our chief instructor—is very good in dealing with our men. He's not at all like the *sous-officiers* I've known. At first I thought he might expect too much, too soon but that has not been the case. Yet he is a strict disciplinarian. I would have to say, Comrade Van, that the training is going quite well."

There were, however, some odd moments as a result of the fact that only one of the three OSS instructors spoke any Vietnamese.

"Tell 'em we're gonna shift t'grenades now," Applegate ordered.

The instructor shouted the order in Vietnamese: "Withdraw grenades!" The training unit shouted back, "Withdraw grenades!" and proceeded to do so. Applegate enjoyed the command and response system. It was the closest he could come to Ft. Benning's parade ground discipline. From time to time, he tried shouting a command in his own Alabaman version of the Vietnamese he'd learned. The guerrillas were too well trained to laugh. Instead, they waited for the other American to translate the command just as if it had been given in English. It was as close as the training came to a humorous interlude. For the guerrillas, though, it made the American top sergeant less of an unforgiving giant. From such things bonds among soldiers are created. The guerrillas were on their way to becoming the new liberation army and the Americans would be their guides.

The fact was that there really wasn't much for Edouard to do after the training program got into full swing. For a while he hung around each site as the three noncoms guided their charges through the various training drills. John was involved in what seemed a constant round of introductions to various Viet Minh political leaders who made the pilgrimage to Kim Lung to meet with Uncle Ho. John was Ho's personal trophy—the living embodiment of the several .45 automatics and the signed photo of General Chennault. The former had been handed out to worthy commanders and the latter was pinned where it could be easily seen above Uncle's little desk. Meeting the American major was a great privilege, but John had to be available on a moment's notice to have it happen, and that moment seemed to come at least twice a day. When Jimmy Tau suggested that Edouard join him on a trip north to look into extending the outreach of the AGAS escape and evasion net, John did not object, though he was admittedly envious.

Jimmy had made these trips often in the past. Guided by Viet Minh escorts and changing local guides, he would travel from village to village explaining the reward system for the recovery and protection of downed fliers. The villagers were also strongly encouraged to pass on any information regarding the presence of Japanese forces. The information on either the fliers or Japanese military would flow through a growing net of couriers to the several AGAS radio teams operating in the bush. These smaller units would be in contact with Mac Soo's base facility at Kim Lung. Another base facility was sought to be established toward the northwest. Scouting out a possible site for this new base unit was a matter of finding not only a secure area, but one which served the geographical and topographical commo requirements. Jimmy Tau described it as a boy scout camping trip.

The trip began in considerable luxury. Edouard was able to sit with Jimmy in a cart filled to the top with bags of rice that were being transported to the many villages they would visit. The bullock that pulled the cart may not have been fast, but he kept up a steady pace somewhere between two and three miles an hour according to Edouard's calculations. Jimmy leaned more to the two-miles-an-hour theory based on his supposedly more expert engineering background. In any case, the slow-moving transportation was preferable to walking the ten hours a day that Jimmy insisted be the schedule. The bullock was led by its owner who rented his rig and animal for the exorbitant sum of four of the large brown hemp bags of rice. The trail taken had to be able to accommodate the wide cart, and this limited the villages Jimmy could visit, some of which were so small that they had only single path trails leading to them. This required Jimmy and Edouard to jump off their coach and trek for a few miles on the forest trail until they reached their intended objective.

During the first two days of the safari, as Jimmy Tau had come to call his mission, there were no side trips. The two Americans would jump off the cart from time to time simply to stretch their legs by walking a mile or two, then back on the cart. By the third day, however, they stopped every four to five miles to venture into the bush to seek out their target village. They travelled with a team of guerrillas and local guides, eight men in all. Edouard thought of his previous experience back in the Vietnamese forest during the Gorilla Mission. This time there was none of the tension which dogged every step of the earlier trek. With Jimmy's area knowledge and basic Vietnamese language skills, Edouard indeed began to feel they were on a boy scout camping trip. Though they had local guides, Jimmy knew the route well enough from many other forays that he admitted he could have proceeded alone without any help. At least that was true for the first several days. By the fourth day they were out of Jimmy's range and the local guides became essential. They bivouacked that evening near a small stream. On Jimmy's advice they arranged a nighttime guard among the guerrillas. This had been the first night that was deemed necessary.

"It's just a precaution," Jimmy said. "I don't think we're in any danger, but who knows 'What evil lurks in the hearts of men?' as The Shadow says."

Edouard laughed at the reference to the well-known radio program.

"Did you listen to that? It's one of my favorites."

"They say it was a kid's show, and no one would admit they were listening. I liked the Green Hornet also. That was because he had this guy Kato, 'his Filipino manservant'. I forget the Green Hornet's name. He'd say, 'Quick Kato, the gas gun' and the Green Hornet would knock out the bad guy with Kato's gas gun. Why didn't the Green Hornet carry his own gas gun? That still bothers me."

The two Americans had finished their evening meal of GI field rations and sat together under canvas they had rigged off the end of the cart to provide shelter from the intermittent rain. Both contentedly smoked cigarettes and the smoke curled up and away from the canvas roof.

"Tell me, Jimmy, how did you get into this AGAS business? I would have thought with your background you could have had some cushy post in Quartermaster or somewhere organizing POL shipments."

"I guess I could have, Eddy, but I got linked up with a couple of other guys when we sneaked out of Haiphong. It just sort of happened. We knew a lot of people in Tonkin from our business and that was valuable to some people, if you get my meaning. We were able to do some pretty good work in those early years before everything got too organized, I guess you'd call it. AGAS became one of our sponsors. Then as things went on, I was encouraged to accept a commission in the field they were offering from Chungking. Actually, I guess I had no choice. The freelance days were coming to an end anyhow. AGAS is filled with operators."

"We found that out... to our benefit. So that's how you know so much about what's going on. You must have seen a lot during your freewheeling days."

"Don't get me wrong, they weren't that free ... we just didn't have anybody to help us. We passed everything we learned through the Chinese at first, but then AGAS came along, and helping our guys find a way home seemed a hell of a lot more important than playing hide 'n seek with the Vichy army and the Japs. But me and my two buddies had some good times."

"So where are they?" Edouard asked.

"Top secret, Eddy. Maybe they retired. I don't know and I don't ask. Mac Soo used to work with us, too. I inherited him. He's the one with the stories, but he'll never tell them. You may have noticed, he doesn't speak much anyhow."

Edouard realized that pressing Jimmy Tau for more personal information would be useless. It took one to know one, and Edouard could spot a guy a proverbial mile away who gabs to cover the unspoken. Accordingly, he changed the subject.

"So, do you think you've seen any good spots for the new base yet?"

"I better pretty soon. We're sort of extending ourselves at this range. I figure we've got one more days' worth of forward recon left and then we'll have to turn back."

"Will it take five days to get back?" Edouard asked, somewhat concerned.

"Nah, maybe three. We don't have to take the same way. The cart's going to be empty and we can move faster. Three days should do it. No stops, just hightailing it all the way, pardner. We really have to stop in one more village and drop off the last of the rice. This is all Tho country. I've never been up here before. This hilly terrain looks excellent, and I've been thinking from the start that it would be my prime candidate for the base radio. The maps I've got showed it to have all the right characteristics, but you can't count on maps."

"John and I have had some experience in that regard. You don't have to sell me."

The next day, they were able to go only a short way with the bullock cart before the guides directed them to a forest path leading to the village. There was something wrong right from the beginning. There were no other people on the track. It may have been a forest but there always was traffic on the pathways connecting the villages. They passed one small collection of huts, but the few tribespeople who were there quickly fled into the surrounding area at the first sound of the approach of the group. The village Jimmy was seeking was further down the trail and Edouard agreed with Jimmy that they should keep their eyes open.

"Believe it or not, there are still tigers around these parts and that could be the reason the villagers are so petrified, although I must admit we don't look much like tigers. Maybe some bandits came through," Jimmy said.

They didn't have to wait long. The smell of burnt thatch was heavy in the air. The smoke odor hurt their nostrils. When they finally arrived at the village, there were only a few huts still standing; it had been completely wiped out by fire. The entire Tho village, empty of people, was smoldering. Whatever happened must have occurred not too long before—at most the previous afternoon. Carefully, Jimmy, Edouard and the guerrilla team searched among the ruins and found bodies lying dead from bullet and bayonet wounds, perhaps ten in all. If there had been a fight, it was pretty lopsided.

"Do bandits do this sort of thing?" Edouard asked.

"Not that I've heard of. They come and steal, maybe kill one or two who resist and get the hell out. There's no profit in wiping out whole villages. This looks more like some sort of revenge thing," said Jimmy.

One of the guerrillas called out in Vietnamese that he had found someone. He had a young woman by the hand, and he was trying to speak to her in Vietnamese. She just cried and didn't answer. One of the guides came up who spoke Tho and calmed the girl by talking to her in her own language. She was still fearful to the point of shaking uncontrollably each time Jimmy came close. She seemed less afraid of Edouard. It took a while before the guide was able to explain that the girl thought Jimmy was a Japanese officer with his Asian looks, uniform and sidearm. The rest of the story obtained through a difficult translation of Tho to Vietnamese, which Jimmy tried hard

216

to understand, eventually was passed on to Edouard in English. Meanwhile several more villagers, men and women, emerged from the forest cover after they heard and saw what was going on. Bit by bit as each tribesperson told their own emotion-filled version, the story of what had happened was pieced together.

A sizeable number of Japanese soldiers, perhaps 20 or more, had arrived at the village. Their coming was not unexpected because their presence in the region had been well reported by hunters for the past three days. The villagers were fearful of what might happen, but had done nothing to offend the soldiers and saw no reason to think any harm would come. They took the precaution of sending their young women and teenage girls off into the surrounding woods that morning, just as they would with any possible banditry. The worst that could happen, they thought, was the marauding soldiers would steal whatever food and goods they could find, maybe slap some of the men around, and leave. That was tradition.

At first that pattern was played out with the usual demand for food and gold ornaments. The village headman came forward to bargain with the Japanese officer. The officer immediately saw the .45 cal. automatic in the holster strung around the headman's shoulders and started screaming at him. He ordered his men to grab the Tho leader and threw him to the ground. One of the man's wives, in a mistaken gesture of offering tribute for her husband, ran out of her hut with a large piece of the extremely valuable parachute silk the American pilot had left and pressed it upon the officer. This only seemed to make him madder. He pulled the .45 automatic out of the holster, and after some trouble managed to get a round into its chamber and shot the man in the head. The officer seemed to be completely deranged, according to the villagers, and proceeded to shoot any villagers close to him. The rest of the Japanese soldiers began to do the same thing as the tribespeople fled into the forest. The soldiers stayed around for a short while more—how long the villagers didn't really know because they were hiding. They smelled the smoke and realized the soldiers had set fire to their homes. They had returned to the edge of the village that following morning, but had not found the courage to go in until they observed that Jimmy's group intended no harm.

"These were special people, Eddy. They had already helped one of our pilots. I feel really bad about this. I knew one of the villages up here had returned one of our guys, but I didn't know which one. This was it. What a mess."

"We've got to get going, Jimmy. We can't afford to run into the Japs. We've only got our few guerrillas," Edouard said more as an order than a suggestion.

"I've got to leave them whatever we can. I'll tell them we'll send more."

Jimmy was devastated. These wonderful people had risked everything to save one of his fliers—just what he had been working toward all these months—and now they had been nearly wiped out because the little reward they had received had given them away. Jimmy insisted on remaining, long enough to send down the trail for the village's intended rice gifts. The guides explained that Jimmy wanted them to get the bags in the cart. Lacking their headman, it was difficult to quickly agree on who should do what. However, the pecking order was settled, and men rushed out with *don ganh*.

In the interim, Edouard urged Jimmy to question the villagers through his guide as to the route they thought the Japanese had taken after their village. Jimmy tried his best to get a sensible answer, but it was clear the villagers had no idea what happened to the patrol after it left them. It was also obvious that as grateful as the tribespeople were for their bags of rice, as soon as the last of the bags arrived, they wanted to get on with the important ceremony of caring for their dead. It was not good to have foreigners, even friendly foreigners, around at spiritual celebrations for the departed. It would be rude to tell them, but the foreigners—meaning anyone not of their clan or Tho—would only contaminate the process.

The choice facing the two Americans at this point was whether to sacrifice speed for relatively greater safety and avoid the established trails. After discussion about the merits, Edouard and Jimmy agreed that going cross country carried additional risks and the best thing to do was to follow an established, though less used, route. They set off with the intention of covering as much distance as possible in the next few hours. The idea was to separate them as quickly as possible from the danger area surrounding the village that had been attacked. They were on the trail for only about a half an hour when a tribal runner informed them that a large force of soldiers was coming up the same trail they were headed down. The boy had no further information and rushed on his way to alert everyone ahead of the Japanese.

"They must have taken some sort of circle route if they're the same unit that attacked the village," said Jimmy.

"Or else there is more than one force," said Edouard. "In any case, we've got to slip into cover in this bush either right or left and go to ground—fast."

"What will we do with the cart?" asked Jimmy.

The matter of the bullock and the cart was solved by the owner. He unhitched the empty cart about 30 yards off the trail and then led the bullock deep into the forest until they came to a stream. He left the animal tethered by the side of the stream. The entire group then moved away another hundred yards to a position where they could cover their own path if anyone tracked them. There was no need to warn the guerrillas to be quiet. Everyone had just settled into comfortable squatting positions when the air was filled with screeching birds announcing the arrival of what sounded like an army crashing through the forest. Without any orders the entire guerrilla group stretched prone against the damp ground.

In a hoarse whisper Edouard warned Jimmy that if the Japanese tumbled upon the cart, the bullock, or any of their tracks, he better be prepared to run or fight or both.

"Let's head that way," said Jimmy pointing through the trees. "I figure that's due east and our best direction."

Edouard marveled at the Bostonian's sense of direction and nodded his head in agreement. The crashing sound drew closer and the boisterous voices of Japanese soldiers could be heard. Edouard could barely make out several of the nearest guerrillas who had virtually buried themselves into the floor of the forest by pulling dead branches and leaves over themselves. He wriggled himself into a depression in the ground and tried to cover the exposed part of his body with nearby foliage. Jimmy had succeeded in uprooting several large ferns and had gathered them strategically around him.

As he lay there, Edouard contemplated the question of whether or not to get in the first shot and take down any Jap near him or wait until they were discovered. The latter situation would be most likely too late. Best would be the use of his knife—if he had the chance. That way he might be able to take down any nearby Jap perhaps without the others noticing. In the end he resolved to stay put until he absolutely had to move. At that point the best thing would be to run as fast as he could in the direction Jimmy had pointed.

Edouard was still reviewing his options when a group of three soldiers talking among themselves like boys on a hike in the country burst through the brush. If these were supposed to be the unit's flanking scouts, they certainly had a lot to learn about patrol discipline, thought Edouard. One of the young soldiers let out a blood-curdling scream and swung his machete in the air. Edouard was sure one of the guerrillas had been spotted and decapitated. The other two Japanese soldiers ran over to their friend who had just bent down and picked up the wriggling body of a tree snake. An argument ensued apparently over what sort of a snake it was. Triumphantly the one soldier stuffed his bloody trophy into his canvas bag, and continuing their happy debate the three crashed on through the woods oblivious to any dangers that might be lurking.

Edouard, Jimmy, and the guerrillas remained carefully out of sight until the last sounds of the Japanese unit passed on through the woods. Finally, Edouard rose to his knees; seeing this the rest of the group did the same. Soon they were gathered together, each talking faster than the other but in very low voices.

"Boy, those Japs don't give a damn about how much noise they make," said Jimmy.

"Why should they? They think they're the only ones around here except for some poor old villagers. But nonetheless you're right. Not very military of them. Ted Applegate would have most likely captured them and put them through punishment drills for their sloppiness. Let's say a little prayer for that sloppiness. Hell, the main body must have been at least a platoon from the sound they were making moving through the area." Edouard brushed himself off as he talked.

There was considerable disagreement among the guerrillas as to which of them had been closest to the Japanese soldiers. Apparently, Jimmy explained to Edouard, one of them swore the soldier who attacked the snake would have stepped on him if the soldier hadn't been distracted by the reptile. Laughing among themselves, the guerrillas now called their comrade "snake-brother"—an apparently uproariously funny name in Vietnamese.

The bullock was located happily standing in the stream, and soon he was hooked up to the cart. The entire group returned to their original trail with scouts far in front and rear just in case the undisciplined Japanese force decided to execute an about-face or had stragglers rushing to catch up. By the time darkness fell it had become apparent they had succeeded in evading the enemy platoon.

The trip back to Kim Lung was not the leisurely stroll of the earlier trip out. Nor did the villagers on the main trail come to greet the travelers as they trooped past. The word had spread rapidly of the Japanese reprisal raid and the normally friendly tribespeople decided it best to not get caught between conflicting interests. The empty bullock cart trundled easily along at a pace considerably in excess of the miles per hour that had been calculated before. The only delays were occasioned by the sending out of scouts from among the guerrillas to survey the mud track ahead for possible ambush. Edouard and Jimmy sat on the back of the cart keeping an eye open for any sign that might indicate enemy presence. It was futile, of course, for if the Japs had wanted to catch them it hardly would have been difficult. The heavy foliage hung over the trail in such thickness that one could see no further than a yard or two on each side. After a day and a half of hard going from dawn to dusk they had reached more secure Viet Minh territory, much to the pleasure of the entire group. Jimmy, however, remained deeply despondent.

"It's not that we can't rebuild their confidence, but it'll take time... too much time. What the hell were those damn Japs doing up there anyhow? It's way beyond their regular patrolling routes. Maybe up closer to the Chinese border, but not where that village was. Eddy, I feel so sorry for those poor people."

"You've been too successful, Jimmy. The Japs aren't dummies, y'know. Our guys are getting shot down, but you're whisking them right out. They have to get a bit put out with that after a while, so they take some guys out to where they usually avoid going and change some people's minds. The fact that the villagers had some obvious American stuff certainly wasn't the only thing that set them off. That stuff could have been recovered from a dead crew, too. No, these Japs were out to hurt people and leave a message. I bet you'll find that they did it to other villages along the way. It's typical anti-partisan technique. Take my word for it. That's our business."

"So you're saying I'm out of business; that AGAS should close up shop. We can't do that."

"No, nothing of the kind. Of course, you've got to keep doing what you're doing. This isn't the first time something like this has happened, is it?"

"Well, Eddy, yes, it is. We've had certain individuals picked up by the Kempeitei, but never a whole village burnt out like this."

"It shows they're getting desperate. They should be trying to get the tribes on their side. Give gifts, rewards, to turn over any Allied personnel that come into their hands. That's what the Japs should be doing. They must have given up on that tactic. That means they're desperate, just like I said."

Edouard's lecture didn't reduce Jimmy's sadness, but it did provide an explanation, and that was a help. The boy scout camping trip had turned out disastrously, but at least the troop was intact, and both Jimmy and Edouard felt John would come up with something to do. Of that they were convinced.

Chapter Twelve

The camp at Kim Lung buzzed with the news of the Japanese raid into Tho tribal territory. John received the report from Jimmy and Edouard at about the exact same time as Thanh did from the returning guerrillas who had accompanied the Americans. Thanh had to wait till that evening to pass on the information to Giap who was gone on another mission for Uncle. Ho was briefed by one of the older political officers shortly after Thanh had received his military report. It was not proper protocol for Thanh to go directly to Ho with tactical information such as this. The arcane political structure of the Viet Minh, and the Kim Lung headquarters in particular, ensured the passage of any important information to Ho with alacrity without disturbing the theory of chain of command. The concept of well-structured communist order incorporating Vietnamese sensitivities functioned far better than any westerner could comprehend.

While John was upset that Edouard and Jimmy had come close to being killed or captured by the Japanese patrol, he was hardly as distraught over the actual happenings at the Tho village. His first question to Jimmy was how long the AGAS officer thought it would take for the net to become operative again in that area. John's initial reaction was strictly a damage assessment and expectation of reconstitution. He felt sorry for Jimmy and AGAS, and could envision the AGAS chief hitting the roof, but there was nothing in the unfortunate occurrence that directly affected his responsibility, the Moose Mission.

Giap, on the other hand, was more than a little disturbed at the news and he knew that Ho would share his view. This was a Tho village that had been hit, and the Tho were long-term allies of the Viet Minh. Many of the best fighters they had were Tho tribesmen. Attacking that village, for any reason, was a direct challenge to the establishment and acceptance of Viet Minh autonomy over northern Tonkin. Such an action could not be allowed to stand if the Viet Minh was to succeed in its longer term objective of becoming the dominant political force in Tonkin and eventually Vietnam. Integral to this was the necessity of the Indochinese Communist Party maintaining control over the Viet Minh. It was all linked, and on that linkage rested the future.

The meeting with Uncle should have included other of Ho's top lieutenants, but they were all off on separate assignments, too dispersed to return in a reasonable time. As a result, the decision would have to be taken solely by Ho Chi Minh with the aid of only Vo Nguyen Giap. It was less of an intellectual absence as it was political. Consensus was Ho's principal tool of leadership and he preferred its applicability on all important matters. Decision making was not a problem, but how it was accomplished was essential to maintenance of control.

"Do we have the strength at this point to prevent actions like this from taking place again, comrade?" Ho asked in an unusually formal manner. They were talking in the privacy of his hut, but his voice was purposely low.

"No we do not, Uncle, but the situation requires us to take a punitive action."

"I understand the theory, but are we merely a flea crawling up an elephant's back in this matter?"

"It is an elephant that has many other problems and would wish not to get further involved with the flea. On the other hand, the flea has to take his bite or else the elephant will ignore him. And, most important, Uncle, we have an even larger elephant as our friend."

"Leaving the intriguing aspects of this zoology behind, comrade, what is it specifically you wish to do?"

"I do not as of yet have a specific plan, but one thing we must do is obtain the assistance of Major John and his unit. We need their expertise."

"It would also be useful to be in action directly with them as an indication of our commitment to war against their enemy, the Japanese. Politically, it definitely has advantages for us. At the same time, though, I am under the impression that our cadres are not yet at the point where they can seriously attempt an offensive action."

"We wouldn't be if we didn't have the Americans to assist us. Remember, Uncle, our team leaders are used to working with them now. It has only been a few weeks, but the rapport is excellent. I, of course, would go along on the mission."

"We are getting ahead of ourselves here, comrade. First, we must decide what our target is. We might have to do that in conjunction with the Americans also. They have a stake in this in their program for aiding their downed fliers. Jimmy must be concerned about that, and so must his superiors. We must wait a day or so in order to allow them to be in contact with their command. Then we have a conference on the mutuality of our interests."

"I suggest we make Comrade Thanh my assistant. He has an excellent military mind as well as equal political skill. I am quite impressed with him and would expect him to be essential in any operation we might pursue in this regard."

"The two American officers, Major John and Captain Edouard, are experienced partisans. They may not know our country, but they have seen a good deal of war and are quite professional. We must remember that in our discussions with them, comrade."

"I shall bear that in mind, Uncle."

Mac Soo and Jimmy Tau had notified their headquarters at AGAS in Ch'ing-hsi as soon as they could of the Japanese patrol action. Mac had been careful to separately encode a personal message to the AGAS colonel from his Lt. Tau with a very pessimistic assessment of future E&E operations in the broad area of Tonkin. Additional reprisal raids, such as the latest event, conceivably could undercut the entire village support structure that Jimmy and other AGAS forward controllers had built over many months of hazardous duty. A reply from their boss, personally, came back with very little delay, warning Jimmy not to overreact and advising that the matter would be studied on a priority basis. In the meantime, runners were sent out to other cooperating villages warning them to be alert for Japanese Army sweeps.

It was obvious to John that the Japanese raid into what was considered Viet Minh territory carried greater significance than simply the possible loss of a portion of the AGAS escape and evasion net. John took Edouard aside to discuss with him what he foresaw as a possible problem.

"As far as I can see, they've got a couple of ways to go. Uncle can decide to ignore the whole thing and simply send patrols up into that area as a sort of 'showing-the-flag' exercise. That way they're in effect saying this Jap operation was a one-time thing and doesn't really mean anything. On the other hand, they can do something stupid like finding some Jap Army base and try to bloody them enough so that the countryside thinks Comrade Van and his boys are hotshots capable of protecting them. Being from Chicago, I understand that mentality. The cops do it that way and sometimes so do the bad guys trying to control their interests. All that happens is a lot of people get killed—usually civilians."

It was the sort of argument that Edouard saw he couldn't argue against and didn't try. John had made up his mind and that was it. John was annoyed that Jimmy seemed to have taken the whole affair so personally. John was in his *maquisard* frame of mind and had little room for sentimentality. Edouard understood his friend. Kim Lung was a nice safe little place with interesting things to do. It was just close enough to the action without requiring too much direct participation. The Tam Dao mission was John's swan song and he meant it to remain that way. That was Edouard's judgement and there wasn't a reason in the world why he should make any effort to change John's mind—nor did he have a right to do so. John Guthrie had paid his dues, and so had Edouard Parnell for that matter. This training assignment with the Viet Minh would be over possibly in a few months and they would be rotated back to Ch'ing-hsi and then head up the SO section at Kunming. It didn't seem too unattractive to Edouard either.

The request for a meeting with the American major and captain came in the unusually formal manner of a handwritten note delivered by Dr. Ho's guard. The time was set for the following day at 10am. Both John and Edouard agreed that the formality indicated a serious matter was to be discussed, and that the chances were the subject would have something to do with the attack on the Tho village. What was interesting was that Jimmy Tau had not been included in the invitation.

Promptly at 10am, John and Edouard presented themselves at Ho's hut. The door was open to let in the pleasant sun of a rare dry day. Inside, a table had been brought in as well as four bamboo chairs. The entire hut had been converted into a conference room. Indeed, this was a serious meeting. An armed guard stood at attention outside the hut adding further to the importance of the meeting. The two Americans said nothing, but the looks they exchanged clearly indicated they both knew they were in for a different sort of session.

Ho, still looking haggard, nonetheless was smiling and vigorous. Edouard thought to himself that even when the man was in perfect health, he most likely would seem drawn and ill. Ho was smoking a cigarette. He was definitely better.

"Welcome, gentlemen," said Ho in his most hospitable English. "I hope you do not mind, but today we must converse in French as our friend, Comrade Van, as you know, does not yet have a full grasp of your language. He tells me, though, that it is high on his list of things to do.

Giap, standing by one of the chairs in his usual white suit, gave a quick smile of recognition and nodded his head slightly toward the Americans. Ho waved everyone to take their seats. A pitcher of water was offered by Ho who motioned toward the cups set in front of each place.

"It is Dr. Len's recipe, boiled 15 minutes, no less, no more. I've been trying to convince Comrade Van that it is good for everyone. Your Dr. Len is a wonderful doctor and we are so grateful he is here. I, in particular. He has become a favorite with all the people of Kim Lung village where he goes each day to check on his patients. But I'm sure you know that already. He has certainly won over Nurse Truyen. I have not seen her in such a good mood before."

This was Uncle Ho's usual way of opening a meeting. There was no telling what was coming next, but it was an executive session had been clearly established by the table and the pitcher of water.

"I have asked you here today in order that we may discuss the serious matter of the Japanese Army attack on the Tho village visited by you, Captain Edouard, and Lt. Jimmy. I have had long talks with Comrade Van on this subject and we have come to the conclusion that we need your help in deciding what to do. I will allow Comrade Van to explain some of what we have discussed."

Giap placed both of his hands palms down on the table and began to speak slowly in his careful French.

"What occurred the other day was unfortunate on several levels. As you may know, we in the Viet Minh have taken on the responsibility to provide to the tribal peoples, especially the Tho, a sense of security, indeed actual security that has not existed for many years. For the most part, tribal people in Vietnam have been ignored. We of the Viet Minh have sought to correct this. In turn, these tribal people have come to trust the Viet Minh and join with us in the struggle for the liberation of our land."

It was not hard to see where this preamble was leading. Giap's manner, undoubtedly left over from his teaching days, tended to the preachy; but what he said was also the truth as he saw it. The presentation was long and unsurprising. In the end, the situation was not unlike what John had explained before to Edouard. The difference, however, was crucial, and that part was stated clearly and concisely by Ho.

"We need your assistance. We shall discover the best place to attack and then jointly, American forces and the Viet Minh, shall teach these Japanese a lesson. It is just as we spoke in Kunming."

While Giap had been involved in his little speech, John's mind had wandered back to his days in law school and a professor of trial law. He had said that a good trial lawyer must be able to listen carefully to the opposing attorney and, without taking notes, collect all his opponent's vulnerable points. Then in rebuttal, each point should be ticked off as if they were the sole elements of the man's case. In other words, restate the opponent's position in such a way as to suit your own needs. John listened to Giap with this mindset. In the end, however, John wasn't in a debating mood.

"I would like very much to accept your suggestion," John said, trying hard to think of the French idiom meaning "to accommodate you." He knew he had to be diplomatic, but didn't like being boxed in. "To begin with, my small team is not an operations group. OG we call them. OG units are commandos. They are the ones who go in and attack things, blow up bridges, communications, etc. We are a training unit. At some later date, augmented with additional specialized personnel, a team such as ours might be converted into an OG, but that is physically a completely different group of people."

"But you did this in France, did you not?" asked Ho.

"That was different. The *maquisards* who I worked with already were capable partisans. I was there to provide coordination and maybe a little specialized *savoir faire*, tactics for instance. To take my small team into action with your people is at best premature and perhaps even wrong... well, strategically. I don't think anyone wants us to get the Japs so mad that they'll send out a large countering force."

"They don't know where we are," replied Giap.

"Now they don't. They may not know about Kim Lung now, but after we hit them they'll certainly find out. They'll capture somebody and make him, or her, talk."

"We'll go further north and west, to Laos if necessary," answered Giap with quiet confidence. He had already thought of that.

"We would have to get permission from Kunming to launch this strike. We would have to coordinate all the details with them," John said knowing full well that if he had really wanted to do it, he could find a way of informing Horse Simpson after the fact—if at all. "And I don't think they'll want this northern Tonkin area all stirred up—at least not now."

Ho could see John was completely negative on the idea, and it was neither smart nor political to counter his arguments at this stage.

"It is best that we think about this matter some more. We do not even have a potential target yet. Perhaps John could communicate with Kunming and introduce the idea in theory. It is important, John, that the Viet Minh do something to restore the trust of the Tho people and the others who expect us to provide leadership." Ho's manner, as always in contentious circumstances, was calm and totally in control. He was Uncle even at this meeting—especially at this meeting.

Edouard decided it was time to speak up.

"Perhaps there is another way to, as Dr. Ho says, restore the trust of the tribal people. They are all in great need of food and other supplies. I could see that from how they reacted at each village when we dropped off a few bags of rice. This is something that AGAS could help out with by parachuting food and other stuff to designated locations. Jimmy's boss is very capable of organizing something like that," said Edouard. "What we need is a list of the sort of things that would be well received—sort of a shopping list. When it was all ready to go, and we had agreed on where to set up the drop zones, Viet Minh emissaries could be dispatched to the various sectors to alert the tribal leaders that these good things would be coming. That way the Viet Minh would be seen as the benefactor, and so on."

Edouard had warmed to his story as soon as he saw he had caught Ho's attention. John also had signified his approval with supportive nodding.

"The point I'm trying to make is that both AGAS and the Viet Minh have a mutual interest in this matter. Arranging air drops of food and other supplies by AGAS is a great deal easier than getting authorization for a military strike from Chungking—because that's where such a request eventually would have to go as far as our organization is concerned. Kunming would be just the first stop. I'm sure you understand that that is how armies work."

Edouard looked deferentially over at Giap who didn't react. The Viet Minh military operations chief turned toward Uncle Ho for guidance. Ho responded with a thoughtful expression and by blowing out a large puff of smoke from his cigarette.

"Captain Edouard has a very good suggestion. It is one of the things we should think about. In the meantime, it would be perhaps useful to inquire of AGAS as to whether such a project is feasible from their side," said Ho, never one to rush to a quick answer. It was also obvious that this was a matter he wished to discuss privately with Giap.

"I know we should think about this interesting idea, but I would not like to have the need for more direct military action put aside. Is there not some way that Major John can communicate with his superiors in Kunming to get a sense of their reaction and what they might be able to do to assist us?" Giap asked.

This was getting a bit beyond where John wanted the matter to go. He wanted the idea of a military operation dead and buried, at least for the moment. A little outright lying was called for.

"I'll make some discreet inquiries," he said, hoping that would end the subject. The last thing he intended to do was to send some half-baked scheme to Simpson to be dissected by Castelli in his plans function for the detachment.

"I should think that your command in Kunming would be interested in this concept as long as we chose an appropriate target that would be useful to them also," said Ho not quite ready to end the discussion. There was a point he wished to reiterate.

"If I remember correctly, this was exactly the sort of thing that the three of us discussed in our little meeting in Kunming and is the point of the whole training assignment which has brought your wonderful team here to Kim Lung. We must find the proper target, but the timing now has become very important to us. I think those are the things we should all keep in mind."

That was a meeting-ending statement. To make sure no one missed that point, Ho stood up from the table. John and Edouard followed his lead and rose to leave. Giap had one more thing to say.

"If my men are to take on serious targets for the Allied command, we must be afforded the opportunity to gain some appropriate experience, combat experience, before we take on more complex assignments such as cutting rail lines, communications, and that sort of thing."

This was an arrow to the heart of the matter. Giap had put his finger on exactly the targeting that had been in the OSS/SO planning from the outset, the original joint operation with the French—the Chen Nan Kuan to Hanoi lines. Whether this was a lucky guess, sharp military analysis, or information gained from informants was impossible to tell. John showed nothing and neither did Edouard, though Giap had caught them both unawares. Why he chose that instance to display his knowledge was also a question unanswered.

"An interesting point, Comrade Van," John said in as innocent a manner as he could muster. "As Uncle says, we must all put some more thought into this issue and get back together."

* * *

Jimmy Tau's communications with Ch'ing-hsi had come at a particularly disadvantageous time for AGAS and all its posts. Bombing operations of the 14th Air Force had picked up substantially and concomitantly, so had the loss of planes and air crews. The need to recover these crews was the highest priority. Chennault was all over AGAS to get this done and AGAS headquarters was not gentle in passing the buck down to the base at Ch'ing-hsi. The last thing they needed at this juncture was to have the E&E net, so carefully knitted together by Jimmy Tau and a handful of other young AGAS officers in the bush, fall apart because of one Japanese attack on a tribal village. As far as Ch'ing-hsi's chief was concerned, northern Tonkin was his property and no son-of-a-bitch Jap patrol was going to mess around in it.

The first thing that the determined AGAS regional commander did was to request some strikes by fighter bombers on selected Japanese troop concentrations just south of Cao Bang. These, he figured, would force the Jap units to withdraw out of the Tho areas southeast toward Dong Dang. At the suggestion of the planners at 14th A.F. headquarters, napalm was used for maximum effect. The second phase of the coordinated plan was to call in some of the markers owed to him by one Major John Guthrie, currently sojourning along with a few of his OSS compatriots amongst the friendly forces of the Vietnamese nationalist league known as the Viet Minh. The AGAS colonel had built his reputation on his ability to reach out and grasp whatever was necessary to get the job done that he was expected to do. This included everything from direct orders from Southeast Asia Command to favors for friends and all things in between. Twenty years in the Minnesota National Guard and two plus years in China had honed his skills, and a negative response to a request from him was virtually impossible for a former beneficiary of his numerous favors.

The message for John arrived two days after the meeting with Ho and Giap. It was direct and clear, even allowing for the usual conciseness of coded radio communications:

"Need soonest direct action inhibiting Japanese patrolling northeastern Tonkin area especially Tho tribal lands. Thanks."

There was no indication that AGAS had cleared any of this with OSS/Kunming. John knew damned well the colonel would not have considered that necessary. He also knew that if there was anything he needed to do the job requested, it would be only a matter of hours or a few days at most before the items were delivered. There was nothing John could do except call a meeting with Jimmy Tau and Edouard. Jimmy knew about the message as soon as Mac Soo decoded it and was already planning a few suggestions for John before he received the word from Edouard about the meeting in John's hut.

"Okay, I've told Edouard about the message from AGAS and I'm sure Jimmy has already seen it." John had a dangerous lack of humor in his voice.

"I've got some ideas, John," said Jimmy eagerly.

"I don't need any damn ideas. I need some logic here."

"We can get out of this by going back to Kunming for authorization," said Edouard, trying to be helpful to his Moose leader.

"That might end up a pissing contest and AGAS's got far more leverage than Horse does or even OSS China Command in Chungking. One word from Claire Chennault and we're on the road. Thank you, but no dice. We owe him—he knows it—and that's it. The question really is do we try and help AGAS out with or without letting Horse know what we're doing."

"I don't see how we can mount an operation on our own without coordinating with Kunming," said Edouard, mostly for Jimmy's benefit.

"You could have Uncle AGAS do the coordinating for you. You have to use our AGAS radio anyhow. I'll bet he'll handle everything." Jimmy Tau said, creating a new name for his boss.

"There are too damn many uncles around here. Uncle Ho, Uncle AGAS, and Uncle Sam who sent us over here in the first place. Frankly, I'm tired of being everyone's nephew."

It was a funny remark, but no one laughed, though Edouard barely suppressed a smile.

"Jimmy, you tell me what you think will do the trick as far as getting your Tho relations back in good shape—I mean good enough so they'll continue taking care of our boys. And we all know the Viet Minh have their own fish to fry."

"Yeah, I heard. Mac told me," confessed Jimmy.

"Mac told you? Told you what?" asked a surprised John.

"You know, about the meeting with you and Ho and Van."

"How the hell did he know about that?"

"Oh, he's got an arrangement with one of Giap's people. He gives them copies of all our communications—going out that is. Not coming in. And he gets useful stuff in return. My CO knows about it. It's the price of doing business here."

"Jesus Christ! You're giving them copies of our classified signals. Are you mad? Ch'ing-hsi must be crazy to okay this even if you get some tidbits in return. Was this your idea?" John had to strain to keep himself from screaming. Edouard motioned for him to keep his voice lower.

"It sort of just evolved as we proceeded to set up this base commo center here. When I first came down it was just me alone. Mac arrived later to beef up the radio side. He's got real good relations with them," Jimmy replied.

"I'll bet he does," said the livid John Guthrie, his Scottish-American temper in high gear. "And you think he isn't giving them copies of the incoming traffic?"

"I know he doesn't," said Jimmy in a hurt tone.

"You don't know shit, Lieutenant. I don't care how long you've been in this country. Which the hell side are you on, Tau?"

"I resent that, sir. I am a commissioned US Army officer and I resent that. My commanding officer approved everything that's been done. We couldn't have the cooperation we do here if we didn't share information with Uncle."

"He's not your uncle. he's not our uncle. He's a Vietnamese communist whose intention is to take over this country with or without our help. And you're not sharing information, you're giving him all outgoing traffic and getting selected items from them in return."

"In fact we send out stuff for them, too. They have a receiver at Chiu Chou Chieh not that far from Ch'ing-hsi. They send in some sort of Vietnamese transfer code. It's not hard to read if you know everyone's code name and the local dialect. Mac's pretty good at it. But they know that and trust him. That's the way they send instructions to their people in China."

"Through us? They send their signals through us?"

"Yes, some of it. Every now and then we get a brief message for them, but they don't receive much. They don't trust the radio for receiving reports. They send couriers mostly. They work in relays and I was told they can get a message down from the border, that's a hundred plus miles, in something over 16 hours. It's pony express without the pony. They really don't need us, but I guess it's convenient from time to time. Major, we're not giving much up. Anything we learn is most often from them anyhow, and what I figure out on my own I would share with them in any case."

"That means that they could drive from Kunming to the border near Ch'ing-hsi, what's that place... Chiu Chou Chieh... in about ten hours easy... slip a report to a relay runner there and it would be in Kim Lung in a little over a day from Kunming. They really don't need the radio much at all. No wonder they're so damn eager to keep the Japs out of that whole Cao Bang/Tuyen Quang triangle. All their commo from China runs through there—literally runs through." John was thinking out loud. He had calmed down in the process.

"John, both sides here need that area. AGAS needs it for their recovery ops and the Viet Minh need it for all their reasons. There really isn't any conflict of objectives here—just different objectives," Edouard said in his usual role as mediator.

"Okay, I grant that. But we damn well don't have the strength to knock over Jap strongholds. I don't think an OG unit would even attempt it. Hit an' run, that's all that can be done. And what the hell do we hit?"

That was of course the main stumbling block. They all knew what they wanted to happen, but making it happen was something else.

"Simply put," Edouard began, "we are trying to discourage the Japs from traipsing through Tho tribal areas as well as nearby regions and scaring the natives. I've heard about places in the Amazon or someplace in South America where the locals keep strangers out—including the gendarmerie—by putting shrunken heads on poles. That's supposed to get the message across pretty well. Have we got anything like that?"

"I don't think we want to get into a brutality contest with the Japs," Jimmy said, "But your thesis is good; make the place inhospitable."

John tilted back in his bamboo chair contemplating the picture Edouard had created of the shrunken heads.

"Jivaro Indians… they're the ones you're thinking of. They shrink heads," he said. "It only works if you're afraid of getting your head shrunk. We need something a little less subtle."

"Here's another one for you," Edouard offered, happy they were beyond the radio business for the moment. "In the southwest US, to keep the Indians from attacking settlers, the cavalry used to send out patrols to intercept raiding parties."

"We've got no cavalry, and if I remember correctly, the horse soldiers were always getting ambushed by the Apaches or somebody." John was not enthusiastic.

"No, wait a minute," countered Jimmy. "Part of this is a show of force for the Tho and other villages. If they see a sizeable unit of Viet Minh heavily armed with things like the machine guns we sent them, plus a stalwart group of foreigners—that's us—they're bound to feel more secure. And if we run across any Jap patrols, all the better. What was it that Eddy said the other day to Len about being a doctor? It's all about image, he said. We've got to project the right image."

"So you're saying that we should get everyone all dressed up like soldiers and march around Tho-land… that will scare off the Japs and make the Tho happy," John said with heavy sarcasm.

"It'll work. I'm sure of it," answered Jimmy.

John looked over at Edouard who sat on the floor whittling a piece of wood with his combat knife. Edouard continued to make shavings. He finally spoke:

"There's a short-term benefit for sure. We should really recruit some Tho and other local tribes as scouts. They've got to feel part of the action." He went back to his whittling. He had a nice little pile of shavings.

"In other words, we don't go looking for a fight, but if one comes up, we have a sizeable force to handle it. And meanwhile we give the local villagers the feeling the cavalry will protect them," John said, showing more interest than before. He seemed to be selling himself on the idea.

"The important thing is that we get moving on this as soon as possible. If Jimmy's worried about the psychological impact on the region of the village being destroyed, we have to counter that quickly." Edouard gathered up his shavings and smelled them.

"What the hell are you doing with that wood?" asked John.

"I'm making a sachet. I've got some gauze from Len and I put the pieces of wood in the gauze. I don't know what the wood is, but it smells terrific."

"I think you've got jungle fever. We're sittin' here worrying about how we're going to solve this problem and you're whittling a smelly piece of wood." It was hard to tell whether John was annoyed or amused.

"It's relaxing," was all Edouard said.

"I think the idea is excellent. I think we should tell Comrade Van. He should go for it also." Jimmy Tau was back to his ebullient self.

"I think we've got something I can live with here," said John, satisfied he wasn't agreeing to a major military encounter. "Just so everyone understands this is a 'show of force' and not some damned punitive expedition up the Khyber Pass."

"Victor McLaughlin, Cary Grant, and Douglas Fairbanks Jr.," Edouard announced.

* * *

Tony Castelli was more than a little disturbed at the news he had received from his designated Viet Minh contact in Kunming. The man had been nearly ecstatic—or as close to ecstatic as a purposefully taciturn individual can be—when he told the SI major of the news he had received that the American training group was leading a large Viet Minh force against the Japanese in reprisal for a Jap raid on a Tho village that had been helping recover American pilots. Tony had given the impression that he had heard something about the operation but held that it was "another section." He made every effort to appear enthusiastic and departed as quickly as possible for Horse Simpson's office.

"This is a new one on me, Tony," said Simpson. "I've not heard one word about anything like this."

"They can't be doing this, sir," said the distraught Tony Castelli. "We have no authorization for something like this. What the hell is John Guthrie thinking of? It's simply a training mission. We don't have any approval for military operations with the communists. Chungking is nervous as hell about this sort of thing. It's the same with the Chinese Communists up north where Dixie Mission is just for liaison and training. They wouldn't OK something for the Vietnamese that they refuse for the Chinese."

"I told you, Tony, I've heard nothing about this. I knew about the Jap raid in the Tho country—so did you. But this so-called reprisal raid is news to me. I'll send an immediate query via AGAS. Maybe your guy got it a little screwed up. It happens, y'know. John's a very careful guy. I'm sure there's a good explanation."

The urgent request for clarification was immediately responded to by Moose Mission. The rather short message stated simply that the Moose team was taking the first class of its training cycle on a "graduation" maneuver in the field as part of an effort to instill confidence in the training group and the tribal communities which assist AGAS. Simpson was quite satisfied, but Tony Castelli remained highly suspicious. At this point, however, he had his hands full with Commandant Jean Sainteny who had just returned from a hectic trip to Paris urging his bosses to maneuver for a more independent role for French forces.

There was nothing positive that came out of the long and difficult round trip to Paris as far as Jean Sainteny was concerned. He'd lobbied hard to arrange a private meeting with Le Grand Charles, but to no avail. He even had a difficult time getting to see his own boss, the head of French Intelligence, who found far more pressing the problems of the immediate post-war European political world. A figurative pat on the head and Commandant Sainteny was sent back to his post in Kunming to be saddled once again with the responsibility—in his own mind—of the future of France in Asia. At least he didn't lack the ego for this self-appointed position for which he perceived the OSS office in Kunming as his principal adversary. The inability to get Montfort and Phac out of Tonkin became Castelli's fault and part of a continuing anti-French plot by American intelligence.

In turn, OSS/Kunming became so preoccupied with the French political obsessions that the Moose Mission was able to proceed unhindered with its own completely unauthorized sweep of northern Tonkin. The additional supplies for the operation were airdropped to Kim Lung by AGAS. This included a large quantity of foodstuff that was intended for distribution by the Viet Minh among the various tribal groups per Edouard's original idea. As a show of his own appreciation, Ho ordered that work be accelerated on the half-finished airstrip. Jimmy predicted that at the new rate of progress the strip would be open for business in two weeks, or about the expected time of the return of the expedition at the end of July.

The heavily armed Moose team set forth on the march, sandwiched between Viet Minh units as much for their own security as military protocol. The guerrillas were led by Thanh, as Giap had been ordered by Dr. Ho not to go on the venture. Comrade Van stoically hid his extreme unhappiness, but he was clearly upset at being held out of this major military mission, even if he understood why. Nothing specific was said but it was obvious that Dr. Ho did not want his top operations officer endangered by slogging around the countryside. Ho protected carefully his intellectual and operational assets. They had taken a long time to develop and the inner circle was of inestimable value to their cause and Party. This was how Jimmy Tau explained the unexpected absence of Comrade Van. Jimmy's knowledge of the Viet Minh and its arcane leadership was no longer questioned.

Jimmy Tau and Mac Soo remained behind to man the base radio and transmit regular status reports back to AGAS. A system of runners on set schedules were established in order to ensure communication with the column in case the portable field radio AGAS had provided did not work properly—always a problem. In addition to the nearly 200 guerrilla fighters in the column there were approximately two dozen Tho tribesmen. They were along as representatives of their tribe, as well as to act as guides. Many of the guerrillas doubled as porters for supplies and ammunition. It was a formidable force.

Not having any specific target, it was agreed from the beginning that the route taken should be balanced on the requirements of the AGAS network in conjunction with known Viet Minh tribal strengths. The aim was to make an extended march through territories important to maintaining Viet Minh political influence and at the same time to reinforce the existing AGAS support structure in the countryside. Thanh had been well briefed by Giap before departure as to key tribal connections to be made, and these were coordinated on the map with Jimmy's network of spotters and cooperating villages.

"If we'd had to clear the planning for this enterprise through channels, it would have taken two months," said Edouard, marching by John's side early the first morning. "As it is, how long has it been since I came back with Jimmy? Two weeks, if that. I tell you this is what I would call a logistical dream."

"It helps when you don't have to request permission. Of course, we also don't have much in the way of support either. This must be the whole damn Viet Minh elite guard, if you want to call it that. How many people... you know, fighters do you think they have overall?" asked John.

"Well, I remember Uncle Ho talking about how he could put a thousand fighters in the field if we could arm them properly. I'm not sure what that meant. I'm sure he's got eager bodies, but whether that translates into bona fide soldiers is a question. You're right, though, John, this has to be considered their elite. That has more to do with the fact that Ted and the boys have done a good job and they've got a few veterans like Thanh to lead them.

"I've been impressed with that young man ever since the Tam Dao raid. He knows his stuff and is cool as hell. How old do you think he is?"

"Haven't the faintest. They all look so young, but Jimmy said he's from the French colonials...."

"Yeah, that's what he told me when I first came down, Jimmy did. What did he tell you about what he was doing just before he joined AGAS? I've wanted to talk to you about that, but there's always been somebody around."

"He's careful but he explains it as an independent operation after the war started... haven't the faintest idea what that means. He and two other guys from the oil business bugged out of Haiphong when the Japs moved in... I guess to avoid internment. I don't know any of the rest of the details. He's pretty tight lipped about what they did, but I guess they were setting up Intel nets... maybe for the Chinese."

"Who the hell is Mac Soo? He barely says a word but is some sort of genius with the radio. Have you ever really talked with him?" John asked.

"I figure he speaks or understands more Vietnamese than he lets on. Also, Jimmy himself has a pretty good understanding. More than he admits. But he's a pretty good guy, don't you think?"

"Oh, yeah a good guy. But he's pretty close to going native. He's been here too long."

"They're interesting people, these Vietnamese," said Edouard wiping some water off his nose. "Do you think it'll ever stop raining? We could use some dry weather for this hike."

"I just hope our guys can handle the trail. They really aren't in great condition... that's why I made such a point of limiting it to ten miles a day. I've no fears about Ted Applegate. He's hard as nails. But the others have been sittin' around on their asses giving instruction. I'll see how they do after the first few days and after that we can tell. Ten miles is enough to start. It's a few miles between villages most of the time."

"We should have some flags. If we're making a show, we should have some flags. It would be twice as impressive," said Edouard.

"Maybe a brass band?" replied John.

"And dancing girls. Now that would be a great way to catch the locals' attention."

The first few days went as John had predicted. Every few miles there was a village. The column would stop; food and gifts distributed and on they'd move. After a while, the news of their coming would be telegraphed ahead by tribal runners and soon the eager villagers were lining up to greet them before they arrived. It was all working very well. Thanh spoke to John on the fourth evening out.

"I don't speak the local dialects, but I've learned from our Tho friends that our presence is having the effect we wanted. There was some fear at first, but the word is going out before us now, and people are talking about how the 'protectors'—that's what they're calling us—are coming. They call you 'the big men'. The protectors with the big men... c'est une bonne image, oui?"

"Yes, a very good image, Thanh. Let's hope it lasts after we've left."

"I think it will, Major John. These may be very simple people, but they are not dumb. They are very impressed with our force. We come as friends and they recognize that. It is a big occasion for them."

It had been decided that the column would stop overnight at a particularly large village situated at an intersection of trails. Several empty huts were made available to the tall white men and room for most of the Viet Minh fighters was made by the village families. The rain had been constant, and it was a great luxury to be sheltered for the night. The village treated the arrival of the sizeable force as a great honor and opportunity. Cooking fires sprung up throughout the hamlet and pots appeared for cooking rice. Villagers quickly gathered offering vegetables and some unknown meat for sale. Thanh explained to John that this was one of the rare chances for these hill people to earn some money. They lived mostly by barter of goods or produce. They were very poor, said Thanh, stating the obvious to make a point to the American major.

John asked Thanh to share the hut he and Edouard had been given. After some strong urging a grateful Thanh accepted the offer. A fire had been started just outside the hut by village children for the convenience of the great men. They gathered at a respectful distance observing John's every move. Edouard napped inside the hut as Thanh spread a ground sheet for his bed. The children watched attentively as John, sitting under a palm frond canopy extending from the roof of the hut, took off his boots and dried his swollen feet. He dug out some extra socks he had brought in his pack and carried the boots to the fire in hopes of drying them out a bit. The boots seemed enormous to the children studying the process as the wet leather steamed next to the crackling fire. The children watched as one would a scientific experiment of great mystery. After a while, the tall man would go over and turn the large boots around to warm on the other side. The palm canopy protected the fire from the drizzle, but every now and then a gust of wind would drive the light rain on to the fire making it sizzle. That only added to the pleasure of the little spectators.

After a hard day's walk, the evening meal of rice, vegetables, and some of the meat of unknown derivation tasted wonderful. Edouard asked Thanh's advice on the meat, and the former Vichy soldier said that he had smelled it and it seemed all right to eat. What it actually came from, he had no idea. For the moment at least it didn't matter; it all tasted delicious. After the meal was over, they drank tea from small wooden bowls that had served also to hold the rice. John opened one of the packages of K-rations that he had had all the Moose men carry with them for emergency purposes. He distributed the three "Spud" cigarettes to Thanh and Edouard and took the last himself. He broke the small energy bar in two pieces with great difficulty, eventually having to cut it with his combat knife. Both Thanh and Edouard accepted their dessert with pleasure, insisting John keep the rock-hard piece of chocolate himself. The children refused offerings of the mysterious other items from the white man's packet. They were content to watch and giggle at John as he tried to chew then suck on the several-year-old chocolate square. The rain ceased as the light faded and the evening darkness took over. The three men sat outside the hut smoking and watching the fire as it dwindled in intensity.

"Tell me Thanh, how long have you been in the Viet Minh?" John asked.

"Only the last few months, really. I was in the colonial forces before that, of course."

"I guess I didn't mean Viet Minh then. I meant how long have you been with Uncle Ho's, uh, group?"

"I have been in the Party for nearly seven years now. Why do you ask, Major John? Perhaps you think I'm too young for command. I agree, but we are a young party, so you see I started when I was very young. I joined soon after I got out of school. And you? Have you always been a soldier?"

"No, Captain Edouard and I only joined our army when the Japanese attacked our country. Have you heard about that?"

"Oh, yes, I have been instructed in that. I do not know your country, but I was told by our Party instructor that they sank many of your big ships. I am a soldier and do not know anything about ships, but I can imagine that it was a great loss. You had to defend yourself, of course."

Conversing in French was an interesting exercise with Thanh speaking his strong Vietnamese accent and John struggling along with his flat American Midwest accent in a French that could be best described as functional. Edouard from time to time would act as interpreter of what was supposed to be a common language. Every now and then he would smile at the pronunciations and try to correct what was said. Neither Thanh nor John were completely successful in getting the sounds correct, but after several tries Edouard adjudged them close enough. It made for a good time in the middle of Tonkin's hill country in what had begun to resemble a large but successful camping trip of a heavily armed collection of motley attired peasants. Even the Americans in their filthy fatigues blended in with the crowd. It was just what John wanted. He wanted his troop of fighters to appear as if they were representative of the villages they were there to protect. A little bit of psychological warfare that fit right in with the people's liberation concept of the Viet Minh. He brought the concept up with Thanh, who enthusiastically agreed.

"It is important for us to work with the strength of the villages to support us. Do you know of Uncle's writings on this matter? He has thought out all these things. I know you are good friends of his, and that is what heartens all of us and makes us want to work harder to learn what you are trying to teach us. We are very lucky to have America help us and in particular to have you, Major John, and you, Captain Edouard, with your excellent men."

It was a small speech straight from the Viet Minh handbook, but Thanh meant it. He was not a complicated young man, but he had already seen in his lifetime enough to persuade him of the injustice of existence under the domination of the foreign oppressor. Those were the words of his tutor in Kunming, but he had not needed his words to strengthen his own conviction of the rightness of the Party's path toward liberation. He truly was grateful for these American friends of Uncle. They had to be good people to be working so hard to train his Viet Minh comrades and to be so trusted by the great man, Uncle Ho. The logic was simple and direct.

Humor played little part in Thanh's life, so he completely missed the fact that Edouard was making a joke when he said he would recommend to Comrade Van that these "expeditions" become a regular part of Viet Minh training. The rain had returned in torrents and Edouard's remark was supposed to be sarcastic. The three retreated into the relative dryness of their little hut. There wasn't even a candle to provide light, so they all sat on the floor barely discerning each other. Thanh, undeterred, was intrigued by Edouard's comment and said so.

"We must talk more about this, Captain Edouard. I believe you have an excellent point." Thanh was clearly prepared to stay up for hours discussing plans for future training.

"I was only..." Edouard began to say and then thought better of it. It was obvious even in the dark that the young Viet Minh officer had completely missed the levity intended.

John laughed and said in English, "He's got your number, wise guy." In French he added, "The Captain always has good ideas for other men to work hard, but I assure you, Comrade Thanh, if there is another expedition, I shall make sure that Captain Edouard goes along."

That time Thanh got the humor in the remark and let out a hearty laugh.

"We shall always be honored to have him," he said still laughing.

That evening changed what had been strictly a working relationship into a companionship of friends. Having learned to enjoy making small jokes, Thanh would sidle up to Edouard on the trail and pretend to have something important to tell him. He would then say something that made no sense whatsoever, burst into laughter, and dash away.

"He's trying to be funny, but he doesn't know how," John explained to a perplexed Edouard. "You've created a monster and it serves you right."

"I'm going to teach him some lawyer jokes. See how you like that," Edouard replied.

The next few days were perfect in every way. The weather turned clear and dry. Game seemed to be everywhere, providing excellent rations for the column and villages along the trail. They had made a circle movement that brought them back on line to return toward Kim Lung. Everyone knew they were on their way home and the entire troop buzzed with excitement over the prospect of the end of their venture.

They were bedded down in a Tho village advantageously located near a fast-moving stream when the headman of the village who spoke some Vietnamese was brought to Thanh by one of his Viet Minh squad leaders. Thanh listened to the man's information and went over to the American team who were just about to turn in. John could see something was wrong from the look on Thanh's face.

"*Quelle nouvelle?*" he asked the Viet Minh officer.

"This man… he's the chief here… says he's received a report from hunters who have just returned to the village that there is a Japanese patrol not far from here. He doesn't know how many, but says they are much fewer than we are, at least according to his hunters. I am prepared to send out a reconnaissance if I have your approval, and I can get one of the hunters to show us where the Japanese are.

"Does the old man have any idea how far away the Japs are?" John asked.

"He said not far, but I don't know what that means to him. I would think it would be under a half an hour."

"I'll send one of my men with your reconnaissance unit, and we'll post extra pickets tonight just to be on the safe side," John said.

John chose his Vietnamese-speaking instructor to accompany the Viet Minh patrol and briefed the others on the news. To his surprise, the reaction of his small Moose team was one of considerable enthusiasm. John mentioned the unexpected response to Edouard as they prepared to get a little sleep before Thanh's recon patrol returned.

"I'm not surprised," Edouard said. "They've been spending weeks talking about just this sort of thing, training Viets to do the job, and so on. It's natural that they would want to see a little action. It's different for each of them, of course. Ted Applegate's a pro… he's always happy to play soldier. The others are, well, eager to take a swipe at the Japs. Do you remember how you felt when you first jumped into France?"

"I was scared shitless. Are you telling me you were all gung ho parachuting into Belgium?"

"I went in by boat. It was pretty exciting."

"I forgot what a nutcase you are," said John, crawling under the canvas of his pup tent. Normally the little tents fit two, but John and Edouard, as experienced field officers, had contrived to have their own tents. It wouldn't have been possible if they didn't have the Viet Minh porters to carry the extra shelter halves. As it was, the chance to be alone at night was not merely a luxury but also a chance to quietly think over the day's events. In John's case this evening it meant trying to consider all the alternative actions that might be required depending on the report he received from the reconnaissance. It was a state of mind not conducive to sleep, but that was exactly what John was doing when he was awakened some hours later by his Moose team instructor and Thanh.

"Sir, sir, wakey, wakey," said the instructor, just returned from his four-hour tour of the nighttime bush.

It took John a few moments to orient himself from his deep sleep.

"So... yes... I'm awake... what's up?"

"We got ourselves a small Jap patrol, sir. Maybe 15 or 20, tops. They don't seem to have any special radio equipment other than walkie-talkies, if they have anything. A couple of automatic weapons, and the rest rifles, all neatly stacked as if they think they're back in garrison in Tokyo. They had two sentries awake, but they were sitting together chatting away like a couple of school kids. I don't know where these guys come from, but they certainly don't think they're in any place dangerous. Some nerve, eh?"

"How long did it take you to get there?"

"I timed it... exactly one hour 42 minutes regular walking on trail and through some heavy cover... not tough at all. Maximum five miles from here... most likely less."

Thanh didn't speak while the OSS man was giving his report in English. He said in French to John, "My reconnaissance leader told me he thought this enemy patrol must be led by a very inexperienced commander because of the way they had bivouacked."

"Yes, my sergeant, here, has told me of the stacking of the rifles and the total lack of proper picketing. Tell your man he did very good work. If we decide to do anything we'll have to get moving right away to get in place before sunrise."

"Are we going to attack them, Major John?" Thanh asked.

"I'll tell you in 15 minutes, Thanh."

John put his boots on and shook Edouard awake in his tent. Edouard's first reaction was to reach for his .45 automatic which was by his side. He had the weapon in his hand about the same time as it took for him to open his eyes. It was a reflex rather than a conscious act. John fell backward in reaction.

"Jesus, Edouard, be careful with that damn thing," said a surprised John.

Edouard apologized, put down the pistol and politely asked if there was anything he could do for his major. John repeated the report he'd just received.

".... and I figure that we can ignore them if we want. They aren't causing any trouble—there's been no reports from the other villages about their shooting the place up. Obviously it's just a routine Jap patrol."

"Are you asking my opinion, John? What is it you're suggesting... that we leave 'em be and go on our way?"

"That's an option."

"With all due respect, oh mighty leader, I don't think it is. I think our Viet buddies expect to kick some—how do you say it in Chicago—ass. Yes, that's definitely what they'd expect."

"Just hit the bastards and forget about it?"

"Something like that."

"You're not worried that it would just stir up everything?"

"I don't really know what'll happen, but one thing's for sure, if we walk away from this little engagement, the Viets will think we're not serious about fighting the Jappos."

"So, we go in and wipe them out."

"That's it, John. I know you're worried about later implications, but it seems you're the only one. Uncle Ho wants us to hurt them... Uncle AGAS wants us to hurt them. Who's left? Nobody. Bengal Lancers old sport. Smash the Pathans and teach 'em what good British steel can do!"

"You definitely are a nutcase, but I guess you're right. Mount up, Captain, we're off."

Thanh held a meeting with all his squad leaders. Having been one himself, he understood well the importance to each of these basic unit commanders of a clear understanding of the intended operation. This had been part of his training as a political officer during the weeks in Kunming, but it also was his personal experience from years in the army. Each squad leader knew what Comrade Thanh expected of him and that would be passed directly to the others down the line. Each squad was accountable for its objective. It was the Viet Minh version of the Chinese term *gung ho*, "work together," which the American forces had redefined for their own use. There are things all armies share.

The Moose team was instructed to stay together and allow the guerilla fighters to take the lead in the operation. Len Sorenson was to remain with the several guerrillas designated to assist him with any medical needs. Ted Applegate, with the aid of his translator, reminded Thanh and the squad leaders of his lessons in setting up the machine-gun positions. There wasn't much time for planning other than arranging the squad positioning so that they wouldn't end up shooting at each other. The recon team that found the Japanese patrol led the larger unit to within a half mile of the site. There were far too many fighters for the operation, and it was soon clear that the numbers combined with the general excitement of the action meant everyone was getting in each other's way. In addition to the confusion, the noise that was made was excessive and, in John's estimation, a potential danger to operational success. He grabbed hold of Thanh who, by pure luck, he found in the dark.

"You've got to get control of your troops. It sounds like a circus out here," John whispered hoarsely into Thanh's ear. Thanh wasn't sure what he meant by circus, but he understood the intent of the order. He nodded agreement and slipped off to contact his platoon leaders.

The plan was to move up carefully while it was still dark and wait for first light and whatever the Japanese considered reveille. Thanh would fire the first shot from his carbine; that would be the signal for the machine guns to kick in and everyone else to follow. No one was to leave their positions to go in after the enemy soldiers until Thanh gave the signal with his whistle. A simple plan with minimal chance for screw up.

The first problem came with the fact that the perimeter of the Japanese bivouac was too small to contain all the Viet Minh guerrillas, tribal fighters, and the Americans. Every man wanted to get a good firing position in the crescent moon of the assault location. Why the two Jap sentries never heard all the rummaging about at the tree line could only be explained by the fact that both men, although sitting up, must have been dozing off. Slowly, far too slowly, everyone got into place and Thanh slithered silently between positions to check on placement. Every one of the fighters knew not to make the noise of cocking their piece until they were given the signal to fire by Thanh's single shot.

The Moose team had a good view of the target from the corner of the crescent. The other side of the crescent across the way was manned by Thanh's most experienced guerrillas, some of the Tam Dao veterans. These were the two sectors most in danger of shooting at each other and the best soldiers were the only ones that could be trusted to maintain fire discipline. The Americans lay in the wet grass that carpeted the forest floor and would move carefully only occasionally as their bodies stiffened. With unexpected swiftness a gleam of light showed through the trees to the east. An indistinct movement occurred on the edge of Japanese camp which certainly would have been noticed if the sentries had been doing their job. As it was, one of the Japanese on guard stood up and stretched, quieting the ambushing force. That sentry shook his friend awake and went off to rouse the rest of the patrol. The light still wasn't clearly illuminating the target area when a single shot rang out and the crescent ambush erupted. Thanh hadn't fired his carbine, as John well knew because he was lying right next to him. There wasn't anything either of them could do but watch as one after another of the Japanese were cut down. In 30 seconds there was no movement in the target area. Thanh shouted in Vietnamese for a cease fire, but it took several commands to be completely effective. It was doubtful that the Japanese fired even one shot.

The first thing John did after the firing stopped was to order the Moose team to maintain their positions. The Viet Minh regulars and the tribal fighters were running all over the Japanese encampment. It took a while, but Thanh eventually was able to enforce discipline with the aid of his platoon leaders. Several of the Japanese soldiers were still alive, though badly wounded. Thanh reported this to John and asked what should be done with these men. At Tam Dao no one asked him, and he wished it was the same this time. He was trying to bring himself to make the hard decision when Edouard spoke up.

"Are any of their wounded capable of walking or is it just a matter of time before they die? Where's their officer?"

"I'll need some medical help to answer that question about the wounded, Captain Edouard… and I don't know about the officer. I'll go back and look while you perhaps can have Doctor Len come forward to check on their casualties," Thanh replied.

Quickly John waved off the suggestion that Len become involved with the Japanese wounded.

"He stays here. His Viet Minh assistants can do that job. I don't want any of our people to be involved in any way," John directed.

Similarly, John made sure none of the Moose team set foot in what had been the Japanese bivouac.

"We are not here," he said to his clutch of Americans. "I don't know what's going to happen, but I sure as hell do not want any of us to be part of it. This is a Viet Minh show, got it? We're just here for the ride. Nobody sets foot over there. No souvenirs, no nothin.'"

In French John continued with Thanh.

"This is your victory. If there are any spoils, your men should have them. Edouard's right. Go check on the wounded and then tell me what you find."

Edouard went with Thanh to find Len and his assistants still remaining some 50 yards behind in the cover of the forest. There were no casualties among the guerrillas except for those who seemed to have lost their minds in jubilation. It had all been too easy and the normally disciplined Viet Minh force that had been on the trail for days wanted to enjoy their success. Even Thanh considered their running around and shouting not inappropriate under the circumstances. It was important to allow soldiers a release after combat. The manual said so—within reason. But the manual also said that they should swiftly be brought under control after the first wave of euphoria. Thanh ordered his platoon heads to have the squad leaders round up their respective commands as well as search for any officer.

The problem of the wounded answered itself as each of the Japanese casualties expired even while Len's medical assistants were trying to patch them up. The search for an officer among the dead Japanese proved futile.

John was sitting in a circle of his Moose men when Thanh reported not finding an officer.

"Ain't that damn near impossible, Major John?" said Ted Applegate. "There's always an officer with a patrol that size. Maybe they just missed the insignia. Ah'll go have a looksee."

"Don't you budge from here, Top. Remember we're invisible. This is a Viet Minh show, like I just told you. Maybe they're short on officers and had a senior sergeant leading," John ordered.

"Never happen, Major," mumbled Applegate.

The Americans were talking over where they heard the first shot come from, when a runner came to say they had found the Japanese officer and John should come quickly. John sent word back that the officer was not to see him or any other Americans. He was not to know there were any Americans at all.

"I thought Thanh understood that," he said.

About 20 minutes later Thanh returned to report that the officer had been caught just on the opposite side of the camp. He had slipped out to the latrine just as the sentries had begun to wake the rest of the camp. The guerrillas found him still holding his pants on with his hands. He apparently froze at the first sound of the attack and stayed that way until he was discovered. Thanh said he spoke only a few words of French but was eager to talk. The question now was what to do with him.

This was something John had already thought of and he was ready with the answer.

"Make a big show of bringing forward your most fierce-looking men. The tribal fighters seem perfect. Do a lot of talking, pointing at the officer and all the dead Japs. Give him the impression you want him to explain to his commanders that they must never return to the lands of the tribesmen. He won't understand all you're saying, but that doesn't matter. We just want to get the point across that this is tribal land and all foreigners must stay out. That's the important thing. He must be carrying back the message that because this is tribal land, they and everyone else must stay out. Do you understand what we're trying to accomplish here, Comrade Thanh?"

"I understand perfectly, Major John. Give the impression that this is all tribal land and no outsiders—whoever they are—are welcome. Excellent. I then let him go, correct?"

"*C'est la guerre psychologique*," said John in his hoosier French.

Thanh gave him a big smile and a clenched-fist salute and dashed off.

"You think it's going to work?" asked Edouard, chewing on a hunk of fruit bar from his rations.

"I'd thought about the idea before we left Kim Lung. I wondered what to do if we captured some Japs. My problem was always that I knew a few lousy Americans would have no impact, and I also didn't want to get you guys involved in the sort of bloody massacre we had at Tam Dao. At the same time, I knew we'd have to run away from any Jap force that we didn't really outnumber by a vast majority. It's all just worked out perfectly."

"So why couldn't we be seen?"

"Well, the first reason is that I'm not sure that we won't face some sort of disciplinary procedure and I wanted you guys as far from the action as possible during the whole fracas. Maybe that's just the lawyer in me setting up a defense before one's needed. But I guess another reason is that I didn't want to, as plain as that. Of course, tactically I was already thinking that if there were any live Japs, I wanted them only to see wild, heavily armed tribesmen. At least in their mind they'd see that. That was the picture I wanted taken back. Like I told Thanh, psychological warfare... at any rate I think I said that."

"'We're not going to get court martialed. Horse loves you,' said Edouard, reaching over and touching John's arm. John said nothing but gave a slight shrug. What was there to say? He knew damn well he'd proceeded without proper authorization.

The Japanese officer—Thanh thought he was a lieutenant—was sent off into the woods. The hope now was that he would make it back to his base with a story of enormous numbers of ferocious tribesmen, something that the Japanese command would just as well not get involved with anymore. If it worked, it would solve both AGAS and the Viet Minh's problem in that area of northern Tonkin.

The news of the great victory preceded the column all the way back to Kim Lung. The return march of several days was marked by repeated celebrations at each of the villages they passed through. The column still had plentiful food for distribution and that added to the joy of the tribal communities. No Roman army had a more triumphal procession. As they were passing through an unusually open area, an observation plane with clear US markings buzzed the line of guerrillas causing near panic. The pilot was lucky that the Moose trainers hadn't arrived at that part of their instruction that included mass groundfire against foreign aircraft. All that actually happened was a mass dispersal into the bush and a great deal of swearing on the part of the Americans who instinctively had thrown themselves into the muddy sides of the trail.

Kim Lung had been notified by runner of the successful engagement and Jimmy Tau certainly would have radioed the news immediately to his commanding officer in Ch'ing-hsi. The observation plane was undoubtedly a welcoming signal from AGAS. When that was realized, the flyover was treated by the Moose team as the congratulatory gesture that was intended, and the mud bath became a continuing joke. They arrived back in Kim Lung late in the evening of the twelfth day of their expedition having forced march the last 20 miles. The Moose team was exhausted but in far better fighting shape than when they had started out. They all felt that they were now veteran jungle fighters who could take on whatever Tonkin could offer. John and Edouard agreed that they were most likely right, though neither were eager to test the conclusion.

Chapter Thirteen

Giap and Ho were delighted with the results of the "long walk in the countryside" as Edouard dubbed the expeditionary mission. The reports from the region had confirmed that the Viet Minh was more than ever seen as the "protector." Jimmy Tau confirmed the fact that the AGAS connections were still all up and motivated. The AGAS chief radioed a personal congratulatory message to John and all the Moose team saying he was recommending John for a promotion and the whole unit for a citation. Everyone was joyous... except John, and as usual Edouard bore the brunt of his unhappiness.

"Use your head, man," John said to his exec officer who mistakenly tried to cheer up his boss. "This means Horse is going to want us to take over the OG assignment against the Hanoi rail and commo lines."

"They've got others already trained and equipped for that," protested Edouard.

"But we're here, we've got the Viet Minh all hot to trot... with a few more guys I'm sure they'll be happy to send down... the rest is a given."

"But Horse said he wanted us back in Kunming to take over the SO section. You heard him. I don't think he'll change his mind on that."

"Maybe, but I wouldn't count on it," said John, firmly committed to his gloomy mood.

There was none of that gloom among the Moose men. Ho had authorized a general celebration in honor of the good work done by Thanh's men and the Moose team. The expectations were high for what Ted Applegate called a real "hooha." The rumor had spread that a bevy of young women would be trucked in from all over to add to the merriment. John asked Ho if that news was true.

"Yes, it's all true, John. It is time for you and your men to relax. Hard work is good, but men need some relaxation from time to time. You deserve it." Ho replied with a concerned look.

"But with all due respect, sir, are you sure you really want this, uh… degree of… mixing. I'm no prude, Uncle, but…."

"What is a prude, John?"

"Well, a prude is someone who is overly concerned with… with everything being, you know, proper. Yes, proper."

"Décent, modeste?"

"Okay, that's good."

"You are not *modeste* or *décent*, John?"

"I think you know what I'm trying to say, sir."

"Oh, yes, I do. You are trying to say that although you are not against intimate relations between men and women, you wonder if I realize what I may be encouraging. Is that correct, John?"

"Yes, that's about it."

"You know, John, I am a student of human behavior. I recognize that men enjoy the company of women, especially when there is something to celebrate. This is true all around the world. Many of our fighters have wives and perhaps what you call girlfriends. Others do not but wish they did. Our own Lt. Jimmy is one of those unfortunates. Our Dr. Len and Nurse Truyen seemed to have developed a… what shall I call it… a special relationship. I know our Viet Minh fighters would enjoy the company of girls if they have no girlfriends of their own. Should your men be any different? Just for this one evening let all our young men… and women… enjoy themselves. I, too, am not a prude."

John knew he had extended the topic as far as he could go. If Uncle Ho was intent on throwing a no-holds-barred bash, there was nothing he could do about it. His duty was done, and it would be absurd to try to order Ted Applegate and the others not to attend.

The night of mad revelry came and went with little noticeable harm other than some really stiff headaches the following morning among the Moose team. Whatever their successes were among the imported girls, their ability to handle the local hooch was definitely limited. More than one was seen stumbling sick as a dog toward the woods quite a bit before the party was near ending. Jimmy Tau, with the assistance of the always courteous Bui Dac Thanh, met a charming young lady who did not dislike his Chinese heritage, and the rest of the Moose team had little trouble finding a giggling partner with whom to share a gourd cup of local brew. Sgt. Ted, as he was known among the guerrillas, had an arm around two young ladies, one of whom carried a large gourd presumably filled with extra refreshment. It was quite a party.

John early on had sent off Edouard to enjoy himself and sat at the doorway of his hut watching the night's festivities. He would have liked to have thrown himself into the affair and followed Uncle Ho's advice, but he just could not bring himself to that degree of lack of inhibition. If Giap had been there tossing back the wine gourds and fondling the local cuties, John knew he would have joined in. But none of the ranking Viet Minh hierarchy were in attendance and that carried a message. This was a night for the young, and John certainly did not feel he was one of them.

John had lived among these Vietnamese for quite a few weeks and still did not feel he had a true understanding of them. In most instances all the people he had met, either ordinary villagers or Viet Minh fighters, were uniformly polite and reserved. They were generous to strangers and extremely hard working. But both at Tam Dao and recently with the Japanese patrol, the Viet Minh fighters, who were nothing but armed and trained villagers, had a ferocity and wildness equal to the most savage of untamed tribes of his imagination. And yet, at the same time, they could be counted on to accept discipline to an equally extraordinary degree. He realized that for the most part he had met the unsophisticated and poorly educated members of Vietnamese society—the ordinary people. In the few instances he had met what might be called elite, men like Giap and Ho, these men seemed to have little in common with nor any relation to those who followed them. Perhaps only the young and competent Thanh bridged the gap. That a communist movement, a people's party, could have leadership so intellectually distinct from its followers seemed to defy political reality. There also was no relationship between the communist *maquisards* in France whom he had known and the Viet Minh fighters of Tonkin. The one similarity—struggling to rid their countries of foreign oppressors during wartime—showed no kinship in a future post-liberation life. It was all quite confusing to a man such as John who, through his own background and education, was disposed to think in terms of workers' rights and equality of opportunity. If Edgar Hallstrom had been right and he had been chosen for this job because of his labor background, somebody had made a pretty damn big mistake.

John sat for most of the evening with his feet dangling off the end of his stilted hut. He watched the world of the Kim Lung encampment, the headquarters of the Viet Minh, the Indochinese Communist Party, laugh, dance and drink their way through the night. One night out of the hundreds of days and nights of a battle for survival. It was the first time in all the time he had been there that he had seen such a display of happiness. Uncle Ho had been right, again. What would happen to all this if there was no Uncle Ho? If he had succumbed to his many illnesses? If Len Sorenson, the delight now of Nurse Truyen's life, had not done his job? If?

Luckily, there was a day between the big celebration and the radio message from AGAS that a plane would be arriving to pick up the Tam Dao refugees and the French soldiers, Montfort and Phac. The completion of the airstrip had been Ho's "*petit cadeau*" to the Moose team and AGAS. Not only was the day used to recover from the previous night, but it was essential in arranging for the transport of the intended passengers. Neither John nor Edouard looked forward to meeting with Montfort again. They basically had ignored the two soldiers after their dismissal of them to the holding facility created by the Viet Minh at Tuyen Quang. Jimmy Tau had visited the area on his AGAS survey work and had reported all well housed, if worried about their future. Nonetheless, the arrival of the first transport plane was an historic moment and it was the Moose Mission's duty to be at the first landing.

The weather was the usual, hot, humid, and gray overcast, but the rain was slight, and the strip was quite solid. The transport plane circled twice and then glided in with plenty of room to spare. It was a much longer strip than the one that the Gorillas had used. It would have to be because with all the refugees on board, the takeoff would need every inch. A detachment of Viet Minh was drawn up as a formal greeting along with the scruffy collection of Moose men and Jimmy Tau. As soon as the plane landed, an officer with French insignia jumped out. John immediately recognized Jean Sainteny. Not one word of notice had been sent telling of his arrival. John could not believe AGAS in Ch'ing-hsi would have allowed that. Sainteny strode over to John, ignoring Montfort and the refugees.

With a big smile, as if they had been long-time friends, the Frenchman extended his hand after a quick salute.

"How nice of you to come out to greet us, Major. I haven't seen you since Lao Cai. What an honor."

With a perversity born of frustration, John decided to respond in English.

"How nice to see you, Major. We weren't expecting you," John said looking right at Sainteny. He then turned to Edouard and asked him to translate, which Edouard Parnell did in his immaculate French.

Ignoring the slight, Sainteny continued on to give his well-worked out explanation of his presence.

"I thought it important that the two French soldiers and the refugees realized that at the first opportunity their country would come to their aid. France is grateful to you and your men, Major Guthrie, for the part you have played in securing the safety of its citizens."

The truth, of course, was that Jimmy Tau had arranged the pickup through AGAS as soon as the strip had been completed. It was an American plane flown by an American crew that would extract all of the French from Tonkin. That Sainteny would have the gall to imply any official French assistance was ludicrous, but that was obviously the position the M.5 commander was taking. John looked over at Edouard who responded with a knowing smile. John did him one better by breaking out in purposeful laughter. The ploy took Sainteny completely off guard and he was left standing with nothing else to say and a confused look on his face. Unwilling to forego the initiative he had just gained, John shouted over to Montfort ordering him to load everyone on the plane. Montfort replied with a salute and a quick "Yes, sir" in English. There was nothing the now red-faced Sainteny could do but accept the fact that John was in command in every respect.

Edouard, always more attuned to diplomatic matters, attempted to soften the scene by inquiring if the commandant had had the occasion to meet with their mutual friend Tony Castelli. Unaware that the one-time buddies were now in a state of undeclared war, Edouard continued chatting away in his most social French as if he was standing on a polo field between chuckers rather than a newly cleared dirt air strip in the middle of Tonkin. The nonplussed Sainteny just stood nodding as Edouard rattled off one anecdote after another. Finally, Jean Sainteny burst forth with the real reason he had hitched a ride on the mercy flight.

"I had hoped that I might have a chance to meet with the great Ho Chi Minh while I was here," the French intelligence officer said in what he hoped was an off-hand manner.

"That's a matter you'll have to take up with the Viet Minh, but there's no one here who can deal with your request," replied John, willing now to speak in French.

"I could wait to make the arrangements," was Sainteny's oily response.

John turned to Edouard and asked if he had a piece of paper. There was none available.

"We could send a runner and have the reply back in an hour if Dr. Ho is available and the plane can wait that long, and I get something to write on," John said to the Frenchman.

"I'm sure the plane can wait that long and I have paper in my musette bag," Sainteny said. "I'm sure something can be arranged," he added. John scribbled a note in English for Ho explaining that Jean Sainteny had arrived on the plane and was asking for a brief meeting with the leader of the Viet Minh. He offered no comment of his own and tried to make the note as un-colored as possible. If Ho wanted to see the Frenchman, it would be his decision without influence by John. The note written on Sainteny's notebook paper was sent off speedily with one of the members of the Viet Minh honor guard that had stood by patiently.

The next hour was passed with the members of the Moose team catching up on all the news from the air crew while Sainteny talked with the two French soldiers, Montfort and Phac, as well as some of the refugees. No one discussed how Sainteny would return to China if Ho indicated he was willing to meet with him and the plane had to take off without him—which it would. John knew now that the strip was in working order, Sainteny could be extracted as soon as another plane was available. He perhaps would have to rough it in the communal hut for a couple of days, though. The image of the neatly turned-out French staff officer sleeping on a straw pallet on the floor of the communal hut was enough of an amusing thought so as to encourage John to want to have the man stay. It never came to pass.

A panting Viet Minh soldier returned with Ho's answer written on the back of the notepaper that had carried John's message. It was a simple statement: "No, thank you. Hoot' was all it said. The fact that Ho had misspelled his name in English did not detract from the definitiveness of the response. Sainteny was more than a little annoyed.

"You explained I was here?" he asked John disbelievingly.

"I wrote you were here and wished to see him... nothing more."

"But I want to see him. It's important."

"Apparently Dr. Ho doesn't agree with you."

"But I have to see him. I've come all this way...."

"Commandant, you have Dr. Ho's answer," said John in a firm tone, not wanting to prolong the matter.

The pilot waved to indicate he was about to start his motors. John pointed that out to Sainteny. Edouard picked up the Frenchman's musette bag and tossed it into the rumbling transport plane. Sainteny continued his objections as the roar of the motors drowned out all but his strongest shouts. Gently, Edouard guided the still-shouting officer to the open door of the transport and helped lift him on board. All the while, he and John kept pleasant smiles on their faces pretending they couldn't hear a word of Sainteny's implorations, and when he was safely on board they gave him their cheeriest wave goodbye. The plane roared off down the strip using every bit to get airborne with its heavy load.

"I'm sorry I didn't get a better a chance to say goodbye to Guy Montfort," said Edouard. "He was a nice guy caught in a bind."

"Maybe," was all John answered.

Jimmy Tau had gone over to talk with Guy Montfort and found that the refugees were of two minds regarding their expatriation. They had been comparatively well treated during their stay in Tuyen Quang. Some even wanted to remain behind now that they were safe from the Japanese. Most of them had spent the better part of their life in Tonkin and there was nothing for them anywhere else. It was only after Montfort explained that they would all be allowed to come back after the war that the entire group agreed to be airlifted out.

"So where the hell did Montfort get the idea that the French will still be welcome after the war?" John asked as the three American officers walked back to the Kim Lung camp along with the rest of the Moose team and the reception party.

"All the French think that way, I'm sure," Jimmy said. "That's the line coming out of Delhi. We hear it on Mac Soo's shortwave receiver from the BBC all the time. The British and French will return soon and make life good again is what they say. I wonder if all the Indians agree with that, and the Malays and the Burmese and all the others?"

"Well, that's not our problem," said John.

"Has Mac Soo picked up anything more on the air raids over Japan? They must be using the airfields on Okinawa that they took last month," Edouard asked.

"We seem to be bombing every day according to what Mac picks up. Okinawa is real close to Japan so that makes the job easier," answered Jimmy.

"We bombed the hell out of Germany, and they kept right on. We'll have to go into Japan next... that is if they don't decide to take a detour through a landing down south near Saigon. That's always a possibility," John added.

"I think the time is ripe to go right into Japan. What's this... the beginning of August? They'll want to go in in good weather... maybe September, early October," said Edouard.

"I think today is actually August 1st," John said. "I figure it took a year from the invasion of Normandy until the Germans surrendered and so it'll be about the same for Japan. It'll be bloody, but that'll be it. Are you planning to spend this next year here at Kim Lung, Jimmy?"

"I hadn't thought about it, John. I've been out here so long that one more year won't mean that much. I think I could use a little time off though. Maybe go someplace to dry out. But this is the key spot for AGAS right here. I know my boss counts on me."

"John and I are going to go back and live the good life in Kunming. You are a very dedicated guy, Jimmy," said Edouard.

"Not really. The accommodations aren't that bad when you get used to the damp and all that. I really don't have anyone to boss me around and everyone treats me great... the Viet Minh, that is. It's much safer than the stuff I did before. All in all, I figure I've got a pretty good deal. Now with the strip operational I'm sure to get more visitors, but that'll be a nice change from you ugly guys."

"Do you trust Mac Soo, Jimmy?" John asked, apropos of nothing.

"I wondered how long it would take before you asked me that, John. Yes, I trust him. But you've got to understand he's Chinese, a real Chinese not a Beantown Chinese like me. His allegiances are personal. I think he has an allegiance to me and to his job. What else and to whom he has other allegiances, I don't know and would never ask. He wouldn't tell anyhow. But I trust him, yes, I do. I understand your question, but the answer is impossible to give. He's not very communicative, but he's a great radio man and that's what counts."

"Did you ever think he might be a part-time Viet Minh?" John was direct.

"You mean do I think it's possible he's a communist? It's possible. He could be a lot of things, but it doesn't change the fact he does a great job for us."

There wasn't any sense in John pursuing that line of questioning, so he changed the subject.

"Do you think Dr. Ho will really take on the Japs or is he just interested in controlling this small area of Tonkin? He's a real clever guy and he wants our support, but he's not going to be one to throw away his military capability to satisfy us and our war. What do you think?"

"You answered it, John. He wants our support—politically and with materiel. He'll allow Giap to hit the Japs where we want them hit, but he won't do it if it means taking big losses," Jimmy replied.

"So that means he wants us to help liberate his country, but he wants it done in such a way that he's able to end up with an even stronger Viet Minh. Right?"

"It's only logical, John. What would you do? He's got a big job ahead of him. He's got to get the Japs out. Then he's got to make sure the French don't come back in. And none of this is going to be handed to him on a platter. On top of everything he's a communist and whatever that means. He'll play ball with us as long as we help him. Nothing new in that. But he likes Americans... I really believe he does. Of course, that is just so we don't get in his way. I've no illusions in that regard, not a one."

The completion of the airstrip and the beginning of its operational use placed the presence of the Moose Mission at Kim Lung in a different context. No longer were they an isolated unit attached to its command only by coded communication. Kim Lung had become part of the network of bush airstrips dotting northern Indochina. The sense of autarchy of the Moose Mission was now past, and it all fed John's growing unease.

"Why were you interrogating Jimmy so hard, John?" asked Edouard when they were alone back in the camp.

"I wasn't interrogating him. I just had some questions that needed answering... and he had the answers. He didn't seem to mind."

"I guess you're right. Perhaps it was your tone. I heard an edge, but as you say, he didn't seem to mind. I guess I'm the one who's edgy."

"It's all changed now. I'm sure you feel it. I certainly do. Things are getting too complicated around here. When I first got down here everything was real simple. We go and clear out Tam Dao and all parties are happy. You guys arrive and we teach the guerrillas to shoot and salute. Swell, again, everyone's happy. We tuck away Guy Montfort and the other bad apple that make Uncle Ho so pissed off, and that one's taken care of. Fine. But then we take off on nearly two weeks of stomping around the forest chasing our tails proving to everyone—including ourselves—we're the toughest guys on the block. Edouard, what the hell are we doin' here? Six guys in the friggin' middle of nowhere waging psychological warfare on the Japanese Army and conning the local peasants who want to think we're their personal US Cavalry. Oh yes, another thing.... Did it ever occur to you what would have happened if Ho had died after Len gave him the medicine? Do you think that we wouldn't have been held responsible?"

"I never thought of it that way. We were just supposed to be a training cadre. But you're right it's much more complicated than that."

"Okay, I grant that we knew from the beginning that we were the first part of a larger push to get Ho and his boys actively operating against the Japs. But we aren't OG, we aren't a bunch of bloody commandos, no matter what anyone thinks. The truth is, we're just plain over our heads. All sorts of things are going on and we damn well aren't in control—but we're responsible. I'm responsible."

"Everything's in good shape, John. Of course, you're right in what you say, but it's all turned out fine so far. AGAS's happy. Apparently, Horse is happy—we've had no complaints from Kunming, and surely there would have been some."

"We set out on a major operation without authorization," John persisted.

"So it's over—all's well that ends well. Anyhow you had no choice. It's all old news, John. You've done a great job." Edouard could see his friend digging an ever-larger hole for himself. He tried to shift the focus. "That bastard Sainteny must have pulled some fast ones to get on board the plane."

"That's another thing. Why do we have to be involved in French colonial politics? We're not the damn State Department. I know I'm sounding like some old woman whining about all these troubles, but it's dawned on me that we've been stuck in the middle of something which is not only way beyond our pay grade—that part doesn't worry me—but we seem to have been made into some type of stalking horse."

"For whom, for what, John?"

"I haven't the faintest idea. That's what's so damned frustrating. Maybe it's me. I like things more black and white. Don't you get the feeling that there's something going on that we don't see?"

"I sure do. But that's because there is. There always is, John. You know that. I just accept it and you don't. You take this responsibility stuff too seriously. You think Horse Simpson loses any sleep over his job. Not one wink. Neither does anyone else. If they were out here they wouldn't be any different than they are back behind the desk in China. You saw Horse on the Gorilla Mission. Did he have a second thought about anything? Not on your life. You and I, especially you, were tied up in knots over the map. He just floated along sure you would work something out. Captain and quarterback, he said. Hell, it was more like coach and quarterback, and you're looking over at the bench for the play to call when the game's on the line and it's fourth down and 30 yards to go and the coach is looking up at the sky. John, you just see things other people don't. I bet you're a great lawyer. I'd hire you for anything. But it's also why you've got an ulcer. Me, I have no ulcer and you can be sure no one in Kunming or Ch'ing-hsi does. Uncle Ho has an ulcer, I'll bet you dollars to doughnuts. But he hides it better than you do. That's why you two get along so well. He's just got 20 years of covering up more than you."

Edouard rummaged around in his pocket and came up with one of the K-ration fruit bars. He took off the wax paper, popped the bar in his mouth and stuck it in the side of his cheek like Ted Applegate did. It was a perfect imitation. John laughed.

"Let's change the subject. What ever happened to the guy who shot off his weapon before the others back at the ambush?" John asked.

"There's a perfect example. I bet you've been thinking about that for days. The answer is I don't know, but I'm sure it's something not allowed under US Army regs. Like maybe getting shot for disobeying an order. At the very least they gave him a hell of a whipping. You know they learned their discipline under the French. It's not pretty, but usually effective."

The following day brought another surprise. A radio message arrived from Tony Castelli indicating that he would like to meet with Dr. Ho for reasons not contained in the signal. As politely as one can do in the clipped language of coded radio traffic, he requested the assistance of Chief/Moose Mission in arranging a meeting. As Edouard said, Kim Lung had turned into a dating service. There was no reason to delay Castelli's request and John immediately passed it onto an overjoyed Ho.

"I remember very well meeting Monsieur Castelli. He was the aide to Colonel Hallstrom. A very eager young man. I would be delighted to meet with him. Do you have any idea, John, why he wishes to have this meeting?"

"The message didn't say, sir. But he is in charge of our intelligence section now and I imagine it has to do with that. Do you wish me to ask?"

"Not at all. I expect he'll be landing at our new airport. Excellent."

It was agreed that Tony Castelli would arrive two days later, barring weather difficulties. Confirmation of his ETA was received that morning and John and Edouard were driven out to the strip in one of the Tam Dao trucks as the message from Tony also indicated that a substantial cargo of supplies would be arriving with him.

"It's a house gift," Edouard joked. "He was too cheap to bring a bottle of good French wine."

The plane was a half hour late due to heavy rains which delayed takeoff. Castelli literally jumped out of the plane before the small ladder could be lowered. He was neatly attired in pressed sun tans and jump boots, his idea of suitable field garb. He also wore a Kunming-tailored bush jacket. The contrast between him and the Moose officers could not have been more stark with their uniforms stained and absolutely not pressed. He also wore an immaculate web belt and leather holster, the Abercrombie & Fitch version of the travelling warrior.

"Tony, you old SOB, good t'see you," shouted John over the still-running motors. "Welcome to the war."

The truth was that both John and Edouard were delighted to see the short round figure of their favorite SI officer, and he seemed happy to see them also.

"I bring greetings from Great Chief Horse and his little friend, Pony Paul. I also have a plane load of goodies for your hosts that make very big sounds and kill many buffalo."

Three guerrillas hopped out of the back of the truck and with the aid of the crew unloaded the plane's cargo. With some difficulty they loaded the boxes into the truck.

"Comrade Van, that's General Giap, will be your friend for life," said Edouard.

"That's exactly what I intended," replied the grinning Tony.

After the weapons and ammunition were loaded on the back of the truck, the three crowded into the front cab and headed back to the encampment along the heavily rutted road that not too long before had been merely a well-worn ox trail. John explained how the truck had come into their possession and Edouard regaled Tony with some of the clever ruses by which the Viet Minh obtained needed gasoline to run the trucks.

"Apparently the favorite trick is to syphon the gas directly from Jap vehicles when they're parked overnight. Now the nearest Jap garrison is in Thai Nguyen about 30 miles away. That's a favorite target. Apparently, kids sneak into their motor pool after dark and drain out the gas just a few gallons at a time. They bring it up here in large gourds. It's really quite enterprising. They can get it on the Hanoi black market also, but at exorbitant prices."

"That's what I'm here for. We have to start developing a better net for information. You know, just those sort of details… how much is black market gas, what troubles the Japs have with their own supplies, all that logistics stuff. I want to explain to Dr. Ho how the Viet Minh can help the war effort with that type of info. And I brought along the rifles and ammo to show we're serious."

"Have you got any grenades? They love grenades," Edouard said enthusiastically.

"I don't know, maybe some," Tony answered.

"Dr. Ho was delighted to hear you were coming. I was surprised, but he remembers you fondly from his trip to Kunming. Naturally, we told him you were totally untrustworthy. Oh, talking about untrustworthy, did you hear that Sainteny, your old buddy, was just down here. Ho told him to take a flying leap. He just pops in unannounced like he owns the place and then gets pissed off when he can't see anybody. He was in and out of here in an hour. How did he get on the plane is the question. Did you do anything to help him?"

"Not me. We're not dating anymore. Seriously, he thinks all Americans are out to steal France... at least Indochina. He's got lots of problems, not the least of which is the belief that OSS is backing Dr. Ho in order to make sure the French don't get back Indochina after the war. I hope you guys haven't been talking in your sleep."

"It's good to see you, Tony. What's new with the war? I just said the other day that it'll be over in a year. What do you think?" asked John as he maneuvered the truck to avoid a wandering goat.

"Looks like we're getting set to invade Japan, though there's still the rumor that there's going to be a landing down south... you know, the old take Saigon story."

They had already reached the outskirts of the camp area and there were small groups of village children gathered to watch the truck go by. They laughed and waved. The big trucks were a favorite.

"Well, here we are. You can bunk in with me," John said.

"Is this all there is to Kim Lung?" asked Castelli.

"No this is just the Viet Minh headquarters camp. Kim Lung the village is nearby the road we just came up. You'll love it, Tony, it has a bowling alley, a movie theater and a small symphony orchestra. You're just in time for our annual art festival," said Edouard.

It was drizzling only slightly but Tony wrapped himself in the trench coat he had brought along. John and Edouard ignored the wet and ordered the guerrillas in the back to unload the boxes. Thanh showed up and directed the men to carry the boxes to one of the bamboo lean-to shelters. When he saw how much there was, he called in some help. John introduced him.

"This is Comrade Thanh. *Il est un homme très important ici.*"

"*A votre service*, Commandant Castelli."

Thanh snapped off a salute and extended a welcoming hand.

Tony returned the salute and shook Thanh's hand. John noticed how confidently Thanh had greeted Tony Castelli. It was a meeting of equals. Weeks before, when he had first arrived, John had come upon a tense young soldier fixed on being correct. He was truly an officer now, sure of his position and relaxed with his responsibilities. John smiled. It was one of the nice things that had happened.

John and Edouard led Tony to John's hut after asking Thanh to notify Dr. Ho that his guest had arrived. Tony was obviously a bit surprised when he saw the stilted bamboo quarters. He was not sure what he had expected, but a wood hilt on stilts was certainly not it. His reaction showed on his face. Edouard couldn't resist.

"You're lucky to arrive this week. We just finished construction of these wonderful homes. Before we had to sleep on the ground. It gets a little damp, as you can see, but one or two native girls makes it snugly at night. Sort of like Gauguin in the South Seas. You know Gauguin, of course. I've taken up painting myself since we've been here. I expect wartime art will be all the rage when we get back after the shooting's over. Don't you, Tony, old chap?"

"Eddy, you're as crazy as ever. So this is it. A bit drafty, but that's good for air circulation, I suspect. I don't know where we got the idea, but we thought you guys would be billeted in some Frenchman's abandoned villa—or something like that."

"Sorry, Tony, this is all you get," said John. "We did send word you should bring your sleeping bag. I take it that it's with the rest of the stuff in the truck?"

"Yes, if they off-loaded it from the plane."

"We have some very comfy straw mattresses if you need one," said Edouard continuing to tease the newcomer.

"No problem, I usually sleep standing up in the field," responded Tony Castelli, not to be outdone.

They all laughed and set about to find Tony's sleeping bag and the rest of his gear that had been left in the truck. A messenger arrived, indicating that Ho wanted to see his visitor. They stowed Tony's stuff in the hut and walked over to Ho's near-identical residence. Edouard thought that it would be too crowded and excused himself to, as he said, make arrangements with the chef for dinner.

As usual, Ho's hut was lit with his favorite candles. Tony Castelli was greeted as if he was an old friend. Ho apologized for the lack of electricity, but noted he preferred the soft candlelight. They sat at the small bamboo table. Ho offered Tony a cigarette, but he wisely declined. Ho's Chinese cigarettes were rougher than Gauloises.

"I want to thank you for bringing so many rifles. I have been informed that there must be nearly a hundred. And also the ammunition. How very thoughtful, Major," said Ho as if he was accepting a bottle of wine and some flowers from a house guest. The SI major had brought the right gift.

"I was amazed at how strong the men were who loaded up the truck. They just carried the boxes like they were nothing. Each box must weigh 60 pounds," said Tony, hoping that it was a compliment for the Viet Minh guerrillas with which Ho would be pleased.

"Oh my, Major Castelli, when I was younger I could move boxes like that all day long. Moving heavy things is a trick. I shall teach you, if you wish."

"Thank you, Dr. Ho. but I'm afraid I am terribly out of shape for heavy lifting. I spend too many hours at my desk. I'm not like Major Guthrie and Captain Parnell."

"You stay here for a while and we will get you in excellent shape. Is that not right, John?"

"Yes, sir. Perhaps a change from the rich food of Kunming will do him good."

Tony took it all in good spirits and was pleased to be able to be accepted so easily into the informal inner circle of Kim Lung. It was important, though, not to overstay his welcome at this very first meeting. Ho helped him along.

"We shall have a long talk tomorrow, Major Tony... you don't mind that I call you by your first name? We are very informal here. You must be tired and also wish to talk with your friends. Until tomorrow then...."

The proper goodbyes were exchanged, and Tony left with John. Nothing more was said about Castelli's reasons for the trip. They expected to talk after dinner that evening with the rest of the Moose team. It was a treat to have someone from Kunming who could fill them all in on the latest gossip and news. Mostly, they wanted to hear about the USO show that Tony mentioned had arrived in Kunming thanks to the 14th Air Force. Ted Applegate had Tony repeat twice the part about the two scantily dressed belly dancers who stopped the show. Tony was a good storyteller when he wanted to unwind, and some liberal doses from Jimmy Tau's wine collection did the trick. They drank and sang on into the late night, thoroughly enjoying the presence of a new face. That face was carried to his sleeping bag by John and Edouard when it collapsed onto the dinner table in the middle of a story.

The morning headache was treated by Len Sorenson who administered a quantity of diluted sodium bicarbonate. That and some cups of hot tea served to edge the SI major back to recovery. After a while, he was able to explain to John and Edouard what he wanted to accomplish during his visit to Kim Lung.

"Basically, I told you what we need when I first got here. What I would really like to see would be an OSS/Viet Minh intelligence net developed throughout Indochina—that includes Laos and Cambodia. We, SI, will supply the money, equipment, whatever is needed, and they provide the agents... a full-scale net. We need an already existing organization to get this done. We don't have the time to build it from scratch."

"That's pretty damn ambitious, Tony. How far up have you cleared this?" said John.

"High up, John. High enough to allow Horse to send me down here to make the offer, and you know he doesn't go off half-cocked."

"What makes you think Uncle Ho will want to do this? What's he going to get out of this?" asked an intrigued Edouard.

"He'll get money, for one thing. He'll get all sorts of materiel support if he needs it. What is it that he wants? That's why I'm here... to find out what it'll take to get him on board. Oh, boy does my head hurt!"

"Have some more tea. You'll feel better if you flush out your system," said Edouard as he filled Tony's mug.

"I wouldn't expect an immediate answer. Uncle doesn't operate that way. Have you any time frame you're working on?" John asked.

"I actually sent up sort of a trial balloon with Ho's rep who I meet from time to time in Kunming. It was a 'what-if' scenario. He seemed to think that it was something that the old man would want to discuss. As far as time frame—yesterday would be nice. As we said yesterday... it was yesterday, wasn't it? We're in the last phase of the war. We need this net to secure this area if there is an invasion in the south. If they go directly into Japan, we'll need it to get a lock on economic and military movements going from Indochina to Japan. There's a hell of a lot of stuff shipped from here even now."

"He's going to be interested in our political support for his liberation goals," John warned.

"Right. I've thought of that and for the moment I have to dance around the specifics. I think under FDR there wouldn't have been any trouble, but I don't know whether this Truman guy will follow the same route. I've heard that DeGaulle is already putting on a lot of pressure to keep us out of post-war IC matters, and on principle Churchill would back him on that."

"What's the principle, if I may be so bold as to ask?" cracked Edouard.

"The principle, Eddy, is that they both want to rebuild their colonies. FDR was the only one who had pushed for an anti-colonial line, and he's dead. No one seems to know how this Truman is going to shake out. He's a longtime senator from Missouri, not exactly a center of international politics. He's most likely never heard of Indochina. I'm not kidding. But changing the subject for a minute... if the Japs are only 30 miles away, what keeps them from coming up here and biting your head off?"

"One, they don't know about Kim Lung. To them it's just another village. Two, they don't venture up here because they don't want to stir up trouble. Everything is kept nice and quiet and they like it that way. They don't know why it's so damned quiet, but they've decided to leave well enough alone. They used to be much more interested in the Tho tribal areas north of here but had pulled back. That's why their patrol that wiped out the village was such a surprise and had to be swiftly countered. There's a delicate balance at the moment. Does that explain it?" answered John.

"Good enough for me," said Tony.

"What day is it today, Tony? John thought it was August 1st two days ago," asked Edouard.

"That was four days ago, you numbskull. Today's the fifth. Excuse the kid, Tony, he never knows what day it is. I think he's got a hot date somewhere."

"John's right, Eddy. It's got to be August 5th because I left Kunming yesterday and my orders read the 4th. Of course after last night, I'm not quite sure what day it is or where I am."

The meeting with Ho was held later that morning. The day had turned warm and sunny after early rains and the heady fragrance of the forest closed around them. Tony remarked on the rustic charm of the encampment.

"It's all quite neat," he said as they walked to Ho's place, "and when the sun's out like this, there's a certain charm."

"The people make it, Tony. They are extremely hospitable. The French were just plain stupid to not treat these people decently. They don't have much, but they'll always share what they have. I know it's funny to say this but it's a very relaxing place," said John.

"How's your ulcer? Still get stomach pains?" asked Tony.

"How'd you know about that?"

"Everyone knows. You thought no one could notice?"

"Well, it's fine. I don't know whether it's the simple food, the lack of meat—we don't eat much meat—or just the way things are around here. But every now and then, of course...."

"Of course."

Nurse Truyen met the two Americans at the door to Ho's hut and John introduced her in French.

"Major Castelli, this is Nurse Truyen. She takes care of Uncle Ho and assists our Doctor Len Sorenson in the medical needs of the community."

Truyen demurely nodded her head and rushed off.

"I can see the attraction extends to the local birdlife," noted Castelli with a raised eyebrow. He didn't have a chance to follow up on his comment because Ho immediately appeared.

"Ah, you've had a chance to meet our Nurse Truyen. An exceptional young lady, don't you think, Major Tony?"

"Major Guthrie just told me she works with his medic."

"Yes, they are quite a team. What is the word when you can't separate something?"

"Inseparable," Tony suggested.

"Yes, that's it. They are inseparable. Correct, John?"

"Yes, sir. Sometimes too much so."

"John is a prude, did you know that, Major Tony?"

"I never would have guessed, sir."

They sat at the table and again Ho offered his Chinese cigarettes. Tony reached into his pocket and brought out a package of Lucky Strikes as a conjurer would a rabbit from a hat.

"These are for you, Dr. Ho. I have a whole carton of them for you with my gear. I shall send them over later when I retrieve them from the duffel bag."

John looked at Tony who was beaming with his little trick that he had kept secret. There was something about Tony Castelli that was ever a little boy. The nice thing about it was that he had no idea. Ho smiled and opened the pack. He offered the cigarettes around and lit one himself. It was quite clear that Tony Castelli had touched the right nerves again.

"I have come down to visit, Dr. Ho, because I have a very important program that we would like to share with you and the Viet Minh organization. We would like the Viet Minh to become partners in an enterprise that could be of particular importance in what will be these last days of the war against the Japanese and also in the following days of liberation of Indochina. The cooperation you and your people have shown in working with Major Guthrie and his team has been a valuable lesson for those of us in the American Army charged with the responsibility of building friendship and common cause with the peoples of Indochina." Tony Castelli stopped for a breath and Ho jumped in.

"I have an unfair advantage over you, Major Tony. I have received already a complete report from my man with whom you have already spoken. He thinks your idea of a joint American/Viet Minh program of gathering intelligence could be an interesting project to explore. Is that not what you are about to explain to us?"

To Tony's dismay John started to laugh. He laughed while trying hard not to laugh. Ho maintained his favorite serious expression and Tony didn't know whether to smile, cough, or just grind his teeth. Somehow, he accomplished all three. Eventually Ho smiled also.

"It is good to see John laugh again. He is a very serious man. He knows me very well, Major Tony, and sometimes the things I do must amuse him. I never thought of myself as a comic person, but one never really knows themselves, do they?"

John gained control and apologized for his outburst.

"You just had such a wonderful speech, Tony, and I knew that Uncle must already know what you were going to say: it was just all too perfect. Again, I apologize to you both."

Tony recovered as well as he could under the circumstances, shrugged, and held up his hands in mock surrender.

"That's it then, Dr. Ho. Down to the basics... what do you think of the idea of your organization building up a large information gathering network with us? Of course, we'll foot all the bills and do whatever training you might need, supply any needed equipment and so on. We're talking all Indochina, Vietnam-Laos-Cambodia."

"It's a fascinating project. You understand that it could only work as long as our interests are the same, mutual, that is."

"Our interests are the same, Dr. Ho. We both want the Japs out of Indochina. The United States wants Indochina to have self-government. You would be an American ally and we would be yours. The rest becomes a matter of details."

"There are many details, of course. But I have to admit to the fact that I am pleased with the idea that a great and democratic nation such as America would think to join with the peoples of Indochina in their liberation."

John picked up the subtle slant of Ho's remark immediately and wondered if Tony also did. Tony might become caught up in the Vietnamese leader's rhetoric just as he had his own—except that Ho's words carried far more meaning and intent. John decided it was best to keep his mouth closed and let the scene play out. After all there was a time to rise to object in court and there was a time to just sit tight. This was the latter.

"My hope was that during this trip I might be able to meet with some of your aides to discuss what they thought might be needed, physically that is. I mean things like radios and other communications materials, and that sort of thing. At the same time, we could go over the types of information we might be interested in and how difficult it might be to obtain it. Just preliminary talks, of course, but it would be a useful start." Tony obviously wanted to follow up quickly on Ho's apparently favorable reaction.

"I would like you to meet with Comrade Van. He's away at the moment but I expect he'll return by this afternoon. I shall talk to him and then we'll see," Ho replied, in a more noncommittal manner that Tony would have liked. Tony reminded himself not to appear over eager.

"Wonderful. I look forward to meeting Comrade Van."

The business details swiftly over, the conversation turned to those things which Ho always found interesting—news of the outside world.

"Tell me, Major Tony, does your new president know about President Roosevelt's commitment to give independence to the Philippines?"

"I'm sure he does, Dr. Ho, and I'm sure he'll honor it," replied Tony.

"The reason why I ask is that so much depends on America following the path set down by President Roosevelt. The Philippines is a symbol to us all."

As usual there was more meant in Ho's statement than the obvious. John was not sure that his friend Castelli understood that fact. John jumped into the conversation.

"I believe Uncle is worried that changing American administrations, whether this one or not, could alter American policy in such a way as to undercut previous agreements. Am I correct, sir?"

"As you may remember, I have been observing American presidents since my first effort to meet with President Woodrow Wilson in 1919... it seems such a short time ago... his Fourteen Points were very important, but I do not think very much happened," Ho commented philosophically in response to John..

Tony rushed to assure Ho that things had changed substantially since that time and the foreign policy of Roosevelt and the US would continue under the new president and even other presidents. He realized he had no Washington guidance, but he was talking about an America that would no longer be isolationist.

"I believe firmly that there have been fundamental changes in America, and we recognize a responsibility we have worldwide," said Tony.

In the great capitals of the world, such a statement by Tony Castelli would have been considered trite. In Ho's bamboo hut in Kim Lung the words had a resonance of truth and import. Ho smiled in understanding.

The conversation moved on to far less important matters such as the heavy influx of journalists into Kunming and the concomitant rise of prices of scotch whisky on the black market. Ho enjoyed the gossip, and the meeting ended with a promise that Ho would send word of the next meeting after he spoke to Giap.

"How d'ya think it went? Okay?" Tony asked John as they crossed over in the sun-heated humidity to John's hut.

"I think it went fine… for a first meeting. As he said it's really in the details. Or was that you who said that? At any rate, it's a big idea and I'm sure they'll give it serious thought. I've got to warn you that it may take some time to work out a complete agreement. There are more guys than Comrade Van who'll have to be consulted."

"I should have said something about keeping the project tightly held… need-to-know I mean."

"No worry about that. Security comes as a second nature to these guys. It's a matter of internal politics really. That's the way Ho likes to operate. He's got close advisers on various things and they get their say. We're talking only four or five and they're used to group decision making. Don't take my word, ask Jimmy Tau. He, by the way, is the guy you've got to have in your new outfit. He's been working this place since the war started. He knows where the bodies are buried."

"I thought he was just the AGAS communicator here?"

"Not at all. I'm sure AGAS in Ch'ing-hsi has all the info on him, but I'm not sure that they'll tell you. Jimmy's a star as far as knowing the inner workings of the politics of the Viet Minh and the old French colonial structure. He's perfect for your project if it gets going and you can wheedle him away from the Air Corps."

Edouard was waiting for them at the hut when they returned. They gave him a quick briefing on the results and mentioned that there was a hoped-for meeting with Giap in the offing. There was, however, something equally important on Edouard's mind.

"I have to definitely know that today is August 5th. Actually, I have to know that tomorrow is the 6th."

"Ok, I'll bite. Why must you know this? There, I asked," said John.

"It will be my most momentous birthday. I shall be 30 tomorrow… if it's really the 6th," Edouard announced triumphantly.

"That's what all this is about? Your birthday?" John exclaimed in disbelief.

"Thirtieth birthday. That's it, a landmark. The only problem is whether being on the other side of the international dateline changes things. Should I celebrate Vietnam time or New York time, that's the question?"

"Definitely Vietnam time," said John mockingly. "Here's where you're 30 and that determines the time. Everybody knows that. Hell, in New York you'll most likely be still only 29."

"Excuse me," said Tony, "if I'd known I would have brought a cake with me. Here I am once again, without a present. You wouldn't mind if I just gave you a personal check?"

"Fine, you guys can make fun, but this is important. I need a proper celebration."

"I don't think I could take another celebration," said Tony.

"Don't worry. There'll be no celebration of his birthday. He's got no proof that's his actual birthday. In fact, it's highly doubtful that little Edouard is 30. If he's more than 18, I'd be surprised."

The kidding carried on through lunch with Edouard continuing his birthday act for the enjoyment of the entire Moose team. Tony Castelli joined in the fun, happy to be part of the group. He already had been anointed a Mini-Moose with, as Edouard put it, "a chance to make full Moosehood if he played his cards right." Tony was invited to go with the training cadre to watch the new cycle of Viet Minh recruits put through their paces. The short SI major was delighted to be accepted in the fraternity of these field soldiers in their sweat-stained fatigues and mud-caked boots. Informality was not something Tony Castelli came across very much in his staff position, and it was a rare chance to feel he was actually part of the war—or at least as much of a war as could be found 30-odd miles from the nearest Japanese soldier.

The invitation for a meeting with Giap arrived just as Tony returned from observing the mock grenade throwing. He insisted on cleaning himself up, proving he had not yet become a true field officer. John went along at Tony's insistence. Castelli was enough of a politician to realize the advantage gained from having the already accepted SO major assuming the role of sponsor.

To John's surprise, the usually dour Giap smiled and warmly shook Tony's hand when he was introduced by Ho. God knows what the old man has told him, thought John. Immediately, John was on guard, but Tony couldn't have been more delighted with the reception. It was too crowded for a meeting in Dr. Ho's hut and it was suggested by Giap that they all go for a walk to the village, as it was such a nice day. John had barely recovered from that unexpected invitation when Ho suggested that John allow the other two to go off on their own. There was nothing to do but accept the suggestion. As Giap and Tony Castelli walked off with the Vietnamese animatedly acting as tour guide, Ho took John by the elbow and explained:

"I want the two of them to get to know each other. It is best if they just talk alone, John. Major Tony speaks good French so they can converse freely."

"As usual, Uncle, you are one step ahead."

"Not at all, John. I'm just trying to make Major Tony have an enjoyable time here in Kim Lung," Ho said with intense seriousness.

It was getting close to dinner time when Tony returned to John's hut. He had a broad smile on his face as he clambered up to the entrance.

"A very smart guy that Comrade Van. He really put me through my paces, but very diplomatically, mind you. I think we have a deal. At least we're as close to one as I can get it at this stage. He's suggesting that we choose a specific sector—someplace not too large—and concentrate on developing that one sector. That way we both learn how we want to run things. He knows a hell of a lot about this business."

John had a mental picture of the short, burly Castelli in his jump boots and sun tans strolling along with the slightly shorter but thinner Giap in his wrinkled white suit. It was quite an image—two accomplished chess players executing their opening gambits.

"Remember, Tony, for you this is a staff exercise which you can run from a distance. For him this is a life and death contest in which he sometimes gets personally exposed and always endangers people he knows."

"I understand, John, that's why I use every chance I can get to come out into the field... you know what I mean. I'm not tryin' to butt in, but when something is strictly in my area—intel, that is—I figure it's best I at least get some sort of feel."

"You've every right, Tony. And all my guys are happy as hell for the visit, but I want you to go back to Kunming with something more than some convenient quick impressions. Oh, yes, and some greater knowledge than the need to lay off the local hooch. I want you to sit down and talk with Jimmy Tau before you go. I think that's real important."

"I'm looking forward to it. I've just seen him briefly at chow. Do you think he'd be available for tomorrow?"

"I guess so. Tomorrow is the famous Parnell birthday bash. God knows what he's cooked up for himself. When were you planning to leave?"

"I figure I'll radio to see if they can get a plane down here the day after tomorrow. That strip really does change everything, doesn't it?"

"It's a whole new world, and you can be sure Uncle Ho knows it. I think in a way, he was protecting his privacy by delaying its construction. I can understand that thinking. In one way it's a big help and in another it just gives too much access to people you don't invite. Sainteny was the first example. How the hell did he get on that flight? At first I thought you might have arranged it, but then you said relations have soured."

"I haven't the faintest idea how he got on the flight, though the fact that they were picking up French civilians as well as military certainly gave him a talking point over at Chennault's liaison office. He's a slick one, John. He waves his Paris connections around like a saber."

It was an early night for Tony, who had begun to feel the effects of the previous night's mind-numbing alcoholic experience the second time around. Ted Applegate referred to it as "the double whammy effect" as he expounded on the properties of all forms of "white lightning" of which he considered himself an expert—and was most likely correct.

The following morning a strategy session regarding Tony's planned intelligence net was held with Jimmy Tau attending. Normally, he would have been excluded from any discussion of the new project on a need-to-know basis. But the fact was that one way or the other Jimmy's long-term status within the Kim Lung structure ensured he would hear about it anyhow. And the truth was, as John had said, Jimmy knew more about gathering information in Vietnam than anyone else.

"So what do you think?" Tony asked Jimmy Tau after he finished his outline of the project.

"I think it's a great idea, but then you'll never have any control over it. They'll take your money and equipment and do with it what they want."

"But that's where we'll exercise control—by being the source of the money and equipment," Tony countered.

"Doesn't work that way. You have to think backwards. That's the way Comrade Van's thinking and so is Uncle. Don't forget they don't have the same objectives as we do. For you this project is aimed at the Japs, right? For them it's aimed at getting the US to support their liberation struggle. They think backwards from there. They ask the question, always, does this help make Vietnam independent? And then they work back from that."

"But that was one of my selling points. I recognized that fact."

"But for you it's tangential. For them it's primary. It makes all the difference in the world when you get down to the operation in practical terms. I'll give you an example: Say there is this Jap official in some region that has some serious personal problems that make him vulnerable to coercion of one type or another. Maybe he's simply crooked, it doesn't matter. From their standpoint this man is an asset that they want to use to protect their own Viet Minh covert structure. You would want him used to provide information of Jap troop movements, mineral shipments, whatever. One requires him to take an active role… giving away Japanese secrets. And the other… their side of the equation… requires him just to exercise passivity, to do nothing that alters the status quo, to not launch any campaign to root out Viet Minh instruments. Which way do you think they're going to go? Every objective will be judged in the light of the same divergence of interests. See my point?"

Tony was about to launch into a rebuttal of Jimmy's example when he realized the answer lay elsewhere.

"Let's say I agree. Then the answer I give you is the same one I'll give them. When we run into a conflict—which I grant we will—all they have to do is let us know and we'll defer to their interests." Tony sat back, pleased with his own cleverness.

"Only one problem with that, Major. They won't tell you of the conflict. They'll just proceed in their best interests and you'll never know what's goin' on. That's how things are done here. Why insult you, they think. Just let it all roll on and everybody is happy. That's Vietnam."

"So you're saying that the project is dead from the start?"

"Not at all. I'm saying that you won't have the project you think you'll have. Remember, you're doing something that will help them. They'll want you to keep doing that. Sooo, what do they do? They do the best they can to keep you on the hook as long as they can. I know because that's the game I've been playing around here. I want to get our guys out and I need their help in doing it. As long as they keep helping me do my job, I let them do what they want to do with what I give them to help me. John will tell you. It works because I make it work. You're going to have to do the same thing, except the game you're playing is more complicated."

To his credit Tony tried no further to argue. He still was not totally convinced, but the fact was Jimmy's logic was based on years of experience in dealing with a culture of which Tony Castelli was only academically familiar. It was also true, and perhaps more important, that Jimmy Tau, MIT grad and petroleum engineer, was a field man and not a desk man. He was what Tony wanted to be but never could be, no matter what the job. But in this case, it was the arcane business of field intelligence operations, and that made it even more beyond Castelli's staff officer ken.

"I told you he'd be helpful," said John deciding the time was ripe for a little of what he'd learned from Edouard in the past months.

"He certainly has been," Tony replied diplomatically if disingenuously. He knew that Jimmy had been right but didn't want to totally believe it. He'd been given an out and he would take it. "As you say, it's a trade-off and I think we should be willing to make it," he said emphatically. Jimmy smiled and said nothing.

John decided he had done his bit and now it was his turn to bow out of a business in which he had no responsibility. This one the SI boys were going to have to figure out on their own. He had already learned his lessons in Kim Lung.

Mac Soo had been sent out on a mission to find and catch the best fish he could for Edouard's surprise birthday dinner. Mac had promised a special treat which did not include the ever-present, highly seasoned *nuoc mam* fish sauce that the Vietnamese so dearly loved. It was his intent to grill the fish on an open fire to which end Ted Applegate was instructed on obtaining the correct wood for the grill. All of this was done in secret in order to carry on the theme of totally ignoring Edouard's own preoccupation with the day. No one wished him a Happy Birthday even when he reminded them that this was the day. One of the instructors even made an important issue over the fact that he had graduated from language school on August 6th of the previous year. Naturally everyone congratulated him ostentatiously on his anniversary. Edouard understood the silence as purposeful teasing and played to it by bringing up his birthday in every conversation, no matter what it was about. Everyone enjoyed the joke, including Tony Castelli who had been left somewhat depressed by Jimmy Tau's assessment of his big intelligence project. In fact, it was Tony's idea to get a melon, cut it in half, and stick a big candle in it in place of a birthday cake.

The preparations for the evening meal had kept Mac Soo away from his radio and left Jimmy to cover incoming traffic of which there was very little other than confirmation of the flight that would arrive the following day to pick up Castelli. Mac usually monitored the short-wave frequencies during the day to find out what was new in the world. It wasn't until around four o'clock in the afternoon when Mac Soo had finished all the dinner preparations that he returned to his radio shack. There still were no official signals so Mac turned on his short-wave receiver and picked up the news that would stun the entire world that day. As the BBC reported, a single bomb was dropped on a Japanese city destroying the entire city. The atomic bomb had been dropped on Hiroshima at 0815 hours, Japanese time that morning. Mac spun his dial and picked up the official Chinese radio service confirming the story. He made a note in his logbook of the information and returned to waiting patiently for the regular 1700 hr service transmission from AGAS. There was nothing other than confirmation of Castelli's departure flight for the 8th. Mac returned to the mess with that information and the news about the single bomb attack which he did not completely understand.

Only Jimmy Tau seemed intrigued by the concept while the others envisioned a large bomb destroying a small town. Tony judged the airstrike to be meant to simply carry a message of worse things to come. There was nothing in Mac's sketchy report that caused them to react differently. They all jokingly agreed it was clearly in honor of Edouard's 30th birthday—completely missing the momentous nature of the new weapon in their eagerness to celebrate their own important occasion. It was not until the following morning and more full coverage on the short wave that reality dawned on the Americans in Kim Lung of the enormity of what had occurred.

Jimmy Tau, drawing on his old MIT physics, tried his best to explain what he could of the nuclear process as it was reported, though he admitted the subject was way beyond his limited study of nuclear theory. Jimmy suggested they brief Uncle Ho on the matter and John told him to go over to Ho's hut and tell him what he knew. Meanwhile, Mac Soo queried AGAS on the meaning of the new weapon. They said they were also trying to find out, but that it looked like a major secret weapon had been unveiled that was reported to be going to end the war quicker. Everyone was delighted at that prospect even though they still didn't understand how this new super bomb worked. They did know now that it was called an atomic bomb and the city was a major industrial center.

Jimmy returned saying that Ho seemed interested but not overwhelmed with the news. Ho's reaction, according to Jimmy, was focused principally on whether there had been any comment from the Japanese.

"Obviously he's thinking about what this may or may not do as far as the Japs in Indochina are concerned," Jimmy reported. "He asked if he could be kept informed."

"I'll make sure you get a detailed report with all the implications so you can brief Dr. Ho when I get back to Kunming. If this means we're going to be close to the end of the war, alot's going to change," said Tony Castelli.

"Whatcha think, Major?" Applegate asked John.

"I think we're getting damn close, Top. If we've got enough of these atomic babies we can blast the Nips off the map."

"'N we can thank Cap'n Eddy for it, him and his birthday."

"You're welcome. You are all welcome," said Edouard happily accepting the credit for the development of the nuclear weapon. Somehow, sitting in the middle of Tonkin, it still wasn't possible to fully grasp the portent of what had just happened.

Chapter Fourteen

The next few days sped by, with each hour seemingly producing new events to change the world. The Moose team hung around the radio shack as Mac Soo spun his dials for the latest information. Tony Castelli left on schedule for Kunming in a heavy downpour, promising to have all the latest news immediately radioed to Kim Lung. By the 9th, Russia had declared war on Japan and Nagasaki had been destroyed by the second atomic bomb. By August 10th, Washington announced they had received the Japanese acceptance of surrender. For the Moose Mission, their war would soon be over. The Americans in Kim Lung were overcome with joy. But as each day had progressed, the activity around Ho's hut grew more and more intense as runners dashed to and fro with messages of Viet Minh activity. John and Edouard realized their role in the Viet Minh community had completely changed as the Americans were effectively ignored.

Giap held meetings with his guerrilla commanders several times during the day as representatives of other Viet Minh fighting units arrived in Kim Lung for instructions. It was quite clear that a major military operation was in the process of organization when Ted Applegate was asked by Thanh to run through the light machine-gun drill once again with the selected gunners. John asked for a meeting with Ho, but unlike previous times he had to wait for several hours. Ho was very apologetic.

"I am so sorry, John, at making you wait. As you can see, we have a great deal on our hands. I am glad you're here, though, because I fear you soon will get your orders to leave us and we still need your help."

"That's what I wanted to talk to you about, Uncle. We have received word that we'll have to pull out in the next few days. There's no timetable yet. I've been waiting to hear what the policy is going to be regarding arranging the surrender of Japanese forces. My guys would love to be in on that."

John was outright lying. He had received unambiguous instructions through AGAS that no OSS units in the field were to involve themselves in Japanese surrender activities. It was in a message relayed by Jimmy Tau who was in the process of closing down his own operation. Mac Soo had already left with most of their equipment in a flight that had stopped at several AGAS bush strips. The speed with which American operations were winding down was extraordinary. It was that speed that allowed John to pretend he had not received a direct order regarding the protocol of surrender. Nothing had come directly from OSS/Kunming. It was a small point, but adequate for his purpose. The Moose men deserved to be in on the end of the game. That's the way Horse Simpson would have put it, and maybe that was why he, too, may have been playing the old Army trick of incomplete communications.

"I agree that your men should have that honor," said Ho. "Comrade Van is planning to secure the Japanese post at Thai Nguyen and I am sure he would want you and your team to accompany him. I, in fact, have organized a meeting in Tan Trao of all the representatives of the various groups within the Viet Minh. It is important that we decide on some things quickly now that the war is over. It has all happened so quickly, unexpectedly, that I'm afraid we have been caught short in our planning. Would you do me the honor of accompanying our group from Kim Lung?"

It was less than a week since the first bomb had dropped on Hiroshima and Ho Chi Minh and his people had already arranged a congress. Key agents had made it down from China in record time, aided perhaps by orders radioed through the cooperation of one Mac Soo. Jimmy admitted as much.

"The message went out before we heard of the bomb, John. It seemed an ordinary enough communication," said Jimmy.

"I was just wondering how all their big shots had been pulled in, that's all," John commented.

"I think the signals to China were just a coincidence in timing, but it wouldn't have mattered. Mac would have sent the message out anyhow. I'm sure he sent out plenty of others."

"Uncle wants me to attend some meeting he's set up for Tan Trao. He also said that Giap was going to arrange for the surrender of the Japs at Thai Nguyen. What do you figure that's all about, Jimmy?"

"Uncle wants to show you off to his chums and maybe Giap wants you in on the final kill. It would be his way of thanking you. Nobody's asked me along. I guess they don't want anyone to see a Chinese face in the crowd. I'd be annoyed if I cared, but I don't. Not anymore, John. I told you before I needed a leave. I didn't expect them to stop the whole damn war just to give me one. I'll fly out in a few days. How are you guys getting out?"

"We've heard nothing, and I don't want to ask just yet. If I ask, they'll have to pass on the orders regarding Jap surrenders. My boys would love to be in on the Thai Nguyen ceremony."

"Who says it's just a ceremony. We've monitored enough Jap traffic to be able to tell that they aren't all buying into the surrender stuff. Mac told me that before he left. He's got just enough Japanese to be able to figure it out. You could be walking into a big shooting match. I would think twice if I were you."

Jimmy Tau had left John with a lot to think about. His first reaction to Ho's invitation was to jump at the chance. It had all happened so swiftly that it seemed the natural thing to do to go to Tan Trao with Uncle for their big get together, then onto Thai Nguyen with Giap. Hell, they'd be halfway to Hanoi by then. Maybe he could get to see their famous capital before the show came to an end. Edouard certainly thought so.

"Correct me if I'm wrong, but the whole surrender business has caught everyone off guard. It'll be a little while before it all settles down. This gives us a chance to—what did Jimmy call it—freelance for a bit. If Uncle is about to make his big political move, it would be fun to be around for the festivities. If he and the Viet Minh are about to show up in Hanoi to take over, then that's the place for us to be. Has anyone told us not to?"

"We haven't made any great effort to get instructions… you have to admit that," said John.

"And they haven't busted a gut trying to contact us either. Where's Tony… what's he doing up in Kunming? He said he'd keep us informed," asked Edouard.

The conversation went back and forth until it was decided to hold a war council with the rest of the team in the communal mess.

"We've been wonderin' bout the same thing, sir," said Ted Applegate after John explained the situation they were in. "I can tell ya we're real interested in bein' in on that Jap surrender."

"We can call it quits right here, Top. It might take a little while but I'm sure Col. Simpson will send a plane down for us. If worse comes to worse, we can always walk back up there. I'm sure we could arrange some Tho guides," John responded.

"I'd like to go all the way to Hanoi with the Viet Minh," said Len Sorenson who rarely pressed his own views forward.

"Of course ya would, boy," Ted said with rare sarcasm. He restrained himself from further comment on what certainly would be a touchy subject.

"Say we go all the way to Hanoi… How are we going to get out of there? I mean, what do we do then?" One of the instructors asked the obvious question.

"We'll find some transportation. The 14th Air Force is bound to set up at whatever airfield they've got down there. For all we know, there's already a crowd of potentates taking the Jap surrender. They certainly won't walk to Hanoi," Edouard replied with his usual optimism. "Come on...it'll be fun. We deserve it."

"We gonna have t'walk down there?" asked Ted Applegate, bringing up a practical point.

"If we agree to go with them, I'll insist we get to use one of the Tam Dao trucks. I should be able to arrange that, but it's a good point, Ted," answered John.

A final vote produced a unanimous agreement to go on down "for some sightseeing" in Hanoi, as Edouard dubbed the trip. The Moose team also agreed to go along with Giap to accept the Jap surrender at Thai Nguyen if there was going to be one.

As the meeting was breaking up, Jimmy ran up from the radio shack.

"Got a message here from Tony. It came in the clear from AGAS. It's for you, John."

The communication was succinct and somewhat surprising:

> Shifting work site to Hanoi next week stop Horse says okay you meet me there to arrange departure stop AGAS says okay you depart with Jimmy stop You choose stop Inform soonest stop MiniMoose

"Well, there it is. Great minds moving in the same direction," said John to the group. "Unless you want to change your minds, I'll signal we'll be visiting Hanoi. I guess Tony isn't sure exactly when he'll get there, but that doesn't matter. He won't be too hard to find."

The next step was to coordinate with Giap and Ho regarding the plans for leaving Kim Lung. To John's amazement, he was informed that the encampment would be abandoned the following day. Arrangements would be made to stuff the Americans into one of the trucks to take them down to Tan Trao. Like everything else that had happened in the past few days there was no time left to proceed on what had become the expected Kim Lung relaxed routine. Duffel bags were filled, weapons secured, and accumulated souvenirs left behind. Len Sorenson opted to walk down to Tan Trao with Nurse Truyen and her medical assistants along with two bullock carts of medical and food supplies. John knew he'd have to put an end to this romance before they set off for Hanoi, but he decided not to make an issue of it at this point.

Jimmy Tau was left virtually alone at Kim Lung.

"When does your chariot arrive, Jimmy?" Edouard asked.

"Tomorrow or the day after. I'll have some of the villagers help me out with the stuff I have left. It's really not that much," he replied.

They tried not to make it a sad goodbye but leaving Jimmy Tau behind just didn't seem right. Edouard tried to encourage the AGAS officer to go with the Moose team to Hanoi.

"Already been there, Eddy... and in better times, I assure you. No, I'll head back to Ch'ing-hsi and Uncle AGAS. But I'll give John some names to contact in Hanoi if you need some help. That's if they're still alive."

The last night in Kim Lung was full of reminiscences of the past weeks—bittersweet times. They were determined to polish off all of Jimmy's wine reserves but didn't even get close. It just wasn't a time for wild revelry. No one said it openly, but the entire Moose team—even the hardnosed Ted Applegate—knew they had come to the end of their war. There was no regret there, but there was a sadness at leaving the special world of Kim Lung with its bamboo huts, Mac Soo's gourmet fish dinners, and the hospitality of the generous villagers. They all knew there was something they would leave behind in Kim Lung that would never be found again anywhere else. The evening broke up early with each man going off to his own thoughts.

Jimmy Tau had lingered after the others had left and took John aside in a conspiratorial manner.

"What's the problem, Jimmy?"

"I've wanted to speak to you alone but couldn't find the correct moment. It's a bit sensitive," the AGAS officer said hesitantly. It was apparent it was something he did not want to have to pass on.

"You make it seem like your favorite aunt died."

"Well, in a way.... This was a big surprise to me, and I wanted to think about it before I told you. Mac Soo gave me this information just before he left. You know he sent through lots of messages for them, the Viet Minh, Uncle, and so forth. They use a code but that never stopped Mac from knowing what he was sending. It was pretty simple to break if you have sent all their transmissions. They must have sent their super-secret stuff by courier anyhow, but Mac could always get an idea of the sense of these things he radioed to their receiver frequency. They'd change the frequency, but the code remained consistent—pretty amateur stuff... as I've already told you."

"I'm dying of curiosity here, Jimmy. What was it?"

"Well, Mac figured out that these messages he was sending were destined for a top agent up in China somewhere in the Kunming area. What Mac told me when he left was that he'd figured out that the most recent ones had been about making contact with the French. Mac hadn't been sure at first, but he finally kept cross checking and that's what it was. Ho has been trying to get in touch with the French. It began weeks ago."

"But Sainteny was here and Ho wouldn't see him," John said, perplexed.

"Maybe Ho didn't want you knowing of the contact. Maybe Sainteny came down without an invitation. Maybe both or something else. Who knows?

One thing's for sure, my friend—Uncle's been playing a game here and we're not in on it!"

* * *

For Bui Dac Thanh, the news of the great American secret weapon that had forced the Japanese into surrender reinforced in his mind the respect he had for the Americans he had come to know at Kim Lung. Theirs must be a great and powerful country, he thought, and the fact that they would send their soldiers to fight with the Viet Minh was proof that the liberation of Vietnam was near at hand. He had told his men just that as they prepared to march south toward Hanoi. He, Thanh, had been honored to be assigned to act as the commander of the special protection force for Uncle Ho while he attended the historic congress at Tan Trao. Furthermore, Thanh had been informed that if they then moved on to Hanoi—which everyone expected they would—he would take on expanded security duties because of his intimate knowledge of the city. The time had truly come when the battle to wrest control away from the colonial masters would begin in earnest and the real war would have begun.

The little town of Tan Trao seemed to be flooded with important Vietnamese nationalists and their closest followers. Thanh had been briefed by Giap regarding the fact that many of these people were not members of the Party and therefore must be watched closely.

"It is important, Comrade Thanh, that you and your men exercise the maximum care not to show how carefully you are observing the attendees to the congress. They should know you are present, but not be made to feel they are under surveillance. Do you understand what I mean, comrade?"

"Yes, comrade, I understand. Keep a careful eye out but do not let anyone know we are doing it."

"The Americans will be here also, so allow them as much freedom to move about as possible except during those times which I will instruct you on. Confidential sessions and the like."

"Understood, comrade."

The problem of security for the congress was part military and part policing. Thanh realized early on that he would have to divide his limited manpower so that some could act as a perimeter guard while others moved freely in small numbers within the town. The larger Viet Minh military formation directly under Comrade Van's command was bivouacked just outside of the town ready to be deployed if an emergency demanded. The presence of the Americans who had arrived in one of the trucks from Kim Lung bolstered Thanh's confidence. He had come to respect the American, Major John, in a manner he never thought would be possible of a non-Vietnamese. He had had a professional respect for his French officers, but that was different. He had never liked them. The idea of liking them was not even conceivable. These Americans, and especially Major John, were to be both respected and liked. It was as if he was a Vietnamese. Thanh wondered if the American major was a communist. It must be so for he was so close to Uncle Ho.

Unfortunately, the Americans did not seem to understand the seriousness of the congress. It was apparent to Thanh that the enlisted men thought it was a large meeting to celebrate the Japanese surrender. They laughed and joked in public and took walking tours of Tan Trao in search of souvenirs. Thanh understood that this was the first real Vietnamese town they had visited outside the small village of Kim Lung, but even so they did not act with the decorum that Thanh expected they should. He still had a great deal to learn about Americans, he decided.

The one American, the medical doctor, had caused quite a bit of gossip and jealousy among the guerrillas who did not approve of the favors bestowed on him by Nurse Truyen. She had always held herself above all of them and now she was, in effect, insulting them further. Thanh had had to firmly silence that talk on several occasions. Doctor Len had done a good job with his care of the guerrillas and villagers, and that had gone far to reduce tensions. However, here in Tan Trao outside the protective environment of Kim Lung, remarks by some of the visitors noticing the relationship between the American and the Vietnamese nurse brought to the fore once again the inappropriateness of the liaison. That Truyen was also Uncle's personal care giver made the situation even more delicate in Thanh's eyes. There was no one he could talk to other than Truyen and that would be out of the question. It would be best, he decided, to put off saying anything until it was clear how long the Americans would be remaining with them. Sometimes lack of action is the better route to leadership. That was also one of the things his tutor had taught him.

This security work was truly taxing. To do the job right, Thanh should have been able to have had an advance party in Tan Trao days before the congress. It also would have been useful if some sort of identification badge could be worn separating the attendees from townspeople. Then there was the matter of diplomacy. Some of the delegates were armed and that posed a problem. Others were just plain obnoxious and that posed additional problems. Sometimes these two factors were combined and that was the worst. One delegate whom Thanh actually recognized as a party member from Hanoi was the most trouble.

Thanh originally had tried to calm down a fracas between the man from Hanoi and another attendee. Thanh had been called over by a young soldier in his inner security team when he was unable to break up the shouting and shoving match between the two delegates. Thanh had forced himself between the two and held them apart. The man from Hanoi took umbrage at Thanh's interference and insisted on seeing the head of the security detail. When he learned that was Thanh, he became even more annoyed. Later the man from Hanoi, who clearly had a problem regarding status and rank, became embroiled in an argument with yet another delegate.

"Comrades, comrades, let's cease this foolishness," said Thanh, having raced over at the first sign of trouble. His choice of words and tone of command did not sit well with the Hanoi delegate, who made the mistake of rudely shoving the younger but far more fit Thanh to the ground. Thanh rose slowly, dusted himself off, and to the surprise of the small circle who had quickly gathered, announced the man was now under arrest. The man laughed at the announcement.

"You can't arrest me. I am a member in good standing of the Indochinese Communist Party, and we are all equal here, young man, whoever you are."

Thanh, who was unarmed, reached over and drove his thumb and first two fingers on each side of the man's windpipe, forcing him to gag and fall to the ground. Thanh had seen the legionnaire Sgt. Vogel do the same on several occasions in the barracks over matters far less serious than pushing a security officer to the ground.

"Comrade, you are under arrest," repeated Thanh. Immediately two of Thanh's soldiers grabbed the delegate from Hanoi under his arms and dragged him off to a small stockade they had requisitioned that previously had secured livestock for sale. The word spread quickly among the delegates of the tough security in place, and there were no further disruptive incidents.

The Vietnamese-speaking weapons instructor was the only OSS man who had any interest in the proceedings of the congress as he was the only one who could understand any of the speeches. Thanh, with whom he had developed a friendly relationship over their weeks of close working conditions, placed his American colleague out of casual sight in the rear of the meeting room so he could listen without standing out. These were the general meetings and contained no confidential discussions which would be inappropriate for an outsider to hear. The revolutionary rhetoric was typical of what Thanh had heard for years and was in his mind quite innocuous. For the OSS sergeant, even with his limited fluency in Vietnamese, the exhortations were shocking. The bloodthirsty calls for death to the imperialist exploiters were seasoned from time to time with some specific references as to how their political and personal bodies would be dismembered. It was rough peasant talk but it was shocking to the American who had not been exposed to anything except the politest village vocabulary. He asked his friend, Thanh, about the language later on. Thanh shrugged it off as typical political rhetoric, but it bothered the sergeant enough that he made mental notes of some of the more outlandish of the remarks.

The small army that Giap had collected outside of Tan Trao had made an impression on all the delegates and the local villagers. Ho and Giap had arranged a rather purposeful show of force as a powerful sign to any delegates from organizations that might seek to follow their own way within the Viet Minh. It was a time when the communist leadership had to be recognized and accepted. Subtlety had no role in the congress at Tan Trao.

The Moose team was housed in a modest-sized wooden building in the center of the town. The important thing about the structure was that it had a solid roof that kept out the rain which had been streaming down with only a few breaks since they arrived. The initial efforts to look around the small town became futile as the soaking progressed. John began to regret his decision to acquiesce to Ho's request that they tag along. For the most part the team hung around enjoying not being rained on, talking and playing cards. John and Edouard went over with their sergeant the details of the meeting he'd attended.

"Basically, they're organizing themselves into a form of assembly and a sort of government with departments. There's lots of speeches, but I got the impression that it's all orchestrated by Uncle Ho and his guys. Lots of talk about independence and how they'll fight to the death and kill everyone to get it. I mean these guys are really workin' themselves up. Thanh said it was all rhetoric, but I don't know."

John had told Edouard what Jimmy Tau had passed on to him. Edouard had been quick to react.

"They're using us, John. If Ho's been in contact with the French all along, we've just been used to keep pressure on them, the French," Edouard had said.

"But we knew that's what they'd do—use us," John had responded.

"But not with the French—not as some sort of leverage with the French."

Other things had begun to surface as soon as they arrived at Tan Trao. Giap's large armed force seemed to have appeared from nowhere. The nondescript guerrillas of Kim Lung had multiplied fivefold and all of a sudden broken out in uniform khaki shorts and shirts. Even the guerrilla girls had matching black skirts and blouses. All sported ammunition belts and other military paraphernalia. The rag-tag partisans had turned into a far larger and better-equipped fighting force than the Moose Mission had been allowed to see.

At first the OSS team members were amused at the transformation. That lasted until it dawned on them that, as Ted Applegate put it, "They been playin' the po' boy t'squeeze all the crap they could outta the US Army. Hell, ah got me an uncle who's a millionaire nearly 'n he goes 'round in these here overalls filthy as a pig jes' t'git folks t'feel sorry fer 'im. Damn!" The heavy drawl emphasized his meaning.

Len Sorenson, who in the first days after arrival in Tan Trao was abruptly jilted by Nurse Truyen, decided that also was tied into the Viet Minh charade. In a way, he was right because Ho had intervened when he learned of the numerous complaints that had come to a head on arrival at Tan Trao. A firm course correction had been ordered. Len was desolated.

John was asked repeatedly by the Moose team what he thought was in the wind and could give no answer. Team morale was low. They wanted to get going. The war was over. John decided to find Giap to find out what was going on. He and Edouard sloshed through the muddy streets of Tan Trao searching for Thanh who would know how to contact Giap. They found Thanh standing with some of his security guards under a lean-to shelter. He directed them to Uncle Ho's office near where the congress was being held. Thanh said that was the only way he could suggest how to find Giap. John really didn't want to bother Dr. Ho, but he had no choice.

The guard, who stood unblinking in the rain, spoke no French and gave no sign of recognition. After being spoken at for half a minute, he turned on his heel and went into the building. The door opened again shortly afterward, and there was Giap in his usual white suit only slightly more rumpled than usual. Politely, he invited both Americans in from the rain and sent the guard back out. Equally politely, he apologized for the absence of Ho Chi Minh.

"I am sorry, but he is giving a speech at this very moment. He shall return soon if you wish to wait. How are you and your men, Major John? I haven't seen you in a few days. This is much different than Kim Lung, I suspect." For Giap that was positively chatty, and John was momentarily disarmed.

"Uh, yes, much different," was all he could think to reply. "The rain is quite heavy, yes… and I was wondering if that has had an impact on your plans for Thai Nguyen."

"I'm in fact going to be talking with Uncle about that as soon as he returns. It is good you are here. Perhaps you would like to offer us your advice."

John looked over at Edouard on whom he was counting to divine any nuances of meaning in Giap's French that he missed. Edouard just smiled and gave no clue. John decided that it was far easier when Giap was his usual laconic self. This pleasant cordial Comrade Van was far more difficult to deal with on military matters.

"We'll wait," John said, with a terseness suitable to the old Giap he had come to know.

Thankfully, Edouard took over the conversational duties, noting how sharply turned out Giap's guerrillas were in their new uniforms.

"They've always had them," Giap explained. "They never had a chance to wear them because we did not yet represent a national liberation army. Now the moment has arrived. It is a small thing but important, don't you think?"

Both Edouard and John nodded in agreement. Neither asked from where all the other newly arrived soldiers had come. John decided not to wait until Ho returned to press Giap on the Japanese surrender issue.

"Have you had any communication with the Japanese commander?" he asked.

"I've sent an emissary, but we have heard nothing back."

"What will you do if they don't respond?"

"We shall attack and kill them, of course," Giap responded.

"Wouldn't it be better to simply isolate them and move on?" John asked.

"Not at all. In fact, I hope they don't reply. We shall have a chance to show to our countrymen that the Viet Minh is liberating our nation from Japanese domination. The road to Hanoi must be cleared and Thai Nguyen is blocking that road. There are lessons that must be taught."

It was a simple enough answer. The Japanese garrison would be seen as a symbol of all foreign presence. The chances that they would be allowed to surrender seemed to John to be quite limited, but he persisted in his questioning anyhow.

"What lessons do you mean?"

"There are many—unfortunately including some of our countrymen as well as foreigners, not you of course—who do not recognize the rightness of our cause. They need to be made to see the people's might. Uncle can explain these things far better than I."

As if on cue, Ho came in accompanied by two others. John recognized them from when the Moose team first arrived, and they were introduced along with other Viet Minh officials at Kim Lung.

"Hello, John and Edouard," Ho said in English. "May I introduce my close comrades who have just arrived...." Ho turned to the Vietnamese saying something in their language. Both men smiled and nodded, restrained but polite.

In French John said, "I believe we have met before in Kim Lung shortly after Captain Edouard and the others arrived. It is my pleasure, comrades."

Perhaps it was the use of the term "comrade" that put the two at ease, for they quickly appeared to relax. John wanted to pursue the line of questioning he had become involved in with Giap, but Ho had other plans.

"It is good you are here, the both of you." Ho spoke in French now for the benefit of the others. "I am sure you'll be pleased to know that we have created the Vietnam Committee of Liberation and I have been honored by being elected president."

"That is excellent news, Uncle. Or should we call you Mr. President? What exactly will this committee do?" said John.

"It is our view that the committee should act as a provisional government until such time as we can hold national elections. There will be many sacrifices, but we have all agreed that these must be made." Ho looked over at the other Viet Minh leaders, his stalwart Party comrades, and they dutifully nodded.

The emphasis on sacrifice was a typical political term and it didn't bother John. What did worry him was what Ho meant by the word. After all, they had just come out of years of hiding in the bush in terrible conditions. What could be meant by sacrifice beyond living in bamboo huts? Edouard in his excellent French put his finger on the issue unstated.

"How long do you think the revolution will take to completely succeed, Uncle?"

"Captain Edouard is a comrade revolutionary in instinct if not in fact, I think. He comes from a great Irish revolutionary family that fought against British colonialism many years ago, comrades. He asks the question of a true revolutionary and I'm sure he already knows the answer. The revolution never ends but it succeeds when the people rule, and the vestiges of colonialism and imperialism no longer exist in Vietnam."

Edouard looked over at John who seemed on the verge of asking something. John's eyes were giving off a warning signal, one that only his friend could discern. A slight narrowing of the lids followed by a purposeful widening and a flash of intensity alerted Edouard that John was about to challenge what had just been said. The man has no sense of self-protection was Edouard's single thought. The "revolutionary" Edouard jumped in quickly.

"You are right, of course, Uncle. And I believe that Vietnam is now close to that point."

It was such a sycophantic statement that John was stopped dead in his tracks. The surprising thing was that no one else in the room took Edouard's remark as anything but gospel truth. Even the usually questioning Ho smiled in acceptance of the compliment. These were all true believers, and such a comment was a simple recitation of dogma. The important thing as far as Edouard was concerned was that it had kept John from speaking. Giap had come close to saying what he really meant and that was apparent to both Edouard and John. It didn't take a genius to figure what "lessons" meant. There must have been close to a thousand khaki-clad liberation soldiers out there—and maybe more down the road—who were prepared to administer these lessons. There was no need for any more questions.

"Is there something particular that you wished to inquire about, John?" asked Ho.

"I was asking Comrade Van about the timetable for the Japanese surrender, but they have not responded in Thai Nguyen."

"No they have not and we shall have to make sure they understand we are serious. Is that not true, Comrade Van?" said Ho, more as an affirmation of an already given order than a question. President Ho was clearly in charge and

Uncle Ho's role had been diminished if not near totally erased. Giap answered affirmatively as a good soldier should, even when he is a field general.

It was time for the Americans to leave and both moved at the same time toward the door when Giap called out.

"Major John, we hope that you and your men will be able to join us in our action at Thai Nguyen as we discussed. I expect we shall be on the way tomorrow."

John hesitated a brief moment and turned facing the room.

"The American Army will always be happy to work with the Vietnamese Army to gain the surrender of their mutual enemies!" John saluted goodbye and followed Edouard out the door into what was now a quite bearable light shower. As soon as they reached a safe distance, John began a string of profanity that would have done his steelworkers proud.

"Goddamn sonofabitch, those bastards are just going to wipe out that Jap garrison for the hell of it. Jesus H. Christ! They don't want any fuckin' surrender. They're off to kill the poor bastards no matter what, and it's just to make a show. It's just to announce the big bad Viet Minh is on its way to Hanoi to take over. The war is goddamn over and they're gonna screw everything up."

"I was trying to get your attention back there," Edouard began.

"Yeah, I realize that now. I felt there was something wrong when Giap started on his lesson thing. They aren't going to let the Japs surrender. It's not half as useful for them. And what makes it worse is that they want us along as part of the cheering section. Oh boy, are we in the shit."

"We've got to get out of this, John. Maybe we could just go as observers...."

"Do you really want to watch another damn massacre? I don't care if they are Japs. The damn war is over. Over means over. I can't believe that for once the brass were right in telling us to stay out of the surrender business. They didn't even know why they were right either."

"Even when they're right they're wrong," said Edouard, as usual seeing humor in the worst of situations. "The problem is, old man, we've got to figure out how to be right, too. I don't see how we can get out of going to Thai Nguyen. It's not like school where you can get a nurse's note."

"Very funny. Do you know anything about the guys with Ho? Didn't Jimmy Tau give us a rundown on them?" asked John.

"One he called a general and Jimmy said he's the big Tho leader. I remember that particularly because Jimmy talked about Giap and this guy as having their own fighters, and I thought that was interesting. The other guy I actually noticed going in and out of Ho's place at Kim Lung several times. I always figured him as some sort of political operator of the old man's—but what the hell do I know. I'd only be guessing. Why do you ask?"

"No reason except that they were there, and I knew we had met them. Obviously, they're part of Uncle Ho's inner circle. He's pulled all his top guys together for this push. That general has undoubtedly come in with all his fighters. That's where some of the extra numbers come from. They've got themselves quite a collection of gun slingers."

They had arrived back at their modest wooden quarters and were greeted by a smoky fire that had been built on the dirt floor. Most of the smoke exited through the open windows but a great deal remained inside.

"What the hell is this?" asked John irritably.

"Len says it'll keep down the bugs and also cut the humidity," said one of the weapons instructors with a smile on his face.

"We'll be hot as hell in here." said John.

"That's what ah told 'em," said Ted,

"Truyen told me about this, Major," said Len, invoking the name of his sainted, all-knowledgeable ex-girlfriend and assistant.

"Well then, it's got to be true," replied John without smiling, as everyone except Sorenson laughed. "At any rate, we can use it to dry our clothes," he added.

They rigged a drying rack from cut bamboo and soon John and Edouard were sitting in their underwear as their soaked uniforms steamed next to the fire.

"So whudda we goin' t'do next, Major?" asked Ted. "We've been sittin' here talkin' 'bout the war bein' over and all, but it don't seem much different to us."

John didn't reply immediately. He sat tilted back in one of the old chairs they had found in the house. Finally, he spoke quietly:

"That's the big question. We don't have much in the way of options. This Thai Nguyen surrender thing may be turning into some sort of fire fight. I don't want to get involved in that and I don't want you guys to get involved either. The trouble is that the only way we can get to Hanoi is with these Viet Minh, and they're determined to go through Thai Nguyen and the Jap garrison. It's very political and really none of our business."

"Yuh mean they wanna wipe out the Japs, Major?" asked Applegate.

"That's about the size of it, Top."

"Well, if the damn Japs won't surrender...." threatened one of the sergeants.

"The Major thinks Mr. Giap and his army are not really interested in their surrendering, and I agree with him," said Edouard.

"Can they do that, sir?" asked Len as he fanned the smoke out the window.

"They can do any damn thing they want to at this stage. That's the problem. If they don't get their way, they're going to war."

"Who are they goin' tuh war with?" chimed in a puzzled Ted Applegate.

"You've put your finger on it, Ted. To begin with it'll be the Japs at Thai Nguyen, but that's just to get everyone's attention. Remember, not

286

all Vietnamese are Viet Minh. They have to be shaped up if Uncle and his comrades are going to take over in between when the Japs leave, and the French try to come back. I told you it was all very political."

"I think we should just take off and go down to Hanoi on our own. Maybe we can swipe a truck," said the instructor who was the former N.J. state trooper.

"Only one problem with that, Sergeant," said John. "We don't know what we'd face on the road. There could be more Japs who don't believe the war's over. There could be Viet Minh who don't know who the hell we are. We might even get blown up by some OG unit of ours. We're all in that truck, and you know the OG guys. They'll blow up the truck and ask questions later."

"We could use an American flag," said Len.

"Thank you, Betsy Ross," said the other weapons instructor. "Where the hell are you going to get an American flag?"

"How about a white flag?" Len persisted.

"I ain't surrenderin' t'nobody," announced Ted Applegate.

"We wouldn't be surrendering, Top," replied Len. "We'd just be showing we're peaceful."

"Seems like surrenderin' t'me," insisted the top sergeant. "What do you say, Major?"

"I say that I don't know, and that's the God's honest truth."

"The problem, folks, is that Mr. General Giap is about to take off tomorrow morning and expects us to be with him. We have to make up our minds by then and be ready to roll," said Edouard neatly summarizing the situation.

"Is he goin' t'lead his troops in that damn white suit?" asked the military-minded Top Kick.

"He'll lead 'em in a tuxedo if he wants," said John. "He's the real 500-pound gorilla in this one. He's got his marching orders from Ho and that's it."

Everyone went quiet. There wasn't much else to say. Ted Applegate broke the silence after a few moments.

"I thought this here guy, Ho, was supposed to be t'be this real peaceful old man that everyone jes' naturally looked up to and respected. That's why they call him Uncle. That's what I thought."

"He is, Ted, but there's much more to it. For one thing that peaceful old man is really not that old and he's a committed communist. Whatever that means in his case, I really don't know. I do know that he'll do anything it takes to get this country liberated—that's his term not mine. That's what you see going on right now. It's not the snug little guerrilla movement we saw in Kim Lung. They're about to start a war just as we're ending ours. That's what happened on the road between Kim Lung and Tan Trao. It's not our war, and frankly I don't want it to be. I wish them good luck, but that's it."

John had said more than he had wanted to, but when he was finished, he didn't regret anything he said. They might as well know exactly how he felt. He wasn't going to get them into anything in which they might get shot—not at this stage.

The next morning the Moose team gathered their stuff together and waited for orders from John. John had no more idea of what to do then than he had the previous day. Edouard waited with everyone else for his friend to say something, anything. Nothing happened. John had gone silent, staring out of the open window. They were all in their combat garb with weapons, ammo belts, and packs. The rest of their gear was carefully piled inside the front door to the building. It had rained during the night, but the morning had dawned clear. Soon a bright sun rose over the small town of Tan Trao giving it a pleasant and tranquil glow. One of the Tam Dao trucks drove up and stopped in front of the Americans.

Bui Dac Thanh leaned smiling from the front seat and asked in French if *l'armée américaine* was interested in a ride. It was another of his attempts to say something humorous to Edouard. Automatically, they began to load their gear in the back of the truck but stopped to turn toward John. He gave a slight nod and they continued. Edouard took John out of earshot.

"We just go along to where it takes us? he asked.

"Looks like it. At least we have a truck," John replied. He then turned to the waiting soldiers and commanded, "Mount up!" The Moose team piled into the back of the truck which they shared with a squad of Thanh's security guard. Edouard and John sat in the front with Thanh driving. They had no idea where they were going.

It was about eight o'clock when the truck set off on the road toward Thai Nguyen about 20 miles away southeast. Giap's force had long since been on the march in the same direction. Other than keeping up inconsequential patter, Thanh said nothing more meaningful than the fact that the main body of troops had pulled out during the night. Presumably, they already would be within striking distance of their target. Giap would have wanted the Japanese to wake up to find they were surrounded by the Viet Minh. The truck drove slowly through the many ruts in the muddy road but was still able to make fairly good time. Thanh loved to drive, a skill he had not much time to practice for six months.

Afterwards they estimated they had been just a few miles away from Thai Nguyen having passed a line of Viet Minh porters when a squad of Japanese burst out of the sides of the road with their weapons trained on the cab of the truck. The timing had been excellent, for the vehicle had to slow around a sharp curve. A tree limb blocked the way and Thanh slammed on the brakes. Edouard and John stepped down from one side of the cab and Thanh the other. The men in the back, with Japanese rifles trained on them, jumped down gingerly from the truck. The Japanese were outnumbered by two to one, but they were the ones in control. Thanh was livid at the embarrassment of being ambushed in this way.

These were not parade ground soldiers. The faces of the Japanese were hard and drawn. The sergeant in charge was a short burly man with the look in his eyes of a wounded bull. He shouted in Japanese at John and Edouard; it was obvious that he wanted the truck and was going to do whatever he needed to get it. The sergeant held a rifle in one hand and gesticulated with the other. Another Japanese soldier aimed his rifle directly at Thanh but would shift off from time to time to aim it ominously at the two American officers. John could see that in the back some five or six additional soldiers had their weapons trained on the Viet Minh security personnel and the rest of the Moose team.

The sergeant reached to take John's .45 automatic from his shoulder holster. He was so close John could smell the man's rancid odor. With one motion and without a single conscious thought, John pushed the man's rifle upwards with his left hand and drew his combat knife from his belt with the other. The level of the knife was chest high on the far shorter Japanese and the angle of the blade rising hit him high in the breastbone and deflected into his trachea with all the force of John's upward thrust. He never uttered a sound.

The nearby soldier was able to get off only one round aimed at Thanh, who took the .25 cal. bullet in a grazing wound to the head. Edouard dispatched him with his automatic and immediately turned on the Jap soldiers in the back. He dropped one of them before they all became entangled with the enraged collection of Americans and Viet Minh security guards. One of the Vietnamese went down with a fatal shot in the chest and another was slightly wounded in the thigh by another Japanese shot, but none of the Americans were hit. Ted Applegate did complain of a strained shoulder after he wrestled away one of the Jap rifles and swung it wildly at its former owner. The entire fracas was over in several minutes. Three Japanese were dead and four were wounded, mostly as a result of being beaten severely.

Edouard ripped open the first aid packet on his web belt and put sulfa powder on Thanh's head wound. Then he wrapped the ex-French Colonial Army acting corporal's head in a tight bandage to stop the blood flow. The other Vietnamese casualty was taken care of by Len Sorenson and his medical kit. It was a few moments later that they realized John was sitting glassy eyed by the side of the road, the combat knife still in his hand, his arm and chest completely covered in blood. Edouard tried to speak to him but got no response. After Len had finished with his patient, he came over to see what he could do with John.

"He's in shock," the medic said. "We must keep him warm. Have we got a blanket? Also, someone get me lots of water and a clean shirt. I want to clean him up right away."

Len and Ted Applegate washed down their major as best they could as Edouard dug out John's duffel to get a shirt. They wrapped him in one of the sleeping bags. He remained that way for about half an hour during which there was a lively debate over what to do with the four Japanese soldiers. The Viet Minh security guards wanted to kill them and leave them by the roadside. Ted Applegate agreed with them, but quickly deferred to Edouard who reminded him that they had not started shooting first—whatever that meant. It was decided that Thanh would pass them on to Giap's people when they were found. The Japanese might be useful for questioning, he admitted. That satisfied the other Vietnamese who couldn't stop talking among themselves about how the American Major had taken down the Japanese sergeant with his knife. As Thanh explained it, they were considerably impressed, as was Ted Applegate who lamented that at this rare moment, he had left his cherished bowie knife strapped to the back of his pack.

John slowly began to recover his rationality and soon unwrapped himself from the sleeping bag. Len decided it would be a good idea if they brewed up some tea, but the implements were not available. In the end they just reloaded the truck, this time with their new Japanese passengers trussed up on the floor and headed off to find the main Viet Minh force. John sat quietly in the front saying nothing but responding briefly to any question asked. Edouard watched him closely all the while. There wasn't anything he could do, but he could watch him. That much he could do.

Thanh insisted that he could continue to drive, and Edouard found it impossible to dissuade him. The wounded Vietnamese was in the back with the rest of the Moose team and security detail. Their dead comrade had been left by the side of the road carefully laid out as if he was resting. The porters who were coming along would take care of the body according to custom. The dead Japanese were rolled in a heap on the side of the road. Other than the bodies being stripped, nothing would happen to them until some village official arranged to have the remains buried. Such things were not considered a priority.

In the back of the truck, Ted Applegate had retrieved his bowie knife from his pack and periodically menaced any of the bound prisoners if they made any moves at all. None of the Americans expected him to use the knife, but the Viet Minh soldiers saw no reason why he shouldn't. In Vietnamese they would urge him along in unmistakable tones. The Japanese knew exactly what they were doing even if they couldn't understand the language. Len Sorenson told Applegate to put the knife away before one of the Vietnamese decided to take similar steps on his own. At first the top sergeant was annoyed at being told what to do by someone of lower rank, but he soon saw the logic and sheathed the enormous blade. When it came to Vietnamese matters, the rest of the team deferred to the only one among them who really seemed to understand. Applegate saved face by saying he most likely couldn't properly use the weapon because his strained shoulder wouldn't allow it. What followed was a lively discussion on whether or not Top would be eligible for a Purple Heart in view of the fact that his skin hadn't been pierced by an enemy instrument and, most important of all, that the war was over, so technically these Japs weren't enemies.

"What the hell are they?" shouted an outraged Applegate.

"They're fuckin' thieves and robbers," said the legally minded ex-cop.

"Assault with a deadly weapon in an attempt to steal our property. I say they get 20 years. Write 'em up, Top."

In the front cab Edouard was totally occupied with watching Thanh to see if his head wound affected his driving and John who continued to sit without speaking. Back and forth Edouard's head would turn as he sat between the two of them. Thanh seemed to be doing quite well while the unwounded John appeared unwilling or unable to react to his surroundings. He was a passenger on a road to nowhere. Edouard knew he would have to talk again with Len Sorenson to see if there was anything at all in his medical supplies that they could give John. He was thinking about how useful some of Jimmy Tau's wine might be in this situation when Thanh let out a shout. Some Viet Minh soldiers could be seen down the road in front of them. They pulled alongside a squad of khaki uniformed Tho fighters who had no idea what Thanh was talking about when he asked them where General Giap's headquarters was.

They continued down the road at a very slow pace because more and more soldiers now marched along single file on each side. Some waved at the truck and Edouard could hear shouts of greeting coming in return from the rear. A little further along the way, Thanh recognized some people and stopped the truck to talk with them. He quickly returned to the truck and continued driving.

"They said they thought there was a command post about two kilometers up this road. At least that's where they were told to report, so I expect we'll find someone up there." Thanh was back in his usual unrufflable state. If it wasn't for the large bandage around his head, it would be impossible, Edouard mused, to imagine he had been shot.

What apparently once had been a sizeable farm building by the side of the road had become a parking lot for several vehicles including the sister truck from Tam Dao. Thanh announced they had arrived at a command post as if he was the guide on a scenic tour. Edouard could see what he thought was a flash of a white suit in the farmhouse, but it swiftly disappeared. He urged John out of the truck and then slipped down himself. The Viet Minh and Moose team all piled out of the back of the truck at the same time. Immediately, a crowd gathered as Thanh's security guards excitedly told the story of the Japanese attempted ambush. Thanh went into the farmhouse and after a short while came out with Vo Nguyen Giap. John saw Giap but ignored him and sat on the running board of the truck lighting up a cigarette from which he inhaled deeply. Edouard spoke to Giap and told him what had occurred.

"I understand. Comrade Thanh has just told me about the incident. Somehow, they must have eluded us. I'll have them questioned," Giap said and ordered the Japanese prisoners be removed from the back of the truck.

Len Sorenson came around the back of the truck with the wounded Viet Minh soldier leaning on him. Giap curtly called for help and some other soldiers took over from Len. They made no effort to encourage the American medic to accompany them and Edouard called Len back when he started to follow the group on his own.

"I'm just going to check on my patient, Captain," Len said, not understanding at all what had just happened.

"I know, Len, but you've got to wait until you're asked. This isn't Kim Lung. If they want you, they'll call. We need you here, by the way. Take a look at the Major," Edouard ordered.

Len Sorenson attempted to do just that and was pushed aside by John.

"I'm all right, dammit," was all John said.

Len looked over at Edouard who shrugged his shoulders and motioned for the medic to come over.

"Have you got something to give him? Maybe a shot of something, brandy or something?"

"Oh, no, Captain. No alcohol. Not now. Some water and maybe some salt tablets. I'll get 'em. That's all. He doesn't seem to have a temperature, but I can't really tell from long distance."

Giap went back in the farmhouse after giving brief instructions to Thanh to stay with the Americans. Thanh was a bit confused and followed Giap back into the house. He came out shortly afterward, somewhat flushed in the face. Edouard inquired as to what was going on.

"*Ce ne fait rien, Capitaine,*" Thanh replied. It was apparent, however, that Giap had held him responsible for what had happened. Edouard decided not to compound the reprimand by asking further questions. There were two things he was really interested in at this point: how to help his friend, John, and getting a report on what had happened with the Japanese in Thai Nguyen just down the road.

The Moose team had congregated in a sort of semicircle around John, talking to each other but keeping an eye on their major. The former cop took Edouard aside.

"I've seen this before, Captain. It happens often if a guy gets involved in a shootin'. The police doctor always tells us t'leave him alone. But this is much worse, I understand. Hand to hand with a knife just ain't the same as a shootin' even at close range. We just gotta let'im be. He'll be okay."

"Thanks. It's a shock, of course, but he's tough."

"Yes, sir, he's real tough."

Giap and a sizeable number of soldiers left the farmhouse and headed down the road in the assorted vehicles parked nearby. He offered no goodbyes, but he did shout something to Thanh as he drove off.

Edouard asked Thanh what Giap had said.

"He said I should bring you safely to Hanoi."

"I don't think we should rush right off. I think the Major needs some rest. We might as well stay here and push on tomorrow morning unless there's some reason to rush."

"There's no reason to rush, Captain. I'll have my people find some food and we'll stay right here," Thanh said.

The Moose team and Thanh's security personnel quickly took over the farmhouse. If Giap had decided to come back they most likely would have to move on, but there didn't seem to be much indication that would happen. Giap and the rest of his army were on their way. Exactly where they were headed wasn't clear, but it seemed in the general direction of Hanoi. It was better to stay behind them than get in front and end up caught between them and whatever they ran into. All the Americans agreed it was a good decision to remain behind overnight.

John showed signs of feeling better. He accepted a cup of tea that was brewed over a fire that Giap's people had left behind. The tea came out of the stores Len Sorenson dragged along for the team. They had enough GI rations to last them for a while, but the Vietnamese had brought along nothing at all. It was by pure good fortune that the porters following the Viet Minh armed force to Thai Nguyen arrived before evening. They were too far behind Giap's troops to be much help to them, but they were in just the right spot to feed Thanh's special unit. The rice and vegetables they carried were magically converted into a wonderful meal for what the porters called "the victorious Vietnamese Army and their friends." They meant to celebrate the great victory over the several Japanese they had observed by the roadside on the way down from Tan Trao. It was not until the following day that Edouard began to ask questions about what happened to the Japanese surrender at Thai Nguyen.

Thanh had gained very little information from straggling soldiers other than the fact that there had been some fighting and the rest of the Japanese had surrendered. It sounded bloody, but no one had any precise details. It was as if that was all old news and no one was very interested anymore. The truck pulled out with Thanh driving early the following morning. He admitted to a bad headache but otherwise insisted he was fine. John took no part in the preparations for departure. It was as if he was just along for the ride. Edouard took over.

It was only 40 miles to Hanoi from Thai Nguyen. Thanh took the road circling the town when they left, so they never saw what state it was in. He explained to Edouard that he was taking this route purposely in order not to get tangled up in any mess that might have been created by "yesterday's affair"—a nice way, Edouard thought, of describing a hell of a mess. The longer route around Thai Nguyen was crammed with Vietnamese going both ways with carts of household items. It was as if they had no idea which way was safety. Several small villages were passed that had been burned. It prompted John's first spoken words that day.

"What the hell is that?" he asked.

"I don't know, John," answered Edouard. "Looks like someone's been burning the villages. Not all though."

Thanh explained in matter-of-fact French. "Some villages are Viet Minh, some are not." He couldn't speak English, but it was pretty clear what John had questioned.

"They're killing their own people, Edouard."

"There might have been Japs in there, John. We don't know what went on."

"Goddammit, it's Giap's lessons. He's on his way to Hanoi and he's teaching lessons along the way. Sonuvabitch!"

While Edouard was happy to see that his friend had rejoined the present world, his black mood had remained. John was right, of course. Edouard could see that. The revolution had begun, and the first casualties had been taken. He smiled at his friend in hopes that would make him feel better. John saw the smile and nodded in recognition. He didn't smile back.

"We're going to want to find any American headquarters that may have been set up in Hanoi when we get there," Edouard said to Thanh.

"Those are my orders—to bring you to them. Safely, I was told," replied Thanh, smiling at his little joke.

The road improved the closer they got to Hanoi. There were surprisingly few people moving about the normally bustling city. Thanh continued his tour guiding and pointed out each new landmark they came upon. As the truck drew closer to the city center the atmosphere changed dramatically. Banners were strung everywhere, Vietnamese were on the street milling about as if they were at a political convention and, most surprising of all, Japanese soldiers stood on guard at intersections and in front of important buildings. The Viet Minh red flag with the large yellow star hung from corner poles and several municipal buildings. Thanh pulled the truck to the front of the Hotel Métropole, the magnificent old hostelry that had for so long housed all important visitors to Hanoi. It was the natural first place to look for an American delegation, Thanh suggested.

Edouard and John stepped down from the truck and went into the hotel, which was crowded with French civilians, some Chinese officers, and even a few Japanese officers. Over in one corner by themselves was a clutch of French officers arguing with what Edouard judged was a hotel manager. An American sergeant appeared carrying what seemed to be a small portable records file.

"We must be in the right place. There's a guy already with a box of admin reports. I smell a US Army staff installation nearby," said Edouard as he and John edged through the crowd toward the sergeant.

"Sergeant, do you know if there's a Major Anthony Castelli around here?" Edouard asked.

"Upstairs, second floor, sir," the soldier answered moving on toward the reception counter.

"A little bit different than last night's accommodations, eh?" Edouard said to John who had seemed to have perked up. "Let's go upstairs, John, and see if we can find Tony."

A Japanese officer, samurai sword and all, came down the stairs. He saluted the two American officers as he passed. They were too nonplussed to respond. They could hear American voices long before they had climbed to the second floor. A lieutenant came laughing out of the open door of an immense room. Edouard began to ask:

"Lieutenant, do you know if...."

John broke in sharply, "Where's Castelli?"

The lieutenant was about to take umbrage at the tone when he noticed both John's rank and facial expression.

"In there, sir," he said, observing also the large blood stain that had dried on John's pants.

"There's a truck in front of this place. There's a bunch of my guys in the back. You go down there and tell them to come up here. Got it? "

"Yes, sir."

"Oh, yes. There's a security guard of Viet Minh with them. Tell their officer—he's in the driver's seat—that we'll be right back to tell him what to do. You speak French, don't you?"

"No, sir but I speak Vietnamese."

"Okay, move out, Lieutenant."

Edouard was as surprised as the lieutenant at John's military briskness, but for different reasons.

"Ah, you've returned to the land of the living," he said.

"I never left," grumbled John. "Let's find, Tony."

The two SO officers worked their way into the large room crowded with boxes and hotel furniture. A large radio transmission system stood partially assembled in one corner next to a table piled high with electronic parts. They spied Tony's short frame on the other side of the space half hidden by a large bulletin board on which was pinned a map and a host of other papers. Edouard called out to Tony who had just hung up a telephone.

"Major Castelli, your disreputable cousins from the sticks have arrived."

Tony looked up and let out a shout.

"You've made it. You've made it. I thought we'd have to send out a search party. It's great to see you guys," Tony said as he dodged around boxes to reach his friends. He gave Edouard a big hug and was about to do the same with John. John's unsmiling face stopped him abruptly in his tracks. Tony took a half step backward seeing the dead eyes of the man in front of him. Unshaven, in filthy clothes, there wasn't any difference between the two SO officers before Tony Castelli other than the blood stain on John's pants—no difference except his look of hardened emptiness.

"The rest of the team is downstairs. They'll be coming up," was all John said. He turned and walked away saying as he left that he had something to do. Edouard was about to go after him when Tony held him back.

"What's going on. Has he been hit? Is he wounded? "

"John's not in good shape, Tony. I'll tell you all about it later. I've got to keep an eye on him."

With that Edouard turned away and followed John down the steps, a concerned Castelli just a few steps behind. The rest of the Moose team coming up the stairs had stopped for a moment as they passed their commanding officer and then proceeded to continue noisily on.

"Where's the Major goin'? He didn't say nuthin', Captain Eddy." Ted Applegate said.

"I don't know, Top. You guys keep going up to the second floor. We'll be with you in a moment. Where's all your stuff?"

"We brought our packs 'n duffel bags 'n stuff into the hotel. They're by the door. That lieutenant is watchin' 'em. Who is he, Major Tony? One of yours? He speaks Vietnamese real good. Of course, not as good as our boy."

Edouard had already dashed down the steps after John, leaving Tony to welcome the Moose men and direct them upstairs. Applegate and the others were so high it seemed that they were drunk. It crossed Tony's mind that they might have been coming from some celebration, but he quickly dismissed the thought, remembering John's look and Edouard's obvious concern. He followed Edouard down the stairs.

When Edouard arrived in the hotel lobby John had already made it out the front door. Edouard slowed down to see what John was going to do. John went over to Thanh in the cab of the truck and the Vietnamese jumped out.

John spoke to him in careful but informal French, between friends. Edouard stood a distance away, but he could still hear most of what was said.

"...so don't forget, *mon ami*, we are all grateful for your help," John said.

"No, it is we who thank you, *mon Commandant*. You have shown great courage to come to help us in our liberation. We shall always remember you. America was the first to help us, and you were the first one. And, of course, Captain Edouard and the others also," Thanh said, seeing Edouard standing some paces away. Thanh snapped out an order and his security detail tumbled out of the back of the truck. Thanh gave another order and they quickly formed ranks. Thanh took up position in front of them, executed a crisp about-face. There in front of the grand Métropole Hotel, the symbol of past French colonial life, Bui Dac Thanh gave the command for his men to present arms. He once again did an about-face and saluted. John and Edouard returned the salute as did Tony Castelli who had come out the front door. Another order and the detail climbed back into the truck. Thanh jumped back in the driver's seat and with a boyish wave to his friend, Edouard, the young Viet Minh commander gunned the old truck down the street.

"He'll make general someday," Edouard said.

John just shook his head and looked down at the ground. He couldn't speak.

Edouard put his arm around John's shoulder and led him back into the hotel. Tony wanted to help but didn't know what to do. It was clear that John had expended his last bit of energy to say goodbye to Thanh. He walked with his head down, the pain in his chest consuming his body. He looked up at Edouard and said,

"I think it's time we went home, Captain."

"I think you're absolutely right, Major."

Epilogue

On September 2, 1945, Ho Chi Minh, President of the Provincial Government of Vietnam, announced the independence of that nation from the colonial control of France. For the next 15 months, Ho attempted to negotiate France's acceptance of this status while the French rushed to rebuild their military and administrative control of Indochina.

On the morning of September 26, 1945, the ranking OSS officer in Saigon, the highly experienced Lieutenant Colonel A. Peter Dewey, shortly after learning that one of his officers, Capt. Joseph R. Coolidge, had been ambushed and severely wounded the previous day, was himself machine gunned to death by a Viet Minh independent action group as he attempted to pass by a hastily constructed road barrier. The guerrillas proceeded down the road to attack the OSS headquarters, but were driven off by accurate American fire and the arrival some hours later of a unit of British Gurkhas. Apologies for this "tragic error" from Ho in Hanoi notwithstanding, the killing of the well-known and popular OSS officer was never forgotten in Washington.

For his wartime loyalty to DeGaulle, Jean Sainteny was rewarded with the position of Commissioner of Tonkin and Northern Annam. Continuing conflict between the Viet Minh and the French military escalated to serious battles in November and December 1946 at Lang Son and Haiphong. Thousands of civilian deaths were caused when the French Navy indiscriminately shelled Haiphong forcing Viet Minh military units to abandon that port city and Hanoi. Ho Chi Minh and his government retreated back to the jungles and mountains of Tonkin where a guerrilla war was waged for the next eight years. The French defeat at Dien Bien Phu by Viet Minh forces under the command of Vo Nguyen Giap was followed shortly after on July 21, 1954, with the signing of the Geneva Accords. As part of that agreement a partition was created along the seventeenth parallel separating North and

South Vietnam. By 1955, the United States assumed the training of South Vietnam's Armed Forces.

The entire OSS team that had spent the last months of the war with the Viet Minh was speedily whisked out of Hanoi in September 1945 and beyond the reach of the gathering world press. They never looked back nor did an American political establishment eager to disassociate itself from the earlier relationship with the communist leadership in Vietnam. The contacts and goodwill created by US intelligence were discarded or purposefully ignored. In later years, the now middle-aged leaders of the OSS mission successfully remained hidden from public scrutiny by dint of their own unwillingness to become part of the controversy swirling around the issues involved in the war in Vietnam. To this day, few people among the many involved on both sides of the war have any idea of what occurred that summer in Tonkin, but there was a time....

About the Author

George H. Wittman joined the Army Reserve in 1950 with the intention of working towards his commission. He was instead recruited into the recently formed Central Intelligence Agency. As his career developed, he undertook extensive sensitive assignments across the globe. In addition, he took over direction of the family's mining and international trade business, which as G.H. Wittman, Inc. would later undertake international security and political risk management. He served as founding chairman of the National Institute for Public Policy, lectured periodically at the FBI Academy in Quantico, VA, and had a consulting relationship with the FBI's New York field office. Even in retirement, he continued to write and offer analysis on international affairs and security matters. He was a regular contributor to several publications including *The American Spectator, The Washington Times,* and *AND Magazine.* In his quieter moments, he found time to write several novels. His first, *A Matter of Intelligence* was published by Macmillan in 1975. Above all, he viewed and presented himself as an American patriot, resisting political affiliation and committed to what he believed was in the best interest of the nation.